A SWORD FOR THE IMMERLAND KING

A Sword for the Immerland King

F.W. FALLER

Second Edition, 2022

KIRRINATH
PRESS LLC

A Sword for the Immerland King

First book of the Portals of Tessalindria Collection.

F. W. Faller

A Note from the Author

It's been almost twenty five years since I started writing *"A Sword for the Immerland King"* on a portable manual typewriter overlooking the ocean on the backside of Monhegan Island, Maine. It was years in the thinking as I made a living, worked at raising three children, taught in the church fellowship, learned to pray and attended to the many details of the life I was blessed with.

I was *learning* to write at that time and for those who know about writing fiction, it's not a trivial exercise. It can take years to develop an author's voice and years to develop the skill. I was fortunate to have the opportunity to publish this book and begin my journey as an author before my voice matured.

When I decided to re-release this book with more knowledge of the publishing, book selling world, and a considerably more developed skill in fiction writing, I found many details of the craft that I needed to fix. I've reduced the length while strengthening the presentation, but have kept the story intact. As I was editing, I found very little that I wanted to change structurally as the story moved along, drawing me in so that I often lost my "editing eye" and had to retrace my steps frequently to stay on task.

I hope that you enjoy this read, because, even after 25 years, the story still makes me cry at the end, and forces me to rethink the core values of a life of purpose and dignity.

Pronunciation Guide

Carnados.....car·'nā·dos
Chronista.....kro·'nis·tå
Eladra.....e·'lå·drå
Eladrim.....e·'lå·drim
Erengnira.....'e·reng·'ni·rå
Galar.....'ga·lar
Haniah.....ha·'nī·ah
Lutaka.....lu·'tå·kå
MahEladra.....'måh e·'lå·drå
MahMoralda.....'måh·mor·'al·då
Mankar.....'mang·kar
Meekar.....'mee·kar
Mirradach.....'mir·rå·dåk
Morahura.....'mor·a·'hur·a
Mordara.....mor·'da·rå
Narahu .....na·'rå·hu
Omberon.....'om·ber·on
Paca.....'på·cå
Patira.....på·'tir·å
Phartang.....'far·tang
Psadeq.....'så·dek
Rapahoogin.....'rap·å·'hoo·gin
Sandihar.....'san·di·har
Sessasashae.....se·'så·sha
Timmanaeus.....tim·ma·'nā·us
Verclan.....'ver·cln
Vishtava.....vish·tå·'vå
Vistorath.....'vish·tor·ath
Vrengnia.....'vreng·ni·å
Windarad.....'win·då·rad

NOTES: -a ... as in cat, hat
-å ... as in Bach, father
-ā ... as in hate, day

Dedication

To every Man, Woman and Child
who has lain on the grass,
stared into the grand infinity
of the night sky and wondered,
"If everything could be different
what would have to remain unchanged?"

Chapter 1

Beginnings

"When the spring of life is polluted and senseless, you must dig deeper. There in the depths, at the source of the fount, you will find a purity of sense that is more profound than your most vivid imaginations."

Tessarandin, Book 13

Narahu shivered. He breathed hard, his lungs burning for air as he lay gasping on the damp earth under the bridge. The frantic terror of the scene behind him had driven him onward in the darkness of the young night. Tal, the smaller of the twin Tessalindrian moons, paled orange as she hung low above the mountains far to the east, offering little light. She had drawn him like a magnet away from the inferno in the smithy to shelter under the bridge.

They would come after him. Images of the events leading to this moment flooded his mind for what seemed like minutes, though he knew it was only seconds.

Fada was—no, had been—a bladesmith for the great King Lutaka of Tessamandria. He worked exclusively for the king, but had no use for the busy-ness and distraction of the castle and fortress, and had set up his smithy a fair distance from it. "Too many people, too many comings and goings. It's good for a king, but not for a smith," he said.

The smithy was half a daysmarch outside the city that surrounded its fortress, separated from the outermost houses by a wild stand of ancient trees. The silence of the nights soothed Narahu's vorn. He could see the stars and the mountains and hear the river wending its way north to places he never expected to see.

King Lutaka had a smithy in the fortress where his smiths made all the weapons of war: the swords, javelins, daggers, spears and other things needed for his campaigns to unite Tessamandria, but he had given the work of smithing other blades to Narahu's father: the knives and choppers for the kitchens, the sickles and scythes for the harvests, the axes, froes, adzes, threshing bars and tailors' shears that were needed throughout the kingdom.

A month ago, late in the evening, they'd had a surprise visit from Alaavar, the commanding general in Lutaka's army. Alaavar knew Fada, but such a visit was unusual. He had come alone in secret. Fada was finishing an experimental thatch cutter blade used for roofing houses.

Alaavar wanted Fada to make thirteen swords, one for King Lutaka and the other twelve for himself and his generals. It was to be a surprise, a special favor for his king. Fada had resisted, insisting that it wasn't his place to make swords, but Alaavar pressed him and offered larger and larger sums of money until Fada had relented and agreed.

The king's sword was to be a little bigger, and if he were to put a special effort into any one sword, that would be the one to favor. "Only the best for the king, you know," Alaavar had said, as he smiled.

Narahu's head spun as he lowered it between his knees. He remembered the vague apprehension when the final sum was determined. Perhaps it was Alaavar's smile that had made him uneasy. It was more of a sneer, really. Fada had looked directly at Alaavar's face when they shook hands. Had he not seen it?

Fada started work on the swords immediately, working late into the evenings after spending long days at his commissioned work. Narahu had worked the bellows, watching and listening as Fada sang the forge poetry, metering each hammer blow and heat by the rhythm of the words as they poured forth from Fada's mind and mouth. The forge poetry for the swords was different from the poetry for the other blades Fada made. Narahu remembered understanding all the words, darker and tangled somehow, as if its origins were from another world entirely. He hadn't liked the sound of it. It wasn't warm and strong like the poetry of the knives and the hatchets.

They had finished the swords two days ago and laid them out on the bench in the center of the smithy, awaiting Alaavar's arrival. Narahu studied them. The master craftsmanship for which Fada was renowned, evidenced itself in the work, but even so, the surpassing excellence of the swords stunned him. Every flawless detail gleamed in the light of the oil lamps that lit the smithy. Narahu doubted that he could discern one from another except for the king's sword, which was a bit larger. He shuddered involuntarily as he pictured the swords laid out on the table.

Fada had sent a message to Alaavar at the fortress. Word came back through a page that he would arrive shortly after nightfall. Narahu sensed Fada's tension. He snapped at Narahu frequently, which wasn't his way, and had exhausted himself in perfecting the swords. Now it was time to be rid of them. He moved about the shop fidgeting with his tools and placing and replacing everything he touched.

Narahu had helped tidy up the smithy for Alaavar's visit. He had set the tong racks in order and swept the floor, cleared the vise bench and filled the slack tub with clean water. At Fada's request he had retrieved extra lanterns from the storeroom and lit them, and hung them about the smithy to illuminate the swords on the table. The swords glowed in the lantern light, casting muted reflections across the beams and walls.

Several of Alaavar's generals accompanied him when he arrived. Narahu could see only four of them, but there were others outside. Those who came in, remained by the door in the shadows. Narahu wasn't able to see their faces, but a certain darkness surrounded them, a darkness that should have been dispelled by the extra lantern light.

Narahu wasn't sure how he knew something was wrong, but his suspicion about Alaavar was confirmed when the commander saw the swords and smiled at Fada; there was evil in that smile, pure and cruel.

Alaavar stepped forward to the bench and picked up the king's sword. As he swung it slowly back and forth, it hummed softly. Fada spoke: "They are the finest—"

"Quiet, little man!" Alaavar scowled as he waved the sword. "These are fine swords. Only the best for Alaavar, don't you think?" The ugliness of the his voice reinforced his sneer. Narahu tasted revulsion in the back of his throat, but there was no time to identify it.

Fada said something about the sword being for the king. Fada must have sensed the same wrongness as Narahu, because when the sword flashed the first time, Fada ducked and the blade struck the post vise where it was anchored to the bench. With a blue flash the sword clove the solid iron as if it were a melon.

Fada leapt behind the forge bed and yelled, "Run, Narahu, run!" Narahu remembered the quick movement of the fire shovel. A shower of glowing coal from the dying fire bathed the commander who howled in pain as he unleashed his fury. "Run, Narahu! Now!" The other generals leapt to the table to claim their swords.

Alaavar's sword slashed through the edge of the forge bed with a blinding flash. Fada dumped a bucket of water into the firepot. Alaavar cursed as the searing steam blasted up into his face. The generals behind him yelled obscenities.

Narahu heard the crash of glass and tin as one of the lanterns near the forge yielded to a blow from Fada's forge rake. Paraffin from the lamp rained down onto the fire and with an eerie *whoosh*, an orange fireball leapt toward the ceiling. More cursing followed, more crashing. Two generals started toward him. *Crack!* The lantern on the wall between them exploded. "Run Narahu!"

"Fada!"

"Run—now!"

Harrraaannngg! The king's sword sang again; another blue flash followed by the splintering of wood. The whole building lurched down as Alaavar severed the support column in the middle of the smithy.

Two generals crashed through the fire from the second lantern. The one in front tripped over something and the other fell on top of Fada, cursing and growling.

"Run—ru—"

Narahu felt the blow that cut Fada down, as if it had cut his own heart out of him. How could he have felt it? He knew what it meant. Alaavar laughed: a hideous, cruel laugh that erupted in Narahu's ears.

It shook the smithy. It shook his vorn, the core of his being. It shook the foundation from under his feet. Narahu turned and bolted toward the back door.

He dodged the stack of anvils and the ring mandrel, then rolled under the rack of iron bars and spare tongs. The thrashing, swearing and growling followed him, like a nightmare against the backdrop of Alaavar's laugh. Narahu ran into the night—into the freedom of the open endlessness of the outside world.

Narahu knew the trail well, even in the dark—every turn, every jog, and dip of the path to the river. The dark shouts of Alaavar's generals made his body light and his feet swift, giving him strength he didn't know he had. They weren't far behind. Something flashed so brightly that for an instant the entire landscape was illuminated as if by Asolara, followed by another burst of profanity. Swords clashed and their guttural curses mingled with other voices, shouting. There were more flashes. Narahu couldn't risk looking back; he dared not, lest his winged feet fail to carry him as fast and as far as possible from the holocaust behind him.

His heart still pounded like a drum in his chest as he gasped in the cool clean air. His hands shook. His head swam in a numbness he hardly had time to notice. They would be coming. He had to keep going, but where? There was no going back. The fiery glow in the night sky him told him that there was nothing to go back to but death. The smithy was Fada's crematorium. He choked back the tears as his body heaved. He threw up between his legs.

"Narahu!"

A wave of terror swept over him as viselike hands gripped his upper arms. He tried to scream but an icy palm clamped over his mouth. "You must not run, Narahu. Listen carefully. There is little time." It was a language he had never heard before, but he understood it perfectly. He tried to break free, but the beings on either side of him clamped his arms tighter. "Are you afraid of the water?"

He tried to shake his head. "Take a deep breath." The hand came off his mouth and he drew in deeply. He knew what was about to happen. Hooves clattered toward them on the road, approaching the bridge. In the next instant he was in the river, still in the grip of his captors as they pulled him deep into the dark water.

"No!" he wanted to shout but he couldn't.

"Stay calm, Narahu. Save your breath and strength." Voices? Under water?

The powerful stroke and kick of his captors pulled him downstream through the watery darkness. He was face up between them, watching the faint glimmer of the surface, surreal and quiet, about three paces above him. "Stay calm, Nara hu...your strength...your breath."

His lungs began to burn. He needed air—had to break free! He started to struggle. Suddenly, the shadow of one of his captor's face pressed down upon him. His breath was sucked out of him and then returned to him before he understood what had happened. The new air was strong and vitalizing and the burning in his lungs stopped abruptly. Cold water rushed past him as his captors swam on, deep in the middle of the river.

Without warning, they turned in perfect unison, like flocking birds in formation. They surfaced quietly under a thick overhang of bushar reeds. As they came up, the hand clamped over his mouth again. "You must remain quiet." The hand fell away and Narahu exhaled softly. "Listen," said his captor's voice in his head.

Narahu listened. Cursing and shouting rolled down the river from the bridge, now about a hundred paces away. The welter of angry voices were yelling at each other—threatening—swearing.

The warriors still held Narahu. For several minutes, they waited silently under the reeds with only their heads above water. Not until the confusion on the bridge abated did his captors move.

"You must head north to the mountains. Travel only at night." It was the being on the right. He released Narahu's arm.

"Do not light a fire. Stay off the roads. There is great danger," warned the other as he released his grip also.

"Who are you?"

"Servants of Mah'Eladra, Guardians of Psadeq. I am Vishtava," said the one on his right.

"And I am Vishtani," said the other.

"Eladra?"

Vishtani nodded. "Your life is in grave danger. Your father is dead. Your mother will be soon. You cannot go back."

Narahu shivered.

"Go north to the mountains, and hide in the caves you find there. Keep moving. There is no safe place for you in Tessamandria. We will be watching," Vishtava said with a smile.

They ducked beneath the surface of the river simultaneously and vanished as quickly as they had appeared under the bridge. Narahu shivered again. He wasn't sure if it was from fear or the chill of the water.

He pulled himself along the bank until he found an opening in the reeds. He crouched low and listened. No sound came from the bridge or the smithy. He'd lost his shoes in the river.

Keeping himself well down in the tall reeds of the riverbank, he removed his tunic and shirt and wrung them as dry as he could, then his pants and socks. He must travel tonight. He would hide and let his clothes dry in Asloara's warmth the next day.

His knees shook as he stood up. He tried to think back, but his mind mercifully blanketed the ordeal with numbness. He headed north. The mountains lay low and barely discernible in Tal's low-slung glow. Somehow, he had to reach them. That was all he knew.

Chapter 2

Trouble

Seven Centuries later ...

"Youth has no anticipation of failure. It watches, not to see if it will succeed, but when."

Karendo Marha,
Journey to the Infinite

Paca watched his father's hammer fall on the hot steel. It fell as it had a hundred thousand times, striking square with a near perfect precision, honed by fifty years of working the forge. It bounced on the anvil with a *ping* and floated up to fall again as the scythe blade took shape under its impact.

The blows stopped as the blade lost its orange glow, and with a swift, knowing stroke from Fada, found itself back in the fire. Paca tugged the bellows toggle. The fire growled as air forced its way up through the glowing pile of coal.

"You're no ordinary young man," Fada said quietly in the moment before he took another blade from the fire. "Though we live an ordinary life, in an ordinary town, you must never settle into the ordinary yourself."

The glowing blade swept over to the anvil. The hammer fell, *pinged*, floated, and fell again. Paca watched Fada's face. He had to look up, even when Fada bent slightly over the anvil. His wise and impassive face was thin, with a neatly trimmed graying red beard. His head of fiery copper hair was cropped short so errant sparks couldn't catch in it, and his gray eyes sparkled under his dark eyebrows in the forge's orange glow.

Paca waited. As soon as the blade was back in the fire, the conversation would resume.

Shiloh was indeed an ordinary town. Paca had thought so all his life and still wondered why Fada had chosen to live there. It was filled with the ordinary people. There were ordinary bakers and butchers, candle makers and bricklayers, carpenters and roof thatchers, merchants, a mayor, a woman who made pies, a couple of tailors—and many others. Paca knew them all well, and being the son of the smith, was well known.

The knife blade slipped back into the fire. Paca tugged. Fada's gray eyes rested on him gently. "You've served me well, but soon that will change." His tongs gripped the third blade in the fire, another scythe for the upcoming barley harvest. Paca watched him pull it from the fire and step to the anvil.

Paca loved Fada and respected him as well. Mada had died in the Timeron Plague two years after he was born, so Fada had engaged him at the smithy as soon as Paca could manage it. From the age of seven, it had been Paca's task to clean the tuyere, chip the clinker out of yesterday's fire, set the tinder and coke in the firepot, and heap the green coal around it. He would soak the coal and light the fire, and by the time Fada was ready, a bright smokeless fire was burning evenly in the forge bed. He tended the bellows, watching intently as Fada fashioned bars of gray steel into prized tools for Immerland.

Fada made the smithy into his school, teaching him about life during the heats and letting the short lessons sink in during the hammering.

"What will change?" Paca queried as the third blade slipped back into the fire.

A hint of a smile appeared at the corners of Fada's mouth, but vanished as quickly as it had appeared. "Remember Lesson One," he said as the first blade came to rest on the anvil again.

Fada had several others who worked for him at his forge along with Paca. They did most of the routine ironwork required for a modest and ordinary town. They fashioned the latches, hinges and knockers for doors. They made the coat hooks, hat hooks, boot scrapers and window latches—gate hooks, horse shoes, hasps and clasps of various sorts, but Fada fashioned all the tools with sharp edges. This was part of their agreement when they came to work for him, and none of them were taught his bladesmithing, except Paca himself, into whom he continually poured his knowledge and the wisdom of his craft.

His works of welded iron and steel were extraordinary. He had a way with steel and an understanding of the fire and forge that surpassed the other smiths in Immerland, and he had become known throughout the country for the keenness of his edges and the gracefulness and usefulness of his tools.

Over his own forge fire, he had a peculiar sign that read:

Imagine any blade you can,
But never a blade to hurt a man.

He called this "Lesson One."

"How could I ever forget Lesson One?" Paca frowned at the blade switch.

Fada eyed him keenly. His lips uttered nothing but his eyes uttered the lesson again.

Fada refused to produce a blade of any kind for a person in whom he perceived evil intent. Never in his life, as far as Paca knew, had he forged a blade whose design was the harm of another person. Each tool he made was designed and fashioned with a specific person and use in mind, and every stroke and movement of Fada was focused into that person and that use.

When a blade was finished, Fada would summon the new owner and place the tool in his hand. Laying his hand on top of the tool, and locking his gray eyes into the eyes of the recipient, he would say:

"Bless this tool to this worker's hand.
Bless it to function at his command.
Bless him to use it as he should.
Bless its edge for a common good."

Paca watched this exchange many times, but wasn't sure he understood it fully. He knew Fada knew he didn't understand. He could see it in Fada's eyes, though Fada had never said anything about it to him.

Paca had asked Fada once. "Fada, why do you bless the tool so? These simple words can't protect this blade against evil use. You pour your vorn into the blade, and it's keen and hard, but now it's beyond your hand and subject to use and abuse as desired by someone quite beyond your control. Do you really believe this blessing does anything?"

Shaking his head, Fada had smiled. "Has even one of my blades ever been used to injure another person?"

Paca wasn't sure. "Not that I have heard anyway. But that may be just coincidence or luck or—"

Fada's eyes cut him short. "Someday you'll understand. There's no such thing as coincidence or luck. Until then, there's still much for you to learn about the making of edged tools."

"The royalty of a being cannot be measured by position, physical strength or its collection of wealth. Royalty is a state of mind that belongs to those who know who they are."

Mindar Colloden,
The Great Fathers

Vrengnia walked behind her father as he ambled along the parapet overlooking the great courtyard of the Immerland Castle. Three advisors walked casually alongside the king: King Sandihar of Immerland. Today there was no hurry. The kingdom was at peace and had been for several years, except for the continual skirmishes with the mountain people along the southern border.

"And what do you think, my dear?" He stopped suddenly and turned toward her, his eyes flickering with mild amusement.

"I—well, I need to think on it a bit more, I..." Vrengnia paused, looking Fada in the eye as it twinkled. "I haven't the faintest idea what you are talking about!"

Fada guffawed uproariously. His advisors snorted and smiled. "My birthday!" he said. "It's going to be my fiftieth, you know!"

"Surely it isn't, Fada!"

"But it is! It is. We'll have a grand celebration—a genuine party—for everyone. What do you think?"

Vrengnia smiled. "I need to think on it a bit more," she said.

"Yes, yes...a bit more. Well, when you've had your thoughts, I would like to hear them." He turned to resume his walk.

Vrengnia could have been embarrassed, but she wasn't. She loved and respected Fada. Her mother had died giving birth to her. She wasn't sure of the details, except that Fada had loved her mother dearly and had poured that love into her own life in response to Mada's untimely death. Since the age of six, she had been following Fada and his advisors, the dors, and the mayors of the towns surrounding the castle.

He was teaching her, but she always thought it must be a bit boring to be king. So many details, mundane and trivial, demanded his attention, almost as if the simplest of decisions had to be made by him; as if everyone feared making decisions in his presence. She had become accustomed to ignoring most of it unless it was serious.

She had known that Fada's birthday was approaching. She remembered his fortieth. She wasn't sure how much bigger a party could be. Besides, it was such a beautiful day. Plans like these should be discussed at night; after dark.

She followed along behind the royal quartet, but her eyes swept out toward the horizon. The soft, late summer breeze bore a potpourri of the stables and the hayfields with hints of lavender and ripening apples. Asolara bathed the towns that surrounded the castle in deep shadow, allowing her to see the busy-ness of all the people about their daily tasks.

These were the last days of summer, and preparations were being made for harvesting the fields that stretched into the distance outside the towns, a patchwork carpet of gold, green, yellow and amber, rolling out to the foot of the hazy blue mountains to the south and east. Perhaps this afternoon she could escape on Mahala, ride through the towns, and visit this busy-ness herself, a welcome change from the controlled ambiance of the castle.

"Should it be in the banquet hall—or the courtyard?" Fada stared at her.

"What?"

Fada roared again. "You're hopeless sometimes. I think you need to get that horse of yours and get out for the afternoon."

She blinked. "If you don't mind—I was thinking that myself."

"Well, you're no good to me in this daydream of yours." He stepped forward and hugged her. "Go! I'll see you at dinner."

Vrengnia bowed and turned to leave. She thought she heard Carnados, Fada's most trusted advisor, murmur something about her being very much like her grandmother. Carnados had always treated her with dignity and respect. He was a good deal older than Fada, old enough to be her grandfather, which is the way she thought of him. He had known her grandmother, the Great Queen, and was the only one in Fada's company with the authority to say such a thing.

The Great Queen, Vorania, had ruled Immerland for forty years. She had built the castle and unified the townships surrounding it. Loved by those who knew her, and well respected by those who didn't, Vrengnia reasoned that there were few others to whom comparison would flatter her as much. Today she would ride out among the people, as her grandmother often did, away from the stultifying formality of the castle and its synthesis of grandeur. She skipped down the stairs from the parapet and bolted across the courtyard to the stables. Mahala, her horse, would be waiting, eager to run as always.

The guard at the castle gate straightened and saluted as she cantered Mahala under the portcullis and onto the drawbridge. The sudden change in the light, or perhaps the freshening breeze, heightened her sense of escape—maybe it was the wide openness of the fields rolling down the hill on which the castle stood. She sighed deeply as the clip-clop of Mahala's shoes on the drawbridge changed to the muted thumping on the softer, more solid ground. She pulled to the left and urged Mahala into an easy gallop.

The castle slipped away as she left its confines behind her, Mahala's powerful gait carrying her like the wind away from...from what? The castle was home, and always had been. It probably always would be. Recently it had begun to feel more like a prison, a place to be escaped at any chance. Something wasn't right. Fada was changing. No, perhaps *she* was changing. The lifelong ambition to be the Queen of Immerland had changed from a bright fantasy of youthful eagerness to a dark dream from which there seemed to be only one escape. It grew darker with each passing month, and her singular relief was the bright otherworld outside the castle. There was nothing particular that she could grasp, nothing to ask about, nothing specific to change, like shadow dancers in a dream, ominous and untouchable.

She looked back as Mahala carried her into the wall of trees at the bottom of the hill. The castle gleamed in Asolara's brilliance until it vanished behind the rich, green foliage streaming past her. She sighed again as she emerged from the other side of the barrier wood and set her face forward into the warm wind. For now, she was free. For now, she didn't have to think about being a queen. For now, the wind and Asolara washed her vorn and she shed the vague haunting of the castle, its effects dropping off her with each rippling wave of Mahala's strong shoulders.

*"As to this day or that, who can tell what will make any one of them important.
Are they not but convenient containers in which we categorize the passage into the
infinite?"*

Oratanga,
Passages

"The very image of her grandmother," Carnados had said.

"Yes," sighed the king as he watched his daughter disappear down the steps, "never missing a chance to get out of the castle for a ride." He turned back to his advisors. He was tired of talking about his birthday celebration. He changed the subject. "She'll be twenty, four days after my birthday, Carnados—on the equinox, remember?"

Carnados nodded.

"I keep waiting for her to grow up."

"There'll be plenty of time for that." Carnados smiled.

"Yes, I suppose so, but even the smallest sign—a tiny change—would be nice."

"Your majesty?"

"That hat! It's got to go." The king laughed as he pictured his daughter. He couldn't remember a time when she was interested in any clothing made for women, and her bright and varicolored clothing selection had given rise to the affectionate title "The Pied Princess." Loose pantaloons and a long-sleeved flowing blouse was the favored choice, cut more for a fanciful soldier than a would-be queen. "It's easier that way" she said of her shortened hair that she kept mostly tucked up under a comical purple and green leather cap, which most thought accentuated her green eyes.

A gray sleeveless tunic bore her grandmother's crest on both the front and the back, three diagonal slashes of cobalt blue, one above the other, with a brilliant yellow sunburst just to the right of them. In the end, though considered a bit odd, the king knew she was loved and admired for her frankness and simple innocence.

"She will lose it someday, Sire." Carnados smiled. Sandihar knew it was genuine. Because of Carnados's wisdom, Sandihar had charged him with the routine running of the castle and the kingdom. Carnados in turn delegated the mundane functions to other advisors and managers of the domestic servants and housekeeping staff; the laundry, the kitchens and gardens, the stables and kennels, the library, the treasury. He oversaw everything with the exception of training and leading the king's army and managing Immerland's retinue of spies.

"She's a lot more like you than you think," Carnados continued. "She's an apt pupil and all that you have been teaching her over the years will rise up in her at the necessary time."

Sandihar studied Carnados, weighing the fullness of his statement. Carnados often seemed to cloak his wisdom in riddles, so Sandihar was never sure if he should be puzzling out some profound meaning, and Carnados, always genuine and sober, never let on one way or the other. Carnados had served and loved Sandihar's mother, and Sandihar often felt small by her stature, even in Carnados's eyes. If not for Carnados's unswerving loyalty and support, Sandihar knew he could easily be suspicious of his motives.

As Sandihar watched Vrengnia bound across the courtyard and disappear through the archway leading to the stables, he changed the subject. "Call Galar," he said, turning back to Carnados.

"Galar?"

"Yes!" The king smiled. He had been pondering something for a while, and it had just occurred to him how it might work. "I have a special errand for him."

Carnados waved and Mindar, the youngest of the king's advisors, swept away from his elders toward the staircase off the parapet.

Galar was the leader of the dors, the military protectors of the kingdom. He could be trusted with this errand. Sandihar had personally selected each of his dors. Whenever he would appoint another dor to his service he would place both hands on the man's head, lock his black eyes into the eyes of the dor and say:

> *"Bless this man to this king's own hand.*
> *Bless him to function at my command.*
> *Bless him to follow as he should.*
> *Bless him now for a common good."*

Often when he brought a dor into his service, he could see the dullness in his daughter's eyes that betrayed her ignorance of what this blessing meant. He remembered the time she asked, "Fada, why do you bless the dors? These words can't protect this man against his own evil. They're wise and true, but now they are beyond your hand, and subject to influences beyond your control. Do you really believe this blessing does anything?"

He wanted to help his daughter understand, but he wasn't sure he understood himself. He was sure it touched some deep truth that eluded him, and he repeated the blessing simply because it was something his mother had always done. "Has any of my dors *ever* done evil to injure another person unjustly?" he asked his daughter as his mother had always asked him

"Not that I have heard, but that is just coincidence or luck or—"

"Someday you will believe in neither coincidence *nor* luck. Until then, there is still much for you to learn about the making of a great and wise queen." Sandihar winced inside when he thought about this answer. It was the answer his mother had always given him, and he was sure that she had understood and believed it, just as he was sure that he didn't actually understand it enough to believe it himself. What bothered him most, was the skeptical look in Vrengnia's eyes, and he had nothing further to offer her. His only consolation was that she seemed content not to press the issue. He dreaded the day she would.

"Dor Galar, Sire." Carnados's voice shook Sandihar from his reflections.

He smiled to himself as Galar approached along the walkway. Galar's long, easy stride conveyed royalty to anyone who saw him. It was royalty that went beyond his height and his service to the king—a royalty of character—a man who knew who he was, and what his business was. Mindar trotted to keep up.

"My good Dor," said Sandihar as Galar bowed slightly in deference to him, "I have a special errand for you, in preparation for my birthday." He let his voice trail off as he looked out over the fields to the south. Galar remained motionless.

"Do you know the town of Shiloh?" He waved his hand toward the tiny hamlet to the southeast, barely visible beyond a small hill halfway to the horizon.

"Yes, Sire, I have been there many times."

"Do you know the blacksmith who forges there?"

"I know his reputation, but I wouldn't say I know him."

"Yes, yes—well, I have been thinking. My fiftieth birthday is coming up, as you know, and..." Sandihar paused, eyeing the dor thoughtfully. Galar didn't move. "Well, I thought that we might ask the good smith if he would make a sword for my fiftieth birthday!"

"And my role, Sire?"

"Well, you would ask him—for me, of course."

Galar hesitated. "Sire, this man is the finest bladesmith in the kingdom—"

"I know." Sandihar smiled as he interrupted the dor. He knew the smith's reputation well.

"He refuses to make swords, Sire; blades of any kind that are designed as weapons. You know this also, Sire."

"He is older and wiser. Surely he won't defy me a second time,"

"I don't know for sure."

"But you will ask for me?" He posed the question somewhere just this side of a command. Galar shifted slightly without breaking eye contact.

"I will engage the smith this very afternoon."

"So soon?"

Galar bowed. "There's no reason to delay." Galar turned and strode off. Sandihar watched him go. He liked a man who knew his purpose.

When the last sound of Galar's descending steps faded in the tower stairway, Sandihar exhaled. "He certainly has a way of confirming his appointment to leadership of the dors."

"Yes, Sire," murmured Carnados, "he does indeed." Sandihar felt that double-edged twinge in the way Carnados said it. He hated it, but loved the man who said it.

"The depths of Moraven deep, the heights of the Crown of Tessalindria; these are but floor and ceiling to the infinite expanse of possibilities for our short lives, and our small world."

Pratoraman,
The Middle Way

Galar loved riding out at this time of year. The world moved slowly and the golden weather filled his nostrils with warm fragrances like no other. Galar took his time, allowing his horse the privilege of an easy walk. Above him, riding the warm eddies from the fields drenched with Asolara's slanted rays, a hawk drew lazy circles on the infinite ceiling of the sky. Its effortless turns set his mind drifting slowly to the circles surrounding the king's request.

The blades of the smith at Shiloh Forge were legendary in Immerland. All the best working blades in the kingdom were made there. These blades could cut chains, nails and bolts without becoming dull or chipped, according to some of the rumors. Such a blade would be a perfect accoutrement for the king, but the smith at Shiloh forge had refused in the past to make weapons for him or any of the dors. The king knew this also.

Galar pondered the king's request. He didn't disdain the king for thinking that perhaps, for his special occasion, he might convince the smith to do him a favor, but the timing was abrupt, and out of character for the king, whose habits were cautious, bordering on banal. Might it be linked to the unsettling reports on the mountain clans that filtered in from the scouts along the southern borders? Yet, it wasn't the king's style to obscure his purpose in that way, and this wasn't the first time they'd had such reports.

A subtle change in the king had occured over the past two years. Until then he had ruled "by the book" as Dor Windarad often joked. Galar smiled to himself at their image of the king and his secret book, given to him by his mother, and containing every wise thing a king could say or do. He envisioned the king hiding away late at night to pour over its pages, searching out how to run his kingdom as she had.

Recently, it had been different. Galar had spent many an idle moment trying to correlate the change to something he could identify. The appointment of Omberon as the captain of the King's Guard had changed something, but Galar wasn't sure if this suspicion arose from his personal distaste for Omberon. Windarad had voiced the same suspicion, but couldn't substantiate it.

The sudden request to open an old wound by asking the smith to make him a sword was more curious than all the rest. Galar chased the tails of vague forebodings through his mind, and the approach of Shiloh was a welcome diversion. He was on an errand for his sovereign. He had a job to do and he did want to meet this smith personally.

The smithy lay on the southern edge of Shiloh, at the end of a lane leading out into the barley fields. The smell of the air changed as he entered Shiloh, laden with the smell of manure and muddy streets, freshly baked bread and the peculiar odor of the butcher shop. Polite hellos and quiet smiles surrounded him as he wended his way through the village, ever closer to the ring of multiple hammers on their anvils.

The doors and windows of the smithy stood wide open. Spirals of smoke curled upward from the five chimneys that poked through the thatched roof. He approached the long, low building and dismounted to the left of the door. As he tied his horse to the dragon's head hitching post, the smell of coal and hot iron drifted from the dark doorway. He took a deep breath and paused, listening carefully to the diverse sounds, anticipating what each might be before entering. Above them all, the strong voice of a man singing captured his attention:

> *"Layer the steel and iron pure.*
> *Heat and hammer the weld secure.*
> *Draw it long and fold it then*
> *Weld, draw, fold—again, again."*

The singing stopped as he entered the shop. One of the smiths laid down his tongs and hammer and wiped his hands on his grimy leather apron. He signaled his assistant to lay off the bellows, bowed and waved to the other smiths. They stopped hammering. "What is your business here, Good Dor?"

"I am Galar, Head Dor to the King. I've been sent to request your hand in making a sword for the king's upcoming birthday."

The man looked up and pointed to the small, carefully carved sign above his forge fire. Galar's eyes flicked to the sign, absorbing it quickly, then back to the face of the man before him.

"I don't make swords." The smith held Galar's eyes in his gaze.

The gray eyes of the smith, deep-set and clear, said without words that he was the man of legend, and some long-held conviction already stood at odds with the king's request.

Galar had to finish his errand. "This is for the king—for a very significant occasion."

The smith looked into Galar's eyes. "...and I don't make any tool for someone who doesn't come to me personally."

"Why?"

"Because I will know the character of the one into whose hands I commend a tool—any tool—that I make."

"So if the king were to visit personally, you might make his sword?"

"I would not," said the smith. He pointed again to the sign above his fire, and turned back to his forge as he waved the other smiths back to work.

The conversation was over. Galar had encountered such men before, though they were rare: a confident, well-respected master of his domain. Galar turned and walked out of the smithy, leaving king Sandihar's desire unfulfilled.

"When we speak in riddles, Tessalindria is confused. When we jest, she is amused. When we speak in anger, she retaliates. When we speak truth simply, we shake her foundations and she trembles."

Sessasha,
It Is Said

Paca always tried to understand Fada before he questioned him, but the abrupt treatment of the king's emissary was far outside the boundary of civility. "Fada, this was a request from the *king*, a good and wise king—surely you can make an exception?"

Fada looked at him, measuring his words. "Goodness and wisdom are perceptions. He *is* the king, but when he comes here, he's *just* a man, possibly good, possibly wise, but wanting a sword. I won't do that to any man."

"Do *what* to any man?"

"Inflict on him the burden of a tool designed for the injury another of the mankind."

"I'm not sure I understand."

"When I make a blade, the intent of the blade is forged into it from the first stroke of the hammer. You know this. If this is not done, then the blade will be a blade much like those made by other smiths of Immerland. My blades *live* their intent into the hands of their owners. This is the greatest secret of bladesmithing. To make a sword for a man, is to inflict on that man the burden of the intent of a sword: to kill others. I won't do this."

Paca stared. He knew Fada well, and he knew more was coming.

Fada continued, "When you understand this, you'll pass from brilliance to greatness in your craft."

Paca's insides churned.

Fada picked up the steel blade again, and turned his attention back to the fire. Paca had heard this many times, in various ways, but wasn't sure he believed it. It lay at the core of Lesson One. Fada's convictions often made Paca uncomfortable.

Right now he was angry, but he held his tongue as Fada raked out the fire and laid the blade flat on it for a new heat.

Fada's gaze engaged Paca's as the song began to flow again. Paca knew it well:

"Pack the edge and pack it tight,
Pack the edge while the blade is bright.
One-two-three, one-two-three, heel to tip.
Tappity, tappity, lickity split.
Bury the blade in the ashes deep;
Overnight, its softness keep."

The discussion had ended. Paca tried to argue with his anger, but that made it worse. There was nothing specific to be angry about; nothing specific he would say to Fada, even if he had the chance. He concentrated on the bellows and giving the fire its breath for Fada's work.

The next day started out like any other day at the smithy. Paca finished his chores. Today, a fire was unnecessary. The blades had been pulled from the ash bin, cold and gray after cooling overnight, and the task for the day was filing and shaping the edges. As he dusted the ashes off the steel, the forge poetry rose up and rolled off his tongue:

"Cut to shape and dress and file.
Apply the lines of grace and style.
Flatten the faces, a gentle wedge.
Smooth the tang, but leave the edge
Sharpen the—"

The door to the smithy burst open, interrupting Paca in mid-sentence. King Sandihar stood in the doorway, his eyes scanning the shop. Paca had seen him before, but never this close. A head shorter than Fada, with light brown hair that grayed around his temples, the king had dark eyes, as black as the forge coal, with small crow's feet extending from their outer corners to his temples, that spoke of a man content. He didn't look content now.

He wore no crown, perhaps to make the visit less formal, but his gold vambraces and his tunic, with its tasseled epaulets and the Immerland crest emblazoned across the chest, left no doubt about who he was. The princess stood just behind his left shoulder. She was almost as tall as her father, but much less royal in appearance. Paca smiled to himself: the Pied Princess. Three other men hovered behind her dressed in long blue robes and white turbans. Behind them, just outside the door, stood several guards, partially obscured by the doorframe and the bright mid-morning rays of Asolara.

The king strode to meet Fada, with the princess a step behind. When she stopped, she was not more than an arm's length from where Paca stood with his hand still on the post vise where he had clamped the compost chopper blade. He could have touched her. She brought with her a fresh scent of the outdoors. It wasn't a perfume that one might expect of royalty, but subtle, and noticeable. Her clothing spoke of gaiety, simplicity and function all at the same time, a rare combination for a young woman. He guessed she was little older than seventeen.

"I've come to request that you make a sword for your king." The king looked up into Fada's steel gray eyes.

"No," Fada said softly, as he turned and pointed to his sign. The king's black eyes darkened as Fada bent to the task of positioning a blade into his filing vise.

Paca guessed that the king was not used to being refused with such authority.

"I'm the king—" the king said, his voice trembling on the verge of rage.

Fada interrupted him without looking up from his vise, "You are a *man* who wants *me* to make *him* a sword. The answer is no!"

The king glanced over his shoulder at the men in blue robes. Paca looked quickly at the princess who stared at him intently. Her eyes spoke of surprise, fear and pleading, as if Paca might intervene in the affront to her father. He knew he couldn't. The white turbans looked away, leaving the king on his own to face Fada who, having tightened the vise, straightened to face the king.

"Your highness," said Fada softly, "We've been through this before. There's no man in the world, not even you, who would be safe carrying a sword I had made for him. If it's your pleasure to have a new sword, I beg of you to request this of one of the other smiths in the kingdom. The smith at Yendel is a fine—"

"No!" interrupted the king. "I will have a blade of *yours* at my side. You have until tomorrow at this time to consider my offer. I will pay you well, but if you still refuse, you'll be imprisoned until you do as I ask."

Fada opened his mouth to speak, but the king turned and headed out the door. His advisors kept their eyes on the floor. The princess hesitated. Paca felt her penetrating gaze for an instant, before she broke it off and followed the entourage out of the smithy. She had reached inside him through his eyes and taken something...no maybe she had left something; what it was he wasn't sure, but now she was gone.

Paca looked back to meet Fada's eyes. Fada smiled reassuringly and bent to his task, adjusting the blade in his vise. Paca waited, sensing a great sadness welling up in Fada. When he didn't speak, Paca turned to the work before him, trying to focus on where he had been before he had been interrupted by the king.

The next day broke upon Shiloh with warmth and exuberance belonging only to the quiet days of the late summer, but Paca could sense the darkness over Fada as he continued working on the chef's new knife. While Fada finished his filing, Paca swept the floor around the forge, arranged the tongs and the fire tools, topped off the slack tub, and set the forge fire. Today they would harden and temper several knives, making the steel edges hard and keen, leaving the back of the blade flexible and springy.

The words of the forge poetry sprang from Fada's lips as the blades lay in the fire. Paca felt Fada's gray eyes fixed into his own, imparting a strength of wisdom that could be had no other way:

> *"Heat the blade to lodestone red,*
> *Even and bright in Timmanaeus's bed.*
> *Slice it fast in the tepid wave.*

> *Slice it straight, its fairness save.*
> *Temper it slowly, temper it true,*
> *The edge to straw, the back to blue."*

Paca knew the words, but something in the intensity of Fada's voice made them new and alive each time.

The steel squealed as his Fada plunged it into the quenching brine—an agonizing but momentary ordeal the blade must endure, a rite of passage on its way to its ultimate purpose. Back and forth the blade went as the cry of the steel subsided into steam. He had barely pulled the blade from the tub, still steaming lightly in the cool morning air, when the door opened. The king strode in with the princess and four soldiers close on his heels. Fada laid the blade on the edge of the forge and pulled the other blades from the fire before dropping the steaming tongs onto the packed clay floor. He stood up straight behind the forge as the king made his way toward him. The two men faced each other, locked eyes, and paused.

"Have you considered my proposal?" the king asked.

"I have not."

"You would defy your king a second time?" the king raged.

"Your Highness..." Fada bowed slightly in deference to the man before him. "It's a privilege to live under your leadership. You've brought peace and prosperity to this land where we live in abundance and freedom under your wisdom and grace. Your people love and respect you and you walk freely among us without fear. You have accomplished all this without a single blade from me—"

"Nonsense," interrupted the king. "Your blades slice my food and most of the food in the kingdom. Your blades chop our wood, they harvest our fields, they shape the wood and cut the stone for our houses and the castle, and in all this, never has one of these blades injured its owner or another. My kingdom is in debt to your workmanship for our prosperity and success. Is it such a large thing to ask you now to make a sword for your king's fiftieth birthday?"

Fada's gray eyes lit suddenly, as if they had caught the fire of Timmanaeus himself. Fada straightened to his full height, his face taking the appearance of chiseled iron.

"I am a man of peace. Each tool I make is forged—from the first hammer stroke to the last stroke of my strop—to be used for peaceful purposes. This intent lives in the blade, and protects its owner and others. If you consider this to contribute significantly to your success as king, I am doubly honored and indebted to you to be allowed to continue with my work in your service. But I cannot impart such life into the blade whose purpose is to take another man's life—"

"This will be a blade of peace—"

"There is no sword that is a blade of peace," Fada said, his eyes dancing brighter. He seemed to grow taller as he said it. "The life of my blades springs from their intent. There can be no intent in a sword other than harm to others. If that intent is *not* forged into the sword, it will be no different than any other sword. If it *is*, then surely there will be no peace. It's been said that you cannot prepare for, and prevent war, at the same time."

Darkness fell over King Sandihar's handsome face, and for the first time Paca noticed the leader of the King's Guard. Paca couldn't be sure if it was a smile or a sneer that lurked behind the crooked nose of that dark face. Something wasn't right. He knew it in the depths of his vorn. He glanced quickly to the other guards. Calm and alert, they were honest men paying attention to the details of their job. He looked back to Fada, imposing and solid.

"You're saying you won't make a sword for me?"

"I will not."

The king whirled around and raised his hand. "Take him away!"

Time froze as everything slowly revolved around Paca. He saw the princess hesitate. Her eyes looked directly into Fada's and he held her gaze briefly until she turned suddenly and followed her father out of the smithy. Paca was sure that something had been said in that brief moment.

As the king and the princess disappeared through the doorway, the captain and two soldiers stepped forward. Shackles rattled. Fada moved forward to meet them. "I'm a man of peace. There's no need for chains. I'll go with you, but I need to talk to my son first—in private."

The captain sneered and opened his mouth to speak, then shut it without a sound as he signaled the other guards to step back and wait. Paca followed Fada to the corner of the smithy. "Fada, you can't let them do this—"

Fada ignored his plea. "You'll take over my duties as the head smith until I return. You know the poetry, and you're capable of managing the other smiths. There's enough steel in the storeroom and coal in the bin for several months. By that time, I'll be out of prison. Of all this I'm confident. But you must promise me one thing—"

Paca looked up into his eyes.

"Promise me that you won't forge any blade for the injury of the mankind."

Paca dropped his eyes. Fada's hand reached over and lifted his chin, forcing him to make eye contact again. "Promise me!" he commanded.

"I promise."

"Promise what?"

Paca knew what he had to do. The nature of psadeq demanded it of him. He felt like a child, but he understood the urgency. Fada would have no peace without Paca's promise. He looked squarely into Fada's eyes and spoke firmly. "I promise not to forge any blade where the intent is the injury of the mankind." As he spoke, Paca felt doubt sweep over him like brine quenching a hot blade.

Fada clapped him smartly on the shoulder. "Good." He looked at Paca thoughtfully. For a moment, Paca wondered if Fada could read his doubt. He willed his heart to be stout for Fada's sake. Fada's grip tightened on his shoulder. "The princess is your friend. I see it in her eyes. Let her be your friend, but nothing more." He turned and followed the soldiers out of the smithy.

Chapter 3

Prison

"Great is the being who, seeing two paths of truth, is able to reconcile them into a single greater truth."

Hispattea,
The Essences of Corritanean Wisdom

King Sandihar stood alone in the tower room. He had been there for nearly an hour, anticipating the arrival of the smith. He'd ridden ahead with his daughter and his advisors, leaving Omberon and his guards to escort the captive. They were taking longer than he expected, and he hated the uneasiness that crept through him.

He created a distraction for himself, looking around the room for the fiftieth time, rechecking each detail. The round room, halfway up the South Tower, was seven paces in diameter and furnished at his command to be sparse, but comfortable. Even with the windows open to the warm, midday breeze, the faint fragrance of mint and pine oil lingered from the thorough washing it had needed after years of disuse. The three windows, set into the thick eastern, southern and western walls, had been cleaned. Their hardware had been checked for soundness, brushed off, and oiled so that its black patina shone against the freshly oiled wood.

A firm, clean bed, a small writing desk with a chair and a leather couch provided a few creature comforts. A wardrobe for clothing stood against the wall between southern and western windows. Beside the bed, a nightstand shadowed a pitcher of water and the chamber pot. He had made the room livable, but couldn't imagine a man staying here by choice.

As he stared out between the heavy bars of the southern window, Sandihar tried in vain to smile to himself, but a gnawing doubt that the smith would grant his request plagued his vorn. Imprisoning a man who had done nothing wrong—except a personal conviction that had insulted him—further fueled his frustration.

Why would a man be so stubborn? He made blades for a living. Why would he draw such a distinction? This thought had kept Sandihar awake most of the night. He sensed the answer floating just beyond his mind's grasp, making him feel like a child again; trying to understand something he wasn't sure he ever would. This was the feeling he hated most of all.

The sound of the approaching soldiers was a welcome relief. He'd never liked being alone. When he was alone, there was little to do but think in small circles that went nowhere. He was a man of action, and action to him was being surrounded by people. This is how he ran his life, his castle, his country and his world. Without them, alone with himself, he felt small and insignificant.

Sandihar leaned back against the window. A small choke rose in his throat as the smith ducked slightly to step through the door from the semidarkness of the corridor. Omberon should have been in the lead.

The smith stood to his full height and scanned the room quickly. Sandihar met his eyes. The smith walked to the middle of the room. With a quick, civil bow, the smith acknowledged him. "May I sit down?"

Sandihar nodded.

The smith sat down on the small couch and leaned back, staring comfortably into his eyes. His opaque expression was void of any anger or frustration. There was no visible passion in any emotional direction. "Thank you for your hospitality. How long do you expect that I'll be here?"

"That depends…"

"On whether and when I make your sword?"

"Yes." Sandihar waited for a response. Nothing. He looked up at the guards. Omberon smirked; three others stood behind him. "Was there any trouble getting here?" He hoped to discover the meaning of Omberon's twisted smile.

"None, Sire. We stopped to get a few things from his house." Omberon tossed a small burlap sack onto the couch beside the smith.

Sandihar glanced at the sack, but found his eyes drawn immediately back to the smith, who still stared at him.

"May I be left alone, Sire?" the smith asked.

Sandihar nodded. "Of course. Anything else you need?"

"Nothing." Still no emotion, not even the slightest hint of resentment, fear or anger.

"If you need anything, knock on the door and the guards will see to it that your needs are met." Sandihar had that feeling again: the child, left wondering what all others seemed to know. He bowed suddenly and stiffly. He didn't know why. It made his ears hot. He whirled and headed for the door, expecting that the smith might say something. Omberon saluted. That crooked smile—was the captain laughing inside? "Follow me…lock the door."

"Pride is the consummate nemesis of clarity of mind."

Hispattea
The Essences of Corritanean Wisdom

"Come, Vrengnia, would you like to visit the smith? I'm curious to see whether he's made any effort to use the forge I set up for him." Dinner had been cleared from the table in the banquet hall, and Vrengnia lingered over an after-dinner sherry with Fada.

Vrengnia set down her glass and stood up. "I should like to see the smith..."

"You seem hesitant."

"Yes...and no. Just seems harsh to lock up a man who's done nothing."

"Nothing? He defied me to my face. This is the second time." A storm gathered in Fada's eyes.

"The second time?"

"Years ago. I should have dealt with him then."

"What happened?"

"I'll tell you about it some other time. It's not important."

Vrengnia wasn't sure, but she realized he wasn't going to explain it now. "He refused to make a sword for you, but what has he done, really?"

Fada rose to face her, setting down his glass in a dramatic flourish of care. "Come along, We'll see if he has *done* anything."

Vrengnia followed him out of the banquet hall. She had spent many hours walking behind Fada, and could read his feelings by the shape of his shoulders. Right now they said, "Sullen."

"I'm not angry with you, Fada, but I don't understand, that's all."

"Ummmhh," an acknowledgment that he didn't like what he was thinking, but didn't know what to say about it. She followed in silence.

Two guards stood at the door to the room below the smith's prison. They stiffened as Fada came into view. "Anything happening in there?" he asked softly.

"Not a sound, Sire," said the tall soldier on the left with a guttural rumble characteristic of the castle guards. "There's been no sound since you left this morning."

"Was he served lunch and dinner?"

"Yes, Sire. both."

"Did he eat?"

"I don't know, Sire."

"Open the door!"

There was no lock on the door, but the heavy bolt was only accessible from the outside. Vrengnia watched the shorter guard pull it back and push the door into the room. The guard stepped in first. Fada followed him. The tall guard waved Vrengnia in behind. She obeyed, and with a quick step stood behind Fada's shoulder. She had always stood there. It was her place, but recently she'd begun to resent it. At the moment, in the presence of the smith it seemed a little silly as well, but she made no effort to move, out of respect for Fada.

Identical to the one above it in the tower, Fada had transformed the room into a crude smithy. It was sad and comical, having seen the intensity and the detailed organization of the smithy at Shiloh.

A small forge sat against the southern wall beside the window. A neat but forlorn looking bench with a small vise stood near the forge with a few tongs and other tools scattered about on it. She guessed that the burlap bag that stood open by the forge was full of coal. The anvil, on its stump to the left, seemed whimsical compared to the great anvil that the smith owned in Shiloh, and the half-barrel of water on the floor beside the forge was leaking. None of it seemed to have been touched. The bulk of the room was empty and echoed with every movement. She couldn't imagine hitting an anvil in this stone chamber.

The king glanced quickly about and his eyes came to rest on the smith who stood by the western window gazing out on the twilit fields.

"Good Smith, I would have thought you would have begun my blade by this time. I'm disappointed." Sarcasm laced his voice, but his face remained stern. "Is something wrong?"

The smith turned, but continued leaning against the window casement. His hands relaxed under his folded arms, as he eyed Fada thoughtfully. He waited before he spoke and measured his words. "Yes, there's something wrong. The coal is bad, the anvil is saddled, there is no flue for the forge, the steel you left me is inferior, the bellows aren't sufficient for the kind of work you require, and I am imprisoned against my will—"

"Details, details," Fada interrupted with an impatient hand gesture. "Instead of telling me what's wrong with my provisions, tell me what you need, so I can get it for you."

"What I need..." mused the smith. "What do I need? I need to be in my smithy with my son, earning my keep making blades for your kingdom—"

"Stop!"

Vrengnia didn't often see Fada angered so quickly.

The smith paused. "By your leave," he began again more cautiously, "I don't mean to be trivial with my king. I consider you a wise and kind man and a good king. You have protected us and our land is safe and prosperous. However, the wisdom of imprisoning me is faulted. It's out of character for you to hold me hostage simply because I wouldn't make the birthday present you wanted, particularly when I have served your kingdom and your person faithfully."

Fada softened as the smith continued speaking. His shoulders dropped ever so slightly.

"I cannot help but think that there's something bigger at stake, something you fear that you didn't fear before. If this is true, a better sword isn't the remedy for fear, and now, I request, as a faithful servant, that you release me to my service to you in my smithy."

The two men stood staring at one another. Vrengnia shifted her weight from one foot to the other. Silence made her uneasy. Fada once told her about the necessity of silence at certain times, but she wasn't sure she understood what he meant exactly. She wasn't sure that he did either.

Fada sighed. "You're a good man, with a great wisdom, and perhaps I have made a mistake in imprisoning you. But I will have a blade from your forge ere I set you free to my service. I will supply anything you need, and you will be well taken care of in my service here, but there will be no release until this task is complete."

He hesitated. The smith turned back to the window.

"When you are ready with a list of what you need, I will spare no expense to get it for you. Until then, you will spend the days here and the nights upstairs."

Fada waited, but the smith remained silent and still, silhouetted in the window against the western sky.

"Take him to his chambers upstairs." He said to the guards. He strode out of the room. Vrengnia followed. His shoulders said, "I'm frustrated." Vrengnia was embarrassed.

"A short sword for the soldier boy,
A long sword for the king.
A wrong sword in an idle hand
Is quite a fearsome thing."

Ancient Mooriman Rhyme

Sandihar smiled at Carnados's question. "I've spent a good part of two hours with him every day since he came to the castle. Why do you ask?

"I was curious what you might talk about for such a long time. Surely not convincing him to make your sword—"

"No—no, nothing like that. He won't let me."

Carnados raised an eyebrow.

"It seems every time we get anywhere near that subject, there's always a compelling diversion that brings us to something else entirely. I usually don't even realize it until after it's happened."

"He is a clever man."

"Clever is too mild, I think. He is knowledgeable beyond his own natural intelligence, but I can't figure out how…or why…or where, or even when he could have gotten such knowledge."

"What do you mean?"

"Remember all the history you used to insist I learn—or at least should have some familiarity with?"

Carnados shifted in the armchair, straightening slightly and smiling. "I seem to remember it ending up mostly the latter."

"Well…yes…well, he seems to know all about all of them!"

"All of them?"

"And I don't even think he can read."

"Impossible. No one could know the ancient literature without being able to read, and the ancient linguals at that!"

"Well, he does. Moreover, he knows the glyphs and runes. I have caught him several times writing on the floor with a chunk of coal. It's always in glyphs. He quotes from Hispattea and Mortag of Horrinaine. Remember when I called Mortag an old windbag? In the smith's mouth his words are a refreshing breeze."

Carnados shifted again and leaned forward, his fingers on his temples, his eyes concentrating intently on one of the floor tiles.

"It goes on and on," Sandihar said. "He knows every detail of Vortang's *Theory of War*; he draws diagrams that would shame Marhaigan and his best pupils. Several times, he has referenced Karamanta's elucidation on the Eladra and spatial infinity. He converses fluidly about the Kirrinath, and he quotes liberally from the *Tessarandin*—"

"How old is he? Do you know?"

"I don't. I have asked, but my questions never are answered. He won't speak of himself."

Carnados looked up briefly and then back at his tile. "Do you suppose he could be Sessashian?"

"It crossed my mind. He didn't say, though it's unlikely he would. He's a natural teacher, without being 'teachy.' When I leave, I feel like a child that has been listened to—that has been, in fact, heard—and I feel like I have been taught, not taught things, but life itself. Have you ever had that feeling?"

"Your mother made me feel that way sometimes."

"My mother…yes, except I never felt like I understood very much when my mother taught me."

"Really?! Do you understand the smith?"

"Yes—and no." Sandihar coughed to relieve the tightness he felt in his throat. "I mean, it all seems so clear when he is teaching, but when I leave, I feel as though the most vital ingredient of the thoughts is left behind, as if he is unlocking them to me, but holding onto the key. I haven't had a decent night's sleep in a week, trying to put together the pieces of some infinite fabric he's weaving."

"Has he spoken to you about his imprisonment? Has he asked for release? Has he asked for *anything*?"

"He seems perfectly content to stay where he is led. He's been no trouble to the guards whatsoever."

"Strange—"

"Worse than strange, he seems to enjoy it. Sometimes I get a vague feeling he is actually in charge, that somehow, from within his cells, he is changing the world around him. Whenever I visit him, he acts as if he expected me. It's frightening, frankly. I have only felt that kind of fear one time before."

"Verclan?"

"Yes, but don't remind me—"

"I don't think I need to."

"You're right, but perhaps you can help resolve—" He looked up suddenly to see Vrengnia in the doorway to the throne room.

"May I come in?" Her tired eyes accentuated the slight frown of her lips. "Am I interrupting something?"

"No...no, come in, sit down." Sandihar never refused his daughter. It had served him well, particularly in the last few years when their relationship had been strained by her advance toward being a young woman.

"Fada, I've been troubled since you arrested the smith, particularly after the discussion he had with you about the greater good behind all this." She circled in front of him and looked directly into his eyes. "What he said that day...I've been unable to get it out of my mind—as if it were true; there is something bigger here, isn't there?"

Sandihar sighed, "There is." He paused. He wondered whether it was wise to continue. Vrengnia stared into his eyes. "What I tell you today you must utter to no other. Can you promise me this?"

"I'll tell no one," she affirmed.

Sandihar didn't want to continue. He wasn't sure he could even trust his daughter. "We've had several reports that"—he struggled to say the next word—"that Verclan is amassing an army, near the southern border, and he intends to attack Immerland again."

"Verclan? Can't we just repel him as we always have?"

"There's more," he said. Vrengnia lowered her eyes. "There are rumors that he may have a smith working for him who fashions weapons that can cut steel like clay and pierce mail like linen. We won't be able to stand against such an assault."

Vrengnia stared at the floor. "Where did the rumors come from? Where did you hear them?"

Sandihar didn't want to answer her question, so he ignored it altogether. She looked up as he continued. "Our hope is in the jailed smith, whose blades are fabled to do the same. My hope is if we can convince him to make one blade, then he will relent and make many—the key is to get him to break and make the one, first." He wasn't sure she noticed his evasion.

"Can't you just tell him of the threat to the kingdom? Would he not be more willing to help us?"

"It would only make him more stubborn, I fear. We have no proof and we don't even know the source of the rumors, but we must be prepared, and the key is this smith." Sandihar paused. His eyes narrowed as he continued, looking squarely into his daughter's eyes. "You mustn't tell anyone. Fear in our people is a greater enemy than Verclan and all his army. There must be no word of this until the truth is known clearly. The only ones in the kingdom who know of these things are the scouts, my advisors and you. Promise me again you will tell no one!"

"I promise to tell no one," Vrengnia said.

Sandihar eyed her thoughtfully for a moment, but said nothing more. Something told him she wasn't sure. It was a feeling he knew well. He had said such things to his mother many times.

"Each must understand, without hesitation or pause, that within the First Cymbic Sphere, complete acceptance and understanding do not have to be sought; they simply are."

The Tessarandin,
Book Four

"What is it like to be in charge here?" Vordar smiled as he sat atop the anvil watching Paca clamp his work in the filing vice.

Paca shrugged. "It's not the being in charge that's different. What's different is not having Fada here. It just seems quiet." He bent over the vise to check the fairness of the thatch knife before he started the finish grinding.

"Yes, quiet is the right word, though your father doesn't do a whole lot of talking." Vordar was a young man, like Paca himself, and a good smith for his years.

Paca nodded. "That wasn't that kind of quiet I was talking about."

Vordar dropped his hands to his knees. "Are you going to the castle again? It's been three days now..."

"I think not—what would be different? If nothing else is different, why would the outcome be different? I've been there thrice. I don't even know for sure that he's there."

"You need to find that princess."

"That's enough, Vordar."

"But we all saw her look at you. Didn't you see it? And then those other visits, I mean—" Vordar grinned.

Paca smiled to himself, but kept it from leaking onto his face. "There's work to be done," he muttered as he stepped toward the huge sandstone grinder by the window. "You should get to yours."

Vordar shrugged and spun around on the anvil, slipping easily off the other side on the way to his forge.

The poetry sprang from Paca's mouth. He never understood exactly how this happened:

"Grind it rough on the sandstone round,
Work with care 'til the hollow's ground.
Pitch in the bevel, constant the length,
Bevel the point, but watch its strength.
Stone it by hand to platinum sheen,
Strop it on leather to make it keen."

He said it through several times, tumbling the pictures associated with each word over and over until he could visualize every nuance of each blade before he started.

In the middle of the fourth time through, on the second blade, a movement at the front gate interrupted his concentration. He looked up through the window to see the princess fumbling with the gate latch. He bent over the grindstone, trying to pretend he hadn't seen her.

Vrengnia had been to the smithy three times since Fada's arrest. The first time to offer condolences following the arrest, and the second was to make sure that everything was going well in the smithy. The third was to bring Paca some fresh bread from the king's kitchen. Each time she came alone, dressed in her comical colored outfit and looking more like a court jester than a princess.

Paca didn't know whether there was any other than her stated motive for her visits. She wasn't like other young women he knew who were always flustered or embarrassed over themselves, their conversation, their actions—just about everything. The princess walked with grace and ease, even in the midst of the smithy. She asked intelligent questions with refreshingly true curiosity, and listened to the answers as if she genuinely wanted to know. She looked into his eyes when he spoke, and her contribution to the conversation was articulate and useful.

In spite of her position as the princess of the kingdom, she carried no hint of this into her dealings with him. When she left, Paca found himself completely at ease with her having been there and completely at ease with her leaving. It was as if she had always been there when she was there, and as if she had never been there when she left. Though she probably knew what was happening to Fada, she never spoke of having seen him, and it seemed inappropriate to ask her.

She approached the door.

Paca pumped the treadle to keep the massive wheel spinning and his attention on the wet blade in his hand.

She entered the smithy, hesitating only to adjust to its interior dimness. She strode directly to him. That fresh, outside scent that always surrounded her invaded his workspace and he looked up, trying to act surprised. Laying the blade aside, he stood to his full height as he wiped his hands on the grimy towel by the wheel.

"We must talk." Blunt, but polite.

Paca raised an eyebrow, as he stared into her eyes quietly.

"Perhaps we can go outside. What I have to say is for you only," she said.

He held out his hand in a "you first" gesture, and then followed her to the door. He looked over his shoulder. With a wave of his hand, he let Vordar know that he was in charge while Paca was gone.

They walked out into the yard and followed the lane leading out of Shiloh into the barley fields behind the smithy's back fence. Asolara flooded the empty road, rendering a glorious potpourri of warm smells: the pungent odor of ripe barley, the drying soil of the fields and the star flowers on the side of the road. Birds sang to one another as they feasted on the fields, embellishing the subtle cacophony of an unseen chorus of insects.

"I need you to make that sword for my father's birthday," she said when they were out of earshot of the smithy.

"No!" Paca stopped short. She took a couple more steps before turning back to look straight up into his eyes.

"Did you say that, or was that your father?" she asked.

"What? Of course, I said it. Fada is in prison, remember?"

"No—I mean—was what you said from *your* vorn, or was it tied to some obligation to be like your father?"

Paca wavered and dropped his eyes.

"I thought as much—come on, we have much more to discuss."

"I'm not sure we do," said Paca quietly. "At least not about this."

She stepped toward him until she was unusually close. "We're both much like our fathers, more than we're comfortable with sometimes. I often wonder if I even *want* to be like my father. He's so strong, so disciplined, so organized—I'm not sure I could bear it—and he's sometimes stubborn to his own hurt."

Vrengnia gestured that they should continue walking and they started down the lane again. "I'm not sure I would have imprisoned your father, for example. I mean—what good is it to imprison a man from whom you want a favor?"

Paca stared into the distance but said nothing.

"Maybe if Fada had taken more time to explain the situation, *your* father would have been convinced to do his bidding."

They walked a number of paces, each waiting, and each listening to the other quietly.

Vrengnia broke the stalemate. "I also believe...that if you examine your vorn, *you* would have agreed to make the blade." She paused. "I mean—as much as we're the same as our fathers, we're also different. We're not so stuck in our ways—"

"Perhaps."

"Perhaps?...Perhaps? Come now. I know you love and respect your father. He's a man worthy of both, but you must forge your own tools. Fada is like that too, but there are some things that, when I'm queen, I will definitely do differently."

"Why?" Paca shot back. "Your father is a fine king! He is wise and thoughtful, kind and gentle, and has led us to great prosperity and peace. What would you do that would be better than this?"

Vrengnia gazed at the horizon.

Paca continued, "Please understand. I wrestle with the same thoughts about my father. There are things about him that I don't understand. I sometimes wonder whether it is just because he is getting older and set in his ways, or perhaps there is truth in his ways that I cannot comprehend yet. Maybe you, too, are underestimating your father's strength, Princess. Perhaps in judging your father, your own arrogance will lead you to miss the greatest gift he has for you."

"I have had many such conversations with myself—about my father. But what about yours? Take, for instance, this obsession with not making weapons—where does *that* come from? What does it do for him? Fada already has swords. His army has hundreds of them. One more won't make that much of a difference! Is it just arrogance? Your father's sword, were he to make one, might be fine, but should he suppose that it would be that much superior to those made by other smiths in Immerland? I mean, would *you* be so arrogant? Are *your* blades so superior?"

"If they aren't, then why are you so desperate to have one?" Paca asked.

The princess softened. "Don't get me wrong. I believe they are better. But are they *that* much better, that your arrogance would leave your father rotting in prison over this issue?" She continued. "Suppose I told you that this was more than just a birthday gift, that there was more at stake, that indeed the safety of the kingdom itself is in jeopardy."

"You hinted at this before," Paca replied. "Is this what you are going to tell me? If it is, I need to know. If you want my cooperation, you owe me honesty."

"It's not quite that simple."

"Not that simple?"

"I made a promise to my father that I wouldn't tell anyone—"

"Tell anyone what?"

"I promised."

"You mean that you have knowledge of a danger to the whole kingdom, that you think I could help with, and you're not allowed to let me know what it is so I *can* help. Why would your father make you promise such a thing?"

"You could help by making his sword."

"I cannot!"

"Why?"

"I promised—" The words had come out before he had time to think about the implications.

"Promised what?"

Paca remained silent.

"You promised your father that you would not make any weapons, didn't you, that you would not make a sword for my father!"

The hint of triumph in the princess's voice should have galled him. "Yes, I did," he conceded. He wanted to feel angry. It wouldn't happen.

They stood staring at each other in the middle of the road. "Let's think about this situation," she said. "I made a promise to my father that I would not reveal this threat to our kingdom, and you made a promise to your father that prevents you from helping me. Are we not both just living out our fathers' stubbornness to all of our detriment? If I were to break my oath, and tell you the need, would you consider breaking yours to help me?"

He stared at the princess, not wanting to believe the situation unfolding before him. It was so easy when Fada was around, but now he was on his own. What were *his* convictions? What was it that *he* believed? "I might," he whispered hoarsely.

"Might what?"

"It depends on the seriousness of the situation."

"Then you would consider it, at least?" pressed the princess.

"Yes."

"Then as a measure of good faith, I will break my oath first, but you must tell no one of this conversation. The purpose of this revelation here is to convince you to help me. If you do, our kingdom can be saved, and your father will be freed from prison without having to compromise his convictions."

"If all I have to do is make your father his sword, then go ahead." He tried to weigh the measure of a greater good, the promise to Fada, his psadeq or...he did not even know what rested on the other side of the scales. Psadeq weighed heavily.

Fada had taught that psadeq encompassed the entire nature of a relationship: trust, faithfulness, love, genuine concern—but it was more than all these things at the same time. It was something that everyone knew, that anyone could grasp and understand, yet it defied precise definition. Its essence encompassed and played into every relationship there was: husband and wife, doctor and patient, brothers, soldiers, tradesmen, father and son—it waxed and waned with the events in a relationship that drew two persons together or split them asunder.

Psadeq was the measure of the "rightness" of a relationship: immutable and binding, but fragile and easily unraveled at the same time. Paca knew its value and knew his obligation to Fada under its laws, but psadeq with the princess was strong also. Though he had known her but a short time, it seemed he should have known her all his life.

They walked a few steps before the princess began her revelation. "Fada has received information from his scouts to the south that Verclan is amassing an army for another attack on Immerland."

"Verclan?"

"The same," continued the princess. "Fada is afraid. He believes our kingdom is facing a threat from Verclan we haven't seen in many years, and there are complications on top of that: it seems that this isn't the first conflict that your father has had with mine, but he wouldn't tell me the details. Now he means to convince—or force—your father to make a sword for him."

Paca listened quietly, trying to sort out the significance of the information being revealed to him. All around him, the world was bright, warm and at peace, but a darkness was creeping into his vorn, a dread, a fear that he couldn't shake.

The princess was talking, but he was only half listening. He thought about Fada in prison and how, by giving in, he could free him. The cost, however, was to betray psadeq with Fada. The alternative was betrayal of the kingdom in a time of great need, unless, of course, none of this was true. He wished Fada were here to hear this; he would know what to do.

"So what do you think?" The princess's words cut into his thoughts like a stroke from a saber.

Paca shuddered. "I—I'm not sure."

"Not sure?"

"Not sure I can help!"

"Don't you see? You're the only one who can help!" The two stopped walking and were staring at each other in the middle of the road. A cart full of barley from the harvest approached along the lane. They stepped back to let the cart pass between them.

"G'morning," said the driver brightly.

"Good morning, good farmer," responded the princess with a smile. Paca said nothing. After the cart passed, the princess stepped forward. "Do you see this? Do you see how happy and content he is? This is the way it is throughout the kingdom now. People are secure; they're happy; they're busy. We can't let all this be destroyed!" She put her hand firmly on his shoulder. "Come, Paca, let's return. You can think about this for a day or so. In two days, I'll return and I'll expect an answer. We have some time, but not a lot."

They started back toward Shiloh. Paca wanted more clarity. "So all you are asking is that I make a single sword for your father?"

"That's all."

A sullen, irritating oppression, flooded Paca's vorn. He sensed that this wouldn't be the end of the requests. "Will you promise that you will ask no more from me if I do this?"

"I promise," said the princess.

Paca chose to believe her, because he didn't want to think any further about where all this led. He sensed a sincerity and simplicity in her persuasion, but the doubt was there. How could he trust a promise from someone who had just broken a promise she had made to her own father? What right had he to judge the princess when he himself was contemplating breaking a promise he had made to *his* father? He saw the trap, and tried to ignore it. "In two days I'll have an answer."

The princes smiled. "Two days it is!"

As they walked back to the smithy together, they talked of insignificant details of their lives, meandering in conversation between everything and nothing. Paca felt defeated and completely accepting at the same time. He didn't want to face the reality invading his life, but didn't want to run from it either. The thought that perhaps this was the purpose of Fada's incarceration sank deeper and deeper into his vorn.

"Decisions are temporal in nature, and eternal in consequence. The path we walk in the infinite consists of finite, decisive steps in the now."

The Tessarandin, Book Seven

Paca carefully left out the details about the sword when he told Vordar about his walk with the princess.

Vordar laughed. "First she comes here to apologize, then to see how you are doing. Next it was that loaf of bread, which, by the way, was very good!"

"Vordar—"

"Then she wants to talk."

"Stop it!"

Vordar stopped and stared at him. A smile lurked around the corners of his mouth. "All you did was talk?"

"Yes."

"For a whole hour?"

"Every minute of it. Look, Vordar, some of what we talked about was business. There is some work she wants from me, and I may need your help."

Vordar was rearranging his fire. "Okay" he said expectantly, as he finished spreading the hot coal out around the rim of the firepot.

"I may have to work at night to keep up with the shop production, and I may need you to run the shop during the day..."

"Interesting." Vordar dropped the fire rake onto the rack beside the forge bed and wiped his hands on his apron.

"Most of all, I need you to cover for me and not let anyone else know what I am up to."

"What is it you are going to do?"

"I'm not sure I am—I have a couple days to consider the offer. It's tricky work...."

"Tricky?"

"I think it best not to actually let you know what I'm doing. Will you help me?"

"I think I can do that." Vordar smiled.

Paca knew the smile was genuine; Vordar was a good friend; one to be trusted if the need for his help arose.

Today was the day of decision. Paca wrestled with it in his mind as he rummaged around the wood-room, searching for stock to lay handles to the four scythes he was finishing for the barley harvest. The endless labyrinth of thoughts trudged toward an inevitable conclusion: He would make the king's sword.

Another thought burned his mind; he wanted to make a second sword as a gift for the princess. On the surface, this was a bit forward; with anyone else, it would have been inappropriate, but it seemed right. It would be a work of friendship and honor, an expression of psadeq.

As he extricated a candidate for one of the handles, the stack of wood leaning against the wall slid to the floor with a crash.

"Are you okay?" Vordar poked his head into the storeroom.

Paca looked up and shook his head. "I've never understood why Fada hasn't come up with a better system for storing all this."

"Maybe you should. You're in charge now, right?" Vordar winked.

"Maybe I should do it today," Paca said sarcastically.

"No, she's coming today, don't you remember?"

"I guess so..."

"Have you decided what you are going to do?"

"I think so..." Paca left Vordar hanging. They stared at each other for a long moment.

"Well?"

"I am leaving the finality of the decision to the moment. I feel I will know whether it's right or not then, not now; but it's on the edge of inevitable."

"Okay. If you don't need any help, I have an appointment with my fire." Vordar smiled.

Paca took comfort in Vordar's acceptance and went back to stacking the wood as Vordar vanished from the doorway.

The real wrestling was more about the conditions under which this task would be carried out. The cost wasn't meaningless, but close to it. How would he achieve this without Fada knowing, or anyone else for that matter? What conditions would he put on the use of the swords? How could he make it clear to the princess that there would be no others after the two? How could he be sure that, having made the swords, Fada would be released?

Paca carried the four handle blanks out into the corner of the shop where the handling was done. He knew it would take the better part of the day to prepare the handles. The balance and fairness of each was critical to the effectiveness of the tool in the hands of the harvester. It would take a critical level of concentration to achieve it, and he wasn't sure that he could hold that focus today.

The princess burned in his mind. It wasn't the silly attraction he'd felt for women he had met on other occasions, but a curiously clear relationship of pure friendship that seemed timeless, not based on how long they had known each other, but simply that they *did* know each other.

He'd had only one other friend like this, Jarish, the baker's son, whom he had met at the first winter festival. They became fast friends. They had much in common and they spent hours together through the years. They could tell each other anything, say anything, share anything.

There was never an agenda with Jarish; the only thing was being together. When they were apart, there was no fear and no anxiety, no matter how long the separation was. When they did find themselves together again, it was as if they had never been apart.

Fada used the word "cymbic" to describe Paca's friendship with Jarish. Paca thought he understood what it meant, but probably couldn't define it or even describe it well. The best words he had for it were "comfortable" and "easy."

The princess made him feel comfortable and easy, in spite of the vast social gulf that separated them. She didn't look down on him, and he sensed no desire in her to use her position to control his affairs. Even the pressure from her to make her father's sword didn't emanate from her position, but from her friendship, and although it seemed demanding, he wasn't anxious. He felt more like he owed it to her as a friend, yet he didn't feel he owed her anything at all.

He was wandering about the smithy looking for one of the sharpening stones for the drawknife when she appeared at the door. He still hadn't finalized his decision. She came alone again. This time as she entered, she walked directly up to him and gave him a brief hug. It seemed right. Vordar started whistling and Paritan dropped a pair of tongs into his empty iron slack tub. The princess took no notice of either.

"Shall we go for a walk?" he asked.

She smiled. "Sure."

They walked down the road, chatting aimlessly about small things: the day, the perfect weather for the harvest, the affairs of the castle and the business of the smithy. Then came the inevitable pause.

"So...what do you think?" the princess began.

"I've decided to make your father's sword, but I don't know why exactly."

Vrengnia listened when she could have said something to give him indication that she heard him. Paca liked the silence.

"It's a matter of trust," he continued. "I don't know you very well, but I feel like I have known you forever. I've no basis on which to trust you or the things you've told me. I have suspicions that I'm being manipulated—" Paca expected the princess to rush to her own defense. It was reassuring that she didn't. "So...I've decided to trust you. I'll make the sword."

"Thank you." He knew she was looking at him. He wasn't ready to look back, so he stared out over the field as they continued walking.

"There are some details..."

Vrengnia listened through the pause.

"I demand the freedom to make the sword as I want it, by my will and design."

"Why would I ask anything else? It is your craft, not mine."

"You must not give the sword to your father until his birthday. No one else must know that I am doing this. When I'm done, there'll be no others to follow it. I'm doing this to secure Fada's release and as a favor for you...out of friendship. Give me your word you won't offend me by asking me to do more."

"You have my word." They walked on in silence. Paca knew that any restatement of anything already said would be distasteful.

"How will I pay you?"

"I haven't thought about that. Perhaps it would be best if I just did the work. Do you feel comfortable deciding what you think it is worth to you when you see it?"

"That's fair. I think you'll be paid well enough."

"I am less concerned about money than the use of the sword," he ventured, still staring at the horizon. "*That* is what makes me afraid...and I am troubled by the promise I made to my father—"

"So am I—I mean with my father. It's a risk I will take for the greater good." She paused and looked at him again. "To be honest, I don't know *why* I think this is good," she said. "Perhaps it's our friendship. I'm not sure I would have asked anyone else. I feel bad for your father, and resentful of mine for imprisoning him, but I've thought long, and this path seems right. Perhaps we'll look back someday and understand the significance of this, but I can't regret it now."

The clarity with which she explained things encouraged him. She was "his friend and no more," as Fada had said, and the friendship was genuine. What he feared was that they, although wanting the best for both their fathers, were missing something that their fathers would have had them know.

She gave him another brief hug when she departed. It left him with an unusual sense of closure on the discussions of the day.

Chapter 4

Rumblings

"When earnest beings speak, one may be right, another may find he is wrong, but all will learn something."

Mortag of Horrinaine,
Of Beings

The king sat on a small stool opposite the smith. They talked in the prison smithy over a simple but hearty lunch prepared by his personal chef. He was pleased. "Why did you decide to start smithing after all?"

The smith swallowed before answering. "There are a few things that I have to make."

"*Have* to make?" Bits of shaped iron lay about on the table: simple in form, elegant, obviously the work of a skilled man, but obscure in purpose. The smith had started the forge for the first time only the day before, the fourteenth day after his arrest, despite the crude arrangement and supplies.

"I am a smith, good King. Sometimes I *have* to smith."

"But it sounded like there was something specific you have to make."

"Indeed!"

Sandihar had spent several lunches with his prisoner and was beginning to understand the way the smith sidestepped direct questions. "Can you tell me what it is you are trying to make?"

"If I could, I would, but I don't know myself."

"Surely, you sport with me."

"No, I don't, good King, have you ever had the feeling that you knew something that there was no way of knowing, but just the same, you knew it?"

"On occasion, but I never let it bother me. Such suspicions are as likely as not to deter real progress and knowledge. What does that have to do with what you are making here in the smithy?"

"Well, I have learned over the years that it's possible and useful to listen to the things you may know-without-knowing. The more one listens, the more he hears, and the more he hears, the more certain he becomes. With practice one becomes sure of what one knows without seeing it."

"And...?"

"I know that I'm supposed to be making something, but I don't know what. Part of my listening is to start working. At the right time it'll become clear, and I'll know what I'm supposed to do."

None of it made sense, but the smith himself seemed sure of what he was saying. Sandihar watched the smith wipe his bowl with a piece of bread.

"My daughter has been to see your son," he announced suddenly. "Several times, I've heard—"

The smith looked up and smiled. "I expected that."

"You did?"

"Of course. They are primary cymbics," said the smith matter-of-factly.

"How do you know?"

"I saw it in their eyes the first time—no, the second time you entered the smithy with her. They have been friends since birth, waiting to find one another."

Sandihar grunted. The smith's confidence was irritating.

"In fact," continued the smith, "their friendship will serve as the resolution to our little impasse."

"Really?" Sandihar scoffed, "And how will that happen?"

"I don't know and it doesn't matter that I don't, but this is the way with primary cymbics. Their trust and acceptance allows them to get past many obstacles that constrain others—they often find a path through."

Sandihar shook his head. Everything the smith said played into his growing suspicion. Just the way the smith looked at him made him feel as if the smith were reading his mind.

"Come now, good King, you're acting like I know something I don't. You know that you have kept me cloistered here in your tower, that no man has spoken to me about what is going on out there." He gestured toward the southern window, "so I know nothing specific—but I know cymbics, and I have great confidence that all this will all work out for the best, even though at first, it may seem to be wrong."

"What if they are plotting something?"

"What if they are? What are you going to do? You can't break a cymbic connection, particularly in the primary sphere! Do you trust your daughter?"

"Do you trust your son?"

The smith paused. "I trust his love for me and his interest in my welfare. I trust his mastery of smithing, his ability and intuition. I'm not sure I trust his judgment. I see this as the time and the place where he must learn judgment for himself. After all, I *am* unavailable, am I not?"

Sandihar nodded.

"A wiser man than I once said," continued the smith, "that 'good judgment comes from experience and experience comes from bad judgment.' I see no reason to be alarmed. In the end, both your daughter and my son will be more of what we want them to be."

Sandihar's respect for the smith had grown, but he still found it a hard thing to learn basic lessons about life from his prisoner. "I have the same trust for my daughter," he conceded. "She'll be a great queen some day. I know she wants the best for me, but she doesn't seem to be in much of a hurry to develop what she needs to reach that goal."

"How old were you, when you became everything your mother wanted you to be?" queried the smith.

Sandar reflected on his life and the mistakes he had made, the errors in judgment and the experiences that had shaped his better judgment. "Your wisdom is fair and good," he said. "Do you think it's best not to interfere with this liaison between your son and my daughter?"

"I think it would be good to let her know you know, but not to interfere. She needs you to trust her now more than she needs your advice."

Sandhar knew the smith was right. He rose and extended his hand to the smith. "Thank you for your time—again. I am sure you have other things to do."

The smith rose and firmly grasped Sandiahar's hand, looking directly into his eyes. "It's always a pleasure."

Sandihar left the prison smithy without looking back. He heard the guards close the door behind him and throw the bolt. He felt like he always did after a discussion with the smith: full, refreshed, inadequate... he couldn't find the word he needed to describe it. Maybe he didn't even have one.

"By fire, by will, by strength of mind,
With focused blows, sure and full, not one errant,
Each delivered as the smith means.
By this is the ordinary transformed
Into the extraordinary,
Where it stands before the eyes of the king."

Timmanaeus

"I start tonight," Paca had said in response to Vordar's question about his task for the princess. "I'm not sure what will happen—I'm not even sure I'll be able to do what I am being asked, but I know I'll need your help. I expect a few long nights."

Vordar had nodded and smiled.

Paca found a new energy in making the swords for the princess. That night he stayed in the smithy after the other smiths had gone. He worked the fire by himself and held his own work while he welded the layers of steel and iron. Working by lantern light added another layer of challenge, meager as it was in the dimly lit smithy.

The solitude fostered a fierce concentration; a focus on the process that couldn't be had in the busy day's activities. He sang the forge poetry out loud, without the self-consciousness he felt in the presence of the other smiths.

He worked each night until his eyes watered and wouldn't stay open. When he left the smithy for the short walk home, the street lamps were out and the town was fast asleep. Each morning he rose early, arriving at the smithy before anyone else to examine the progress of his work in the daylight.

The days were filled with the tasks of running the smithy and producing the blades on order for other purposes. The peculiar thrill of making the swords kept him pressing forward against the grueling schedule.

The princess came frequently; nearly every day. She never asked about her father's sword and Paca never volunteered. When the time came, they would speak. She brought food from the king's kitchen—none of the delicacies that were the fare of the king and his advisors—but rich dark bread and hearty stews. There wasn't a lot of it, but enough for Paca's dinner. Did she know he worked at night? He wasn't sure. She never asked.

"I remember the second day that I came here with my father," she said during one of these visits. "Your father was singing something when we interrupted him. What was it?"

"Forge poetry."

"Forge poetry?"

Paca looked up from the blade he was straightening on the bench into Vrengnia's inquiring eyes. "It's a poetry that helps the smith who uses it to know his way. It's a map of sorts—no, more like a path."

"Where did it come from? I mean, did someone write it?"

"No, it's not written anywhere, I don't think. I believe it was Timmanaeus that first spoke it."

"Timmanaeus...." She said it like a statement, as if she was searching deep in her memory for a long forgotten piece of history.

"Timmanaeus was the greatest of all smiths, perhaps more of a legend than a real being. He lived among the Great Fathers. It's said that he learned smithing from the Eladra, that they gave it to him as a gift, for him to give to Tessalindria.

Though others had tried working the metal, it was Timmanaeus who brought it forth as a viable trade and art."

"And he was the first to sing the forge poetry?"

"So it's said. I learned it from Fada, and he learned it from his. That's as far back as I know."

"Never heard of it."

"Not all smiths use it, or even know it. Blacksmithing as a trade can be learned and passed on without it. My father insists, however, that one cannot master the smith's art without it."

"And you?"

"I...I'm not sure. When my father sings it, he changes, and the energy of his work increases...his focus, his precision...it's hard to describe."

"But that doesn't happen to you?"

"No, but the poetry helps me to concentrate and remember the steps." Paca bent to the task before him. The blade had warped slightly in the quench, and needed a precise series of blows from his straightening mallet to make it true. It wasn't a trivial task. Vrengnia sat still as if she suddenly knew that he needed to focus. As he applied the first blows of the heavy wooden mallet, he marveled at how simple and clear it all seemed.

There were few interruptions in the smithy late at night, so the work on the swords progressed rapidly. The initial stages of preparing the blade steel were no different than for any other knife, except for the quantity of it. The sword had to be a good deal longer than most common tool blades, except those of the great scythes used in the harvests, which he had never made.

The roar of the forge fire, drawing breath from the great double-chambered bellows, along with the solitude of the night smithy, engendered a queerness, a sense not of disproportion, but of a truth he had never before achieved. He sang the poetry of the firebed, and the fire obeyed his song. He sang the verses about welding, drawing and folding, and the glowing, malleable steel obeyed the touch of his hammer without hesitation.

Paca's strength welled up from deep inside, from a reserve he didn't remember tapping before. His grip was sure, and the tongs never lost their hold on the work. He found yet another new strength in imagining Fada beside him at the forge, guiding him, encouraging him. Even in his utter solitude, he didn't feel fully alone.

He felt his strength and awareness growing, but it was on the sixth night, as he was drawing out the blades to their final length, that the sudden and sublime transformation occurred.

He had the king's blade laid in the long, narrow fire as he worked the bellows, envisioning the hammer strokes for the next heat, when a gust of wind burst open the door of the smithy and blew out the lantern between the door and the forge. It backdrafted the chimney, blowing coal smoke and ash back across the forge bed. Paca had seen a backdraft before, but never quite like this. The hot smoke seared his face and he stepped back, dropping the bellows toggle and shielding his eyes with his arm.

He tried to blink away the pain, uncovering his eyes as soon as he could see, scanning the smithy through his tears to see if an errant coal or ash had landed where it could start a fire. A quiet uneasiness crept into his vorn. Something was different. He re-lit the lantern, secured the smithy door against the night, and headed back to the forge. Without the bellows breath, the fire had cooled to red and the sword still lay there, a black silhouette floating on the glow. He took hold of the bellows toggle and the fire was soon roaring again.

He waited patiently for the sword to come up to heat. It was taking longer than usual, so he worked the bellows harder and raked a few coals over the top of the blade. He had removed the clinker from the bottom of the fire only fifteen minutes before, and it roared like dragon's breath, but the blade remained black.

An echo of some unsaid phrase floated through his mind. *Sing—sing.* He opened his mouth to sing to the blade, but he couldn't remember any words and no sound came forth. *Sing—sing the song of the sword*, his mind shouted. He opened his mouth again and a song burst forth:

> *"Argen tyven wi ri kiren*
> *Kara toum a para kaant*
> *Mira, Mira vola torren*
> *Kenta kuolo viri paant."*

The blade flashed as its blackness yielded suddenly to the bright orange of a forging heat. He dropped the bellows toggle and snatched the blade from the fire and stood trembling, the tongs gripped tightly in both hands and the sword quivering in the air above the forge bed.

Paca's mind reeled. He'd never heard the words before, but he knew what they meant. Roughly translated they said:

> *"Put the blade over a deep fire,*
> *The bellows steady and low.*
> *Keep turning it over the embers*
> *Until it resembles the sunset."*

He stood transfixed as the blade began to cool. He dropped it back in the fire, his mind still racing. The words tumbled and turned and the strange language receded, slowly being replaced by words from his own language:

> *"Lay the blade in fire deep.*
> *Work the bellows firm, but low.*
> *Turn it, turn it; let it steep,*
> *'Til it takes the sunset's glow."*

He recited the new words again and again, burning them into his memory as the original faded from his consciousness. He sang out, his voice strong and confident. It was new poetry, strong and deep, welling up from an unknown source. It stirred his intuition; it stirred his vorn. He kept the breath of the forge steady, turning the blade slowly, over and over until it glowed like the sunset. He pulled it from the fire and laid it on the anvil. Suddenly, more new words flowed from the spring deep within him. He raised the sledge and began confidently hammering out the sword before him.

The smith sat upright on his cot in the tower. For six nights now he had been able to hear the distant ring of an anvil late into the night. He knew anvils by their ring. He knew all the anvils in Immerland, who they belonged to and who was working them by their sound. As a blind man reads the footsteps of an approaching friend, so the smith knew that his son was working on *his* anvil late into the night. Each night he lay awake until the ringing stopped and he drifted into sleep.

Tonight there was a new sound, the sound of a voice long forgotten, stirring his mind. He listened, probing the deep silence until the singing started again. He ran to the south wall of the tower chamber and threw open the window. Through the bars he could see the moonless night sky, brilliant with stars. Everything was in darkness and all but the voice was still. Far away in Shiloh, there was a single speck of light. The voice sang again. He gripped the bars for balance as from somewhere deep inside a voice rose to his throat. He began to sing:

> *"Waha olen ir con fira malen*
> *Winda ha o'la se vrama boren*
> *Korla hama, Korla vorna,*
> *Korla vinda hama sinden..."*

His voice swelled and resonated in the prison chambers. Unconstrainable, it flowed out the window and rolled down over the dark castle. The smith held onto the bars as he sang as if, were he to let go, he would collapse from the weight of the song itself. He alone knew what was happening, and alone in the stone chamber, he yielded himself to it.

"Of all the curious and divergent capabilities of the beings of our world, the strangest of all would have to be the ability, without any previous exposure, to comprehend the original language."

Mortag of Horrinaine,
Of Beings

Sandihar rolled over, opened one eye, and bolted upright. The last watch had been at midnight, but what was this? A voice, a strong voice, singing, flooded the castle with its haunting melody. It rose and fell like wind rushing through a forest, or like a waterfall—

"Lights!" Sandihar shouted. Two attendants rushed in with torches and started lighting the lamps around the room. "What's happening?" he snapped.

The attendants flushed. "It started about ten minutes ago, Sire," one of them ventured. "We think it's coming from the South Tower, but everywhere we go, it seems to be coming from somewhere else."

"Guards!" Sandihar yelled. "Advisors!" He pulled on his tunic, as he strode to the large window overlooking the castle courtyard. Everything was black, except for the stars and a few other lights in the lower castle. No lights shone in the South Tower. All the walls of the castle resonated with the timbre of the voice; it filled the whole courtyard. It was deep and strong, light and melodious, sad, but full of conviction and power. He could hear the words distinctly, but recognized none of them.

The princess burst into his chambers, followed by Omberon, a second guard, Carnados, Cordas and Mindar. "What's happening, Fada?" She ran to his arms.

"I'm not sure." He looked to his advisors as he answered. The ashen faces of Carnados and Cordas emenated fear; Mindar trembled. Omberon's brow furrowed deep, his black eyes darker than usual, and his mouth turned down into a frown from his perpetual sneer.

Carnados bowed and took a step toward him. "By your leave," he started, "it seems that the prisoner is a taralang." He bowed again and stepped back.

Sandihar felt his face flush with anger. "Impossible! We've not had a taralang in Immerland since before my mother's time."

Carnados bowed his head. "We seem to have one now—and he is in the South Tower prison!"

The king understood better than he wanted to. "What is he saying?"

"He is singing in the original language, Sire. I didn't hear it from the beginning, but the song is a great story about war and sorrow, of horror and fear, of bloodshed upon bloodshed. In places he is singing poetry about his forge—he's a smith after all."

"I know that!" snapped Sandihar. He strode to the window again. "Who else can understand what he is saying?" An uncomfortable silence followed his question.

"I can," whispered the princess.

"So can I." Omberon said.

He whirled to face his advisors. "Who else?" he demanded.

Carnados looked up at him. "We're not sure, Sire. Supposedly, many still understand the original language, though only the taralangs speak it. Some animals understand it also, strange as that may be. Many believe it has to do with purity and simplicity of one's vorn, but most learned men consider that conjecture."

"What is the 'original language'?" Vrengnia asked.

Sandihar shrugged, waving his hand in deference to Carnados.

"The original language, child, is the language that Mah'Eladra themselves gave to our world. All our beings used it at some time, but as the corruption of the vorn slowly gripped the world, people started making their own language instead—out of pride—to separate themselves from others. They used it as a tool to rule over other tribes and nations, to enslave the animals and to enslave one another. Eventually, they abandoned the original language altogether in favor of their inferior invention. They stopped talking to the animals and the animals stopped talking back. At certain times, the taralangs appear. Using the original language, they sing to those who can still understand it."

Seething anger gripped Sandihar. Why couldn't he understand but Vrengnia could? Why Omberon? Why was he, the king, left out? "What should be done?" he asked a he ground his fists into windowsill.

"Nothing can be done right now, your majesty," Carnados said gravely. "He must finish his song. However, in the morning, I would set this man free. It wouldn't be wise to keep him in your prison."

Sandihar stared out the window. The sonorous voice rolled on filling everything: gentle and strong, rising, falling, completely unintelligible to him.

After several long minutes, he sighed and turned back to face the small group. "We'll let this taralang finish his song. Send word throughout the castle that no one should be alarmed. Those who understand should try to capture as much of what is being said as possible. Everyone else go to bed. We'll make any decisions in the morning—"

They all hesitated. Omberon's scowl had deepened and Sandihar knew he wanted to say something, but as captain of the guard, didn't speak unless addressed by the king.

"Omberon, you seem troubled."

"May I speak freely, Sire?"

"You may, Captain."

"The prisoner must be silenced, Sire."

Carnados's face fell. "Silence a taralang? Why, that—" Sandihar cut him short by a wave of the his hand.

"I would like to hear my captain's view of this affair," Sandihar said. "Why must he be silenced, Captain?"

"The song of the taralang is treasonous, Sire." Sandihar wondered why Omberon's rough voice grated on him so much. It seemed almost otherworldly at times, as if it didn't belong on Tessalindria.

"Treasonous? In what way?"

"I would speak with you privately, Sire."

Sandihar suddenly felt very tired. He also wanted to hear the rest of the song, still cascading over the castle. "We will hear the taralang out, and we will speak in the morning."

Carnados spoke cautiously. "Sire, there are many strong images being sung here, but there is no treason in them." Sandihar looked at him. Was it fear in his eyes? Betrayal? Defensiveness? He'd never seen that look on Carnados's face.

"Begone! All of you," he said. "We will discuss this in the morning!"

The guards and advisors moved at once. Vrengnia stayed until everyone else had gone. "I wish to stay here with you, Fada," she said.

Tears welled up in his eyes as he turned to face his daughter. "I would like that," he whispered hoarsely.

"The mountain man, on a mountain horse, is to be feared and respected."

Old Immerland Saying

"Stand still!" commanded the lead horseman in an urgent whisper. The rider following him stopped his horse. They were riding together along the ridge trail through the mountains on the southern border of Immerland. "Keep the horses quiet and wait here," the leader whispered. He dismounted silently, sprinting up the trail to a turn where a large pine tree rose above the others on the crest of the hill. With the grace of a cat, he climbed to a clearing in the branches near the top. The night sky spangled with stars, but the countryside was dark, save for several points of light in the castle, far to the north.

Everything was silent. He held his breath, waiting in the darkness. He did this several times until at last he caught the sound he had been listening for: the ring of an anvil and a faint but firm voice. At this distance, he shouldn't have been able to hear the sounds, but such is the nature of the original language. Such is the nature of the forge poetry to a smith. From the sound of the anvil, he knew that it belonged to the smith at Shiloh Forge. Listening intently, he strained to hear what was happening. After about fifteen minutes, he made his way down the tree into the darkness of the forest and sprinted back to the horses. "There is mischief at Shiloh Forge!" he exclaimed as he leapt onto his horse.

"What is it, Fada?" the second horseman said as he mounted. They started back along the trail.

"I'm not sure, but it sounds like someone is singing sword poetry. It's *not* the smith—the beat is wrong—but it's *his* hammer—on *his* anvil. We must find out what is happening."

"It seems to come from within. It rises from the belly and bursts upon the lips, as if it is carried within you. It is, however, the gift of the Eladra."

Timmanaeus

The new poetry that welled up inside him energized Paca as he worked the swords deep into the night. Each step brought new verses into his mind and his voice. His thoughts focused them into the two blades. Each hammer stroke was new, each heat was different, and each placement on the anvil, unique. This poetry was very strong. He had little time to think about it, but in the back of his mind, he knew that it was the poetry for making swords, and it was leading him along a path he had never traveled before.

At times, clairvoyant visions that accompanied the poetry burst upon him; bright, intense scenes of slaughter and carnage unfolded before his mind's eye. Fear tore through his mind, but to escape it seemed futile, so he worked on. His hammer hand froze, cramped onto the hammer while his tongs hand, gripping the blades like a vise, ached to his shoulder. He sweat profusely as the forge poured its heat into the blades. Exhaustion crept through him like a winter chill, but he pressed on relentlessly into the night.

As dawn broke, he finished forging the blades. Exhausted, but still driven by the fury of this peculiar night, he wrapped the blades in his apron, grabbed three files, and headed home before the first cock crowed in Shiloh. He stowed his secret under his bed and collapsed into a fitful sleep.

"The presence of evil does often go unnoticed by those who refuse to acknowledge, that it is not simply a void in the goodness; it is a presence all its own."

The Tessarandin,
Book Twelve

Morning broke in Immerland dark and wet. Sandihar woke from his sleep at the first glimmer of gray. As he stretched, he noticed that he had inadvertently left one of his windows open the night before. He crossed the cold stone floor to close it. Looking out, he could barely see the lamps in the courtyard below, lit so the castle workers could begin their morning chores. Muffled sound from their progress rose out of the fog that hid them from his view.

A gentle rain fell on the windowsill from the wet sky that smelled of the sea and clung to his nightshirt, heavy and cold on his shoulders. He shuddered as he fastened the window shut.

He hadn't slept well. He remembered the singing, but knew only vaguely when it stopped. Vrengnia, fast asleep on the couch where she'd chosen to stay the night, breathed peacefully under an orange quilt she'd found in the wardrobe.

For her sake, he didn't call for his attendants, but dressed himself and slipped out of his chambers. He made his way toward the South Tower. The only sound along his short journey was that of the rain spattering on the windows of the hallway as he passed them. He wondered if the taralang and his singing could have brought on this cheerless morning. The mood it set seemed to match the darkness that had crept into his vorn. What had happened last night to trigger this event?

As he came around the corner of the corridor leading to the tower, he startled the guards at the foot of the stairs. They snapped to attention. "Omberon?"

"At your service, Sire."

"I didn't expect that you would be here. Is there trouble?"

"Only that which occurred last night."

"The smith. He's still in his room?"

"Yes."

Sandihar looked at the other two guards for any hint that something else might be wrong. They looked scared. Undoubtedly, they had never heard a taralang. "Come, I want to have a look—and a listen," he added as his slipped off his sandals, motioning to the guards to do the same. He looked at Omberon. That brooding I-want-to-say-more look clouded his dark eyes. Sandihar looked away deliberately, motioning for the captain and his guards to follow him.

They padded quietly up the stairs to the smith's room. Sandihar guessed that the smith was still sleeping. He motioned to the guards, and they followed him down the stairs to where they had left their footwear. "What do you think happened last night?" he asked. He directed his question to the two guards, leaving Omberon out of the request.

They glanced at each other. "We're not sure," one of them said.

"Well, what did you see?"

"Nothing."

"Did you hear anything?"

"Yes, Sire, we heard a voice—singing in the castle somewhere."

"Somewhere?"

"Yes, Sire, but it was hard to tell where—it just was there."

"Did you understand what the voice was saying?"

The guards shifted and looked at each other. "I understood some of it," said the one on the right, "but I wouldn't say I know what it meant."

The other guard looked at the floor. "I didn't understand it at all," he said.

Sandihar nodded and stood up. "Dismiss these men for the day, Captain," he said. "Get some sleep."

They hesitated, looking at Omberon. He waved them off. He only had to do it once.

Sandihar looked down at his feet until the sound of the guards faded from the dimly lit hallway. "What is it, Captain?" Sandihar said, looking up into the captain's dark face.

"May I speak freely, Sire?"

"Of course, as always," Sandihar said.

Omberon leaned closer, and his voice became strangely smooth. "It's good, Sire, that you imprisoned this man."

His closeness crowded Sandihar, but he held his ground.

"If he is indeed a taralang, then it's wise to keep him here. History has shown that the taralangs have always spoken against the rulers of a country."

"That is an odd way of putting it, Captain. My understanding is that they have always spoken when there's a need for change. You imply that change is always bad for kings and rulers."

"Well, Sire, when subjects of kings want change, there are usually serious repercussions against the kings themselves. The lower classes don't have the capacity to separate the need for change from the ones who create the conditions they live in." A touch of scorn glimmered on Omberon's smile.

"Be careful, Captain," Sandihar said. "I have a higher regard for my subjects than that."

"You said I may speak freely, Sire. It's always the notion of kings that their minions love them. 'Tolerate' is probably more accurate. Search deep in history and make sure you aren't deceived."

Sandihar respected Omberon, but he sensed an agenda that extended beyond the welfare of Immerland underlying his words. "How will keeping the taralang imprisoned stop him from singing? He was in prison last night, and the whole castle, and maybe even others, heard him."

"He must not be allowed to sing."

Omberon's imperious tone jarred Sandihar; he suddenly wanted no more from the captain. "I will consider your suggestion, Captain."

Omberon bowed. "You will find it best, Sire" he said confidently.

"Perhaps so. You're dismissed."

Omberon hesitated.

"Is there something else, Captain?"

"By your leave, Sire, am I to post no guard on the prisoner?"

"Is the bolt secure on the smith's room?"

"Yes, Sire."

"Then he will require no guard today."

Omberon's eyes narrowed, but he saluted smartly.

"Thank you for your advice, Captain." Sandihar strode off toward his chambers without looking back.

"Three little wise men,
Attendants to the king,
He often called these three wise men,
And made them dance and sing."

Old Tessamandrian Rhyme

Carnados huddled with Mindar and Cordas in the kitchen, taking refuge from the cold, damp morning air with mugs of hot spiced tea, at a table most agreeably situated near the fire. They were having a hushed, but spirited, conversation about the events of the night before and what they would say to the king.

"We should have guessed," said Carnados. "I mean—look at the evidence. From the moment he set foot here, anyone could see the smith is different. No one could stand up to the king as he has and keep his composure under such circumstances. He's been in control since the day he was taken, even as the king thinks *he* is in control."

"Do you think the king will set him free?" asked Mindar.

Carnados stroked his beard. "I think he *should* free him—but he probably won't." The others eyed him quizzically. "I don't believe the king understands what is going on. He is also a stubborn man sometimes, as you know, and this is just the sort of thing he will continue to be stubborn about."

They brooded over their tea.

Mindar broke the silence: "What, exactly, is the role of the taralangs? I mean, who are they? What are they for?"

One of Carnados's strengths was bringing clarity out of detail. "No one knows for sure. They are usually from the working class of the people, though sometimes not—the Great Queen is believed to have been a taralang, but it was never confirmed. She was so strong and directed; perhaps she never needed to reveal herself. They live ordinary lives, although they aren't ordinary people. When there is great need among the people, they reveal themselves—almost involuntarily, it seems. It's believed that their use of the original language draws together the strength necessary to face whatever is threatening. The threat is often obscure, to be revealed only in time—in hindsight when it becomes very clear." He paused, staring into his tea and swirling it gently.

"So we just have to wait?" queried Mindar, a small irritation breaking through in his voice.

"Yes, we simply wait," said Carnados, "unless...unless you have some clarity on this subject that I don't."

Mindar dropped his eyes, took a sip of the tea, and said, "No, I don't."

Cordas spoke for the first time. "There was one thing, though it's only indirectly related."

"What was that?" asked Carnados

"It seemed to me that Omberon took an unusually keen interest in what was happening."

"I didn't notice..."

"First of all, he understood what was being said..."

"So did the princess—and you and I, as well," Carnados said.

"But the look on his face was different. You and the princess seemed to be hearing it and enjoying it. Omberon looked afraid. He always looks so smug and leering; but not then. It was as if he had seen a NarEladrim warrior."

"Hmmmm. That I did *not* notice."

Several minutes of silence followed. Carnados was absorbed in his own thoughts, his own fears and his own questions.

The king appeared in the midst of this revery. "Just the men I needed to see!" He had come looking for them without a summons, and Carnados found it strange to see him in the kitchen. It flustered the kitchen servants.

Carnados rose and bowed. "Sit with us, Sire," he entreated. As the king sat down heavily on the fourth stool at the table, Carnados called, "Tea for the king!" sending several servants scurrying to the task. Carnados turned to Sandihar. "It was an interesting night, was it not, Sire?"

"'Interesting' might be the right word; 'alarming' might be better. Tell me, each of you in turn. What should I do—and why?"

A servant approached; Carnados waited until the servant had placed the mug of tea gracefully in front of the king and left. He leaned forward, "By your leave, Sire, you must certainly set this man free. There is something that he is supposed to do, and he must be free to do it. It is the way of the taralangs. You must set aside your differences with the smith and allow him to go back to his service at Shiloh Forge." He stopped and settled back on his stool.

"Hmmmm," rumbled the king as he turned his gaze to Cordas.

Cordas opened his mouth to speak and then stopped.

The king sipped his tea and gently set down the mug. "Well?"

"By your leave, Sire, I think you should ask the smith what he wants, what it is that he should be doing. Perhaps he thinks he should be in prison for some reason; maybe there is something going on that we don't understand."

The king chuckled with a quick, amused smile.

"I'm serious," continued Cordas earnestly, "If anyone knows what this means, it is probably the smith. After all, if he is a taralang and if he is as powerful as it is believed he should be in that role, why has he not left the prison himself? Do you think your prison could hold him? I mean, you never actually arrested him. He came along without shackles; he rode his own horse to the castle gate; he has never complained and never tried to escape. Is he really our prisoner? Perhaps we are his."

The king's eyes narrowed and he tapped his finger on the tea mug. "Well said, Cordas, well said." He turned his eyes to the youngest.

"I think we should wait!" Mindar said.

The king studied him. When it became clear that no more was forthcoming, the king leaned forward and said with a twinkle in his eye, "Just wait?—wait for what?"

Mindar looked for support to Carnados and then Cordas. He stared into his tea for a moment, then looked back to the king and held his ground. "By your leave, we should wait. We may not know what we are waiting for, but this is the way with taralangs. *He* may not even know what he is waiting for. For the good of the kingdom—for Immerland—we must wait and see what needs to happen." He looked up into Carnados's eyes. "Isn't that what you were saying only moments ago?"

Mindar's stare begged Carnados's support as the king turned toward him expectantly. Carnados thought for a moment and studied the king's face.

He was still arranging his next statement when the king slapped the table and stood up. The noise and the abruptness of it startled him and scattered his thoughts. Raising his mug of tea in a mock toast to his three advisors, Sandihar proclaimed loudly, "Wait we will, then. Wait we will!" Leaning his head back, he drained the mug and brought it down heavily on the table. Without another word, he turned and walked out of the kitchen.

Chapter 5

Poetry

"Of acquaintances, we may have many; of close friends, a few. But the one true friend, with whom the vorn holds no fear, and the mind needs no boundaries, there love is found in its purest and perfect form."

The Tessarandin, Book Four

When Vrengnia woke, Fada had already left his chambers. She sensed an urgency to escape the castle without anyone seeing her. She dressed in the clothes she had worn the day before and skipped breakfast.

Mahala stamped and snorted when she arrived in the stable. "Ready for a run?" She whispered as she slipped the bridle over his head. He tossed his head and snorted again. "We have to be silent," she added as she cinched his girth. "Silent." She knew he understood. A retired Cortimane, a trained war horse from Mythinia, Mahala knew many things that ordinary horses didn't know. One of them was how to be quiet. She led him out through the courtyard to the drawbridge with hardly a sound.

"Going somewhere, Princess?"

The voice made her heart race as the looming figure emerged from the shadow of the portcullis. The suddenness alarmed her, but not the huge man himself. Vrengnia knew him well: Vishtorath, the gatekeeper.

"I'm going to Shiloh to visit the young smith," she said.

Vishtorath nodded.

"I need to speak with him about the singing last night."

"The taralang?"

"How did you know?"

The giant paused, reaching up to stroke her gelding's ears. "I know many things, Princess. You know that." His voice was soft and strong. Vrengnia loved it. It gave credence to the fabulous legends surrounding this singular guardian of Fada's gate.

"Mahala wants to run this morning. He will carry you to Shiloh quickly, but don't leave the main road."

She never asked Vishtorath for advice, but he always gave it as if she had. His advice was always worth heeding, even when she didn't understand it. "I will."

He cupped his hand in a simple gesture to give her a lift into the saddle. She put one foot obediently into his massive palm and he lifted her as a man might lift a cat. She swung her other leg up and over Mahala's back to find her seat in the saddle. "Please don't tell my father. I think he'll worry," she said looking down into his kind face.

"Only if I must."

Vrengnia knew he would keep her secret. He had a way of doing that sort of thing. "Thanks." Vishtorath turned his back and vanished into the shadows.

She urged Mahala across the drawbridge. He *was* ready to run. As they left the bridge, he pulled at the reins and pawed the damp soil of the road until she gave him the go ahead with a gentle tap of her heels.

The off and on rain in the thick fog made for a wet ride, but the water brought out the subtle odors of the fields, and the wind blended them with the smell of the ocean and Mahala's wet body. His strong, confident gait surged beneath her as they galloped toward Shiloh, leaving the castle, Fada, his advisors and the taralang far behind in distance and mind.

Vishtorath burned in her thoughts. He had been the castle guardian ever since she was a child, since she could remember. He was the only gatekeeper the castle had and the only one it needed. He had a reputation for being a one-man army with "eyes that could read a being's vorn through their armor."

He knew every detail of every person that walked through the gate, and was thoroughly equipped to handle the toughest of assailants. On one occasion, he had been attacked at the gate by five men seeking entrance to the castle. One of the attackers managed to put a spear though his belly. He broke the spear in half with his bare hands and, pulling it out through his back, slew all five with the two pieces of the spear he wielded in both hands. He retired to his small room beside the gate and was back on duty the next morning.

Vishtorath seldom spoke, carrying out his business with silent precision. Most people respected him with a measure of healthy fear. Vrengnia loved him. He spoke with her often as she came and went. He was always interested in her destination, but never seemed to pry, and she always let him know where she was headed. Somehow, she felt his presence with her. It was he who had saved her on that one desperate occasion—he'd never even told Fada. Neither had she—she didn't want to think of it any further.

She smelled the coal smoke from the smithy through the fog. It wasn't a pleasant smell, as odors go, but distinctive, imbued with a sense of hard work and mannish things she liked so well. Breathing deeply, she tied Mahala to the hitching post outside the door and stepped into the shadowed warmth of the shop.

Vrengnia was well known and accepted there, and she looked around without hesitation. The main forge was vacant. She stopped, bewildered, leaning on the great anvil. It was still warm. She looked up to see one of the other smiths watching her. "He sent word that he would be out today."

"Who are you?"

"My name is Vordar, Princess, at your service." He bowed his head before looking up into her eyes.

"Where is he?" she asked.

"Not sure—just not here." Vordar eyed her thoughtfully as he spread scoops of pea sized coal about the top of his forge bed between phrases: "He may be at home sleeping—his fire was just dying when we arrived this morning. It seems he was up all night."

"Where does he live?"

"He lives here," said Vordar with a hint of a smile. "He sleeps and eats in the last house on the right, on the lane leading to the western barley fields. It's a small place—you will know it's his."

"How?"

"You'll know."

Vrengnia found the lane to the barley fields with little difficulty. The last house on the right was indeed small, designed more as a place to sleep and fix a little food than for living. Whitewashed stone formed the frame, with dark stained trim. It lacked a front garden that decorated other houses in the town.

As she slid off Mahala, she understood what Vordar meant. The ironwork was extraordinary in its simplicity and function. The elegant hitching post put the one in the castle courtyard to shame and the iron gate swung noiselessly on its hinges and latched behind her with a solid click. The stout banded door displayed an impressive iron knocker, out of place on the simple dwelling. She ignored it, choosing to rap gently with her knuckles.

The house remained silent. She waited and knocked again, this time with more resolve. Still no answer. She pushed on the door, but it was latched. With some trepidation, she tried the handle. It was sturdy but yielded easily to her touch and the door swung open, stopping quietly against the wall. She peered into the darkened interior of the house. *Clearly a man's place.*

It was stark and simple. Three coat hooks decorated the wall by the door, one of which had a smith's leather apron hanging on it. She expected to see a vase with flowers on the small table just inside the door. Instead, it held several pieces of sculpted iron, each half finished, as if they had been dropped there after a long, unsatisfying day at the forge. Two pairs of boots lay on their side on the hall floor. A subtle mannish scent diffused over the threshold. It wasn't unpleasant, but the exact word for it escaped her. It smelled somewhat like Fada when he had been out hunting.

"Paca?" she called softly. The thick silence fed her discomfort. She hesitated before crossing the threshold, anxious, but resolved to find the smith. Straight in front of her, down a short hall was the kitchen. Just before the kitchen, on either side of the hall, two doors led to the left and to the right. The one on the left was closed and the other stood open. She walked softly down the hall. The manliness of the place enveloped her now, strong and quiet, with a stillness she could feel.

She looked cautiously into the open door. The bedroom was neat, and empty except for a long narrow bed, a nightstand, a chamber pot and several hooks hung with trousers and shirts.

She stepped back into the hall and then into the kitchen. On the right was the fireplace, swept clean as if it were rarely used, with storage cabinets for food or dishes against the wall on either side of it. Straight across from where she stood was a long, low cupboard with a washbasin set into the top. It spread itself under six tall windows facing south. Along the left wall was an eclectic collection of pots, pans, utensils and tools, many of them unfamiliar to her. Except for a large sturdy table that filled the center of the floor, and two stools, the kitchen contained little else.

On the left end of the table, a small area had been set aside for eating, with the two stools pushed under it. Files and rasps, various punches, chisels and odd tools she had never seen before littered the other end. Massive iron vises, the kind she had seen in the smithy, commanded the two corners. Experimental bits of iron and steel; cut, punched, and twisted, lay strewn over the table and floor. Some were grotesque in shape; others were beautiful. *A smith's idea of a kitchen*, she smiled to herself.

As she turned to go back into the hallway, she ran headlong into Paca. She yelped and jumped back.

"Welcome to our home," he said as he stepped past her, sauntering around the table toward the washbasin.

He began splashing water on his face and he spoke to her between splashes. "Your horse is lathered and shivering in the yard—I'll rub him down after I...get you something to eat...you must be hungry." He had grabbed a towel off a hook and wiped his beard. "*Are* you hungry?" He smiled as he put the towel back on the hook.

She wasn't sure what to say. Maybe it was a poor idea to have come here, after all, but she didn't want to admit it; and she *was* hungry.

"I'll take that as a 'Yes.'" He headed out the back door of the kitchen. Alone again, she sat down on one of the stools to wait. The uncomfortable feeling melted away as she reflected on Paca's ease at her unannounced arrival at his house. It faded into a quiet sense of acceptance that she realized she had felt nowhere else. In the castle, she was the princess. Outside the castle, she was still the princess. Paca had a way of letting her be Vrengnia. He didn't fear her. He wasn't in awe of her, or wanting anything from her. She didn't know what to make of it, because it refused to fit into any of the jars she kept her feelings in.

When he returned, he carried a covered, clay pitcher full of fresh milk. As he rummaged through the cabinet beside the fireplace, he rambled off various contents: "Lets see, dried apples, dried peaches, oats...whole barley...cracked corn...figs...no...raisins...oh wow, an apple as well..." He kept going. He was so out of his element, even in his own kitchen. She started to laugh. He turned. "What?"

"You."

He smiled gave a little bow and gestured to the cabinet. "Your turn; I'll go take care of your beast."

Vrengnia rummaged through the various cabinets and prepared a small porridge with oats, barley, a bit of cinnamon, and some dried blackberries she found in a jar to the right of the fireplace. In the cupboard by the washbasin she discovered a collection of herbs in small glass bottles. She scanned the shelf quickly and, selecting some spearmint, wolf flower petals and raspberry leaves, brewed them into a light tea. It was a recipe that Hanniah had taught her to combat fatigue. *Paca might well need it,* she thought as she puzzled over why the smith would have such a collection. Her thoughts were interrupted by Paca's return from grooming Mahala, with fresh cream to pour over the top of the mash. They sat down and ate breakfast together.

Vrengnia found a comfortable quietness in the smith's kitchen. She had the feeling that no one except Paca and his father had been in there in many years, but if Paca was at all uncomfortable, he hid it well. "I was expecting you—I mean not *here* exactly—and not this early..." He trailed off.

"I had to come!" she exclaimed, looking into his eyes.

"Had to?"

"Yes, had to. I mean, after last night—I didn't want to be around Fada—and I wanted to see how it's going with his sword."

Paca sipped his tea, watching her eyes. "What happened last night?"

"Why, didn't you hear it? The singing, I mean..."

He stared at her, somewhere in the netherworld of confusion and disbelief.

"Your father...last night..." she prompted.

"My father? What happened?"

She set down her teacup and related the story about his father's singing. She told him all the details: the comments by the king and the advisors; how they said he must be a taralang and how there hadn't been one in Immerland for many years; that it signified something serious, but no one was exactly sure what. She left out nothing. "I was afraid at first; it was so strange. Then I realized that I could understand some of it."

"What was it about? I mean, the part you understood."

"Some of it was about swords...like the forge poetry you described...."

"And?"

"Well, some of it was terrifying, about war and killing...." Paca's eyes drilled into her, and she looked down as she continued. "The other parts were comforting and warm. But it wasn't just the words...it seemed to reach in and put the thoughts inside me. I could feel the words...I was living them." She stopped. Her hands trembled.

Paca reached down and took hold of them gently. "Go on." His hands were callused and strong. She had never felt hands like this before. Even Fada's weren't like this.

"My father was angry because he couldn't understand any of it. I was afraid, but I couldn't stop listening."

"What were you afraid of?"

"I'm...I'm not sure. I've only felt it once before. I didn't like it then; and I didn't like it last night."

"Have you ever been afraid to die?"

"We're all going to die," is what came out, sounding hollow.

"I know...I know, but have you ever feared that *you* would die *soon*...perhaps in the next few minutes?"

Vrengnia looked up into Paca's eyes. "Perhaps that one time...but last night it was something else...maybe it *was* the fear of death...but not my own."

"Whose?"

"I don't know." His grip tightened on her hands.

"I had similar visions last night," Paca began. He was looking past her into the nothingness in the corner of the room as he spoke. "Some were ugly, and related to swords...to killing. Some were not. I felt the fear of death...I know that's what it was, and as you said, it was not my death, it was someone else's...I thought perhaps my father's. I've often wondered what will happen when my father dies, but I've never felt it..." His voice trailed off.

He rose and moved to the window and, leaning on the cupboard, stared out across the barley fields to the mountains on the horizon.

"Do you think my father is in danger because of this?" he asked, turning to face her again.

"I doubt it," she said quietly, "they all seemed to be quite afraid of him—even Omberon. Carnados wanted to set him free immediately."

"Who's Omberon?"

"The captain of my father's guard. The one with the sneer, if you ever see him."

"Oh, yes. He arrested my father. That face...."

"He doesn't seem to be afraid of anything. If he is, *that face* hides it well, but last night was different."

"Do you think your father will listen to...to...."

"Carnados? I don't think so. I think he's too stubborn."

"That's not good, but it adds urgency to what I must do to finish your father's sword." A sharp gleam she had never seen before came into his eyes. He told her what had happened in the smithy the night before, sparing no detail. "The two events must be related," he concluded. "The first song came to me just after midnight—but now, there's not a moment to waste."

"What do you mean?"

"I'm not sure, but I feel it. I only have tonight to finish it all. You must leave now, Vrengnia. Walk your horse for a bit before you ride him. The trip down was exhausting, even for him. Come back early tomorrow evening and I'll have the sword finished. Don't let anyone follow you. Come here; don't go to the smithy. Is this clear?"

"But why...why the rush?"

"Again, I"m not sure, but by tomorrow evening, if there *is* anything to explain, I will have the time then."

She hesitated. "Are you still my friend?" she asked suddenly.

He touched her arm. "Vrengnia, I'll always be your friend." For an instant, she thought she saw his father in his eyes. It was just a flicker, but it was real. "I think you have always *been* my friend—but now, as a friend, I beg you to go. The day is long before me."

She started for the back door, but paused before leaving, looking back at Paca.

He smiled. "One more thing: if my father sings tonight, don't be afraid, but listen carefully." She turned and made her way through the door. The fresh air felt good. The rain had stopped, the fog had vanished and the clouds tumbled eastward before the long thin line of blue that crawled upward along the western horizon. Asolara would be a welcome friend for the journey back to the castle.

"Can you separate the smith from his tools and still have a smith? Is not his hammer only the extension of his one arm and the tongs the extension of his other?"

Timmanaeus

Sometime following the noon watch, Sandihar decided to visit the tower prison. The events of the night before burned in his mind, distracting him from all but the most necessary of his daily tasks. With these behind him, he wanted to talk directly with his prisoner. He drew the heavy bolt and opened the door slowly. The smith stood near the southern window of the room, gazing out over the landscape. He remained unmoving through several moments of uncomfortable silence, so the king cleared his throat. "May I come in?"

The smith turned his gaze in the direction of the door. "It's your castle, good King. You may come and go as you please."

Sandihar was unsure what he wanted to say. So many questions remained and few answers were forthcoming, and there was no good place to begin.

"Good King," said the smith gently, easing the burden of the first word from Sandihar's shoulders, "I want to start my smithing now."

"But you have been smithing."

"No, I have been scrapping iron. The time has come, but I will need certain things from my smithy."

"Will you make my sword?"

"I didn't say that." The smith was smiling. "I said that I will start my smithing, and I will need certain things from my smithy."

Sandihar was annoyed, but kept his reserve. "What is it that you need, good Smith?" he asked.

"I will make a list for my son, and he will bring the items here to the prison forge. I should meet him there at the noon watch tomorrow."

The smith's voice was firm, but not threatening. Something wasn't right, but he hadn't the nerve to say no to the smith today. Instead, he stepped out of the room and called for scribes.

As he waited for them to arrive, he broached the question that he now wanted to ask most of all. "My good Smith," he said coming back through the door, "I will have arrangements made to have your goods delivered here, but I want to know what you plan to do with them. Has this new desire to start your smithing anything to do with the singing last night?"

"I don't know the answers to your question precisely," said the smith. "Much of what was sung last night I don't remember. Some of it wasn't about or for me. Of what I do remember, very little of it has anything to do with what I have to do in the smithy downstairs." He was staring out the window so Sandihar couldn't see his expression. His voice was gentle and genuine, so Sandihar, though not wanting to believe him, felt compelled to accept his explanation for now. "As to my work downstairs, I don't yet know what I shall do. All I know at this time is that I need certain tools from my smithy in Shiloh."

A moment later, two scribes came scurrying up the stairs behind him, armed with parchment, inkhorn, quills and sharpening knives. Sandihar took them from the scribes and after walking across the room to the window, handed them to the smith.

"By your leave, I cannot write," the smith said calmly. Sandihar spread the parchment out on the small desk.

"Tell me your list." Sandihar motioned to one of the scribes who promptly sat down on the small stool and took notes for the illiterate leaning against the window.

"Seven sacks of my finest coal. My two sledges and my large flatter—my son will know what these are. Three bars of steel from the bottom shelf. Four billets of wrought iron from last year's stock. My anvil—"

"Slow down, Sir," interrupted the scribe. "Four billets...your anvil..."

"My flat blade tongs, the two small box tongs and a jar of welding flux—no, two jars." He paused until the scribe caught up with his dictation and looked up. "I will need my cross and straight peen hammers, the ones I use all the time—Paca will know."

"Hmmm...that's it?"

"For now."

Sandihar took the list from the scribe and read the list back to the smith, who nodded with each item. "It will be done as you say," he said as he handed the list back to the scribe and, with a wave of his hand, sent the two men on their way. "Tomorrow at noon!"

Sandihar hesitated to see if there was anything else the smith would say. He was eager to get out of the room suddenly. He was afraid, not of the smith, but of the unknown that surrounded him. Sensing nothing forthcoming, he turned to leave.

"Good King," the smith said softly.

Sandihar turned to meet his gaze.

"The captain of your guards—"

"Omberon?"

"Is that his name? I was wondering how well you know him."

"What do you mean?"

"Have you known him a long time?"

"Four years and then some."

"How long has he been your captain?"

"A little more than two years. Why do you ask?"

"He doesn't seem like an Immerlander...perhaps Tessamandrian descent? Or Mooriman?"

"I'm not sure...I never asked. Does it matter? He has served me well in all things. I have had no reason to probe into his life's history."

The smith nodded to himself and shrugged as he turned back to the window.

"You think I should, don't you?"

"I was just curious." That was all. Sandihar knew they were through. He turned to the door and left, pulling it shut and drawing the bolt securely behind him.

He stood for a moment in the semidarkness of the tower stairs and took a deep breath, closing his eyes and exhaling slowly, trying to cleanse his vorn of fear.

The voice sprang from the darkness to his left, "Sire."

His heart jumped. Omberon emerged from the shadows of the stairs. He must have been waiting there.

"You startled...me."

"I apologize. I didn't mean to. May I speak freely?"

Sandihar cringed and nodded at the same time.

"Is everything okay?"

"Yes...yes, speak freely my good captain, only let us walk as we do, away from this place."

"I sat on the steps outside the door because I know you were alone with the smith and I wanted to be there if there was any...trouble."

"There is no need to explain, Omberon."

"Sire, I did overhear your conversation with the smith. May I speak freely?"

"By the lightning on the Crown, Captain, yes...yes, by all means, speak freely!"

"I think it unwise to allow the smith to have his tools—to let him smith at all."

They walked together down the stairs. Sandihar let the statement hang as he thought through an appropriate answer. What he felt for the smith was a peculiar blend of emotions that he hadn't fully unraveled. He wasn't afraid of the man.

The smith had never even hinted at a threat of reprisal or violence. He had no grudge against the smith, save for his refusal to make the sword, and even that was more an issue of rebellion than not having the sword. He would have freed him in a moment, were it not for his determination not to let any man in his kingdom defy him to his face as the smith had. He respected the smith for his knowledge, his wisdom, his insight and his patience—many characteristics he wished he himself had in a greater measure.

In addition, he had no particular fear of letting the smith ply his trade in the tower smithy. If there were any hope that he might make the sword, that would be the only way he could do it.

"I'm not sure I understand the urgency of your statement, Captain."

"The smith is up to some...treachery."

Sandihar stopped on the stair and turned to face Omberon. "Treachery? Name it!"

Omberon looked him straight in the eye. "I can't—yet."

Sandihar raised his hands in a gesture of despair. "Well, when you can, I want to listen." He turned and started down the stairs. He could hear Omberon behind him. "You seem to have an agenda with the smith, Captain. You might as well tell me what it is."

"I fear for your safety, Sire."

Sandihar stopped and turned to Omberon again. "That's the *right* agenda. That's what I pay you for. Now is there anything else, I mean, beyond that?"

Omberon opened his mouth to speak and then closed it suddenly, pausing briefly before he spoke again. "No, Sire, nothing."

"I appreciate your concern. Why don't you take some time off, Captain." He deliberately said it in a manner to end the conversation, and turned down the stairs. Omberon didn't follow him this time. By the time he had gotten to the bottom of the stairs, it had occurred to him that Omberon had made no mention of the smith's question about his history. He wondered why the smith had even brought it up.

"And where does one see his true self? Is it not in the darkness, when no one else is watching? When the full freedom of possibilities presents itself and he has to decide who he really is in that vast ocean of opportunity?"

Oratanga,
Passages

Paca worked steadily and carefully, singing the new songs over and over quietly while he filed the blades for the swords. The time flew by. In the middle of leveling the bevel on Vrengnia's sword, he heard the galloping hooves of several approaching horses. They stopped at the gate. What now? He wrapped the swords in the parcel leather and stood the bundle in the corner by the mop and broom. The first urgent knock came as he rounded the table: five rapid strikes of the heavy knocker. Before he got to the door, it struck again seven times.

Two of the king's guards and a herald stood outside the door. "By the king's orders, we offer you this summons," said the herald and shoved a rolled parchment into Paca's face.

He stepped back. "Are you sure this is for me?" Paca said.

"Are you the son of the smith, imprisoned in the castle?"

"Yes—"

"Then it's for you!" the herald said.

Paca took the parchment, broke the seal, and unrolled it, glancing at it for a moment before handing it back.

The herald's face showed his impatience. "Well?" he demanded.

"Well," Paca said with a smile, "I cannot read—if you would be so kind—"

The herald sniffed, and with a condescending flourish, unrolled the parchment and read:

"By order of King Sandihar of Immerland: Pacahara, the son of the proprietor of the Shiloh Forge is hereby ordered to procure from the Shiloh Forge the following items, to be delivered to the smith at the Immerland Castle by the noon watch on the morrow..."

The herald read the list through.

"Can you read it through slowly again? I want to make sure I get everything ready."

The herald obliged with another sniff.

"How will it be delivered?" Paca asked.

A cart would be brought to the smithy by nine o'clock. He let the herald know that he needed to have men available to help move the anvil onto the cart, and he needed to be there to be sure that all the correct supplies got loaded. With these arrangements made, the herald and the soldiers left. He closed the door quietly.

He stood for a moment with his back against the door and his head thrown back in disbelief. Tomorrow, by this time, Fada's great anvil and the best hammers and tongs would be gone. What was happening? Why did Fada want these items? Was it to stop him from finishing? Whatever the reason, he had only tonight to finish his work on the swords. Now he understood the urgency he had felt the night before. There was still much work to do.

He moved swiftly to the kitchen and unrolled the blades again. He set to work, filing, grinding, and polishing, perfecting the blades for the evening's work.

"Grind one way, then grind the other,

First one side, then its brother.
Grind toward the edge, but not too thin,
Grind this hollow, then its twin."
"File crossgrain, 'til scars are gone,
Cross-file again, 'til shape is won.
Polish the flat and polish the back
Leather and rust 'til leather is black."

The hours slipped away into twilight as he pursued the perfection of the swords; singing and filing; singing and polishing.

As twilight settled over Shiloh, Paca straightened his back over the workbench in the darkening kitchen. He'd finished the filing and sharpening. The handle needed to be completed before the blades received their final tempering. The swords would be made of steel; no inlay, gold, silver, or stones. He stretched again and bent down to look at the sky through the kitchen window. With the disappearance of Asolara, the sky had slipped from deep blue to the rich blue green that appeared just before the darkness settled it into night. He sighed and stretched again. His favorite color.

He arrived at the smithy in the dark, lit a lantern, and set about preparing the forge for another long night. As he did, his thoughts drifted to Fada. A taralang! Could this be true? What was he up to? Why had he ordered that the tools from the smithy be brought to him at the castle? Was all this connected to his own work on the swords, and if so, how did Fada know and what did he know? The princess wouldn't say anything. Why would she? He sensed that all this was connected, and that it would all be clear at some point. Something new would happen again tonight, because the swords had yet to be hardened and tempered, the most critical steps of all.

As the fire developed, he selected the steel for the hilt, to be tempered to withstand the most brutal sword stroke. He also selected the iron for the handle, sculpted and swaged into the contour of the hand, shaped and textured so that any hand that gripped it would have control on the sword from the butt to the tip.

The poetry started before the process of forging, flowing up from deep within, erupting in that strange language, then slowly evolving into intelligible rhymes in Immerlander. Though he had hardly slept the night before or that day, he felt strong, and the energy he needed flowed from the poetry. Whenever the activity lulled, he slipped to the door, opened it and listened for Fada's voice. He heard a dog barking once. Otherwise, no sound broke the stillness of the cool, clear night.

He finished the hilts some time after midnight. Three hours later he completed the handles as the poetry drove him onward. He stared at his work in the lantern light. As he wrapped his fingers around the grip, it fit perfectly in the hand. As he held it, the sword came alive as an extension of his arm, almost as if it held itself to his hand. So sure was the grip, that he knew that if ever he wielded such a sword, it would only be taken from his hand by death.

He picked up the princess's sword. It was smaller and lighter, but not by his design. He swept it from side to side. He had a vague sense of its superiority over the king's, but how? He wasn't sure and it didn't matter. He studied each sword carefully, making sure they were perfect. He had never seen anything like them. He had never *made* anything like them.

Selecting a small spot on the handle of the princess's sword, Paca engraved in miniature the three slashes and sunburst from the front of her tunic. He didn't know what it meant, but he was sure it meant something to her.

He first heard the voice while waiting for the fire to mature for hardening. At first, it was faint. He laid the swords down on the bed of the forge and sprang to the door, throwing it open and stopping short to listen. Was it really there? All he could hear was his heart and the far-off barking of that dog.

Then it came, almost imperceptibly, then clearer and clearer until he could hear every syllable. He couldn't make out the language, but he heard every thought. It was forge poetry, for the hardening and tempering of swords, mingled with other verses about war and death, life and wisdom. It was beautiful and haunting at the same time, far away, but clear, like a fine bell.

The hammering was over, so he wedged the smithy door open with an old axe head and leapt to the forge. The fire roared as he tugged on the bellows, and it seemed to sing as he laid the king's blade into the long narrow trough of coals. Above it all, he heard the singing. He listened and watched, his gaze fixed on the steel. As it began to glow, the voice crescendoed. He turned the steel at the bidding of the poetry; he pushed it back and forth to even the heat. He turned it again—and then again. It was close to quenching temperature...another minute...a few more seconds...NOW! He raised the blade from the forge bed and held it vertically for an instant as it quivered in his hands and then, with a quick slicing motion, plunged it into the tepid slack tub.

The blade whistled as it hit the water, sending a cloud of sweet smelling steam into the shadows of the smithy. The blade's song blended with the distant voice for a moment, etching itself into Paca's memory forever.

Then the song shifted abruptly: it repeated itself. Vrengnia's sword! Into the fire it went, the tasks repeating themselves. Paca watched and listened. For nearly an hour, the voice guided him through the steps until both swords lay on the workbench, hardened and tempered for the king and his daughter. The singing stopped.

Paca ran to the door to listen again, but all was still. In the east, he saw the first hints of dawn. Dawn: more a threat than a blessing. There was still more to be done. The king's wagon would be there in three hours.

Chapter 6

Swords

"Psadeq is a concept so ingrained in the cultural fabric of our small planet that, were it not for the freedom we have been given to reject it, one might postulate that it is, in fact, an instinct. Its fundamental nature was confirmed by the progenitors of our dispersed dialects, that they, finding no words suitable to capture its essence, left it one of the few words we have that is a direct descendent of the original language."

Mortag of Horrinaine,
Of Beings

Vrengnia listened outside the door to the smith's prison. She had carefully waited during Fada's breakfast with the smith that morning, watching the comings and goings of the attendants, the waiters and servants, the clean-up crew and finally, the guards. Everything had been quiet in the tower for about half an hour, and she felt safe. She wanted to talk with the smith alone.

She knocked. No response. There were no guards. The single bolt on the outside of the door had no lock. Apparently, Fada was unconcerned about the smith trying to escape.

She lifted the latch and slid the bolt back. It creaked slightly and she stopped to listen again. The door swung inward without a sound and she stood looking into the circular room. Only yesterday, she had been standing in front of this man's house, looking into the silent hallway. She had the same feeling of intrusion, but knew she had to enter, so she stepped forward just enough to look around. It only took a moment for her eyes to find the smith. He was sitting on the bed looking back as if he were expecting her.

"I thought it might be you," he said gently, a slight smile flitting across his lips as he spoke.

"You were waiting for me?"

"Not exactly, but you certainly weren't one of the guards—the way you waited at the door; the way you drew the bolt—something said to me 'Ah, the princess!' Come, sit down." He gestured to the sitting chair by the small desk.

She sat down facing him. "I'm...I'm not sure why I'm here," she started.

The smith leaned back on his elbows and said nothing.

"I visited your son yesterday—" she said.

The smith smiled warmly. "How is he?"

"He's tried several times to visit you here, but Fada refuses to let him near." She looked at the floor, ashamed as she said it; ashamed that Fada would treat such a gentle man in this way.

"I miss him," said the smith, a faraway look crossing quickly over his face. "I most certainly would rather be there at the smithy than here."

She looked up.

"Your father has treated me well—in fact we had quite a breakfast together this morning."

"I know," she said, looking down at the floor again.

"And he *is* having some of my tools brought to the smithy he built for me below this chamber."

"Why?"

The smith smiled, "I asked him to."

Vrengnia laughed. "You just asked him?"

The smith nodded. "And he seemed more than eager to comply. He thought I might make his sword after all. He was a bit disappointed when I told him I wouldn't."

"Yes—I'm sure." Vrengnia wondered what to say, and the smith seemed content to wait.

When the silence became uncomfortable, he embarked on a new direction of his own. "Princess Vrengnia," he began, as he stood up and walked to the southern window, "how well do you know my son?"

"I only just met him, really. I met him the day my father and I first came to your smithy about the sword...and then...well, we didn't actually talk."

"But you have been to see him several times since then." Vrengnia wasn't sure whether it was a statement or a question. "Your father told me this," he continued, "but I could have guessed it would happen from the way you looked at him the next day."

"When my father arrested you?"

"Yes—so how do you feel about him?" The smith stared out the window at nothing.

"Well," she started tentatively, "it's a little different." She continued searching for the proper words. "I mean—the first time I looked at him and he looked at me, it seemed like I knew him—as if we were friends and had been for a long time. With other men, that look scares me, maybe it angers me, but with Paca, well, it...it accepted me—no those aren't the right words—"

The smith turned to look at her, resting his elbows back carelessly on the window sill.

"Ordinarily, I would never have talked to your son again, but I felt compelled to go back and find out what this meant. I was nervous. When I got there, it seemed like I almost belonged there. What was strangest of all, was that Paca seemed to feel the same way. I haven't talked to anyone else about this—"

"Not even to your father?"

"Well, Fada knows I've visited the smithy and spent some time with Paca, but I've never discussed this strange connection with him. I don't think he'd understand it very well." She looked at the floor again.

The smith waited until she looked up. "Have you ever heard the word 'cymbic'?"

Vrengnia gasped. "You know what it means?" she asked. "I have heard it, but have never understood it. Can you tell me?"

Her eager interest lit a fire in the smith's eyes. "Yes," he said softly, eyeing her for a moment before turning to stare out the window again.

She waited.

"Are you comfortable?" he asked, turning his head toward her over his shoulder.

"I'm fine."

He turned to face her fully and leaned back against the sill, framing himself in the window. "We are surrounded by other people. Everywhere we are, unless we've chosen to be isolated, there are people that come and go, passing through our lives, coming from all directions, going in all directions. Some are like props in a play at the theatre. We accept them as part of the scenery, but we never know their names, their lives, their being-ness—they're almost like shadows in our awareness, in our vorn."

Vrengnia nodded.

"With others, we have some commerce, perhaps they come into our shop to buy goods or they serve us our food at dinner. Still, we don't know their names and our relationship to them based on this commerce is purely functional and fleeting. You have seen this before?"

"Yes."

The smith moved, walking back and forth in front of the window, his left hand on his chin and his elbow cupped in his right hand. "At another level are those with whom the nature of the connection is more substantial. We know their names, perhaps where they live, what they do to survive.

"We may smile when we see them because we know this little bit, but in the end, were it not for some trivial circumstance, a twist of the path of life, we would never have this connection, and we would never miss it. In fact, when such a person disappears from our life, we may not even notice the event.

"This isn't wrong, it is just the way of things. Our lives are arranged with many such layers of relationships, and concern for each level varies from person to person. Some people never experience layers that others do. Again, this isn't wrong; it is just different."

The smith paused and looked at her. "Does this make sense so far?"

"So far."

"At the other end of the spectrum of relationships are the cymbic relationships." He paused. "They're characterized by a certain timelessness, in two senses. First, they are timeless in that they seem to have always been there and second, cymbics know they *will* always be there."

Vrengnia looked up at him. She knew *this* feeling too. She hadn't known it had a name.

"Cymbics may not see each other for many years, and they are able to pick up almost where they left off. The cymbics have 'natural' relationships, if you will. They don't need the approval of others, nor do they even expect it. There is a simple rightness to the cymbic relationship that others often don't understand. Psadeq is given, and accepted from both sides without hesitation: it doesn't need to be earned; it doesn't need to be created; it doesn't need to be proven."

"Are you saying that I have a cymbic relationship with Paca?"

"It would seem so. Maybe you should tell *me*."

Vrengnia tried to identify her feelings in this new context. "I wasn't sure what to make of it. Honestly, I thought I might be falling in love—but I have thought that before and it was a bit different."

"In what way?"

"At other times it made me shy and foolish.... I did and said stupid things. That doesn't happen with Paca."

"The awareness of your self disappears?"

She had to think about that for a few seconds. "Yes, maybe that's it."

"It *is* part of it. The genuine love—that foundational, personal concern for another being that transcends your own interests—is characteristic of cymbic relationships." The smith stared at her curiously. "You have another question."

"I have many questions—"

"Ask."

"If this is so, why am I almost twenty and have never been taught this?"

"Ahhh...." The smith nodded and turned to gaze into the nothingness outside the window. "In the course of a well-lived life, in the countless interactions that have the potential for such a relationship, we may only encounter a few—a small handful—of beings with whom we do have such a relationship. It is rare enough that it is often mistaken for something else, such as 'falling in love.' Other times, social dogmas prevent its realization. What if your father had forbidden you to go to the smithy to follow up on your first sense of the relationship?"

"He wouldn't have done that."

"Perhaps not. Many others haven't been so fortunate. As a result, there are many—no probably most—who could have cymbic relationships, but don't."

"*Could* have?"

"Many people, even with the opportunity, cannot have such relationships. We don't know why. It seems to only be given to some. Perhaps it is the nature of the diversity of personalities...but those who lean toward cymbic relationships but never find them, live as strangers in their own cultures. They can be very lonely."

Vrengnia understood. She looked at the floor. The realization was comforting and disquieting at the same time.

"As a result of all these influences, many refuse to believe that cymbic relationships exist. They are treated like myths and met with disbelief and hostility when they're encountered—but you have another question!"

"Yes...." She looked up. "My father—does he—I mean, do you think he understands this?"

"I will never be one to categorize a person unfairly, but the fact that he has never told you any of this, leads me to believe that he does not. My personal experience confirms this also."

Vrengnia knew the smith was right. He stepped forward and sat down on the edge of the bed, leaning toward her as he continued. "Cymbics fall into three categories; they are the 'cymbic spheres': the primary sphere is the strongest, the most 'natural' of them all. In the primary cymbic sphere of another, there is total acceptance, even across all kinds of boundaries. There's no fear; no hesitation. The psadeq is natural, with no need to please the other, to prove rightness or wrongness in anything. It is the purest of friendships."

"I'm beginning to see it," she said. "It makes more sense than how I have heard the word explained before."

"But you still have questions?"

"Well—can cymbics be or become enemies?"

The smith raised his eyebrows. "Yes, under unusual circumstances. Beings change over time, and those changes, or perhaps a singular event, will turn cymbics into bitter enemies. Curiously, they remain close friends in the cymbic sphere, that is—they know each other, respect each other in the timeless cymbic way—but oppose one another in their pursuits of their life. The conflict this fosters in their lives creates a bitterness that few people understand. They submerge it beneath a veil of goodness and false psadeq that makes it very hard to detect. It consumes them from the inside out. Unless there is reconciliation, it will eventually destroy them."

Vrengnia stared at the floor again. "Destroy them?"

"Inwardly at first. Psadeq is eroded and the peace it brings is lost. Sometimes this happens very slowly so that the individual doesn't know it is happening. If psadeq is destroyed, the consequences can be physical: ill health, fatigue, sickness."

Vrengnia didn't want to look up now. She felt a growing fear that she wanted to escape, but didn't know where to turn. It seemed to have been sparked by the truth the smith was speaking, but was being fed from somewhere within. She feared the pain of it would overwhelm her if she were to look directly at him.

He redirected the conversation. "Yes, I believe that you have a cymbic relationship with my son in the primary sphere. Do not fear it, but you must be wise about it."

"In what way?"

The smith was at the window again. He turned to face her, leaning back on the sill with his elbows. "The psadeq of cymbic relationships, though natural and easy is more precarious—more fragile."

"I don't understand. If it is so strong, how can it be fragile—or precarious."

The smith smiled. "I never said it was strong; only natural and easy. It is deceitfully weak at first, and this is what makes it fragile."

"I'm still not sure that all this makes sense," she said, shifting slightly to make herself more comfortable.

"You mentioned that you thought that you might be falling in love, but noticed a difference, did you not?"

"Yes."

The closeness of the cymbic relationships can be confusing at first. Unless this confusion is clarified, it can lead to mistakes that violate psadeq. This is particularly true in a cymbic relationship between a man and a woman." The smith stepped away from the window and sat down again on the bed so that he was looking up at her. Her eyes met his. He continued: "The laws of psadeq in any relationship are immutable, even one which is cymbic. Cymbics seem to lose sight of this more easily."

Vrengnia looked down. "It seems backward," she said. "I mean, I would think that it would be stronger."

"And that is the danger, exactly," said the smith with a smile as he leaned back. "Perhaps it's arrogance, self-confidence, a misguided understanding of what psadeq really is, or belief that its laws don't apply. I'm not sure. Either way, when psadeq is violated, much pain is brought into our world."

The talk of relationships with men and woman surfaced new questions. "Does any of this change when people get married?"

"Cymbics remain cymbics," said the smith sitting up again. His eyes shone intently as he placed his elbows on his knees and leaned forward. "But the laws of psadeq are different in marriage, so cymbic behavior must change to stay within its boundaries. This is another mistake that cymbics make: they naturally feel that their relationship doesn't need to change and this is a grave danger. The closeness and specialness of marriage must be honored and guarded. Cymbics often lose sight of this. It's not uncommon for cymbics to make the mistake of justifying the violation of a marriage relationship because of strong cymbic ties, but it is a violation none-the-less."

Vrengnia thought she understood, but had to admit that she didn't understand marriage very well, having never seen one up close. For now she didn't have to think about it. As she stared at the floor, she felt a silent fear closing in upon her, but couldn't identify its source or give it a name. Was it the fear of her relationship with Paca?

The smith reached over and lifted her chin gently, forcing her eyes to meet his. For a long moment, she stared into his eyes until she felt tears forming and a tightness growing in her throat. Not knowing whether to unleash her fear in a flood of tears or to turn and run, she stood up and stepped back, stammering, "Thank you...for your time, but I must be going. I'm not sure that my father would appreciate my being here."

He stood up. "Love your father, Vrengnia, but don't fear him. He loves you deeply."

He opened his arms and she fell into them. His strength and the warmth of his arms encircled her. They spoke comfort and relief without words for the moment she stayed there. When he relaxed his arms, she turned away without looking at him and headed for the door.

"One more thing," said the smith quietly. She stopped and faced him again, tears streaming down her cheeks. "I need a piece of leather, square by about the length of your arm. Could you get one for me?"

She wiped her face with the back of her hand. "Yes, of course."

The princess pulled the door to the smith's prison shut behind her. As she drew the bolt on the door, more tears flowed down her cheeks. As the iron bolt clanked into the hole in the stone doorway, she wondered whether she was locking the smith in, or the kingdom out.

"There are few gifts greater than one into which the giver has vested his vorn, and then has given without hesitation or expectation of like return."

Hispattea,
The Essences of Corritanean Wisdom

Paca sat at the kitchen table which he had tidied up for Vrengnia's visit. He had taken the time to make a small vegetable stew and had picked up a loaf of dark rye bread from the baker just fifteen minutes earlier. It was still warm. The front door was open so she wouldn't have to knock.

He had a vague sense of anticipation. It was odd that he actually knew she was coming. Until then, she had always just shown up. He wasn't sure what to do, so he sat where he was at the table.

Paca's mind drifted back over the day. The removal of the great anvil from the shop had had more of an effect than he expected. He had purposely avoided involvement in removing it, having assigned Vordar to coordinate that with the other smiths. He couldn't remember a time that the anvil, the centerpiece of the whole smithy, hadn't been there.

The hammers and tongs, the familiar ones, the best ones, had all been taken by strangers to a place he was forbidden to go. It hurt inside when he thought about it. The pain was a blend of helplessness, emptiness and anger, fueled by the unforgettable image of the captain of the King's Guard, leering as he entered the smithy to appropriate the tools. Paca wasn't sure where the line was drawn between hurt and hate, but if he were ever asked if he hated anyone, the captain would probably come to mind.

He had tried to fill the emptiness of the missing anvil by focusing on the task of finishing the two swords. It had taken nearly three hours to grind the edges onto the swords. The steel on their edges was harder than any tool Paca had ever worked. The polishing process was equally arduous.

Try as he might, the best he could achieve was a dull sheen. It was beautiful, but not the mirror finish he had hoped to produce. He etched and pickled the handles, buffing them off to produce a contrast of bright steel highlights with dark lines and features. By late afternoon he had finished them both and rolled them carefully into the muslin cloth, the bundle that now stood in the corner of the kitchen against the back wall.

Vrengnia arrived as close to six o'clock as Paca could guess. The slow and measured cadence of the horse's hooves echoed gently as they came down the lane.

She entered without knocking. As she stepped over the threshold, he heard her call softly, "Paca?"

"In the kitchen," Paca said as he stood up and pushed his stool back. By the time he got to the kitchen door, she was there. She held a large basket in both hands.

"I brought some supper from a friend," she said, handing him the basket. "We should eat it while it's still warm."

Paca smiled. "You must thank your friend for the kindness," he said as he carried the basket to the table, laughing. "Why don't you unpack it while I get some dishes?"

"What's so funny? Don't you want dinner?"

"Oh, no," he said, amused. "I am relieved that you don't have to eat what I prepared."

"You made dinner?" she asked, as she raised her nose and inhaled.

"Well—" He laughed at the comical sight of the Pied Princess sniffing the air.

"C'mon, get it out. We will eat like kings and queens tonight," she said as she began unpacking the basket onto the table.

"You should know," he said and set about finding his best silverware and bowls.

They sat down to dine together, the princess of the kingdom with the son of a smith: lentil stew, corn bread, cranberry raisin jelly on dark rye bread, fresh pears dressed with fresh cream whipped with honey, and oat cakes drizzled with tamarind syrup. They talked about everything and nothing. They laughed at each other and with each other. They laughed at all the people who never laugh because they are so serious about their lives. They laughed about princesses, kings and queens who had never tasted oat cakes and tamarind syrup, about blacksmiths who had never met princesses.

It wasn't until the dishes were clean and the lamps had been lit in the kitchen that Paca turned to the princess and said, "I have a gift for you."

"A gift?" she teased.

"Yes, a gift," he said as he started unrolling the muslin bundle he had fetched from the corner. The first sword to appear was Vrengnia's. Paca stopped. So did Vrengnia. There on the soft cloth, dully reflecting the dim light of the lanterns lay the simple sword. Paca reflected that it wasn't the kind of sword a king would wear, but he was still enamored with its elegance. Vrengnia stared at it, as if frozen for a moment. "Well?"

"May I touch it?" she whispered.

"Careful—it's *very* sharp."

She touched the blade gently and jerked her hand back. "It's deathly cold!"

"Try the handle."

She reached out gingerly and laid two fingers on the handle. Paca saw her pause with a surprised look on her face before she wrapped her hand around it. As her fingers settled around the grip, the sword lifted from the table. "I...I've never felt anything like it." She swung it back and forth gently. It hummed as it moved through the air. "I...it...it sort of...well, I'm not sure whether I am holding it or it's holding me," she said, her eyes bright with excitement. She held it straight out in front of her toward one of the lanterns. It gleamed in the light. "It's...it's perfect—" Her eyes fell, "Well, for me at least—but my father's hand is so much larger—"

Paca put his hand on her shoulder and guided her to the table. "Look carefully at the handle," he said. She held the sword close to the lantern to examine the details of the grip. He watched every movement of her eyes as she scrutinized it, turning it this way and that to get the best light. She gasped suddenly and stood up straight, her eyes wide.

"I told you I had a gift for *you*." Paca smiled. "This is *your* sword."

"What about Fada?"

"His is right here." Paca unrolled the remaining muslin to reveal the second sword. It was of the same design, but a little larger and heavier. The details were perfect. She laid her sword carefully on the muslin, stepped toward him, and hugged him tightly around the neck. Stepping back, she started fumbling for her purse, which she had tucked under her tunic.

Paca stepped forward and took her by the arm, stopping her. "Vrengnia, my friend, this is a gift—for my friend. The other is a gift for my king. There is no payment to be made." She pulled away and started for her purse again.

He grabbed her hand more forcefully. "I meant what I said."

She heard it this time and stopped. Tears formed in her eyes as she stood looking into his. "Thank you, thank you, thank you!" she said. The words were unnecessary, but he nodded in recognition of her gratefulness.

"Come, now, it's time for you to be getting back," he said, "I'll wrap the swords in something more fitting." Under Fada's bed he found a piece of finely tanned leather. It was soft and supple and would serve well to protect the swords on their way to the castle. He brought it back to the kitchen, laid it out on the table, and started putting the swords in place to wrap them.

"What are all the markings on the leather?" she asked.

Paca stopped and flipped the corner of the leather over, glancing at it matter-of-factly. "It's a parcel leather—have you never seen one before?"

"No—I don't think so."

"He started to roll the edge of the leather around the king's sword. "Fada uses them all the time to deliver things to others. The markings are the glyphs of individuals who..." Suddenly, he stopped and looked up.

"What is it?" she asked, puzzled.

"There is one more thing," he said slowly. "Hold out your hands."

He picked up her sword, and balancing it deftly before him, he faced her. He lowered the sword into her outstretched hands and said slowly, with all the conviction he had:

> *"Bless this sword to this woman's hand*
> *Bless it to work at her command*
> *Bless her to use it as she should*
> *Bless its edge for a common good."*

"It's beautiful," she whispered. "I mean—the poem. It's similar to something my father says to his dors when he appoints them."

"I think it a very old blessing. Fada always says this when he delivers a tool. I never understood why. But I think I do now."

"What about my father's sword?"

"I don't know what to do. Fada always delivers his tools in person—I guess it will have to wait—or maybe you can do it."

"I'll try." She laid the sword back on the leather wrap and Paca rolled it up, tying it securely with a short leather thong.

After they had safely stowed the bundle on the back of Mahala's saddle, Paca walked the princess to the edge of the last stand of trees before the castle gate. They chatted randomly for the whole hour's walk. When they finally stopped, she gave him a quick hug, and then, with the grace of a trained horseman, she swung up into her saddle and set Mahala into a canter across the field toward the castle gate.

He saw her stop at the gate and get off her horse. She stood for a long while talking to the gatekeeper. It was longer than a simple, pleasant hello, and he wondered what it meant. A twinge of jealousy was working its way up to his throat from somewhere in his belly, an ugly feeling that he hated and relished at the same time. He knew it wasn't right. He had no claim on the princess; she had given him no indication of anything except appreciation and pure friendship. He continued watching, slowly forcing the ugliness back into its lair by sheer will of mind.

He watched until she vanished into the dark throat of the castle. He turned and headed home. Tal hung low in the sky to the east as Paca walked toward Shiloh in the quiet starlit night, pondering the everything and the nothing of their recent conversation and celebrating the relief of having delivered his burden into the princess's hands.

"He who seeks understanding without a true willingness to find it, is like a man who seeks water everywhere but in the stream."

Hispattea,
The Essences of Corritanean Wisdom

The hammer had been silent for about half an hour. Sandihar concluded that the smith had finished for the evening. He ordered that the smith be escorted back to his room and dinner taken to him.

Now another hour had passed and Sandihar headed for the tower. The guards were still outside the smith's door. Sandihar said nothing, but waved for them to follow him. He led them down to the smithy door. "Did anyone visit today?"

"No, Sire."

"Did he take anything with him to his chambers?"

"No, Sire...uhhh...except his tools."

"Tools?" Sandihar stepped closer to the guard.

The guard took a step back. "Yes, his two hammers and his tongs and...I think that is all, Sire."

"Why would he take his tools with him? Is he going to sleep with them?"

The taller guard frowned. "I wouldn't know, Sire."

"Open the door!" Sandihar wanted to see what the smith had been doing. The warm, acrid smell of the fire lingered in the air as he strode through the door into the dim interior. A curious assortment of worked pieces, all beautifully detailed but completely unrecognizable, lay about on the small table.

There were hooks and pointed spikes with barbs on them, many of them finished with small eyes in the end as if they might be fishhooks or spear points. On one end of the table, an array of flattened loops, with curled-over ends paraded across the surface, each one slightly larger than the last. Another pile of unfinished or perhaps rejected pieces, and several small blocks of stacked plates that were fused together with a short rod sticking out of them, sat together in the middle of the table.

"Does this make any sense?" he asked the guards.

The guards shrugged and shook their heads, stepping to the table as if a closer look would reveal the answer.

The pieces were arranged in some odd pattern. The king tried to imagine how they might fit together, if they were meant to fit at all. He dared not touch them.

"I give up," he said in exasperation. "Let's go. Check that the door upstairs is bolted, then you can leave for the night. The smith isn't going anywhere."

Before he started down the tower steps, he faced the guards one last time. "You let no one in, correct?"

"Yes, Sire, no one entered or left until we escorted him upstairs to dinner."

"Good," said Sandihar. "Now, in addition to this, I don't want him taking anything in or out of there either, is *that* clear?"

"Yes, Sire. Nothing in or out," affirmed the taller guard.

"And his tools?" asked the shorter guard.

"He may take his tools, but nothing else."

"Nothing else," the guards echoed.

The taralang didn't sing that night, and the king slept well for the first time in three days.

"Who is the greater prisoner: the caged man whose mind transcends his physical boundaries, or the untethered being whose mind holds him in a cage?"

Hispattea,
The Essences of Corritanean Wisdom

Vrengnia dismounted in the darkness on the drawbridge.

"Good to see you, Princess." Vishtorath's vibrant, rich voice, flooded warmth. She wondered why so many people feared him. He stepped forward out of the shadows. "Was your trip worthwhile?"

"It was very pleasant, thank you." Mahala had stopped when Vishtorath spoke. "Has my father been looking for me?"

"No, Princess. I haven't seen him today. He's preoccupied with the smith."

"I know. Do you think it odd, this preoccupation?"

"He's the king; he may do as he likes."

"I know that too," She paused, "but—it seems...unusual."

Vishtorath remained silent.

"What do you know about the singing the past few nights? Have you ever heard a taralang before? I mean, no one seems sure that that is what he is." The giant shifted. His answer came slowly.

"I have heard...many taralangs."

The way he said it was more of a confession than a statement. "Many?"

"I am old, Princess. You know that."

"How many times have you heard a taralang?"

A long silence shrouded the huge man. Was he counting? Was he weighing the truth or fomenting a lie? "Twenty."

"Twenty? How old *are* you?"

"I don't know."

She had to imagine his eyes in the darkness as she found herself staring up into the shadow where they should have been. "Did you understand when he sang?"

"Every word. Every thought. Every intention."

Was Vishtorath quoting something? It sounded familiar. "Can you tell me what—"

"It is forbidden." He interrupted her again.

Vrengnia wasn't sure she should ask anything else, so she moved the conversation to another place before leaving him to his post. "Have you met the smith's son? He said he's come here three times looking for his father and was turned away at the gate."

Vishtorath shifted again. "Princess, the king forbade his entrance."

"But you did meet him?"

"Yes. A fine young man. He is standing now in the shadow of the trees on the road. He is waiting to see you safely into the castle."

Vrengnia turned to look. The horizon, shaped by the dark line of trees between the field and the sky with the snaking ribbon of road disappearing into it was all she could see. No detail distinguished the bands of black that formed the night landscape. She turned to face him again. "How can you see him?"

"I see many things, Princess. Please come in. I awaited your return before I lowered the portcullis for the night."

Mahala suddenly started walking toward the stable. "Thank you, Vishtorath," Vrengnia said as she fell in step beside her horse. The portcullis creaked as it dropped slowly behind her in the darkness.

Vrengnia took her parcel to her chambers as soon as she left the stables. There were few people about this late and no one asked her about the package. It was an unusual package to be carrying around the castle, but she *was* the princess and she had rights to a certain privacy.

When the swords were stowed safely in her wardrobe, behind the bright pantaloons and pied blouses, she left her chambers to deliver the leather to the smith. Vrengnia had acquired a different piece of leather for him, but left it behind, under her bed, thinking that the piece that had wrapped the swords was his anyway.

She pondered how she had come to have this piece of leather. She was beginning to discern patterns in things that happened; she found herself discounting congruent events as coincidence less frequently, and she saw a grand design slowly evolving out of the linear perception she had had of her life.

It didn't matter that she had no idea why the smith wanted the leather. What was most striking was that just when she was to bring him some, this piece had fallen into her hands as part of an unrelated subplot of her life—or was it related? There was no way to know. Fada maintained that he didn't believe in coincidence, she knew that, but she wasn't so sure.

She climbed to the tower completely unchallenged. The smith's door was bolted securely. She stood for a long time, wondering whether the smith would know that she was there. She threw the latch and drew the bolt, pushing the door open as abruptly as she could.

"Come in, Princess." His warm voice reassured her.

She remained outside the door. "How did you know it was me?" she asked.

"You waited so long and then threw the bolt so quickly." His voice smiled. She gave up and walked into the smith's chambers. He was gazing out the window.

"Come here, Princess," She walked over to the window where he was standing. "Do you see the mountains on the horizon?" She stared into the darkness for a moment.

"Barely!" she exclaimed. "My eyes aren't used to the darkness."

"Keep looking. When you can see the mountains, look for the lights that shine out from them periodically. I just noticed them for the first time tonight. Do you have any idea what they might be?"

"I think...no...yes, I see," said the princess. "They're very far away; they are probably outside the boundaries of Immerland. They could be anything."

"Or something," rejoined the smith.

The princess looked at him. "Why do I get the feeling that you know what is going on there?"

"I do know, Princess—and so do you; and so does your father for that matter...but come, why are you here?

She held out the leather and pressed it into his hands.

"Ah, the leather." He unrolled it and snapped it briskly to straighten it out. "Hmmmm...this looks familiar. You were there today?"

She nodded.

"And he just gave you this?" He had walked over to his bed and spread it out flat on top of it.

She leaned against the wall by the window with her hands behind her. "He made a gift for me and wrapped it in this so I could bring it back here safely."

The smith raised his eyebrows. "A gift of friendship?"

"Yes—pure friendship." She was suddenly dreading the direction this conversation was going.

"And what sort of gift was it, exactly?"

The "exactly" part was most annoying. She wasn't ready to tell him about the swords. "May we leave this for some other time, good Smith?"

"Of course," he said. "Whenever you're ready."

She was beginning to like the smith almost as much as his son, although the connection was different somehow. His gentleness, confidence and ability to defuse the stickiest of situations were amazing.

"So, when is your father's birthday, exactly?" asked the smith.

"Eight days from now, when Tal is full. There will be a great feast. He will be fifty, you know."

"Yes, I knew that. It's rather remarkable, is it not, to live fifty years...." He was staring out the window again. "And how old are you, Princess?"

"I'll be twenty on the equinox."

"So soon?"

She nodded.

"Have you chosen your name?"

It suddenly occurred to her that she hadn't even thought about it. The twentieth birthday was important. It was the time when the childname was shed and a new name was chosen to carry into adulthood. The childname was given at birth. One had no choice in its designation, but the adultname was by choice, a chance to stake a claim in the adult world. "Not yet...I kind of like my name as it is. I guess I have just been putting it off."

"I see. You may want to give it a bit more thought. You know how important it is." The smith walked to the window again. It seemed almost like a magnet to him.

"I know. I guess I'm not sure I am ready to be an adult."

"An adult? Or a queen?"

Vrengnia flushed, caught somewhere between embarrassment and anger. She held her tongue, trying to find the right words. The smith turned to gaze out the window. She said, "I will give it due consideration...and you? How old are you?"

"I'm not exactly sure. By my closest accounting, I am about fifty five; my son is twenty-three." He stopped, concentrating on the scene out the window. "Princess, come quickly!"

She ran to the window. "What do you see now?" She strained to see into the darkness. One of the brighter spots on the distant mountain was flashing on and off, in an irregular sequence of light and darkness.

"What is it?" she whispered.

"I'm not sure. It may be a message of some kind," said the smith, "but I think you should go tell your father, now."

"Why do you want *me* to tell him?"

"In spite of what he thinks of me, I'm not his enemy, but he'll hear this better from you. Don't tell him that I pointed it out to you."

As he walked her to the door, he said , "I will need your help two nights hence about this time. Will you be able to come?"

"Yes, of course," she said.

"And Princess...." She turned to look at him again. "Don't fear." She wasn't afraid, but wondered if perhaps she should be as she drew the bolt on the smith's prison, locking him away again, so that the rest of the world would be safe from his wisdom and gifts.

Chapter 7

Mountains

"The value of the man who speaks sincerely to his king is weighed on the barley scales, and not on the gem cutter's balance."

Mindar Colloden,
The Great Fathers

Sandihar didn't like what he saw. "When did you first see this?" he asked Vrengnia.

"About ten minutes ago...from the windows in the hallway near my chambers. What are they, Fada, and what do they mean?"

"I don't know...but they can't be good. Advisors!" he shouted. The irregular pulses of light, came from two places. It seemed to be some kind of signaling. What and who were they for? Sandihar and Vrengnia were still watching when the advisors arrived.

Sandihar pointed out the window. "What do you make of all this?"

Omberon appeared at the door.

Carnados, Cordas, Mindar and Omberon stood at the windows and watched for several minutes in silence. The advisors scratched their heads and stroked their beards, stealing glances at one another. Omberon smiled. After a short and hushed conversation, the advisors turned toward him. "May we speak freely in front of the princess?" Carnados asked.

"Of course!"

"We have had reports from the field, Sire. Verclan is stationing many men in the southern mountains. They seem to be scattered here and there in the hills, but more dispersed, in small pockets; highly mobile bands, if you will, possibly small raiding parties. Our scouts have also seen these fires but haven't been able to determine what they are for."

Sandihar's anger rose to fury. "Why wasn't I told of this earlier?"

"We were on our way here to inform you when we were summoned," replied Carnados. "The scouts came in only half an hour ago. There's much confusion—we haven't pieced it all together yet."

Sandihar stared out the window. "What should we do?"

"They are signals, Sire." Omberon's interruption rang with confidence.

"What kind of signals?"

"It's an old Tessamandrian fire code. Someone from the mountains is in Immerland now. He will be able to read these signals from anywhere that they are visible, which is probably most of Immerland."

"Do you know what they're saying?"

"I only caught the end. 'All clear, Mordan, Shiloh, Yendel'. There were a couple of words I didn't recognize."

"I'm open to suggestions," Sandihar urged. He turned back to the window.

"We suggest that you prepare the army for skirmishes along the southern border." Carnados paused. "We also think that you should try to establish some communication with Verclan himself."

Sandihar whirled to face his advisors. "No!" he shouted. Carnados stepped back. "He's a brigand and a murderer. He can't be reasoned with. And I told you before to never make that suggestion again."

"But, Sire—"

"Don't 'But, Sire' me! Do you understand?" Sandihar thundered. The advisors backed away.

"The area surrounding those three towns is quite large," Omberon said. "We may be dealing with just one or two persons—it may be a small army—it may be a scattered group, and it would be useless to search for them in the dark."

"Go on," Sandihar pressed.

"We should send the scouts out to investigate in the morning. By afternoon we'll know if there's been any mischief."

Sandihar eyed the captain. Omberon stood his ground, his impassive face unmoved by the royal scrutiny.

"So it will be," Sandihar said. "Find Rapahoogin. I want him here tonight."

"Every event in life, every peak and every valley on the path we choose, strengthens us or weakens us according to whether we live in the Psadeq of Mah'Eladra and the inevitable collection of beings that surrounds us."

Karendo Marha,
Journey to the Infinite

Exhausted from two long nights and the following days' activities, Paca stood idle in the gloom of the silent smithy. A dark melancholy set in about him. The delivery of the princess's sword and his blessing of it were troubling his mind. He had returned to the smithy after leaving her near the castle.

Sometimes he liked to sit and think. Right now, he wanted to just sit. As he lit the lantern over the slack tub, his mind wandered through the events of the day and his eyes gazed into the darkness to the left of the forge. He sat down on the empty anvil stump. Time dissolved; so did the world around him as he listened to his vorn, not sure whether he could trust it.

Something had been violated, but he wasn't sure what. Maybe he was just tired. Perhaps it was the letdown after all the intensity. Somewhere inside he knew that this wasn't the end of the matter. If this wasn't the end, what was next?

The quiet knock on the window at the back of the smithy startled him. The rapping had been gentle, nothing to cause alarm or fear, so he took the lantern and walked toward the window to see what it was. When he got there, he held up the light, shading his eyes from the lantern's reflection on the smoky glass. He could see nothing. Perhaps he was imagining things.

He made his way back toward the front door, holding the lantern in front of him to make sure he didn't trip over anything. As he passed the forge he looked up to see a man sitting on the anvil stump, exactly where he had just been.

Paca jumped back, grabbing a fire rake from the forge bed. He stood facing the stranger. The man was motionless and calm. Paca couldn't see how tall he was because he remained seated and his dark cloak covered his torso and legs. In the dim light the man looked gaunt and tired, but also well built and powerful. His face wore a sad, kindly expression, yet his eyes sparkled. Neither moved.

"Where's the smith?" asked the stranger.

"Who's asking?"

"An old friend." The voice was gentle and sad but carried a deep sense of affection.

"And this friend's name is?"

"That's not important now. Where's the smith?" The tone was more commanding, but still soft. Not a muscle of his body moved except in his face. "I must speak with him, now!"

The stranger wasn't from within Immerland, because he would know about Fada's incarceration. Paca remained silent. The man rose off the anvil stump to his full height and dropped his cloak backwards in one simple motion. Paca took a step back and raised the fire rake.

The other turned his palms toward him in a gesture of openness and Paca could see that he was unarmed. He wore a simple brown linen tunic with a black silhouette of a crow across the front, girdled with a belt that supported neither dagger nor sword, and leather leggings with soft leather shoes laced up his calves. They stood facing each other. It was the stranger who spoke first.

"If you are the smith's son...are you?"

Something about the stranger's manner calmed his mind and quelled the natural fear he should have felt. "I am."

"I have known your father for many years. Your father served as a farrier in the service of the Great Queen, the mother of your king. You knew this?"

"Yes." Sandihar wasn't this man's king?

"I and your father were close friends, and worked together on the farrier's staff in the queen's stables." He leaned back against the stump again, stared into the dead forge coal, and crossed his arms across the black crow.

"Your father had a gift with steel. He could make anything, and his talent was wasted on the farrier's forge. He taught me more than you can imagine. We were separated when I was sent off by the prince to serve the cavalry in the wars for the southern border. Your father refused to go and was dismissed by the prince.

Your father set up here in Shiloh to work his craft, still within the queen's domain, but a fair distance from the prince." He paused, continuing to stare into the dark fire pit. Paca remained motionless, still holding the lantern and the fire rake.

The stranger's eyes darted up to meet his own. "I need him now."

Paca took a step back. He tensed again.

"Lay down your weapon, son," the stranger said gently. "You have nothing to fear from me."

Paca eyed the man then laid the rake carefully onto the forge bed, and raised the lantern to a hook on a ceiling beam. "If you tell me your name, I will tell you where my father is."

"If I tell you my name will you promise not to touch that fire rake?"

Why would this stranger ask such a question? The dark man continued. "If you do, you'll be shot through before you get it off the forge bed."

"I won't touch the rake."

The stranger paused, then said, "My name is Verclan. Now, where is your father?"

Paca glanced about uneasily, straining to see through the windows and the door. Verclan! The leader of the rebellious mountain clans. What did he want with Fada?

"You promised. Where is my friend?" The voice seemed to be coming from somewhere far away. Paca sat down heavily on the swage block beside the forge. Looking hopelessly down at the floor, he uttered, "He's in the king's prison."

Verclan unfolded his arms; his eyes narrowed and burned with anger. "Is there a reason?"

"He refused to make a sword for the king. So the king has imprisoned him until he does."

Verclan threw his head back and laughed. "That would be your father!" Verclan exclaimed with a wide smile on his face, his arms open. A smirk twisted into the words as they came out.

"He never would make a weapon. Not ever! That's why the prince—who's now the king—discharged him. And with good reason, mind you. He always said that his blades would be too dangerous as weapons." He shifted his weight on the stump and faced Paca full on, his eyes gleaming in the light of the lantern.

"We just thought he was prideful and arrogant. It cost him his job, but looking back," Verclan ran his left hand through his thick, dark hair, "he probably made the wiser decision." There was a faraway look in his eyes as he sat motionless for a moment.

The vague forebodings Paca had been mulling over before Verclan's arrival coalesced. Would he have had the courage to make such a decision? In light of the sudden revelation of this odd stranger, he regretted the path he had chosen.

Verclan clapped his hands onto his knees and stood up suddenly as if he were finished with his business. "It is good to know that he is still as stubborn about this as he used to be, though I wish he weren't in prison for it—but that would be the king, too!"

"You know the king?" Paca said.

"Of course. We were friends, also, but in a different sphere. I served under him when he was just the prince. He was in charge of the cavalry. I shod his horses. As your father is with blades, so am I as a farrier. Only the best for the prince, don't you know?"

"He regards you as an enemy now."

"Yes, he does. We have our differences, to be sure. Someday you will learn that every man has a story. Unfortunately, history is often determined by who gets to tell his story. Perhaps some day I will get to tell you mine." He paused and looked into Paca's eyes. "And you, young smith, what is your story? Do you understand the steel and the fire as your father does? Can you forge an edge and breathe life into it and the blessing of peace, or do your blades threaten the lives of honest men?" He paused.

Heat rose under Paca's collar. He shifted his weight and looked down at the floor.

"Do you carry the banner of your father, seeing the wisdom in refusing to participate in the study of war? Or do you yield to the king in his pursuit of my life?" Paca looked up again. The dark eyes flickered brightly in the dim light of the smithy. Verclan was standing at full height, waiting for a response.

"If you were friends with the king, why does he seek your life?"

"That is one of the strange paradoxes that surround our lives. Suffice it to say, that we are friends *and* he seeks my life. Now, answer my question!"

Paca pointed to the sign that hung above the forge, but said nothing. Verclan glanced at the sign and smiled. "Why do I have a sense that you are lying to me? But, for the honor of your father's name, I will press this issue no further." He raised his hand, glanced at the door, and snapped his middle finger smartly into his palm.

Through the door came a tall young man, powerfully built and proud in bearing, carrying a woodland bow with a long arrow nocked on the string. Paca guessed that they were about the same age. "This is my son, Patira," said Verclan. "He's a smith like you. You'll employ him in your smithy for a time to make sure that no blades for the king are forged here."

Paca's eyes narrowed. "I don't need another smith!"

"Yes, you do," said Verclan matter-of-factly. "I know that without your father, your work is lagging. Patira is a fine smith, as good, if not better, than any you have in your employ already. He knows the art of the blade and much of the forge poetry—and he knows that no blade made by you or your father should come into the hands of the king."

"I won't have him here!"

Verclan leaned forward. "Let me tell you part of my story, then—but only part. Your father knows the blade and the edge, but have you ever wondered where he gets his steel? Have you ever wondered where gets the coal to make his fine blades?" Paca stared at him silently. He did know. Fada bought them from the old trader who came through Shiloh about once a month. He was a strange man who never spoke. Fada selected what he wanted from the cart and paid the man in ironware from the smithy. "Have you?!" commanded Verclan.

"No—I mean—yes," stammered Paca. Verclan's close intense energy intimidated him.

"He gets them from me. It's my hand that provides the blade steel that your father uses and my mines that provide the only coal he wants." Verclan paced back and forth before the forge. "And besides his impenetrable determination not to use his extraordinary gift to make weapons, he has vowed to me that he would never supply them to the king!" He stopped pacing and turned to face Paca squarely. "I don't think that you've fully accepted the lessons your father has been giving you, and I don't trust you. Therefore, Patira will stay in your employ until I need him to come back to my service. Otherwise—" He raised his hand and slowly drew a finger across his throat.

Paca leaned on the forge heavily, wanting to break eye contact, but not daring to do so. Verclan turned to leave, then hesitated. "One more thing! No one is to know who Patira is or why he is here. Is this understood?"

"It is very clear," he said, trembling.

"Patira will start in the morning." Verclan wrapped himself in his cloak and addressed his son. "Check the fires."

"I have—we're clear for now."

Verclan and Patira disappeared silently into the night. Paca sat for a long time on the anvil stump. A great storm gathered. Between the king and the princess, Fada, Verclan, Patira, and undoubtedly the mountain men that followed them, he was now a common link. He just sat, staring at nothing; hearing nothing; seeing nothing; trying to feel nothing.

"The handiest tool of a good smith is an able assistant, who moves and breathes to the rhythm of his master's stroke."

Timmanaeus

Patira was sitting on the stone step outside the door of the smithy, leaning against the doorframe, when Paca arrived. "Good morning," he said.

"So it is." Paca was early—earlier than the other smiths, but he was now wishing he had been there even earlier.

Patira stood up and shook his hand vigorously. His grip suggested extraordinary strength. "It's good to be here." His voice was gentle and reassuring, more like a genuine friend than a spy. Paca couldn't tell how good it all was, but accepted Patira's sincerity.

In the daylight, he could see Patira better: a handsome young man, with dark eyes and short hair so dark that Paca couldn't be sure whether it was black. His face was perfectly featured, thin and delicate but strong at the same time. The breadth of his smile extended over his whole face and his teeth flashed white behind an olive flesh tone. He wore a black tunic with brown leggings and soft leather shoes molded tightly around his feet. Sun-darkened, muscular arms, bare to the shoulder and banded at the wrist with wide leather braids, heightened the visage of a lithe and agile youth.

"Come on," Paca said, pushing open the smithy door. He hung his coat on the hook just inside the door. "The other smiths will be wondering what's going on. I haven't been here the last two days, and the soldiers came only yesterday to take my father's anvil and some of his tools to the castle."

Patira nodded, reassuring Paca that he was listening and interested.

"Not sure why, really. They said that my father needed them. Anyway, we need to get another anvil. C'mon." Paca led the way through a door behind the main forge to the storeroom at the back of the smithy. "So the other smiths—I'll introduce you to them—we'll just have to ignore their curiosity."

"By the fires of Timmanaeus!" Patira whistled softly when he saw the pyramid of anvils stacked against the back wall.

"Fada believes that a blacksmith can never have too many anvils. Whenever he can, he picks them up and stores them in here. C'mon, help me find one suitable for the main forge."

Paca thought he knew anvils, but Patira proved to have a strong sense of selection. "Too small." "Not enough ring." "Not flat enough." "Too worn." It took nearly an hour of heavy lifting and three narrow escapes with their fingers before they finally found one that suited them both. Patira agreed with this particular choice because of the sound. "All things being equal, the sound of its ring is the final arbiter for the integrity of the anvil," he said.

Paca liked it more for the quality of the surface. It was smooth, though not perfect, and the horn still had the right shape to its point. By the time they hauled it out of the shed and set it on the stump, the work of the smithy was in full swing. As Patira and Paca adjusted the anvil until it was level and solid, they could feel the furtive, curious glances of the other smiths. A voice at his right queried cheerfully, "A new assistant?"

"Vordar! This is Patira," he said heartily as Patira took Vordar's hand. "He is the son of an old friend of my father, a farrier and bladesmith. I thought we needed the help. He'll be working my fire."

Vordar's eyes narrowed with a slight suspicion, but addressed the newcomer graciously. With a shallow bow he said, "Welcome to Shiloh Forge. We can always use the help." Paca turned and started pointing out the other smiths, calling them by name and introducing them to Patira. Each nodded and started back to work with no further acknowledgment of his presence. "If you need any help, be sure to let me know," Vordar said and, with a wink, delivered his final remark, "Paca can be tiresome to work for, and he has a bad habit of drinking out of his slack tub."

Patira was quick. "Does he stir it first?" Paca felt the flush in his ears as all the smiths guffawed. Patira smiled in amusement.

Paca was beginning to like him already. "C'mon, we have to work sometime."

For the rest of the morning, they worked the anvil, grinding and polishing, polishing and grinding, filing the horn, and then polishing again so that the anvil's newly exposed surfaces gleamed.

Paca busied himself with preparations for the day's work while Patira cleaned out the forge and laid the fire. Paca watched Patira as he worked. He had an easy manner and a quick mind, particularly related to the forge work. He was younger than all the other smiths, but seemed to have a curiously broad grasp of details. The fire was burning bright and clean as quickly as Paca could imagine doing it himself; and Patira had several tricks that Paca had never seen, as if he had learned his trade in a different country altogether.

As he laid the first blades into the fire, Paca struggled to resolve his emotions about having Patira there. There was nothing offensive or arrogant about his presence; he fit in well. Paca couldn't have found a more apt and eager worker. Patira knew how to be quiet, he knew when to speak, he listened well and he offered his opinion only when it was appropriate. *All in all*, Paca thought, *this isn't going to be so bad*.

Patira worked the bellows and the fire with great skill, anticipating every move that Paca made. He was always in the right place; he worked the fire perfectly around Paca's needs, adding coal at the right time and never disturbing the flow or timing of the work.

It was late afternoon when they heard the clip-clop of a horse's hooves in the lane: the princess. A quick wave of panic fled through Paca's mind about the princess meeting Patira. He decided not to worry, then thought it strange that he could make this decision so quickly. There wasn't much he could do anyway, and Vrengnia had never embarrassed him before.

Vrengnia entered the smithy gaily, striding up to the great forge without hesitation. "I brought you a raisin cake from the kitchen...well, actually I *stole* it from the kitchen." Patira looked at Paca quizzically. Paca had gotten used to her peculiar fashion habits, but Patira's look made him realize all over again how unusual it was.

He bowed slightly and smiled. "Thank you, my friend." He gestured to Patira. "Princess Vrengnia, this is my new assistant and fire keeper, Patira. Patira, this is Princess Vrengnia, daughter of King Sandihar of Immerland." He glanced at Patira to see if there was any surprise. If there was, it didn't show. Patira nodded his head and smiled. Vrengnia stuck out her hand and she shook Patira's vigorously, saying, "You couldn't have chosen to work for a finer smith than my friend here."

She paused before she looked at Paca and said, "Do you have time for a piece of this purloined cake?"

"I am sure we do. Is there enough for everyone?"

Vrengnia scanned the smithy quickly and laughed as she walked out the door. She returned with a large bundle in her hands. Paca was amazed, "You stole *that* from the king's kitchen?" he asked incredulously.

"Well, I *am* the princess, don't you know—got a knife?"

Patira laughed, "That's like asking your father if he has a page." Paca took one of the mostly finished blades from the workbench, washed it carefully, and handed it to the princess. All the smiths took a break and had raisin cake together in the smithy.

For a few minutes, they all chatted idly. Paca was thankful for his friendship with the princess. It never seemed to go wrong, even in the awkward places.

"I saw your father last night," said Vrengnia in the midst of the gaiety. She had caught him with his mouth full of cake. "He had asked me to get a piece of leather for him, so I gave him the piece you gave to me yesterday. I hope you don't mind."

Paca swallowed. "Not at all," he said. "And how's he doing?"

"He seems quite content and at peace—I mean, my father is treating him rather well—for a prisoner." She took a small bite of cake. "He recognized that piece of leather instantly. I hadn't noticed how beautiful it was until he shook it out."

"What did he want it for?"

"He didn't say," said the princess. "He just said he needed a piece of leather."

The smiths had devoured the cake and the princess busied herself with cleaning up the crumbs.

"Did you come all this way just to bring cake to the smith?" asked Patira suddenly.

"Why, yes," Vrengnia smiled. "It isn't really that far, on a good horse." She hesitated. "You seem suspicious, Patira."

"Just curious; it seems a bit...I mean, the Princess of Immerland bringing a raisin cake to a smith?"

"Paca is my friend and has been for some time. This is what friends do, is it not?" Paca detected her defensiveness mingled with a touch of resentment.

Patira looked at her thoughtfully. "Of course," he said. "I was just curious."

The conversation drifted back to the mundane as the smiths returned to their work. Patira, Paca and Vrengnia chatted for a few more minutes and Vrengnia bid them goodbye. She left as she came, without fanfare.

Paca was silent for a while as he worked. At a pause in the work, he looked up at Patira and said, "You made quite an impression on the princess."

"Oh?"

"I have never seen her react so quickly to anything."

"Does she come here often?"

"Fairly—usually just like that. She drops by, hangs around, chats and then goes back to the castle. She's just like that. She's not your ordinary princess."

"That, I could see," said Patira with a slight smile.

They went back to work, and for the rest of the day spoke no more of the princess.

"Wrap your vorn in a mountain cloak,
Close by a mountain fire,
In hemlock stand, in shadowed night,
Warmed by flame, and drawn by light.
Let no one speak, that each one may
Discern the truth, the mountain way."

Dorvatica,
Mountain Song

The scented wind threatened to chill Verclan's men as they sat around the fire. Wrapped in their cloaks, they sat shoulder to shoulder on makeshift benches in a clearing in the dense hemlock canopy. Shadows cast by the fire danced on the dark trunks of the surrounding trees as they waited. The usual banter had run low and no one moved as they stared into the fire.

At the first faint sound of hoofbeats, Verclan sat up straight, listening intently.

He rose as if to hear better. "It's my son," he announced confidently. "At least it's his horse." he smiled as he sat down again. Everyone remained quiet as the sound of the approaching horse grew louder. Patira emerged from the darkness into the light of the fire and dismounted. Verclan rose again and greeted him with a hug. "Come, sit with us and have something to drink."

"Sounds good," said Patira. Verclan watched patiently as Patira tied his horse to a nearby tree and joined the ring around the fire. Patira would know everyone there; they were Verclan's most trusted advisors. He handed Patira a jug with a diluted apple cider mixed with spices. "Maclin?"

Patira took the jug, paused, and took a long draught. It was a drink concocted by mountain herbalists to strengthen the mind and stimulate clear thinking in times of fatigue. Bitter to the taste and burning slightly as it ran down the throat for the first time, it was what Patira would need after the long ride from Shiloh.

Verclan wouldn't have to ask Patira to start. Patira would know that this is why they were gathered and Verclan waited patiently for Patira to begin as he stared into the fire without moving.

"I saw nothing unusual at the smithy today. There was no indication that any of the smiths are working on any kind of weaponry, offensive or defensive—not any armor either." He paused and took another drink of the maclin. "I waited for two hours after the smithy was shut down to see if there would be any night activity, but there wasn't. It seemed like a rather ordinary day at the forge."

"How was the young smith?" Verclan asked.

Patira took another sip from the jug before continuing. "He's very talented. He has a strong intuition for the steel. He's easygoing, good with the hammer, and fast. He can do more in one heat than most smiths would do in two or three." No one spoke so he continued. "He has a curious style. I was trying to figure out whether that might be because he is left handed, but I think not."

Verclan took advantage of the pause: "Did he accept you? Did he seem suspicious?"

"At first it was a bit awkward—he had me working the fire. I think I did a passable job and after a while we fell into a rhythm that seemed to suit him. We actually got a lot done. At the end of the day, he thanked me for my help." Patira smiled into the fire. "It was good."

"So there was nothing unusual or suspicious that happened?"

"There was one curious thing. I wouldn't call it suspicious, just unusual."

Verclan raised his eyebrows. Several of his advisors shifted slightly in their places, but said nothing.

"We had a visit from the princess," Patira announced casually.

"*The* princess? Vrengnia?" Verclan leaned forward intently. "You don't call that suspicious?"

"Well, at first I did think it was odd, but it seems that she has some sort of friendship with the smith's son. She visits him often, riding down from the castle just to say hello and stay at the smithy for a while. Then she goes back. Today she stole a raisin cake from the king's kitchen and brought it down. We all took a break and ate it right in the smithy. Then she left."

"That *is* odd," mused Verclan.

"The other smiths confirmed that this is *not* unusual. Occasionally she'll convince Paca to go for a walk down the lane to the barley fields, but never for very long. It seems that they are friends. Don't know how long they've known each other. I got the impression it's been a while."

Verclan took a minute to think before he spoke. "Perhaps we will learn more tomorrow," he said quietly. "In the meantime, everyone get some sleep. My son and I need to talk. We'll hold council one hour after daybreak for a discussion on these things."

None of the advisors had spoken since Patira had come into the circle. Most of them were wise men who knew that listening was of much greater value than talking. There was always a time to talk. They got up. Some of them stretched as they pulled their cloaks around them, and disappeared silently into the woods.

Verclan waited several minutes, allowing time for both him and Patira to think privately, watching the fire and waiting for the right moment to continue the discussion. "Tell me about the princess, son," he said when the moment came.

"I don't know a whole lot. I mean, I only just met her today."

"No, I mean your impressions. What is she like?"

"Well, she didn't act like a princess. She was unpretentious and accepting. She came into the smithy almost like a child. It's as if she doesn't care that she's a princess. And the way she was dressed, she wasn't even like a woman, much less a princess, in baggy men's trousers and a blouse streaked as if someone spilled dye on it. And this gray tunic over it all, with blue slashes and a bright yellow starburst...very peculiar."

"That was her grandmother's crest," Verclan said.

"And the hat was the strangest; green and purple leather, more like a cap, but larger and flopped over to one side."

"Was she attractive?"

"She was not...let's see...it's hard to say. She wouldn't stand out in a crowd, except for her clothes, but she wasn't ugly, if that's what you mean." Patira fell silent. Both continued staring into the fire, comfortable with the silence between them. Verclan knew there was more, but he knew Patira, and he knew to wait.

Several minutes passed before Verclan spoke again. "Do you remember the other day at the smithy? I offered to tell the young smith my story some time." He looked Patira in the eye.

"Yes."

"It occurred to me then, that I've never even told *you* my story. I wanted to do this on numerous occasions, but your mother and I agreed that we wouldn't tell you until the time seemed right. Now I feel you need to know.

"Why now?"

"Today you met the princess. As I told the young smith, the person who gets to tell the story, defines history. Every story has two sides. I want you to hear my side first."

"What does the princess have to do with it?"

"Well, the princess, undoubtedly, has only heard the other side of the story, and—"

"You know the princess?"

Verclan looked up into Patira's questioning eyes. "Let me start at the beginning."

"The ever-expanding tapestry of true history is far too complex to be represented by the linearity of a single man's understanding of its strands."

Mindar Colloden,
The Great Fathers

Patira watched Fada, who sat to his left, his eyes fixed on the flames. In the firelight Verclan's visage was accentuated by the sharp contrasts of the orange flames against his olive skin and the dark folds of his mountain cloak, wrapped close to ward off the night chill. His face looked tired and he suddenly seemed old in a way that Patira had never noticed.

Fada pushed at the base of the fire with a stick and a shower of sparks leapt into air. How many times had they sat like this under the mountain sky? Five hundred? A thousand? Patira couldn't even begin to count. His eyes followed the shower of sparks down into the heart of the fire.

They remained silent for a time, waiting and listening to each other as only mountain men do, breathing deeply of the moist, hemlock-laden air and the dry, faintly acrid smoke from the burning wood.

"I worked for the King of Immerland once—" Fada began.

Patira shifted on his bench without taking his eyes from the fire.

"It was many years back—before you were born. He was still the prince at the time and his mother, Vorania, the Great Queen, ruled Immerland."

"I was a farrier in her stables." Fada looked up from the fire. "It was there I met the smith. We were about the same age. He just showed up one day. I'm not sure where he came from. I never asked. He needed a job and there was plenty to do. Queen Vorania had dozens of horses. She loved horses.

"I realized that the smith was an extraordinary craftsman, particularly when it came to blades. I've never seen anyone like him anywhere. After hours, when we were done with our shoeing, he would work into the night on his blades."

"What kind?"

"Anything: shears, knives, scythes. He became known and his reputation spread quickly." Fada paused, then pursued his story. "We were friends from the moment we met. I remember our first handshake. I can still feel his grip. Something inside me latched onto him. It seemed as if I had known him all my life in that instant.

"It was in this service that I met your mother. She was a riding instructor to one of the queen's handmaidens, Viarda. We became close friends because of the hours we spent together in and around the stables and the horses. It was through your mother that I was able to meet Viarda. Viarda and I had a special friendship. It was different from any relationship I ever had with a woman. We spent many hours talking about everything and nothing. I shod her horse—she often brought me little gifts from the kitchen. The smith called it a cymbic relationship—it was...it was so different.

"The prince also liked Viarda and set his eye on her to be his queen. I loved your mother—she was the one to be my wife, and Viarda was...well, she was part of the court and understood royalty. She knew what it meant to be a queen from her service to the prince's mother. All in all, the prince made a good choice and she fell very much in love with him. Viarda and I had never thought of being anything but friends."

Fada paused and stretched, adjusting his cloak around him. Patira thought he saw a greater sadness settling into the lines on Fada's face as he rocked back and forth gently on the wooden bench. He seemed to struggle with what to say next.

"When the queen died, the new king took Viarda for his wife. That was good for both of them, except that the king was insanely jealous. Though she loved him deeply, Viarda and I remained friends. It was soon after that I asked your mother to marry me.

"Your mother understood my friendship with Viarda, but the king did not. I had several discussions with him about it." Fada stared past the fire into a nothingness behind it. His voice grew distant. "Each time he grew more hostile. Though I had no romantic desire for Viarda, he couldn't understand it or tolerate it.

"Finally, he forbade Viarda to have any communication with me and in a fit of spite, ordered me to serve in the cavalry with his army, fighting the mountain people—our people—for the foothills to the south of Immerland.

"He did the same to the smith...but *he* refused to serve in the cavalry, so the king released him from his service in the stables. The smith left and settled in Shiloh. I think he did this to be comfortably far from the king." Fada shook his head and smiled at the irony of the current situation between the king and the smith.

"I continued to court your mother. Whenever I could, I got back to the castle to see her, and whenever I did, I always ran into Viarda. We never did anything wrong, at least not in a certain way. Your mother will attest to that. But we were young and I was arrogant and unmarried. I didn't understand the special psadeq of marriage, nor did I have the wisdom to know that our relationship needed to change because of her marriage. The smith warned me, but I didn't have the sense to respect Viarda's new position as a queen and as a wife.

"After Viarda became pregnant with Sandihar's first child, I took a small gift for her during one of my visits to the palace. I don't know to this day how the king knew about our meeting in the stables. Viarda had just opened the gift when Sandihar attacked me. She tried to intervene on my behalf and Sandihar, in his jealous rage, pushed her out of the fray. She tripped and fell against a hitching post—"

Patira felt the pause—and saw the sadness settle onto Fada's shoulders.

"The king had a sword. I was unarmed. Your mother saddled a pair of horses while we quarreled, and she and I barely escaped. To this day, I don't exactly know how. I do remember the king's last words: that he would kill me if he ever caught me."

"Kill you?" Patira echoed in disbelief.

"Yes...kill me. Queen Viarda went into labor and died in childbirth. She named the princess Vrengnia just before she died. Sandihar blamed me for her death and banished me from the kingdom of Immerland. He's never forgiven me."

Fada's voice trembled at the last sentence and trailed off, gripped by some deep pain. Patira knew there was little to be said, if anything, and little to be gained by looking at Fada. He kept his eyes in the heart of the fire.

Fada breathed deeply and sighed. "I fled to the hills to the south. Life was hard in the mountains. The mountain people were suspicious. Fortunately, being a farrier, I hadn't been engaged in direct warfare with them or they surely would have killed me. I earned their respect because of my skill as a farrier, and your mother, because of her skill as a horse trainer. Through a series of curious opportunities, we ended up serving princes of the mountain clans. They all wanted *me* to do their shoeing.

"The hard life became harder when Sandihar discovered where I was. He captured the foothills and took all the arable land up to the base of the mountains. There was no land for the mountain people to grow food. Winters were lean and challenging and many people starved. Resentment for the king grew strong here in the mountains.

"Because all the mountain warriors and princes came through my smithy for shoes, it became the central meeting place for raiding parties that marauded the lowlands for food at harvest time." Fada stirred the fire absently as he talked.

"Sandihar viewed these raids as attacks on his kingdom, and blamed all of it on me." A smile appeared on Fada's face. "Not wanting to be blamed for something I wasn't doing, I began organizing the raiding parties myself. I knew Immerland, and I knew the king and his army. We became so successful that I was able to unite several clans. The king, in his folly, created a greater enemy in the mountain people than he ever would have had if he had left us alone. Curious, is it not?

Interestingly, our cause wasn't to oppose the king as it was a fight for survival of the mountain people. Sandihar has never understood this." Fada smiled sadly, shaking his head and looking up into the trees.

"By this time we had opened the mines, finding our own supply of iron and coal. I kept in touch with the smith, secretly of course. He is the best there is for testing my new alloys and forge coal. The smith, in return, has provided food and other goods that were hard to come by in the mountains.

"I haven't spoken to the king since the day he drove me out. I have a hope that we will be able to speak one day, that we can resolve this. That's why whenever we catch one of his scouts, we send them back with that same message. The king has never agreed to meet."

"Ever?"

"Never. He keeps sending his army."

"I know."

"Perhaps the princess is the key to reaching the king." Verclan mused at the end of his story.

"Perhaps," said Patira, "but she is a feisty one and although she may seem a bit odd and small, she has some fight in her."

"Knowing the king, she is probably pretty handy with the bow and the sword. I have heard that he is raising her more like a son than a daughter—she's his only heir."

"She didn't seem to recognize my name when the smith introduced me to her," Patira said.

Fada looked up with a hint of a smile. "Well, I know that the king knows about you and undoubtedly he knows your name. Either she did not recognize it because she didn't expect it, or the king hasn't told her his story yet. Soon, however, he'll have to do that."

"Yes, I suppose so."

Patira sat and pondered what Fada had said. Finally Fada peered up through the trees at the stars. "Time for bed," he said slowly. "Past time for bed. We will speak more after we've slept."

Chapter 8

Alliances

"We are forever doomed to suffer with histories defined by those who are able to shout the loudest."

Mindar Colloden,
The Great Fathers

Vrengnia eyed Fada. "You haven't even touched your dinner," she said. He had invited her to a private supper, saying he hadn't had much time to see her lately with all the worries about the kingdom. Now he was sitting at the other end of the table, preoccupied with his own thoughts and hardly acknowledging that she was there.

"It's hard to be hungry these days," he mumbled as if he knew it wasn't true, but had to say something.

Vrengnia took advantage of his attention. "Was there something particular you wanted to talk about?" she asked as she raised a glass of wine for a sip.

"Well, yes—and no—I mean, it just seems like I haven't seen you around a lot lately and, it is nice to spend time with someone who doesn't want something from me."

She set down her glass and looked at him.

"Everyone who comes to see me wants something. They all have their schemes and many of them pretend to be after something entirely different from what they really want. It's exhausting and frustrating trying to figure it out."

Vrengnia waited.

"You don't come with an agenda, so it is nice to spend time with you."

She let herself smile.

"So that is the 'no' side of your question. But yes, there is something specific."

She wasn't surprised. Although he appreciated her straightforwardness, whenever he wanted time with her, it was usually because *he* had an agenda. He was the king, after all; his whole life was an agenda and hardly anything was spontaneous. Sometimes she wondered if it *could* be. Now when she became queen—

"I hear that you've been sneaking off to visit the smith's son down in Shiloh." He was trying to be stern.

"I would hardly call it sneaking. I didn't have anything else I was supposed to be doing. And I haven't tried to hide it either."

"And you stole a raisin cake from the kitchen?"

"Yes," she hesitated, "but there were seven of them, and I thought the smiths at Shiloh would appreciate them more than your advisors and attendants—and I think they did, honestly," she said with a faint smile. It was her way of letting Fada know that she thought his sternness was unwarranted.

He backed down. "All right, all right—just tell me what's going on."

"Okay. Will you promise you won't laugh?" she looked over the flowers in the center of the table.

Fada laughed. "Okay, okay."

"But you're already laughing."

"I'll stop—right now." He tried to put on a serious face and ended up laughing even harder.

Vrengnia saw the opening and jumped up, grabbed the heavy armchair she had been sitting in and dragged it the length of the table to the spot just to the left of Fada. "I always hated this long table," she quipped as she sat down. "Now I can tell you. Where should I start?"

"At the beginning—no, wherever you want," Fada said.

She started with Fada's first visit to the smithy, and ended with her last visit with the raisin cake; everything except the swords. *That* had to remain a surprise until his birthday.

"So anyway, yesterday when I took that raisin cake down to the smithy, there was a new assistant there. Paca introduced him to me, but didn't say much else." She reached for a cluster of grapes on the table in front of Fada. "He had an odd name. I think it was—Patira." Fada's eyes narrowed, but otherwise he didn't flinch.

"Hmmm. That *is* an odd name," he said thoughtfully. "Was there anything else odd about him?"

Vrengnia detected a slight shift in his attitude, but she kept going. "Well, his clothes were a little strange, but then I suppose that I'm not one to talk about that."

"Indeed." A flickering smile faded quickly into seriousness.

She had hit some nerve. "Let's see, they were more like clothes you would see on a man who lived in the mountains, dark; no—"

"Have you ever seen a man from the mountains?" he interrupted.

"No," she said cautiously, "but it just seemed that way, if you know what I mean."

Fada stroked his chin, a habit he had when he wasn't ready to say what was on his mind.

"And he seemed a little suspicious of me," she continued. "He wanted to know why I had come all the way down to the smithy just to bring a cake to Paca. He actually had the nerve to almost interrogate me about it."

"And well he might," Fada said angrily, standing up and walking to the window.

"You know him?" she gasped.

Fada stared out the window at the mountains in the distance.

"Not personally," he said. "I'm not sure. That is, I have no proof yet, but this might be the son of Verclan himself."

"Verclan?"

"Yes, *the* Verclan. He has a son by that name and he would be from the mountains. The question is, what is he doing in the smith's shop? There's something...in the back of my mind...I..." he snapped his fingers as if it would jog his memory. He did it again.

His eyes lit up. "Yes! The smith and Verclan were friends; they served together as farriers in my mother's stables. I sent them off to serve in the cavalry but the smith refused to go. I figured that they had lost contact when I exiled Verclan, but perhaps not."

Vrengnia still stood by the table. Fada turned to her. "You mustn't go near that smithy until I find out what's going on, no matter what else you do. Promise me this!" The command was firm.

She wanted to say no as firmly as he had issued his edict, but took a wiser direction. "I need an explanation before I'll agree to that."

The king walked back over to the table. He leaned forward on his whitening knuckles. "Explanations about what?" he asked. His countenance brimmed with rage.

Vrengnia had seldom seen Fada so angry, but she decided to hold her ground. She leaned across the table to face him. "You can start by giving me an honest story about Verclan. I mean, why did he have to leave? What happened between you and him?" Fada turned and walked back to the window. She pressed her advantage. "*You* have never told me." She followed him to the window. He was staring at the lights in the mountains. "You keep saying that you will someday, well—*now* would be fine!" They stood facing each other for three minutes. She waited, knowing that she had to, but unsure whether Fada would break down or explode.

A tear rolled down his cheek. Vrengnia stepped forward and laid her hand lightly on his left shoulder. He shook it off and sniffed, and gesturing to the table, he said, "Sit down. It's a long story."

They walked to the table and sat down. After pouring himself some more wine, he leaned back and slid down in his chair with the flagon sitting on his belly. The posture he took suddenly made him look weak and old. Was she changing or was he? Something was happening between them that she didn't understand. He looked vulnerable and broken in a way she had never noticed before. Perhaps it was that *she* was growing up and gaining strength. Vrengnia wasn't sure she was ready for either one.

Fada's words cut into her thoughts. He was already in mid-sentence before she noticed he was talking. "In the beginning," he started. "Though I'm not sure exactly where the beginning is," he said. His eyes looked far away and filled with a sad anger.

Vrengnia leaned forward, not wanting to miss what he was about to say.

"It started when I was still prince and my mother ruled Immerland. My older brother had disappeared, and I knew I would be king eventually."

"You had a brother?"

"He was four years older. He left one day when I was fourteen; heading for the coast. We never saw him again." He looked up into her eyes and took a sip of wine. "So I knew I would be king, but didn't know how I could possibly learn how to do it. I followed my mother around and watched carefully, but it was difficult to figure out what she did. It seemed so effortless for her." He paused and sat staring into the nothingness just to the left of his feet stretched out before him.

Vrengnia waited.

"She would meet with various people, the dors, her advisors, friends—whomever and just talk. She might ask their opinion, maybe advice. She seldom told them to actually do anything. Somehow, it all just worked. Everyone seemed to know what to do, and did it." Vrengnia detected a quiet frustration in his voice, almost desperation. "She never seemed to be busy and always had time for doing things she wanted to do.

"She loved riding, just for the joy of it, and never needed a reason to go riding, She would just take the time and do it! Her stables had the best horses, the best groomsmen, the best stable hands, and the best farriers." He paused. The way he had said "farriers" carried an angry edge. "She paid them handsomely to maintain her horses and stables. Her sense of the best—on which she insisted in everything—included character as well as skill. She once dismissed the best cook in the castle because of a small indiscretion.

"When I asked her about it, she simply said that the nature of the lie he told her indicated a corruption she couldn't tolerate in the castle. I never understood it." He stopped and looked into Vrengnia's eyes.

She nodded to reassure him she was listening.

"Anyway, there were three workers in the stable that are significant to this fragment of history: First, there was Verclan himself, the finest farrier in the kingdom, though I never understood how she tolerated him on her staff. He was as arrogant as the day is long. I don't think she ever saw it that way. It was said that he could take a horse he had never seen and shoe him blindfolded, and if you asked around, you could probably find someone who would claim they had seen him do it." Fada shook his head sadly and lapsed into a faraway stare.

"And?"

He shuddered and sat up, taking another quick sip of wine. "Working the forge beside Verclan was the old smith, then a young man, with talent to make the blade that was unsurpassed. He knew a good shoe and how to fit it and Mother paid him well to forsake the blade-making to work her stables. My mother had an odd relationship with the smith. He was somewhat of a favorite in the stables when she would visit, and they often spent extended time in conversation talking about everything and nothing at all, so it seemed. I think I understand that better now. He is a very compelling individual."

"Where did he come from?"

"I don't know. Mother found him somewhere. She had a knack for attracting talent. Anyway, the smith and Verclan had a peculiar relationship. They were always together and always stood up for each other. They seemed to have the sense of twins. They worked together as a team on the farrier's forge and could shoe a horse in a third the time that any other team could do it. The horses they shod never threw their shoes. I have never believed in magic, but this pair was the closest thing I have ever seen to it. They were the best." He took a thoughtful sip of his wine before continuing.

"Now, one of the finest riding instructors in the my mother's service was a young woman by the name of Mordara. The stable hands joked that she was born on a horse. She knew the ways of horses and was particularly skilled at teaching others what she knew. She was selected as the instructor for the beautiful Viarda, your mother, who was my mother's handmaiden at the time.

"When Mother went riding, Viarda was always there and Mordara would ride along with her. The two became best friends and spent many hours together beyond the riding lessons." There was another pause and another sad, faraway look. Vrengnia guessed that Fada was remembering many things that weren't directly part of the story he was telling, but were part of what had shaped him. She waited.

"All this was well within the ordinary, but the odd thing that came out of it was that Verclan and Viarda also developed a relationship. It would have been of little consequence, except that as handmaiden to the queen, he should never have been nearly as forward as he was with her. Your mother was extremely beautiful. I was often in her presence. Obviously, we fell in love. We tried to be discreet. I don't think my mother would have approved."

"Why?"

Fada sighed deeply and looked into her eyes. "Your grandmother was very traditional in certain ways. She loved Viarda, but Viarda was still a handmaiden. Princes do *not* marry handmaidens." He took another sip of wine.

"Did you ever talk to her about it?"

"No, it would have been useless."

Vrengnia decided not to press it further.

"I knew she loved me too. I wasn't in a hurry, and mother was getting old. We secretly decided to wait until she died to marry. The only hitch was Verclan."

"Verclan?"

"Your mother kept insisting they were just friends ...."

"You were jealous—"

"Yes, yes. I suppose so, but with good reason. A woman who has agreed to marry someone should *not* have that kind of friendship with another man." He drank deeply, quelling his anger behind the rim of his flagon. Vrengnia's thoughts drifted back to her conversation with the smith.

"I tried to reason with Verclan—to keep him away from Viarda. And I tried to reason with Viarda, but to no avail. They insisted they were just friends. Finally in desperation, I had Verclan reassigned to the cavalry. We were engaged with the mountain people over the farming rights in the foothills to the south. I sent him there, to be a farrier for the cavalry.

"When mother died, the stables weren't used nearly as much, so I tried to reassign the smith also. He refused to serve in the cavalry, so I dismissed him from service to the castle."

"So that's how he ended up in Shiloh?"

Fada nodded. "Your mother and I married, but somehow the connection between your mother and Verclan continued, through the agency of Mordara. I knew it was there, but tried to ignore it. It was beyond resolution, so I just tolerated it.

"Just before you were born, Mordara arranged a secret meeting between Verclan and your mother in the castle stables. Ostensibly, it was so that Verclan could deliver a small gift to honor her expected child, which of course, was you. I heard about it through one of the other attendants who had overheard a conversation between your mother and Mordara.

"I accosted them in the stables and challenged them. Verclan grew violent and attacked me. He was much stronger than I. Fortunately, I had brought my sword. When your mother tried to intervene, Verclan pushed her aside. She tripped and fell into a hitching post, where she was mortally wounded.

"Verclan fled. I pursued him, but the treacherous Mordara had already saddled two of her best horses for their escape and they fled to the mountains. The castle doctors delivered you, but your mother died in the birthing." The faraway look returned to Fada's eyes. "I have never been able to forgive him for the death of your mother."

Fada sat unmoving for a long time, collecting thoughts which flitted across his face, never surfacing in words. Vrengnia waited. The weight of Fada's story descended on her; a weight of anger, and hatred, pressing from all sides. If his tale were true, then his loathing of Verclan could be justified, but she found, in her vorn, a peculiar strength pushing back and repelling her fear. It was doubt, working from the inside out; doubt that this was the whole story; doubt that the simplicity of it could lead to the level of fear and resentment he carried.

Fada continued. "Verclan is a clever man, and it didn't take long before he had aroused the mountain people against me and began raiding the border villages, systematically rallying the outlying boundaries of Immerland against me also. Many of my scouts disappeared, tortured and killed by the outlaw and his followers. I knew that there could be no peace in Immerland unless this man was brought to justice and his followers disbanded."

Fada shifted from sadness to anger. Vrengnia wanted to sympathize. It would have been easy to do a month ago, but having met the smith and Patira and being engaged with Paca in his endeavor to make Fada's sword, she found a tangle of emotions woven so tightly around her inner doubt that she could not. Even the idea, buried in Fada's vorn and withheld from her for so long, that Verclan had killed her mother, seemed like a restless cloud, driven overhead by the gale, but powerless to drop its rain.

A new determination was awakening in her vorn, a determination to move forward rather than sympathize. "Fada," she queried, "have you ever tried to seek peace with Verclan? I mean, talk to him, find a better solution than fighting?"

"Impossible," he snorted in disgust, "He is a madman, a renegade and a traitor. He killed my wife and *your mother*. He can't be trusted and he deserves to die. Even now, our scouts are reporting a massing of small bands of men, waiting in the hills. That is what all the lights are—their fires. They'll attack again. It is just a matter of when and how."

He rose from the table where they had been sitting and walked to the window again. "So, my darling daughter, that is why you must not go to the smithy until we know why Patira is there."

Vrengnia bristled. She hated that appellation. Fada only used it when he was trying to get some unwarranted control over her. "Fada, you have no proof that this Patira at the forge is one and the same with the son of your enemy." Fada glanced at her with a mixture of disgust and anger, but she pressed on. "Secondly, I don't see a reason to fear. Patira gave me no indication, no threat—"

Fada interrupted her in a burst of rage. "When Patira went to the forge, he had no idea that you would be going there. By now, he has undoubtedly conferred with his father and they are laying a plan of what to do if you show up again. Open your eyes! This is the real world. Though we are royalty—the *king*, the *princess*—in many ways we are just pawns in the vast scheme of things, and you must trust my intuition about this man Verclan." He turned back to the window.

Vrengnia fumed, but she saw the wisdom in what Fada said. She waited until she could answer appropriately, more like a queen than a child, then said, "I will refrain from visiting the smithy—and the young smith—out of respect for your authority as king, until you have ascertained the truth about Patira. However, I wish to send a message to Paca explaining that I won't be visiting."

"Why?" asked Fada without turning from the window.

"Because he's my friend. He would wonder if I didn't come to visit for some time."

"That's fair," Fada said, "but it mustn't say why."

Vrengnia thought she understood, "It won't state why. Goodnight, Fada." She turned and headed for the door of the great hall where dinner remained uneaten on the table.

She headed straight to her chambers. Anger raged inside, but she knew Fada was right, in spite of his fear. She stared out the windows at the mountains. The lights were still there. She wondered what they really were, what they really meant. Then she looked up to see the sky, full of lights, peaceful, eternal. *They* were no threat to her or Immerland. Should the lights on the mountains really be any different?

She called for an attendant and made her way to her writing desk and wrote a simple note:

"Paca, because of certain circumstances here at the castle, I won't be able to come to the smithy for several days. I look forward to the time I will be able to come and see you again. I hope that it will be soon. Vrengnia."

She rolled it carefully, sealing it with hot wax and impressing it with her ring. When the attendant arrived, she handed it to him. "See that this is delivered to the smith at Shiloh forge first thing in the morning." The attendant bowed and disappeared down the hall.

She prepared herself for bed and lay down. In spite of her exhaustion, she couldn't sleep. She was still half-awake when she heard the midnight watch called from the parapet across the courtyard.

Somewhere in the nether world between wakefulness and deep sleep she heard a peculiar sound she had never heard before. It was a slight creak and a click just outside her door. It was curious and different, but she fell asleep without making the effort to discover what it was.

"Courage is not found in the one who does not fear. It is born in the heart of the one who knows fear, but does not let that fear dissuade him."

Pratoraman,
The Middle Way

Patira was sitting on the stoop of the smithy door when Paca arrived. The uneasy conflict between the simple joy of seeing a new friend and a subtle fear emanating from who this friend was, swept over him. He greeted Patira casually. "How long a ride is it to...to wherever you are staying?"

"Perhaps an hour. Maybe a bit longer. I had to be more careful today. The king's scouts have been snooping around since early this morning."

"Do you know why?"

"No, but it doesn't matter." Patira seemed relaxed. He stepped in front of Paca and opened the door. "What's on the slate for today?"

"We have to finish those barley scythes." Paca hung his coat. "We need an edging fire, long and not too hot." He knew Patira would do exactly what was needed.

They had worked together only one day, but Patira had proven himself well. Patira headed for the forge as Paca gathered the four roughed-in blades from the previous day's work. He took them to the window to examine them while Patira cleaned the firepot and laid the new fire.

Paca couldn't help wonder what the king's scouts were up to. He wondered if Vrengnia had mentioned Patira to her father, though he doubted that she knew who Patira was, and nothing had been said to give him away. If this were the case, then Patira's cavalier attitude seemed out of place, particularly if the scouts were after *him*.

He looked toward the forge. The fire was already burning. Patira was focused on arranging the coal on the forge bed. "Long and low!" Paca called as a reminder. Patira turned and smiled.

Paca worked the blades in and out of the fire; four at once. Patira tended the air and the coal perfectly while Paca pounded out the details of the blades. Paca sang; Patira listened.

By mid-morning Paca had all four blades cycling through the fire under Patira's expert care, when suddenly, as he looked up, Patira had vanished. The bellows toggle was still swinging where he had left it. Paca hesitated and glanced quickly around the smithy. There was no sign of his helper. He was about to say his name when the door of the smithy burst open and the captain of the King's Guard lurched through it. "We're looking for Patira," the captain growled, squinting in the dimness of the smithy.

Paca thought quickly. "There's no one here by that name," he said as he put the blade he had been working back into the fire carefully, reaching up to work the bellows himself. The captain seemed to know little about smithing, so the absence of an assistant to the head smith wasn't noteworthy. The other smiths were good men, wise and perceptive, and they kept working without a hint of hesitation.

The captain's eyes narrowed. Those ugly eyes. Where had the king found a man with such ugly eyes? The edge on the captains's attitude only made it worse. The resentment of the interruption rose in Paca's vorn, and it made him more determined to not let this rude man take advantage of him.

The captain continued: "There was a man here by the name of Patira. He is a sworn enemy of the king. I want to know where he is!"

"So would I," said Paca casually. "If I did, I would hand him over to you, and you would get out of my smithy so I could continue my work."

The captain scowled. He strode toward the main forge and stopped close enough so that Paca could have touched him.

Paca kept his eyes focused on the man as he spoke. "Perhaps you could describe this scoundrel, and I could tell you if I have seen him."

The captain leapt at Paca and pulled the bellows toggle from his hand in desperate anger. "I'm not fond of games," he growled.

"Neither am I," Paca said, reclaiming the toggle from the captain's hand by sheer strength and quickness. "Now. I am late delivering these blades for the barley harvest and I don't need any further interruptions. Describe the man you are looking for, and I will tell you whether I have seen him. I have no quarrel with the king about this, but if these blades are any later—"

The captain put his fingers in his mouth and whistled. Four more guards, armed with swords bustled through the door. The captain motioned with his hand and they began to search the smithy, poking their swords into every space that they couldn't see. The captain turned to face Paca again. "We don't have a very good description. None of us have ever seen him. All we know is that he is tall and dark, and dresses like one from the mountains."

Paca turned from the blades in the fire and tugged on the bellows. "There was a man like that here the last two days. He came in volunteering to help to make up for time lost since my father was imprisoned—I never turn down help like that. But I had no idea he was so dangerous to the king, and I haven't seen him recently and I have no idea where he might be. Feel free to poke around."

The captain eyed him coldly for a moment and then joined his men in the search. Paca went back to work, working only two blades and tending his own fire. When the guards were satisfied that there was no place in the smithy that hadn't been thoroughly searched, they filed out into the yard and circled the building, checking everything again.

The captain, still brimming with irritation and suspicion, came back inside to speak to Paca: "One of the king's scouts saw this man enter your smithy this morning, before you or the other smiths were here. He didn't see him leave. We will be watching. If you are lying, we will take you in as well."

"So be it," Paca said. "Fare thee well, Captain."

The captain stepped through the doorway, dragging the heavy door closed behind him. The frame of the smithy shuddered as it slammed shut. Paca shook his head and went back to work. He was as mystified as the captain, but in a different way. He had no idea what happened to Patira and he wasn't sure he wanted to know. Patira had to take care of himself.

*"The sum of what one is and does
cannot be held in Hjarvin's Jars."*

Tessamandrian Proverb

The beam Patira lay on shook when the door slammed. He hadn't seen the man's face but could tell from the voice and the attitude that it was someone he didn't want to know.

He lay comfortably on the beam above the smithy pondering the events of the last few minutes. In his mind he could picture Hjarvin's jars, lined up in rows on the shelves in front of him. He was searching for the enemy jar. He knew it was just a couple of rows down and a little to the left of center. The jars were numerous and all looked the same except for the hand lettered marking on each one. As soon as he found the enemy jar he could safely put that voice in it. Hadn't the man claimed him as an enemy, and could he not justifiably put him in the jar?

Fada had said many times never to do this; that the story of Hjarvin and his famous shelves of jars showed so clearly the injustice in our desire to quickly and prematurely categorize beings.

Even if it had no true basis in fact, the story was a good one: Hjarvin lived shortly after The Beginnings, and was given the gift of clear thinking by the Eladra. His fame as a philosopher brought many wise men and truth seekers into his presence. To keep track of all these beings he encountered, he took to writing his observations on scraps of white bark, which he then stored in clay jars. Each jar was loosely categorized with characteristics that Hjarvin developed based on his observations.

After a while there were many such jars and he spent innumerable hours rearranging them and creating new ones to accommodate his changing understanding of beings.

One day, when he returned from his trip to the market, he found that someone had come into his home and shuffled the jars as well as the scraps of bark that were in them. As he began the process of sorting out the confusion before him, he realized how impossible and unfair it was to create such categorizations, that beings by nature are unique and deserved to be treated without prejudice of being placed in a jar with any label on it.

The smithy below resumed its rhythm. No one was talking, and it gave him space to think. He knew that "jarring" the captain of the guard based on his voice and his attitude was wrong. The king had undoubtedly sent him. It was his task to make an arrest. All he would know about Patira would have been told to him by someone else who had put Patira in the "enemy jar" of his own mind. Now he was in the enemy jar in the captain's mind. Everyone knows that enemies are dangerous, that enemies are to be treated in a certain way, that enemies have lots of characteristics that Patira didn't consider himself to have.

Patira didn't want to be in anyone's enemy jar, but he had no control over how others categorized him. The only control he had was *not* to jar other people unfairly: the king, the captain, Paca, and the princess were all individuals who deserved fair treatment in his mind about who they were.

"So, where do you think he went?" Patira recognized Vordar's voice, and he heard Paca breathe deeply. They were not ten feet from him, though he couldn't see either.

"I haven't a clue," said Paca. "I was hammering out an edge, and when I turned back to the forge, he was gone."

"I didn't even realize he had disappeared until the captain said his name." Vordar said. "I looked over and he just wasn't there."

All the hammering stopped immediately. Paca must have given some sort of signal. "Did anyone see where Patira went?" he asked.

"No."

"Not me."

"Me, neither."

"Thanks for not letting on to the captain that he had been here," Paca said. "I'm sure we will find out sooner or later what happened."

"What I want to know is how he knew they were coming?" said Vordar.

"Me too," chimed a voice from the corner. "I mean, when they crashed in here, he was already gone."

"We'll have to find out—but not now; there's a lot to be done." The rhythm of the five forges resumed.

Patira smiled to himself. *Flatlanders!* These people had grown up without having to be aware for their life in every second of existence. He had sensed the danger several minutes before it threatened him, and he knew exactly when it became a real threat. He had surveyed the smithy early that morning and had found his escape route and how to get there should any danger arise.

The smithy's post and beam construction, with heavy timbers, supported a thatched roof. It's tricky to have a thatched roof on a smithy, and so, large animal skins had been stretched across the ceiling just under the roof beams to prevent errant sparks from catching the thatch.

The gap between the skins and the thatch was a pace thick with large support beams crossing between them. Away from the forges, near the walls of the shop, the skins ended, and one could climb up into this space, which offered numerous places to rest undetected from the smithy below.

Flatlanders never look up when searching for anything. It was a common failing when they were in the mountains. If a man were just a few feet above eye level, he could remain unseen as long as he was quiet. None of the soldiers searching for him even considered that he might be "up" somewhere.

Patira decided that he wouldn't come down until everyone had left and it was dark. Whatever mystery there was to his disappearance, he wanted to preserve. Besides, if Paca thought he was gone, he might find out things he would never know if he was working there. He settled in to wait. Perhaps he would nap a little. His mind drifted to the princess.

He found himself drawn to her in a peculiar way. He hadn't put the princess in a jar. He hadn't even struggled with it. Why? That morning on the ride in from camp, many of his thoughts had been about her. They were good thoughts, most of them centered on the connection they had through their fathers. He wondered how different life would have been had that singular encounter between them in the castle stables hadn't happened. He and the princess might have known each other since they were both young. As it was, now they had met only one time, and that was notably brief and unremarkable. How was it that this single, short encounter carried so much weight in his thoughts?

Fada had taught him that coincidence was never actually coincidental. There was always a point, a reason. His encounter with the princess the day before was significant, but he would probably have to wait to discover why. *Romance is out of the question,* he reasoned. In the whole of Immerland and the mountain realms, there couldn't be a more unlikely pair than the son and the daughter of these men. Still, he found himself attracted to her and to the idea of getting to know her better. But how?

Somewhere in the thought circles about himself and Vrengnia, of Fada and the king, of romance and friendship, he drifted into a shallow sleep, stretched out comfortably on a rafter above the ceaseless, rhythmic din of the smithy below.

Chapter 9

Shifting

"The twilight of childhood descends upon us when we begin to understand the weakness and failings of our elders, and realize that we may be walking the same path."

Oratanga,
Passages

Asolara had been up for some time when Verengnia opened her eyes and sat up. She walked to the door of her chambers to call for an attendant, but as she pushed on the door to open it, it wouldn't move. She pushed harder. She sat down on the stool by the door, stunned. She didn't even know that there *was* a latch on the door to her chambers. *It must be on the outside. This is ridiculous.* She knocked on the door and waited, but there was no answer.

Vrengnia wasn't one for self-pity or grieving her circumstances, so she checked each of the windows. They could be opened, but each was barred on the outside. She had always thought this was for her own protection—to keep others from getting in—but the bars suddenly seemed different. For half an hour, she searched for a secret door in the back of the closet, a loose brick in the wall, or a floor tile that could be pried up, but found nothing. She threw herself onto her bed. Was it so simple to become a prisoner in one's own chambers?

It didn't take long for her to reason that Fada wanted to make sure that she didn't warn Paca and Patira. The realization of his lack of trust surfaced the rising anger within her. Something was happening to him. She'd never seen this dark side of him before.

While she dressed she remembered that tonight was the night she'd promised to help the smith with something. She didn't know what it was, but knew somehow that she had to honor her commitment.

While she waited, she sat down at her desk and tried to think of something to write. She went through her wardrobe, mentally cataloguing her various outfits. Her hunger began to gnaw at her. She drank another mug of water from the pitcher on the nightstand…

Shortly before the change in the noon watch, she heard horses at a full gallop. From the window she saw Omberon and four other guards approaching the castle from the south. If they'd been to Shiloh to find Patira, they'd failed. She sighed, and went back to her desk, but still there was nothing.

The sound of shuffling feet in the corridor, and the soft click of the door latch awakened her where she had fallen asleep at her desk. The door opened, and Fada strode in with his arms wide and a warm smile on his face. "My daughter, Princess of Immerland."

Vrengnia bristled like a cornered cat. "Don't you 'my daughter' me," she raged. "What is the meaning of imprisoning me in my own chambers like a common criminal?"

"There are times—" Fada began, as she ducked past him into the hallway. "Wait!" he cried.

She shouted over her shoulder as she rounded a corner, "There are never times for the likes of this."

She wanted something to eat and could feel the gnawing hunger inside. Fada was unlikely to look in the kitchen, since he seldom went there himself, nor was it one of her usual haunts. As she entered, the head baker smiled and raised his eyebrows. "Ah, the princess herself—" She knew that the baker liked her, so the look in his eyes evoked an immediate twinge of guilt . "I'm sorry about the cake the other day."

His eyes smiled and twinkled at the same time. "I knew you needed it—just let me know next time—you seem troubled, what do you need now?"

It caught her off guard. "I just need something to eat," she stuttered, "and to stay away from my father."

The baker smiled again, wiping his hands on his apron. "Both should be easy." There was always a pot of something-or-other soup on the oversized stove and extra bread on the table for the kitchen help, so he found a bowl and served her. She sat on one of the large stools of the loaving table to eat and to think about her new situation. The table was tucked in the back where no casual visitor to the kitchen would see her, especially if she was sitting down. It was a warm, comfortable place to be right then.

The baker left her with her thoughts. The terror that crouched just beyond the horizon of her mind eluded her. As her thoughts swirled, she found that she wasn't surprised at the recent events. She should have been angrier than she was, but somewhere, lurking just behind that unseen terror, she sensed a greater strength that overshadowed it all—surrounding and engulfing her, the castle and even Fada.

There was no name for it, no jar into which to drop it in her mind. The vagueness of it should have distressed her, but instead, was giving her courage and peace. Somewhere in the middle of it all, she sensed the presence of the smith.

She savored every mouthful, waiting for clarity that eluded her. When the last drop of soup had been mopped out of the bowl with the final crust of bread, she wasn't sure she was any better off except for her full stomach.

She thanked the baker and took her leave. *To the stables,* her mind said. Fada would not think to look there. Although she knew how to ride well, horses for her were utilitarian, and she wasn't one to waste time in the stables. As she crossed the courtyard, she realized that hiding was only part of the reason she wanted to go there.

She needed to find out more about Verclan. She knew somehow that she had only heard a small piece of the story; there *was* more, and the most likely place to find it would be the stables.

About twenty people worked at the stables, and during any day, a good number of them would be there. She found several of the grooms, still brushing down the horses of the king's captain and his men. "They look tired," she said, stroking the chestnut mare down the nose.

The head groom was angry. He spat on the ground. "They should never have ridden them this hard—all the way from Shiloh without a break—and for no good reason, mind you. Trying to catch some mountain man outlaw! They failed and took their anger out on the horses."

The terror on the horizon inched closer with the confirmation of the party's purpose. "That's part of the reason I'm here. I'm wondering if anyone can tell me more about Verclan." The head groom spat again and turned away. They all fell silent, not wanting to look at her. "I think they were after his son," she said. One of the older grooms looked up, caught her eye and winked, but turned back to his work without saying anything else.

Vrengnia pitched in, uninvited, to help with the various chores. She was sure that the old groom had something to say and just needed a place to say it. There was plenty to do and lots of time. The work was a good way to forget the specter in the distance and she also thought it might be encouraging to the stable hands to see royalty carrying oats and shoveling manure.

Just before the dinner break in the stables, the old groom shuffled past her and, with an almost imperceptible wag of a finger, beckoned her toward a small door at the back of one of the stalls. He drew the latch on the heavy door and pulled it open. She followed him out through the low doorway, glancing over her shoulder to see if others were watching. No one seemed to notice or care.

The small passage led through the castle wall and when they emerged, they were in a small courtyard just outside the wall that looked like it hadn't been visited in years. There were closed gates on either side, overgrown with vines, and the lane between the gates was filled with untouched grass.

"The Great Queen used to have her buggy pick her up here when she went riding," said the old groom as he stepped to the right and dropped himself onto a small bench propped up against the wall. "It hasn't been used since she died."

He patted the seat beside him. She sat down. "I come here when I need a quiet place. No one will disturb us. Few people know this even exists." He stared out into the fields beyond the courtyard, resting his hands on his knees, and exhaled a sigh. "Now, princess," he began in a low voice, tired with many years, "what is your interest in Verclan?"

She honored his age with a brief pause. "Last night, my father told me the story of Verclan for the first time. I mean, I knew he was an outlaw from the mountains, but never knew that my father knew him personally...I never knew how my mother died either. I thought perhaps someone here might know something more about what happened. No one seems to want to talk about it, or maybe they aren't allowed to..."

The old groom smiled. It was a slow sad smile, and then he began, staring far away to the horizon as he spoke. "Verclan was a remarkable farrier, and he was well liked by all of us in the stables. He was very strong-willed and had a reputation for it. He had what we called 'Verclan's way,' but he would smooth it over so that it wasn't distasteful to people who knew him. He loved the horses, he loved the forge, he loved his work, and he loved all of us. He got crossed up with the prince—your father—somehow. Not that your father is a bad fellow, mind you, but he never had been able to understand Verclan's way and let him *have* his way. Verclan never did your father wrong. He gave him the best he had and your father knew it." The old man shifted, putting both hands down on the edge of the bench and leaning forward. His eyes still stared over the low wall in front of them as he continued:

"The final straw between Verclan and your father was his relationship with the Lady Viarda, your mother. Viarda was your grandmother's handmaiden and was being instructed in her horse handling by Verclan's sweetheart, the beautiful Mordara. Viarda and Verclan had a special relationship. Do you know the word 'cymbic'?" he asked, turning to look at her.

She nodded.

"They had a strong cymbic friendship about which your father took issue with Verclan at every opportunity. When the old queen died and your father became king, he married Viarda and dismissed Verclan from the stable."

The story went on, more or less as Fada had described it to her, except that the old groom was much more sympathetic towards Verclan. From *his* perspective, it was Fada who had pushed her mother in the final confrontation in the stable.

"And you witnessed this yourself?" she said.

"I was in the corner cleaning a saddle. I was some distance away, but I saw most of it. It was quite a ruckus."

"Would you call Verclan a 'ruthless villain'?" she asked.

"Ruthless? Well ...." The old groom hesitated then turned to face her. "Aside from the smith who used to work with him at the forge, I've never met a more peace-loving man. His lack of wisdom and his stubborn refusal to listen to the smith's advice about his relationship with Viarda when she got married, cost him his place in Immerland. They say when he was banished that he went bad, but I have never found that easy to believe. A man of his character and strength doesn't go bad like that." The old man shook his head.

"There must be some other help around here who remember Verclan. Why won't any of them talk about him? I mean, everyone got so quiet when I mentioned his name."

"Well, the king—your father—doesn't want us talking about it. I've never understood why though. It just seems like he has this obsession with Verclan. Everything else he does is wise—kind—kingly if you will, but this strangeness toward this one man, his unwillingness to forgive, seems much out of character. Some say it will be his undoing."

"I am beginning to wonder myself," Vrengnia said, trying to coax more talk from the old man.

"If he were to come and ask me, why I'd tell him to forget the whole thing." The old groom seemed pleased with the idea of giving advice to the king. He leaned forward and pushed himself up with his hands. "If you have any other questions, you know where to find me." He winked again at her. "Make sure you draw the bolt on the door," he said and shuffled back through the wall.

Vrengnia sat still in the courtyard. The pieces of the strange puzzle were starting to fall into place, but the picture that it was making wasn't what she expected, and there were still parts missing. Where would she find them and how? Where could she go next?

She decided to remain where she was until it was time to visit the smith. She could hear his anvil ringing in the tower. Her terror, held at bay by the conversation with the old man, began creeping back in, but each round of hammering from the tower seemed to drive it back. She remained in the gathering twilight, sensing the pulse of a world surrounding her that she had never allowed herself to see.

She watched the stars come out one by one before the hammering stopped for the last time. The sky faded through its colors from day to night, and the warm grass mingled its scent with the ubiquitous lavender of the small, unused courtyard, as the air chilled into evening. No one disturbed her reverie in this tiny, private spot. No one would ever find her if she came here again.

She sat until she was sure that the smith had moved upstairs and the guards had left, then padded her way through the hallways to the tower, trying to avoid contact with anyone. Though the rage about her imprisonment had subsided, she wasn't yet ready to meet Fada.

There was no one in the tower, as she expected. This time when she got to the smith's door, she only paused for an instant and drew the bolt in an ordinary way. When she pushed the door to, the smith said, "Good evening, Princess." He was sitting on his bed with a knowing smile. "I was expecting you this time," he said.

When she was safely inside the door and it was shut behind her, the smith jumped to his feet. "We don't have much time," he whispered. "I'm also expecting your father, and I'm expecting that he will be angry." He reached under his bed and pulled a leather parcel from underneath it. She recognized the leather as the piece that she had brought back to him from his own house. It seemed smaller, and it was wrapped into a parcel that she could slip into her tunic. It was stitched so that one of the odd symbols on the leather was centered on the front: four simple lines that looked like a pair of mountain peaks. He handed it to her.

She nearly dropped it. The smith's strength was deceptive and so was the weight of the package as he held it. She could tell that it contained several pieces of his work. "You must take this to Haniah, the hermit, who lives off the southern road to the mountains past Mordan—do you know of her?"

"I should be asking that of you!" she exclaimed. At every turn, the smith amazed her. "Haniah is a dear friend; I know her well."

"All the better," continued the smith. "There will be less suspicion about your going there. Give this to her and tell her I sent it. Don't give it to anyone else. Is this clear?"

Vrengnia nodded.

"If she's not there, leave it under the writing table to the left of the door. Leave a note—you can write, can't you?"

She nodded again.

"Leave a note saying it was from me, but don't sign your name. If you speak to her, give her my best. Go quickly now; before your father arrives." As she started to turn to the door, she heard the muffled voices of Fada and his guards coming up the stairs.

The smith leaned forward, took her arm and whispered in her ear. She did exactly as she was told. The smith seemed to know that Fada would stop in the smithy first.

She waited until her father's party had entered the smithy, and she slipped through the smith's door, closed it, and drew the bolt quietly, then headed up the stairs outside the smith's prison to wait until Fada had left.

"Mah'Eladra sit on the staircase to the Infinite and close their eyes to listen. In the midst of the relentless cacophony below, the true nature of each being is found and proven."

Karendo Marha,
Journey to the Infinite

Vrengnia sat on the stairs above the smith's prison, out of sight from the activity developing just below her. Because of the stone walls and stairs, she could hear everything clearly, but could see nothing.

Several sets of footsteps plodded up the stairs. She guessed it was Fada and a couple of guards. "Keep your voices low; we don't want to disturb the smith." It *was* Fada.

The bolt was drawn on the smithy and the door creaked. What followed was a series of noises that indicated that they were rummaging through the articles on the wooden table. She could hear iron hitting iron and wood intermixed with shuffling footsteps. The conversation was hushed and intermittent.

"Look at this."

"I wonder what it is."

"Don't know." Carnados! She knew his voice well. Fada had his advisors with him.

"Hmmm...curious."

"What?"

"This thing—"

"What a strange shape."

"Do you suppose that this—"

Something fell to the floor and the clang echoed up and down the stairway.

"*Shhhhhh!*"

"Sorry."

"Did you damage it?"

"Don't think so."

"Be careful."

"Sire," Carnados said, "I looked into Omberon's history as you asked."

"And?"

"Well, it's a bit cloudy."

"Cloudy?"

"Clouded, perhaps...as if he didn't have a history at all."

All the noises stopped. "Exactly what do you mean?"

"The earliest record of him in Immerland is only from about ten years ago, Sire."

"Ten years?"

"Yes. He has no birth records, no family. He just appeared."

"Appeared where?"

"His first records are in the army, Sire. There is no record of his joining the army or being commissioned or conscripted. He was just suddenly there—in with all the other foot soldiers."

"That's very, very odd, indeed!"

Vrengnia visualized Fada stroking his beard with his eyes cast down, staring into the infinity of the floor as if it were glass.

"What do you suppose it means, Carnados?"

"I have never seen anything like it."

"Yes, well—we'll have to keep an eye on him." The conversation dropped off and something else fell to the table. "Something seems different here tonight, I—" Fada paused.

"How so?"

"Well...the pieces look almost the same, but there seems to be fewer of them...."

"Or perhaps different ones."

"You see what I mean?"

"I was thinking the same thing—"

"Ow! O-oh...ah-h...ow-w-w!"

"What happened?"

"My toe....."

"Are you hurt?"

"Not really...just stubbed it on...hey! Look at this!"

There was a sudden commotion, and she heard Fada swear angrily. "Guards!" he yelled. "Guards!" His voice boomed up and down the tower staircase, echoing several times in the otherwise still castle. Footsteps hurried up the staircase.

Fada's fury was palpable.

Fada accosted the guards verbally. "What is this...do you know what this is?" his voice was condescending and angry.

There was a hesitation. "It's the smith's tool bag, Sire," said one of the new voices.

"Yes—I know it's the tool bag—so what is it doing here?"

"Well," said the second guard cautiously, "he must have left it here tonight."

"And why would he do that?" pressed Fada.

"Well, maybe he didn't need it."

"Why did he ever need it?" Fada shot back. The guards were silent. "Why didn't he take it with him tonight? He has every other night, right?"

"I thought he did take it with him," said one of the guards, "but I could be mistaken."

Fada closed the trap. "I think he did take it with him, only it wasn't *it*! Did you check his tool bag to make sure it was actually his tools? Did you?"

"I think we did," said one of the guards. "We always have, but since the bag is obviously here, I guess we didn't."

"No!" shouted Fada. "Don't you get it? Sure he took his tool bag, only it wasn't his tool bag—it just looked like it. It was full of whatever he was making—and you let it slip through the door."

One of the guards spoke to defend himself. "I don't think so, Sire. Look! All the things he was making are still on the bench."

"Yes, except they aren't the *same* things," Fada said."Come on, let's check the smith's room upstairs. It can't have gone far."

The hushed voices were mingled with their hurried footsteps as they came up the stairs. The bolt was drawn and the smith's door was kicked open by someone. The princess guessed it was Fada himself.

"Where is your tool bag?" demanded Fada.

"Why, I left it in the smithy tonight. I was done with my work later than usual, so I just left it there." There was no fear, no resentment, and not even a hint of worry.

A long pause followed. Vrengnia guessed that Fada was trying to get a grip on what to do in the face of the smith's calm. "Search the chambers," he said forcefully to the guards. "You—sit on your bed."

No one spoke as the guards rummaged through the sparse accommodations of the smith. Someone closed the door in the process of the search. She seized the opportunity and crept past, carrying the burden that the smith had given her. She fled down the remaining steps and headed for her chambers.

"Under the Tal's pale light they sat,
And wept again, for knowing,
That if they ever met again
'twould be in Meekar's glowing.
With friends as foes, their families' feud
Such time would not be soon,
That they would meet to speak again,
Under a different moon."

Ramonmara,
The Legend of Mishla Mira

As Vrengnia approached the hitching post in the lane, she realized it was the only indication that anyone lived near there at all. She was south of Mordan by half a daysmarch, on the seldom-used road to the mountains. They loomed closer than usual and they made her uneasy.

She turned Mahala to the right at the post and he stepped over the broken down stone wall onto the path to Haniah's soddy. There was no hurry. No one would see her now and it didn't matter anyway. Haniah was her friend and she came here often.

The strange brilliance on entering Haniah's land caught her off guard as it always did. She had no word for it; no way to describe the sensation, but everything seemed lighter, a bit fresher. Each time it was as new and refreshing as the first.

Her thoughts drifted back to the first time she had ever visited Haniah. She had found out about her from one of the royal physicians. He had given her some herbal concoction for an illness she had, and her recovery had been just short of miraculous, so she had asked where the good doctor had gotten his herbs.

He was given to long rambling conversations, particularly with patients who would listen, so the doctor spoke freely. "My friend Haniah, she lives south of Mordan, you know. She makes the best herbal remedies in Immerland," he'd said. "Been at it for years, don't rightly know exactly how long, but a good while. She makes the best herbal remedies in Immerland, don't you know."

"You said that."

"Yes, yes, well, she does."

"I believe it, and if they are all like the potion you gave me—"

"They're the best."

"Do you suppose she would mind if I visited her one day? I mean, I am often out and about, and always looking for a new place to go and herbal treatment has always been an interest of mine."

"It *is* a bit of a hike—"

"I'd ride my horse."

The doctor had chuckled. "I can give you directions—perhaps a map would be best. Do you have a piece of paper?" He had droned on as he drew the map: "You go down the lane south of Mordan past the old wooden barn, the only one in those parts, you know, and you come to this hitching post on the right—it's the only one around; you won't miss it. You cross the broken down stone wall ... let's see ..." he began counting on his fingers, "and then go across a field, don't you see, then you go across another field and there is sort of a path through the woods that leads to another field, which you also cross. Then there is a crooked little path through another wood and there is *another* field. Haniah's house is on the other side of *that* field." She remembered thinking, *How many fields was that?*

It was all somewhat vague, but when she got there, she managed to find it. She'd been there many times in the three years since she first met Haniah. Mahala knew the way.

As they ambled through the second field on the way to the first path, she pulled the bundle out of her tunic. Mahala's gait was easy and confident so she dropped the reins and took the time to scrutinize the strange package. How would the smith have known Haniah? "Of course—the vials of herbs in Paca's kitchen. Strange connection," she said aloud. Perhaps it wasn't so strange after all. The smith was a remarkable man, seeming to know almost everything. If Haniah was the best in the land, it stood to reason that the smith would know of her. It was a small step to imagine he knew her personally. Another question crossed Vrengnia's mind. What, exactly, was it, that she was carrying to her?

There were markings all over the leather, some of them apparently dyed into it, and others pressed in or stamped. Still others seemed to have been lightly burned in and some carved with the tip of a knife. Many were very old. In the center of the side away from the mark she had seen earlier was a freshly burned mark that resembled a crow's foot, and just below it a small bow drawn back. The bow had no arrow in it and there was a small, five-pointed star just to the right and above it. They were glyphs of some sort.

There were many people in Immerland that had glyphs, personal marks that were used as signatures. It was an old tradition, predating written language and generally only used as ornamental symbols on letters and personal clothing. They spoke of something simple; fundamental. The package in her hand represented the genuine use of glyphs. She had never seen these before and couldn't tell what they were or to whom they might belong.

There were at least two pieces inside, maybe three, but the leather was wrapped so tightly that she couldn't tell what they were. The whole thing was a little larger in diameter than the flat, spread hand of a large man. It was stitched together using strips of the leather.

Mahala stopped suddenly and dropped his head to eat. She was there. Everything was still, and Asolara cast a brilliant warmth across the field. There was no breath of wind to move so much as a blade of the grass, and the air was heavy with the scent of drying grass, mint, and hazel breath. The stillness made it like a painting in the great hall at the castle.

She slid off Mahala and left him to graze in the rich grass in front of Haniah's small sod house. As she walked toward the door, she passed Haniah's outside table. It looked as if it were set for dinner.

Bowls, flagons and cutting boards, hand carved scoops and stoneware plates adorned the table, all neatly placed as if Haniah were expecting a dinner party. It seemed odd for a person who was so removed from the mainstream of people, but Vrengnia didn't know all of what Haniah might do in her remote habitat.

She knocked gently on the door of the soddy. "Haniah?" No answer. She didn't wait to knock again. She pushed on the door; it yielded gently and she stepped into the semi-darkness of the peculiar dwelling. "Haniah?"

The hut was made of sod, from top to bottom, stacked in such a way to make a solid wall about a half a pace thick, except for the occasional window openings that lit the interior. Inside the floor was dirt, but packed so hard that it was almost polished with the wear. A small stove for winter heat sat in the corner, but today it was covered with nuts and small bowls of drying grains. Beside one of the windows to the left of the door was the writing desk.

Vrengnia guessed that Haniah was off foraging for nuts or roots in the woods on the other side of the stream.

She wanted to stay and wait, but decided that it was best to leave the note as the smith had directed, and get back to the castle. She hadn't seen Fada since he had freed her from her chambers the morning before and she knew it past time to find him and resolve the matter. The thought made her shudder.

There was a small scroll of bark on the floor next to the stove, so she took the quill pen from the inkwell on the desk and wrote simply and neatly:

"To Haniah, from the smith at Shiloh Forge."

She shuffled out of the soddy, wishing that Haniah would have been home so they could talk, even for a short while. Under the circumstances, she knew it was best to leave. She snugged the door shut behind her.

Vrengnia walked the few paces from the door past the neatly laid table and looked up. Another horse grazed calmly beside Mahala. It was a beautiful black mare, fully saddled with the reins neatly draped in her mane. Vrengnia whirled around, glancing about for any sign of a second rider. Nothing moved. The peaceful stillness had become a threat. She slipped toward her horse, as if being quiet made any difference.

She stroked Mahala's mane and swung up into the saddle. The horses were so close that she could hardly get her leg between them. As she swung her leg over the saddle, another rider appeared as if from nowhere onto his saddle.

Vrengnia tried to shriek, but the other rider reached out with his left hand and covered her mouth, while deftly grabbing the reins of her horse with his right. It all happened so fast that she didn't have time to do anything. "It's okay, Princess," said a voice that was calm and much in command. Patira!

He had a firm command on Mahala, though she wasn't sure how, and he had grabbed her right arm. "Where did you come from?" She stammered.

"It's an old mountain trick," he said. "I was hanging off the other side of my horse waiting for you."

"How did you know it was me?"

"I recognized your horse; a fine beast and well bred. He didn't even move when I rode up beside him."

She remembered that Patira's mother was a master horse trainer so Patira would likely know a good deal about it also. It would explain how he had gotten control so quickly.

"I'm glad you are here," said Patira. "I was wondering when I would see you again. I am sorry I made such a brash introduction at the forge. It really wasn't me. Do you have a few minutes to talk before you leave?" Although he still had control of her horse and a vise-like grip on her arm, he didn't seem like he was threatening her at all.

"If I let go of your arm and your horse, will you promise not to try to get away?" he asked.

"What do you want to talk about?"

"Well, after meeting you at the forge the other day, I asked my father about what he knew of you. He told me quite a story. It seemed to me that we ought to know each other and should have long before now. Were it not for the stubbornness of our fathers, we might already be good friends. I decided if I had the chance, I would like to make up for some of that lost time."

"I promise I won't try to escape." Vrengnia had had similar thoughts about Patira.

Patira let go of her arm and slid from his horse , never letting go of Mahala's reins. He held out his hand to help her off the horse and she obliged, sliding to the ground beside him. He dropped the reins and they left the horses to graze. He led her to the table and sat down in one of the places. "This is my seat," he said. "You can sit wherever you want."

"Your seat?"

"Sure, whenever we come to eat with Haniah, I sit here. My mother sits there, my father sits there and my two sisters sit on the end. Haniah sits on this end."

Vrengnia was stunned.

"And now good Princess, why are *you* here today?"

Vrengnia couldn't quite grasp what unfolded before her. Patira was polite and disarming. Even if she had anticipated such a meeting, it would all seem upside down. She decided to not worry about it until there was something specific to worry about. She started by telling him about her relationship to Haniah over several years and how she came here occasionally just to visit. She told him about the discussion with Fada and the old stable groom.

He recounted his escape from the captain of the King's Guard and how Paca had snuck him out of the smithy in the dark later that night.

She shared about her encounters with the old smith and how wise and knowledgeable he was; how he refused to make the swords for Fada, and his imprisonment for that refusal.

He explained about his father and how he developed his steel and sold it to the smith.

She related how she had come to know Paca, but she didn't tell him about the swords.

He told her about his mother, and that if she were able to stay a little longer she could meet her. Patira's honesty and simple view of life refreshed her.

Finally, she stood up to leave. "I must really be getting back to the castle," she said. "Fada has been in a bad temper lately, and I've not seen him since yesterday morning."

"Yes—the king," Patira intoned. "You know, I have been thinking, that were it not for the king and my father...Is there any way we could get them to talk to each another?"

Vrengnia looked at the ground. A flush of embarrassment and a twinge of fear coursed up around her neck. "I don't know," she said, "Fada is consumed with his hatred for your father. I tried to talk to him about it...I can try again." She looked up. As she spoke the words, she sensed the struggle within her between the strange, natural trust she felt with Patira and her responsibility to Fada and the kingdom. It was similar to that which she felt toward the smith, that though both of them were at the very center of Fada's conflict, they also seemed to be at the core of its resolution.

She walked over to her horse. Patira walked alongside and she could feel his presence. He helped her up into the saddle. She felt his strength. It seemed as if she had known him somewhere else, although that would have been impossible. She smiled warmly. "May we meet again, under a different moon." It was an old Immerland saying, fitting in this situation.

"A brighter moon!" he said. She pulled the gelding around and set him into a gallop across the field and into the trees at the far edge. She wanted to look back but decided against it as the line of trees between the two fields eclipsed her view. If more time were to be had together, it wasn't for her making right then. It would have to be a different moon, a *much* brighter moon.

"For many, the greatest fear is that of looking at oneself in the glass, and being as ruthless with our own reflection as we are with those who challenge us."

Pratoraman,
The Middle Way

Sandihar felt much better. After he accused the smith of spiriting away some of his work, the smith refused to do any more in the prison smithy. The lights in the mountains had disappeared the night after the smith stopped. This mystified the king, but also relieved him. It was now only four days before the celebration of his birthday and the less aggravation from all these little details, the better. There was still much to be done. He wasn't responsible for most of it, but he had to make sure that those who were in charge did their job.

His birthday party was to be the greatest celebration that Immerland had ever had. The best of the best was being prepared for it, and there was an excitement in the air as everyone did double duty in preparation.

The mayors and elders from each of the nine towns surrounding the castle had been invited, and had confirmed that they would be there. The entire castle staff was included, though not everyone was invited to the main banquet. Food was flowing in from all over the kingdom. He had declared a two-day holiday following the "big night"—as it had come to be called—in which everyone in the kingdom was relieved of their tasks. Gifts were being readied, not just for the king, but for everybody.

In spite of all this, trouble lingered on the edge of his mind. The smith remained imprisoned, having refused to make the swords, and Sandihar wasn't sure what to do. Perhaps he would free him for his birthday. Patira hadn't been caught, though the frustration of that was fading in the growing excitement of his party.

He hadn't seen Vrengnia in the two days since he let her out of her room. Other people had, but she had eluded him somehow. He wanted an opportunity to explain himself.

He had often told Vrengnia that one should never explain: "because your friends don't need it and your enemies wouldn't believe you anyway." He reasoned that Vrengnia must be his friend, but he *had* treated her rudely by locking her up without explanation. She wasn't an enemy (at least he didn't think she should be), so now he wasn't sure what to say when he finally found her.

She sauntered into the hall in the middle of breakfast. "Good morning, Fada." She sat down at the other end of the table. Her place wasn't set because she hadn't been expected. She seemed as if whatever had happened was past, so he smiled, and played along.

"Did you sleep well?" he asked.

"Well enough, thank you. May I have something to eat?" When she entered, Sandihar had motioned to the servants, and they were already bustling about in the kitchen getting together the table setting and foods they knew she liked for breakfast.

"I'm sure it's on its way," Sandihar said. "I haven't seen you in a couple days," he continued, not looking directly at her but at the eggs on his plate.

"Well, it certainly wasn't any fun being imprisoned in my *own* room by my *own* father."

He knew he had to look up. She glared at him.

He looked down again. "I'm sorry, but I had to make sure that no one, not even you, tipped off the young smith or Patira. I had a feeling that you might."

"It's not much of an apology when you have to say 'but,' Fada."

She pressed her position. "Can't you just admit that it was a ridiculous thing to do. I told you that I wouldn't visit the smithy or send a warning!"

Sandihar said nothing.

"So, in the end, did you catch the scoundrel?"

"No." He scowled. "He tricked us and got away."

"Tricked you? Maybe he wasn't there at all," she said with disgust. "And maybe he isn't the enemy you think he is anyway."

"What are you saying?" he shot back as he stood up.

"What I am saying is that just because Verclan is your enemy, it doesn't necessarily make him mine."

"He is an enemy of our kingdom—of Immerland!" Sandihar thundered, bringing his fist down hard on the table to emphasize his point.

Vrengnia ignored his tirade. "And just because *Verclan* is your enemy doesn't mean that his *son* is your enemy. When all is said and done, if Patira is *your* enemy, it wouldn't necessarily make him *my* enemy. And even if Patira is *my* friend, it wouldn't make *me* your enemy, would it?"

Sandiahar's rage restrained his tongue. He couldn't argue with her logic. "You're missing the point," he said, trying to deflect the conversation to anywhere else.

She held her ground. "Just what *is* the point, Father?"

He threw up his hands "Someday you'll understand," he said, trying to find a way to end the conversation.

"You could die tomorrow. Then I would have to be queen—I want to understand *now!*"

Sandihar collapsed heavily into his chair. There was nothing to say. This had been happening a lot lately, not only with Vrengnia but also with the smith, with his advisors, with—everyone. Was he changing or were they? He needed time to think.

The princess wouldn't let him have it. "Fada, why won't you meet with Verclan and try to find a resolution to all this? You won't listen to your advisors—you won't listen to the smith—" The last phrase hung over him, suspended like the executioner's sword before the final downward stroke.

Ordinarily he would have dodged the strike or fought back, but he didn't want to engage Vrengnia any further today. There were too many other things to do and deep within he knew she was right. "I will give due consideration to your request after my birthday celebration. Until then we will speak no further of it." He looked at Vrengnia, trying to guess what she was thinking. She remained still, opaque to his gaze.

She stood up without breaking eye contact. "Thank you, Fada," she said and strode out of the hall without eating. Sandihar remained in his chair for a long while. Now he had his time to think, but he didn't want to.

Chapter 10

Gifts

"When pieces of the puzzle that is our life do not seem to fit, should we deny that they are, in fact, part of the puzzle? Should we not suppose, instead, that perhaps we are trying to put them in the wrong place?"

Hispattea,
The Essences of Corritanean Wisdom

"What's in the package?" Mordara asked as the horses plodded across the field, leaving Haniah's hut behind them.

Verclan looked up at his wife. They rode beside each other as they often did when traveling together, and close enough to touch one another. "I'm not sure, but it *is* from the smith."

"Isn't he in prison?" Her eyes sparkled and widened as she said it.

Verclan loved watching her face. She was a beautiful woman by everyone's account, and he often wondered how she had chosen him from all the men she could have selected in and around the castle. Part of her peculiar beauty was the expressiveness of her face when she spoke. She had a dark complexion and coal black eyes that complemented her long, straight, raven hair. Today she had it pulled back from her face and tied behind her neck with a purple leather thong, but the long tresses still draped forward over her shoulders.

"I believe he is. I'm not sure how he would have gotten this to Haniah, however."

"How do you know it's from the smith?" Patira asked.

"It has his mark—the bow and the star; and it's wrapped in parcel leather. The Immerland merchants don't use parcel leather."

"Perhaps it was the princess," Patira mused.

Verclan turned in his saddle and stopped his horse. "The princess?"

"Yes. She was there today," Patira continued, "in the soddy when I arrived. I hid side-slung until she came out. You should have seen her face when I came up into the saddle."

"You said that the princess had been to the smithy in Shiloh. Perhaps she knows the smith and did this as a favor," Mordara interjected.

"Perhaps. Did she tell you anything?"

Patira shook his head and smiled. "Nothing about the parcel or any such errand. We talked for perhaps an hour."

"About what?" Mordara's voice was deep, sonorous and gentle with her son.

"Oh, lots of things. She says she's known Haniah for several years and comes to visit quite frequently. We talked about events at the castle. Her father's birthday is coming up. There's going to be quite a celebration. The king is busy with preparations."

"The king's birthday?"

"His fiftieth. He wants it to be a grand occasion."

They had reached the trees and had moved to single file. Verclan led, followed by his wife. Patira's sisters, Verice and Tangar, fell in behind their mother, and Patira brought up the rear.

"I think Pati likes the princess." Verice announced as they crossed a small stream. Verclan smiled to himself.

"How do you know?" asked Mordara.

"He smiles when he talks about her."

"I don't think he can have her though," chimed in Tangar. Then she added with a snicker, "Besides, she is probably very ugly!"

Verice giggled. Verclan looked over his shoulder at Patira. His son knew when to be quiet.

"Yeah, really ugly, I bet," said Verice.

"Girls!" chided Mordara.

"And she's a *princess*. Pati couldn't marry a princess." Verice giggled again.

Verclan turned in his saddle so he could see the discussion behind him. He smiled. "Why not? Your brother is a prince. It would be a perfect match."

"Well, I don't think the king would like it one bit," said Tangar.

"Why do you think that?" asked Mordara as she looked into Verclan's eyes. She had a hopeful look; that special look that men know in their wives' eyes.

"The king doesn't like you, Father, and I don't think he would like Pati either."

"Okay, okay. I think it's time to be quiet now." Verclan spoke with his fatherly authority. He was sure that they wanted to continue the discussion, but there were strict rules about being quiet in the woods. When it was time to be quiet, no one spoke. He turned to look at Patira, ten paces behind him.

Patira sat straight in his saddle. He smiled but said nothing. Verclan turned back to the path in front of him. He knew that look also. His thoughts drifted back to the first time he had seen Mordara. They were friends in the stable, but she was always so busy with the castle staff and the queen that they seldom spoke.

One afternoon, she had some free time and asked him if he would like to go riding. Although he was a farrier, he didn't consider himself much of a horseman at the time, but the invitation from "the beautiful Mordara" as she was called, was enough to make a horseman out of anyone. They had gone out riding for perhaps two hours and they chatted about the castle, its people, Immerland, the queen, the prince, the stables and the horses. The time flew by. As they returned over the crest of the small rise obscuring the stable, she spurred her horse to a gallop.

He followed, about ten paces behind. The horses were fast and the fresh crisp air whistled past him as he rode. They were about a hundred paces from the stables when she reached back and pulled the hair pin from the knot of hair on the back of her head. A shower of dark hair leapt into the wind and streamed out behind her. Verclan had never seen her, except with her hair neatly tied back for riding and working around the stables. It was a moment he would never forget and the moment he first *saw* his wife.

The family rode on in silence until they came to a turn in the path where it met a swift stream. "We'll take a break here," said Verclan, "and take a look at the smith's wares."

They tied their horses to a small birch tree by the bank and sat down beside the swift water. Patira opened his riding sack and brought out some cheese, dried apples, and two small cups for water. He handed them to his sisters. "Find the best water in the stream for your mother and father." The girls giggled as they headed to the edge of the stream.

Verclan studied the package, knowing it was significant because it was from the smith. He turned it over several times, weighing it in both hands.

"If you open it, you can better see what it is," Mordara said as she draped her arm around his neck and shoulder. She was sitting beside him where he could feel her closeness.

"I know. I just..." He had unsheathed a short knife to cut the stitching in the parcel. "Whatever it is, he wanted to make sure no one knew until it was delivered." After cutting the thongs, he unfolded the layers of encasing leather.

He held up the first piece. It looked like the hilt of a sword but there was no sword in it. On one side, it was polished smooth and the bare metal shone. On the other side, it was hollowed out, as if something was made to fit into it. He examined it carefully and handed it to Patira. "What do you think?"

"It's a sword hilt without a sword," echoed Patira. "It seems a little odd, don't you think?"

"Yes, at first sight. However, knowing the smith, there is a precise purpose to it, no matter how odd it seems."

Verclan lifted the second piece slowly out of the leather folds. It had the handle of a sword, but where the blade was supposed to be, there was a fan of metal tines, each very close to the other, and all emanating from the place where the base of the blade of a normal sword would have been. Each of the tines was sharp at the end, but not dangerously so. Between the tines were tiny barbs, facing each other, so that if anything entered between the tines, it wouldn't be able to get back out. Verclan picked it up and held it by the handle. It balanced perfectly in his hand.

"What is *that*?" Patira asked.

"It looks like an eel spear," Mordara interjected, "like the ones used by the fishermen along the western coast—but the handle's too short."

Verclan marveled at the piece as he held it up. He knew *what* it was. The question in his mind was why? "It's a sataliin," he said, waving the piece back and forth, allowing Asolara's rays to glint off its faceted surfaces, "a Tessamandrian sword trap—but I have never seen one quite like this." He snapped one of the tines with the back of his finger and it rang like a bell.

"A sword trap?" Mordara and Patira spoke at the same time.

Verclan leapt to his feet, pulled his sword from its scabbard, on his saddle, and handed it to Patira. "I'll show you. Take a swing at me—not real hard—as if your were trying to strike me down."

Patira hesitated.

"Go on."

Patira took a step back and brought the sword over his head as if to strike him across the shoulder. Verclan had used a sataliin before. At the last moment, he raised it up into the path of the descending blade. The sword slipped between the tines of the sataliin and jammed tight, and with a quick flick of his wrist, Verclan flipped the sword out of Patira's hand and into his own. In the next instant, he had the point of the sword planted against Patira's chest. Patira blinked, but didn't move. Mordara gasped, raising both hands to cover her mouth.

Verclan smiled. "Tessamandrian warriors developed the sataliins to carry on their belts in case they lost their own swords. I would never have guessed that the smith had ever seen one." He took his knife and scratched one of the tines with its tip. It left no mark, "This steel is hardened beyond my knowledge," he said with a hint of incredulity in his voice. "I wonder..." He handed the device to Patira. "This other thing..." he continued, picking up the first piece again. He tried to slip it over his sword blade but it didn't fit. "Get me your sword," he commanded.

Patira stood up, unsheathed his sword, and handed it to him. Verclan took the strange piece and slipped it over the blade of Patira's sword. As it came down the blade, it fit perfectly over the hilt and jammed around the butt of the blade, covering the existing hilt as if it belonged there. He tried to remove it, but it wouldn't move. He lifted the sword by the handle and waved it back and forth. It had remained perfectly balanced. He looked up at Patira and smiled. "I believe we found what it's for—we'll have to wait to find out why it was made." He looked at Mordara.

Her eyes told of her fear. "I don't like this," she said, looking down the stream where the girls were throwing water at each other using the cups Patira had given them.

Verclan handed the sataliin to Patira and sat down beside her. Putting his arm around her shoulder, he drew her to him. "I don't either, but we will have to wait to see what it's all about. In the meantime, we cannot fear. Life must be lived and we must trust that Mah'Eladra are working; that there is a plan, and that it's all for the best."

"A being whose psadeq is mature cannot be mocked."

The Tessarandin, Book 2

On the morning of the big celebration, Sandihar stood in front of his wardrobe and stared without comprehension into the welter of options that hung there. The festivities were supposed to begin about noon and he was getting ready for his part in it. He had to select his best royal garb, something that would be fitting for a fifty-year-old sovereign. This was no easy task for a man who had never had to select his own clothing. Today he decided that he *would,* and he found himself in a quandary. Since this was the only thing he had to do that morning, he felt ridiculous. He had been at it for an hour already, wondering how he ever accumulated such a collection of silly clothing, when someone knocked on the door.

It irritated him because he had given specific instructions not to be disturbed until he was ready. As he strode toward the door, ready to give the intruder a sound piece of his mind, it opened by itself. "Fada?"

"Come in, come in," he said, opening his arms to his daughter.

"Fada," she said as she accepted his embrace, "I have a special favor to ask."

"Will it cost me anything?" he quipped as he sent a smirk across his face, trying to look impish. He was actually in a good mood this morning, except for having to choose his clothing.

"Only a few minutes of your time. By the way, what are you planning to wear to the celebration today?" He must have frowned. She caught it and laughed. "I'll help out in a few minutes, but come, I have a gift for you."

"The gifts are to be—"

"—given after the cake," she answered, "but as your daughter, I wanted to make mine special, and give it to you before everyone else, and I didn't really want everyone to see it."

"Are you worried that I won't like it?"

"I hadn't thought of it that way. I mean, it's different. Come on!"

"Okay, okay, but no more than ten minutes."

He followed her into a small sitting room just down the corridor from his chambers. In front of him on top of a small polished oak table was a folded blue velvet cloth, embroidered with silver thread. It was bathed in full rays of Asolara that streamed through the window—a magnificent piece of cloth. Sandihar wasn't sure what to do. What was it for? Vrengnia seemed to catch his bewilderment and jumped forward, grabbing the cloth and lifting it free of the table. There was a flash as Asolara struck something on the table. He blinked and looked more closely. It was a sword, shimmering in the light, and he had to move to the side slightly so that he could actually look at it.

It was an ordinary sword, in fact less than ordinary. It had no gold or silver, nor ivory or jewels; it seemed to be made completely of iron or steel. As ironwork, it was superb, beyond any imagination of what iron could be. Not a single surface of it was fully polished, but it glowed softly wherever Asolara struck it.

"Be careful, Fada. It's very sharp," she warned in a whisper, as if talking aloud would be irreverent.

The king reached out and touched the blade, and instantly pulled back his hand. The blade was as cold as ice. "The handle is warmer," she suggested.

He touched the handle. It *was* warmer. *How can this be?* he wondered to himself. The sword seemed to float into his hand as he wrapped his fingers around the handle for the first time. It became a part of him, an extension of his arm. He stepped back. The sword hummed softly as he moved it slowly through the air. He had never felt a weapon so perfectly matched to his touch.

He stared at her. She smiled back.

"Where did you get it?" he whispered.

"I had the young smith make it for you," she responded. "For your birthday. And he made this one for me, on mine." She stooped down and pulled a second sword from under the table.

The king gazed at the second blade. "But how? Why?

"He is a friend of mine. I asked him to do it and he did."

"You just *asked* him?"

She nodded and smiled.

The king looked back at the blade in his hand. He didn't have time to play with it just now. That would have to wait. He laid it gently on the table, and the princess laid hers beside it. He stepped forward and embraced her. "It's the best present I could possibly have gotten," he said.

He stepped back, his hands on both her shoulders. "The smith," he exclaimed, "I meant to set him free this morning in honor of my birthday. Come on—to the tower!"

He started off down the hall, the princess close on his heels. "No, wait!" He stopped short and she plowed into him. He laughed. "The sword! I want to bring the sword."

Vrengnia caught his sleeve. "No, Fada. Please don't bring the sword."

"Why not?"

An intense earnestness in her eyes pleaded with him. "There is no reason to mock the smith. I mean, he doesn't know about it and wouldn't—"

Sandihar thought for a second. Mock the smith? Why, the smith had mocked him, had he not? The sword had been made in spite of him. He *was* the king, after all, and it was fitting that the smith should learn that one shouldn't mock the king. He pulled his sleeve out of her hand and turned back to get the sword.

"Fada, please!"

He ignored her. When he got to the end of the corridor, he turned to look at her. She had disappeared.

The swords were still on the table where they had left them. The king paused for a moment as he laid his hand on the larger of the two. Should he take both? No, out of respect for his daughter he wouldn't bring hers. He felt a little foolish, but only a little. As he turned and headed back to the tower, he shook off the foolish feeling.

His guards snapped to attention at the bottom of the stairs. They fell in behind him as he led the way up. After drawing the bolt on the door himself, he pushed it open. The smith was standing by the window, watching the preparations in the courtyard below. As Sandihar entered, the smith turned to face him.

Sandihar smiled. He was happy for the smith and he was happy for himself. He had always felt uncomfortable having this man locked up and it felt good to be setting him free. He held the sword casually but conspicuously in front of him to make sure the smith would notice it.

"Good Smith," he began, as if he were about to make a proclamation of some import. "You are hereby free to go, in honor of my fiftieth birthday." Sandihar bowed slightly and, stepping aside, flourished his new sword toward the door.

The smith studied him; neither moved.

"Do you not want to leave?" he said as boldly as he could.

"Good King," the smith said quietly, "if you will leave the door unlocked and unguarded, I will take my leave when I am ready. But not right now. To leave hurriedly would insult your majesty's hospitality, which has been more than adequate. In the meantime I would like to examine your new sword."

A curious mixture of emotions flooded Sandihar. He was delighted that the smith took an interest in the sword, but frustrated that he didn't seem inconvenienced by his imprisonment. It left him with a strange sense of emptiness, and there was something else. It wasn't fear, for the smith had never given him cause to fear him personally. It was a more groundless apprehension.

After a moment's hesitation, he decided that there was no substantial reason not to fulfill the smith's request. Perhaps in doing so his unease would be allayed. He stepped forward, both hands outstretched with the sword laid across them, the uncomfortable coldness of the blade in his left hand and the warmth of the handle in his right.

As the smith stepped forward to take the sword from his hands, the smith's eyes engaged his own and locked on them. The eyes didn't let go until the smith had the sword in his huge left hand. He thought it was best to take a step back and let the smith have some space with the sword. A wave of genuine fear rolled over him as he realized he had no idea what the smith might do.

The smith waved the sword slowly from side to side. It wasn't a casual movement, but choreographed, sweeping through some sort of strange ritual that Sandihar had never seen.

Sandihar sensed that the sword was in the hand of a master swordsman. One hand on the handle, then two, waving the blade this way and that. He would stop, holding it still in various positions, examining details of its construction and design. He lifted it high over his head and stared intently down the length of the blade. He stepped and turned this way and that, and each time the sword swept through the air, it sang an eerie song.

The smith paused and stared. The king followed his eyes to the door. It was of solid oak, and swung into the room on massive iron hinges. It stood a little more than half open. The smith raised the sword straight above his head and looked up its length.

"Woren dorren, vahat barra." The words sprang from his mouth. Sandihar was startled by the abruptness of the eruption, but he understood the meaning. "Vegen sor ahurat marra." Without warning, the smith sprang past him. The sword's song was followed by two bright flashes as it sliced both hinges at the knuckles in a single, driven stroke. The door dropped onto its bottom, hesitated for a moment and then, losing its balance, crashed face down into the room with a thundering slap. The guards had to jump out of the way to keep from being flattened by it. The smith turned to face him, holding out the sword in the same way that he had held it.

"My son did a fine job for his king, " said the smith. "May the king, in his wisdom, bear it for good and not for evil." Sandihar reached out and took the blade. The smith turned to the window again. "Now get out of my chambers!"

Sandihar flushed with anger as the smith delivered the command, but he knew that it was time to leave. He waved to the guards and they followed him out of the room, leaving the smith as they had found him, staring out the window into the courtyard, and the door lying flat on the floor.

Halfway down the tower stairs, when they were safely out of earshot of the smith, one of the guards said, "Sire, what was it that he said?"

"Open door, may you stay this way, may you never imprison another," Sandihar said.

"The turns we encounter on the path of life can be as abrupt as those on a steep mountain trail. How we accept such unexpected re-directions, tests and reveals who we really are."

The Tessarandin, Book 8

Vrengnia sat at dinner with Fada. The day had been long. Festivities had started at noon with a grand parade through the courtyard of the castle, followed by a proclamation by Fada concerning the festival and the two-day holiday. For those who knew Fada personally, there had been a huge banquet.

Mayors and dors, alderwomen and prominent merchants from throughout the kingdom, many of whom Vrengnia had never seen, sat at the enormous banquet table. They ate food that she had only heard about in legends and washed it down with an endless flow of wine and ale. The cutting of the huge cake was followed by a long parade of gifts to the king, as the nobles competed with one another in the extravagance of their gifts.

Vrengnia had spent most of the time ignoring all the formal posturing and wandered about the crowded courtyard with the townspeople. She tasted the wares of every food hawker's cart that had been squeezed into the castle. She sang with the musicians and danced with the actors on the makeshift stage by the drawbridge. Having wandered out into the field outside the gate, she had run in the three-legged race, competed in the spear-throwing and archery contests and helped build the huge bonfires that would be lit when darkness descended on Immerland.

Now she sat alone with Fada at the dinner table in the dining room. Having encouraged others to continue in their revelry, he had withdrawn after the banquet. Vrengnia eyed him. After all the food, this "dinner" seemed to be but a time and place to escape. There was no need for a meal so she was trying to figure out why they were even there. Fada didn't look unhappy, but he didn't look happy either. He was simply quiet.

"Are you content, Fada?" she asked at length.

He looked up. "What?"

"Are you happy? I mean, it *has* been a great day hasn't it?"

Fada smiled. "It's been terrific. But I was just thinking, of all the things that were given to me today—and some of them *are* very nice—the best was definitely the sword."

"Thanks" she said.

"I took it to show the smith. He seemed pleased with the work of his son."

"I should think that he would be; the swords are beautiful."

"He didn't seem surprised though. It's almost as if he knew about them already."

"No one knew of them except Paca and me." she said simply. "Even the other smiths at the Shiloh smithy."

"Even Patira?"

"He did not even show up until after Paca had given me the swords. I am sure he didn't know, unless Paca told him—but I doubt it."

Fada's brow was furrowed in thought. "I have been giving considerable thought to the questions you had about Verclan," he said at length. "Perhaps it *is* time that we met." Vrengnia wasn't sure she'd heard correctly. Fada continued, "I mean—I'm fifty now and I am getting weary of all the conflict."

She remained quiet.

"Do you suppose that he would come and talk with me after all these years? I mean, if he were willing to meet me, do you suppose that we could work things out?" Vrengnia was still not sure what to say. "Come dear, what are you thinking?"

She held her tongue for a moment. "Fada," she started, "it seems to me that any attempt at reconciliation would be good. In the worst case your fears, your thoughts, your position would be confirmed, and in the best, they would be proved wrong. The only thing it would cost you is your pride." She looked straight into Fada's eyes.

His eyebrows rose and a hint of offense flared in his nostrils, but he backed down. "Yes. Yes, that would be all right." He shifted in his chair, staring down at the floor as he spoke.

It encouraged her. "Think of how much—" She was interrupted by a sudden commotion in the corridor outside the dinner hall followed by an urgent pounding on the door. Fada sat up in his chair and set down the glass he had been holding. "Enter!"

One of the king's attendants burst through the door followed by a short wiry man dressed in black from head to foot. The only thing that was not black was his face: Rappahoogin, head of Fada's scouts.

He made straight for Fada, glancing at the her on the way. "Sire," he whispered, "we must speak." He was gasping as if out of breath.

Fada stood up. "Speak freely my good man." Rappahoogin looked again at Vrengnia again. Fada clapped him on the back. "Speak man, it's appropriate that she hears."

Vrengnia didn't like the scouts. They were by nature suspicious men whom Fada paid to be even *more* suspicious. All in all, they were a strange lot, well suited to snooping around to the king's advantage. She had never liked them—any of them, and for the most part, they were suspicious of her.

Rappahoogin bent over and put his hands on his knees, breathed deeply to try to catch his breath, and began speaking in that nasal, droning voice that gnawed at Vrengnia's vorn: "Reports started coming in about an hour ago of large scale raids on the barley and wheat fields along the southern border of the kingdom, Sire. No one was hurt; in fact, no one was even there to see it. Everyone was at the festivities here at the castle.

"When the crowds went home, they came back with the news. We think Verclan's men raided the fields and harvested large amounts of the ripe grain. It was all very neatly done, and there is no damage to buildings or fences; and no animals were hurt.

"As soon as I heard, I sent whoever I could find to confirm the reports before we came to you. I myself went down past Mordan." The little scout continued. "It seems that all in all, about fifteen acres of wheat have been taken and another twenty-four of barley. In addition, many vegetable gardens were raided. How many, it's hard to tell. It was all done very subtly."

Fada sat down hastily. Vrengnia saw his rage as he tried to hide it. He looked at her with cold, angry eyes, then turning to the scout, said, "Do we have any evidence that it was indeed Verclan?"

"No proof, Sire, but perhaps in the morning—"

"I want proof. Put the best men on it. *Now!*"

"The best men. Now." In an instant, he was out the door.

Fada's wave dismissed the attendant without a word and he left, shutting the door behind him.

As Fada turned toward her, his eyes were narrowed. "I think I have underestimated his gall again, and one time too many. Should I really try to reason with such a—" He stopped, and a smile played across his lips. He raised his hand as if he was going to speak and gesture somehow at the same time, but no words came out of his mouth. A peculiar look flitted across his face as he stared at her.

He put his hand down. "It's time to meet this man face to face and resolve this once and for all." His voice was quiet and resolved, but the glint in his eyes was full of anger and passion. He strode out of the room without so much as a glance back at her. She stood speechless behind the table. There was nothing more to be said to him anyway.

Vrengnia collapsed back into her chair. Was there no relief? Was there no justice, that just when a small flame of progress seemed to be catching, it would be mercilessly snuffed out by this coincidence? What was it the smith had said? "There is no such thing as coincidence," and "All things work together for the good." How could this possibly be good?

She stared into the candle on the table in front of her. She thought she understood Fada's anger. Certainly, if Verclan had indeed perpetrated this insult on the kingdom, then Fada would be justified in his anger, but there was something twisted in the way he had ended the conversation. The sudden shift and resolution he had shown as he walked out of the room were disquieting. She thought it had something to do with the sword, but she didn't *know* what.

She *had* wanted to give Fada the sword. It had been made for him and *she* had convinced Paca to make it. She remembered the twinge of fear she had felt just before she led him into the sitting room to give it to him, but in the end, she had decided that the reluctance was not based in sufficient clarity to justify withholding the gift. However, when he had insisted on taking his new sword to show the smith, she had left, driven away by a deep shame in Fada's desire to gloat over his victory over the smith.

Now she wondered what it all meant. The only thing she was sure of was that she had tried to do something special and good, but now, what was good was being twisted beyond her control. It made her dizzy to think about it.

She sat alone in the huge room for a long time, the events of the recent weeks tumbling and cartwheeling through her mind. Like so many gymnasts on the lawn outside the castle that afternoon, they never stopped to rest.

Quite suddenly, noticing how alone she was, she stood up. "Somewhere, anywhere, but not here," she said aloud and headed for the door.

"The heart of a man is fully revealed in how he looks upon his children."

Hispattea,
The Essences of Corritanean Wisdom

Verclan sat by the fire in the clearing with Patira and his advisors. The air was damp with the first dew of evening as the cool wind flowed down from the heights of the mountains towering over them. "Chronista?"

"Seven acres of barley sir, from the fields south of Mordan, from the edge of Haniah's land south and to the mountain road. We also gathered thirty pumpkins, four sacks of cucumbers, four baskets of beans and two pigs."

"Pigs?" Verclan smiled.

"*Two* pigs, sir. The grain is being transported to the eastern camp behind Mount Martak."

"Well done, Chronista, well done. And where are the pigs?"

Chronista smiled. "They're in a small pen beyond the rise over there. We thought we might have them for dinner."

"Let it be so," said Verclan.

The small circle of men erupted in applause for the prospect of pork for dinner. "Phartang?"

Phartang stepped forward. He was a huge man, nearly a head taller than all the others and known for his feats of strength and daring. His hair was long and tied behind his shoulders. Two long scars ran diagonally from his left ear to his chin where he had been attacked by a bear as a young man. He had escaped by killing the bear with a stone. Of all the leaders of the clans, he was the most highly respected.

"We worked the fields south of Shiloh, sir. Two acres of barley and nine of wheat." The men cheered. "It is stored in carts in the foothills awaiting direction about where you would like it taken. We were also able to get fresh melons—to go with Chronista's fine Immerland pork—a cartload of apples, tomatoes, several sacks of late corn, and about half an acre of merrinath."

"Merrinath? Are you sure?" The rare grain, grew only far to the south and even then with great difficulty. It was valued for its unique flavor and herb-like qualities.

"Yes, sir, I'm sure. It was hidden in the middle of a large barley field." A ripple of applause ran through the men.

Verclan stood up, bowed briefly and held his hand out to Phartang, saying merrily, "To Phartang. Should we have expected less?" Everyone laughed. Verclan sat down. "Mortaga?"

Mortaga stepped forward, sweeping his cloak back over his shoulder. He was the oldest of the clan leaders, with a full head of white hair and a white beard. His fierce, keen eyes matched the rasp of his voice. "Seven acres of wheat. Some radishes, celery, peppers, and eggplant—and a cart of rutabagas, sir."

"Well done, old man, and where is it now?"

"Most of its being taken to the eastern camp. Some of it's on its way here for the celebration."

"Celebration?"

"Sir, we are going to celebrate tonight, are we not?" Mortaga's eyes sparkled as he held out his hands in a questioning gesture to the group surrounding him. Several men hooted and everyone applauded.

Verclan bent to write the amounts and smiled. Looking up he said, "Of course, a celebration. Tonight. Patira?"

Verclan looked up as Patira stepped forward. Pride in his son rippled through his vorn. Patira was the youngest of the raid leaders by at least fifteen years, but he had earned his position among them. Verclan had struggled to not favor Patira, but Patira had proven himself many times over in cunning, skill, and courage. His mind drifted back to the defining moment for both of them in their place among the mountain people.

Acceptance of outsiders by the mountain people was slow and hard to earn among these fiercely noble clans. Having gained their trust as a farrier and having built the mines that supplied the clans with coal and iron, Verclan had established his place in their midst. Patira had been less successful at being accepted by his peers, the sons of the mountain warriors. As a result, he had taken to spending his spare time in the woods alone, tracking the warriors and learning on his own about how they lived.

It was spring, four years ago, that Patira had been following four trackers as they wove their way along the foothills on the Immerland border. The trackers were ambushed by a band of the king's men. There were about twenty soldiers in all who had been waiting for them who, in spite of their skill, were all captured. They had been bound and gagged in a small clearing and awaited the march into Immerland. Their captors made sport of them while they ate lunch.

Through a series of clever distractions and daring maneuvers, Patira had scattered the soldiers, wounding them and frightening them to the point where they fled back into Immerland without their captives.

Patira never spoke of what happened or what he did. However, the four trackers told and retold the story in the fine oral tradition of the mountains, and Patira became a legend of daring and cunning, unmatched by any woodland hero of his generation.

"Nine acres of barley, sir, loaded and on their way to the Urland store houses." Verclan smiled to himself as he wrote.

Patira continued, "Six bushels of white beans, some cucumbers, a cartload of apples and six kegs of Red Talion Wine...and no injuries."

"You found them while you were harvesting?"

"They were in the town hall at Yendel. We went to get a drink at the well there and a couple of the men—well—I think it should be very good wine."

All the men laughed. Verclan smiled at Patira.

The reports were good. Forty-five acres of grain had been harvested and moved up into the mountains where they would feed his people through most of the winter. No one had been hurt. As far as he could tell, no one had even been seen. Carefully planted clues would tie the raid directly to his hand, but there was no direct action the king could take except to meet personally with him. There were no scouts to capture, no army to rebuff, no risks to be taken by any man. He had left a specific request for the king, an invitation to meet him on neutral territory, without fanfare and without an army. A personal meeting to discuss differences and possible solutions.

"So all we have to do now is wait—and thresh the barley." Verclan smiled and the all the raid leaders laughed.

Patira popped the cork from a jug of mountain barley ale and took a sip. "There will be plenty of this, this winter," he called as he wiped his mouth with his sleeve. "To the barley harvest—Long live the king!" Everyone laughed again while Verclan proudly took the jug from Patira. He raised it to his lips and drank freely to the applause of his raid leaders. He knew this was where he and his family belonged.

"Sometimes, silence is an answer all to itself."

Old Tessamandrian Proverb

Paca strolled down the lane through the woods in the darkness. He'd been at the castle for the entire first day of the festival and had seen enough jugglers and minstrels for one day. He had eaten enough for all the next. It was quite a celebration and he had enjoyed the energy of the crowds and the joy of the people, most of whom cared little about the king's birthday, but had gone to be part of the event of a lifetime. He had stayed late, watching the people and hoping he would get a glimpse of the princess.

By now, she would have given her father the sword. He tried to imagine what the king's reaction might have been. More than that, he wanted to know if the king had freed Fada and whether Fada had been at the feast. Paca hadn't seen him. Somehow Paca knew that he wasn't at home yet, so he was in no hurry to get back, but the subtle disquiet of all these unknowns dominated his thoughts.

The walk in the warm darkness invigorated him and helped alleviate the quiet melancholy that had set in since he left the castle. Meekar hung over the mountains to the east. She was nearly full and Tal's glow could be seen faintly behind the distant peaks. It wouldn't be long before she too, would be casting her light over all Immerland. The twins always gave a sense of comfort to the night, and Paca was looking forward to having both of them up.

The revelers streamed away from the castle, heading home. Many still rode the energy of the crowds, silly from having had too much to drink and tired from the endless activity. In spite of the crowds, Meekar and Tal, he felt lonely. He wanted to talk to someone he *knew*.

As he neared line of trees that would swallow the castle behind him, Paca heard the voice. Wondering for a second how he heard it above the hubbub of the people moving along the road. He stopped. No one else seemed to notice. He headed back toward the castle and as he did so, others seemed to suddenly hear it also. They stopped and looked back, as if there were something to listen to, but nothing they could hear.

Fada's voice rang like a clarion call above the throng. Every syllable was uttered with the utmost clarity, penetrating the murmur of humanity with a curious vigor.

An old donkey, carrying empty pack baskets from the festival, stopped suddenly in front of him and turned to face the castle, her ears standing straight forward. The elderly merchant who held her bridle was a short, stocky man with a permanent scowl creased into his face behind his beard. He swore and switched the animal with the stick he was carrying. "Stupid beast, come on!" he yelled, yanking on the animal's halter.

Paca strode over to the man and grabbed his hand. "My good merchant, let your animal listen to the taralang," he said.

The merchant pulled his hand from Paca's in a rage. "You insolent dolt," he replied, "what right have you to interfere with my affairs? Listen to the taralang. Rubbish!"

"Can't you hear the voice?" Paca was incredulous but firm.

"What voice?" The merchant asked, still angry. Paca could tell now that he was drunk; the smell of ale was heavy in his breath.

"The singing—from the castle."

"They've been singing at the castle all day, why should this stupid donkey want to listen now—and no, I don't hear any voice!" The merchant tried to pull the donkey's halter, but Paca had a firm hold on it.

"No!" Paca said. "You will let this animal listen until she has heard what she is to hear!" The donkey's ears were turned toward the castle and she seemed to almost be in a spell, listening intently and oblivious to the two men arguing over her.

The old merchant lashed out at Paca with a clenched fist. Paca saw it coming, caught the fist in his right hand, and began to squeeze. The old man had never felt the crushing power of a smith's grip and fell to his knees, begging Paca to let go. "You'll let this animal listen as long as she likes," Paca said angrily. The merchant begged again and Paca let him go. Paca and the donkey stood silently beside each other, listening to Fada's voice sing out its lilting and somber melody. The merchant collapsed to the ground, nursing his hand and his grudge as the crowds swept by, most of them oblivious to the taralang's song.

Chapter II

Taralang

"Kor-Alura, the original language, speaks to the deep corners of the vorn."

Mortag of Horrinaine,
Of Beings

When the singing started, Sandihar was sitting by his bed in his chambers, examining his new sword. He leapt from his seat and ran to the window in anger. *How dare he sing tonight! Why didn't he go home after I freed him?*

Sandihar's anger melted as he realized that he understood some of the words. Parts of it remained unintelligible, while whole verses painted their understanding on his mind. Beautiful and powerful, it rose and fell like the West Sea on the shore at Minsora, lilting like the waters of Rinort in the spring. Sometimes it sounded like the wind in the tops of the forest trees.

....
"The swords of war are lifted high
Royal banners carried forth
Warriors in battle array,
Listening, listening,
Waiting for a different Moon."
....

Several lines the king didn't understand followed; then more that he could.

....
"Not to stand by peace alone
Waiting until they see all men standing
Waiting for a sword to crush the enemy
So that fighting would cease.

Not that the death of any man is the answer
But that sometimes necessity lives
To be the reminder of forgiveness
In the face of timeless wonder."

His advisors burst into the room as if they all wanted to get there first. "Sire—"
Standing by the window, he held up his hand. They fell silent. More lines followed that Sandihar couldn't understand. The rhythm of the verse was perfect in tone and tempo and the words rhymed meticulously in the strange tongue.

Peace, Peace there must be before,
Strong the ruler of the people stands;
Righteous, wise, and equal to all who listen.
To lead in unity, to quench the famine,
Light the fire that shows to all who wonder.
Power, strength and virtue in hand.

....

Its gripped Sandihar's vorn.
In the courtyard below the celebration had stopped when the singing started and a calm stillness hung over everything. Many sat down to listen as others started to leave, as if Immerland itself swayed under the voice of the enchanter. What did it mean? Why now, and how long would it last tonight?
Sandihar held onto the windowsill and closed his eyes, trying to make sense of what he heard and felt. Understanding some of it comforted him, while it terrified him at the same time, as it reached parts of his vorn that had remained untouched for years. Tears formed in his eyes and rolled down his cheeks and his shoulders trembled. He lifted his chin and breathed deeply, as if inhaling the song helped him understand not only the words, but himself.
His advisors stood close behind him. They could wait; they needed to wait. As he opened his eyes again to look up, Meekar filled his vision—and the stars—how long had it been since he had looked up at the stars? He shuddered again as the voice rolled over him on the cool, dew laden air. He didn't move. He didn't *want* to move. Some distant longing made him just want to stand there and listen.
Omberon's gravely voice crashed into his solitude. "Sire?"
Sandihar whirled to face the intruder. Omberon stood beside Carnados, as impassive and smirking as ever. "What is it, Captain?" he snapped.
"Do you want us to stop him?"
The voice halted.
"No! Not tonight." As Sandihar turned back to the window, the singing started again.
"He should be stopped, Sire." The voice stopped in mid phrase.
Sandihar turned again to Omberon. A wave of disgust mingled with anger flowed over him. Omberon's words surged against the unrelenting desire to hear

the rest of what the taralang had to say. Near perfect silence closed in around him, as if Immerland awaited his decision. Few times had he felt such anguish. He understood neither of the forces waging war within him. His mouth wouldn't open so he turned back to the window, hoping to loosen the grip on his throat with the fresh air. As he did so, the voice resumed.

Something about it unleashed the power to speak. "No," he shouted, "the taralang must finish tonight!" He didn't turn back, but he sensed Omberon's retreat. The voice continued—singing to Meekar and Tal, to the infinity of stars in the bright Tessalindrian sky, to his people, and to him, the king and sovereign of Immerland.

"The power is not in the words themselves, but in that they are words given by Mah'Eladra."

Mortag of Horrinaine,
Of Beings

Vrengnia retired to her chambers after her discussion with Fada. She wondered about Paca. Had he come to the celebration? She had wanted to see him, or for him to see her so they could talk. Amidst all the nonsense and gaiety, she longed for his friendship. She held his sword in her hands, marveling at its craftsmanship, when the first lines of song rolled out over the courtyard.

She didn't understand much of it, but the lines she did understand were very clear. It cascaded out of the tower as it had the other nights, settling gently over Immerland. After laying the sword down on the nightstand, she moved to the window, captivated by the words. She remained unmoving for a long time, when one of the phrases sprang into her mind with unusual clarity:

....
"Standing in the lane, listening, waiting
The father speaks to his son freely.
Come close to listen, listen, listen
Wait now, wait until all is said properly."
....

In an instant, she knew what she was supposed to do. She turned from the window and left her chambers, running down corridor and stairs as fast as she could. She sped through the thinning crowds of people in the courtyard and out through the open portcullis.

"Princess!" Vishtorath's voice arrested her flight.

"I must find him," she gasped as she leaned over with her hands on her knees before the giant.

"He passed here not twenty minutes ago. He may be past the trees." She looked up. She couldn't see his eyes in the darkness, only a deep shadow under his helmet. "Do not go beyond the trees, Princess. If you need help, I will get him for you."

"Thank you," she gasped again.

People stared at her as she sprinted down the lane toward the woods, the warm evening air streaming past her. She would find him—she had to find him, but how? Meekar's light helped to illuminate the road but there were people everywhere.

She slowed to a trot as she came to the woods. It was darker here, and she needed a little time to adjust to it.

A vise-like grip caught her arm. "Vrengnia! Where are you going?"

Paca was holding the bridle of a donkey with his left hand and her arm with his right. She couldn't see his eyes in the darkness but she knew they were looking at her. "I ... I ... was coming ... to find ... you!" she gasped. She threw herself on him in a hug. "Quick, you must ... come with me!"

"Why?"

"Come on!" She grabbed his hand and pulled.

Paca looked at the old merchant, still sitting in the road in frustration. "Let the donkey listen!" he commanded.

"Hurry!" said Vrengnia. "We have to get to the castle."

Paca yielded and trotted along beside her. "What's going on?"

"I'm...not sure." Vrengnia was still out of breath because of her run from the castle. "But you need...to come and talk...to your father."

"But he is in prison."

"My father...set him free...this morning."

"Why didn't he leave?"

"Don't know that...either."

The voice continued its singing as they slowed to a walk at the portcullis. She thought she saw Vistorath nod, but he said nothing. They walked quietly through the courtyard together. As she looked up, she saw Fada standing in the window of his chambers. *Please stay there a little longer,* she pleaded.

The voice rolled on, ever changing, singing out words that were heard throughout the kingdom by those whose vorns were meant to hear them, whose minds were open to the direction they gave. She and Paca hurried on, the only movement in the immense stillness of the castle, as it listened to the taralang.

"Our world tires quickly of a being who gloats."

Mortag of Horrinaine,
Of Beings

Paca struggled to breathe as they started the final ascent to the tower. The rapt attention of the entire castle on the voice of the taralang had allowed them to arrive unnoticed. The stamina of the princess amazed him. She never slowed on the entire journey and now seemed to have a burst of energy as they approached the last set of stairs to Fada's prison.

Without warning, the singing stopped; they kept running. As Paca came through the doorway, he saw Fada standing by the window, holding onto the bars as if he were faint with exhaustion. He ran to him and wrapped his arms around him. The big man almost fell, but Paca caught him under the arms, supporting his weight. He helped him over to the bed, where the smith sat down heavily. "Fada, are you all right?" Fada smiled and nodded his head indicating that he should look toward the door.

Paca turned his head to see Vrengnia standing on the heavy oak door, examining what was left of the hinges fastened to the wall. He jumped up and started toward her. "What happened here?" he whispered as he saw her staring. The knuckles of the hinges shone bright as if they had been sawn and polished, perhaps sliced through with very hot blade. He grabbed Vrengnia by the arm and pulled her back toward Fada.

Fada was standing. "The sword you made is a terrible weapon—flawless in its design, and terrifying in its purpose and power." His voice was strong. It cut into Paca's vorn like a dagger.

"Did the king—?"

"No," continued the smith, "I did that."

Paca stared at him.

"The king came here gloating over his new weapon—I borrowed it from him to examine it." Fada moved to the window and stared out into the courtyard. "It's a fine piece of swordcraft, and its first act was to keep this room from ever being a prison again." He turned back to Paca and the princess, beckoning them to sit on the bed. "Come, we haven't much time. Your father will be here shortly."

"Son," Fada began, "you must sleep at the top of the stairs tonight. Take this blanket for warmth. Princess, you must return to your chambers. Paca will visit you later this evening to confirm your plans. Do you both understand?" He looked from one to the other as they nodded their heads.

Fada continued: "Paca, we'll talk more after the king has left. You will both meet at sunrise outside the gate to the castle for an errand that I will explain to *you*, Paca. Now go, quickly!" There was an intensity and urgency in his voice that c ouldn't be denied.

Paca rose and held out his hand to help Vrengnia stand up. They headed toward the door. Paca was used to taking orders from Fada and he started up the stairs, but the princess hesitated. Paca heard Fada say firmly, "Princess, there isn't time now. You'll know in the morning."

"Silence creates a deafening roar in a troubled vorn."

Mortag of Horrinaine,
Of Beings

To Sandihar, in his chambers with his advisors, the taralang seemed to stop abruptly. He wasn't sure if this was his own paranoia, but he didn't remember him stopping like this the other two nights when he sang—yet, he couldn't remember *those* nights clearly either.

He turned to his advisors questioningly. They seemed confused. He *was* confused. "I understood some of it this time," he said. "And you?"

All three nodded, but said nothing.

Sandihar continued, "At first I was angry that the taralang was going to ruin the festivities—" He stared out the window to the courtyard. "But it seems that much of Immerland stopped to listen. Perhaps it was a fitting end to the day. Still, I'm not sure I know what it all meant."

His advisors shifted on their feet as he looked back at them. "Come," he said, "we must visit the smith once again."

He waved for them to follow, and they headed out into the corridor. As they rounded the corner to the tower stairs, he ran headlong into his daughter.

"Fada," she burst out, "did you hear the singing again tonight?"

"I did—and I actually understood some of it!" he said. Suspicions flared. Where had she been? He guarded himself against a thought he didn't want to have.

"I hardly understood any of it but it seemed so beautiful!" She smiled and gave him a hug. "Anyway, I am going to bed. It's been a long day." She brushed past him.

Sandihar loved his daughter, though he had to admit that he didn't understand her very well. She seemed to be changing and growing beyond his reach. She was becoming more and more like her grandmother, the Great Queen. She seemed to take everything so easily. The king sighed and shook his head. "Someday she'll have to learn the burdens of being a queen." He smiled to his advisors and turned and headed up the stairs.

"We must be gentle when we speak hard truth. There must be much love, for this is the way of Psadeq."

Sessasha,
It Is Written

Paca crept up the stairs toward the tower's parapet. He had taken about six steps when he heard something drop on the stairs above him. It made a small metallic sound like a coin or a key. He stopped to listen. All he heard was his heart pounding, and from below he heard the king's entourage making its way toward Fada's chamber. He dared not speak.

He slid upward against the inner wall, wanting to get far enough up so that he couldn't be seen by the king, but not too far to encounter whoever was there. When he was high enough he sat down, trying to listen upward. There were no other sounds in that direction, but he had the feeling he was being watched. The skin on the back of his neck crawled. He wanted to run down, but he knew he couldn't.

He turned to look up. There was nothing there except the gray stairs climbing into the darkness above him. For a moment he sat still, unsure what should be done, then with careful movements, turned himself so that his back was to the inner wall so he could see up and down the stairs easily. As he stretched his feet out in front of him on the stairs, his left hand brushed something small and loose on the stair above him. He picked it up and felt it. It was a disk of metal, about a thumb-length in diameter, with a hole through the center and small blunt points around its edge. It had various details stamped into its surface that he couldn't see in the darkness.

Whatever it was, he was sure he had never seen anything like it. He thought for a moment that this must have been what had fallen while he was climbing the stairs. He clamped it into his hand. If anyone would know what it was, Fada would. For now he had to concentrate on the events evolving below him. The king, and whoever was with him, were almost to the door of Fada's chambers.

From where he sat, he could hear the entire conversation.

"Good evening, good Smith!" said the king.

"Good evening, good King," Fada's voice returned evenly. It startled Paca to hear the difference between the voice with which Fada addressed the king, and that with which he had addressed the princess. It was unguarded and accepting, but empty of warmth, as if he had little to give to the man before him.

If the king noticed, he ignored it. "You sang again tonight—it made a fitting end to the first day of the big celebration!"

"Perhaps," Fada said.

"But that isn't why I—I mean we—are here." A moment of silence followed and Paca imagined Fada's eyes penetrating the king in that peculiar way he had of asking a question without saying anything. "No, we came to get some advice from you." A hint of triumph echoed in the king's voice, as if in asking advice he had overcome some grand obstacle.

"I have told you before. I cannot reveal what the taralang has said."

"No—no. This is real advice," smiled the voice of the king. He paused as Fada asked another silent question.

"Listen, good Smith, I know that you were friends with this brigand Verclan—"

"Brigand?"

"Well, with Verclan—many years back in my mother's stable."

"Yes, I remember it well," said Fada with a remote warmth.

"Well, this Verclan has taken it upon himself to organize the mountain clans into a significant threat to the peace of Immerland." There was another pause. "Most recently, in fact this evening, he took advantage of my festival. He apparently raided the barley and wheat harvest and disappeared with forty acres of grain."

"Apparently?" Paca could see Fada raising his eyebrows to the king.

"Well, we don't have proof, but I am sure it was him." Another pause followed. "So, I am at a little bit of a loss as to what to do—and I thought you might have some insight for me."

"Are you seeking my advice, or are you looking for an accomplice?" came the blunt reply.

"Accomplice to what?"

"The question was rhetorical, good King. I am simply trying to discern whether you really want my advice or whether you want me to play into your plans somehow." Paca detected a new warmth in Fada's voice; a hope, perhaps, that the king really wanted his advice. "I only give advice to people who sincerely want it."

In the pause that followed, Paca felt it again. Someone *was* watching him. Waiting in the darkness; silent and without a name. It created a kind of terror inside him that he had never felt before.

The brief pause gave way to the king's measured voice: "Good Smith, I have come to have the utmost respect for your wisdom. I see that you have much to offer and I sincerely need your advice in this situation."

No one else had uttered a word. Paca wished he knew who they were and could see their faces to know what they were thinking.

"My good King, do sit down." A chair dragged across the floor. Fada's voice flowed with warmth and confidence. "My advice to you is simple: Make peace with Verclan. This is the road to peace for all Immerland. The way of the sword leads only to death and oblivion."

"How is it that you are so sure about these things? We have successfully repelled Verclan's minions with the sword in the past. You speak of peace. Well, we have maintained peace with our swords."

Fada sighed. "My good King, let me tell you my story. Perhaps I can convince you of your folly."

"Perhaps." The king's tone was facetious.

"My father was a great smith. He was the head blade maker for Lutaka the Great."

"Lutaka?" The king must have stood up. Paca heard the chair fall onto the floor. "Lutaka was one of the Great Fathers. He lived before The Grayness—"

Fada's commanding voice interrupted the king. "Sit down, Sire, and let me finish my story! Indeed, what you say is true. And if you will accept the impossibility of that being true *and* what I will tell you as *also* being true, you will be much the wiser.

"One of Lutaka's commanders came to my father's smithy and asked my father for swords for himself and all the generals under his command. The order was for thirteen swords of the finest steel to be used for the defense of the kingdom of Tessamandria. The Grayness had started to appear at that time, although we were not aware of its power or the awful toll it would take on Tessalindria.

"My father was not accustomed to making weapons, because up to that time weapons were of little need in Tessamandria. My father had been taught his smith craft by the Eladra, who had instructed him to never use his skill to make weapons, but at the commander's request, my father, beguiled by the convincing words of the commander, made the thirteen swords. Twelve were made together and the thirteenth forged after the others had been completed. The thirteenth was by far the best. No one, not even my father, knew the danger that he had unleashed into Tessalindria with that sword. "The commander's name was Alaavar, but he took the name Mankar when he usurped the throne from Lutaka—"

Paca felt a movement above him on the stairs. It was subtle and vague, but something had moved, as if the name "Mankar" had unsettled the watcher. He trembled.

"The Sword of Mankar is a legend," interrupted the king with a sneer. "You speak as if it were real!"

"The Sword of Mankar is *very* real. My father forged it. I watched him do it. In doing so, my father broke trust with the Eladra. Mankar came with his generals to acquire the swords and after they had been delivered to him, he slew my father with the sword he had made."

"Why? How?"

"In that sword lay Mankar's key to power and he knew it, so by killing my father, no more such swords could be made. He hewed my father to pieces in his own smithy. So began the reign of terror that Mankar brought to Tessamandria and all Tessalindria in the end; the dawn of The Grayness."

"And how did you escape, good Smith?" The king's voice hinted that he was humoring Fada. The king's tone infuriated Paca, but he was fascinated by Fada's story. Fada had always taught him that there was fact behind the fiction in the legends. "One man's fact is another man's fiction," he had often said. "Discerning the difference is always the challenge." The king seemed unwilling to treat the legend as anything but fiction.

"I fled out the back of the smithy; the Eladra protected me as I escaped. I was sixteen at the time. Mankar and his generals pursued me relentlessly. He knew that I alone had the knowledge to destroy the swords. I eluded their search for four years, living in the caves in the mountains, and watching the destruction of Lutaka's kingdom at Mankar's hand. I made a solemn pact that I would never make a weapon designed to inflict pain on another man.

"Finally, Mankar found my hideout and trapped me in a cave in which I had taken refuge. I fled back into the cave, farther and farther. One of Mankar's generals was on my trail, but, having lived in the caves so long, I was able to elude him. It was in my efforts to escape that I fell through the Trestal Portal. When I came out of the cave, I was in a different time and different place."

Paca could hear the muffled and hurried voices of the others, but couldn't understand what was being said.

Fada continued: "It took me a while to understand what had happened, the legend of the portals being fiction to me at the time, until I fell in with Sessasha—he helped me to put it all together."

"You knew Sessasha?" Mocking incredulity laced the king's voice.

"I saw him die," Fada said. "For two years longer I stayed with his followers. With the help of an old friend who had one of Lonama's maps, I came through another portal to Immerland. Shortly afterward, I began serving under your mother with Verclan."

"Why Immerland?"

"That is my business, good King—but my advice to you is still the same: make peace with Verclan. The way of the sword will lead to death and more death after that."

"So, why did you let your son make the swords for me and my daughter?"

"Swords?"

"Why yes. He made a second one for Vrengnia. Didn't you know?"

"I was in your prison, good King. I asked my son to promise me when I left the smithy that he would not make any weapons, but it was his decision to do so. Given that he has, he, along with your daughter, will have to learn its consequences. It's part of his education. He would not have done this had it not been for some greater good, which none of us can see at this time."

"You are saying that there is some fate waiting for Vrengnia and your son for violating his promise to you? Are you saying that someone will die, and that is a greater *good*?"

"There is no such thing as fate, just as there is no luck or coincidence. Nevertheless, there are consequences for every decision. Each being must take responsibility for the decisions that he makes. Vrengnia and Paca will someday have to take responsibility for theirs, just as you must assume full responsibility for yours in regards to Verclan.

"Every being is destined to die, good King, the only question is when. Swords are designed to kill people. Should it surprise you that some being's untimely death would be associated with your new sword? Or with Vrengnia's? Are you in a position to say that that untimely death might not be part of a greater good? That the death of *one* might not prevent the death of many others? That the death of *one* might not save but one other, through whom a greater goodness is brought to many? Surely you do not set yourself up in judgment of history before it has happened and question the leadings of Mah'Eladra." Fada's reasoning hung in the long pause that followed.

"The man is a murderer and a thief," said the king, trying to control the rage that crept into the edge of his voice. "There can be no peace while he continues to plague my kingdom!"

"My good King"—Fada's voice was still gentle—"the decision is yours. I have only offered my advice. You may take it for whatever you think it's worth. But you will own that decision."

"Exactly what is your current association with Verclan?" asked the king.

"He is my friend, a cymbic in the first sphere. We love each other deeply and respect one another. He provides me with his finest steel and coal from the mountain mines and I provide his family with food so that they do not starve in the winter. The sword you possess, and Vrengnia's too, were made possible by Verclan's toil." Silence reigned for a brief moment. "Believe it or not, good King, Verclan isn't the enemy you have made him to be."

"What are you saying?" asked the king.

"Have you ever been to the mountains? Perhaps you have spent a night there? Have you ever tried to imagine what it must be like to *live* there?"

"That is ridiculous!"

"So you have no personal understanding of what you inflicted on Verclan when you banished him from Immerland, am I correct?"

"I suppose—"

"Why do you *suppose* that Verclan raided the barley and wheat harvest last night? Was it to spite you? Was it to start a war with you?"

"Yes, I think it so—but how did you know about the raids?" The king's voice betrayed his anger and suspicion.

"No, it was not!" said Fada firmly. "Your daughter told me about the raids—she was here just before you this evening. Verclan raided the fields because his people would starve this winter without that grain. It's as simple as that. You, O King, have taken all the arable land up to the mountains and have left nothing for these people to live on. The attack was as simple as survival! Though you are seen as a good king in Immerland, you are viewed as an oppressor of the poor in the mountains."

There was another long pause. The watcher shifted again, a silent movement in the non-shadows of the black stairway.

"Verclan murdered my wife, the Queen of Immerland," began the king. "The princess barely survived."

"If this is about a personal vendetta, then settle that with Verclan himself." Fada's voice was becoming stern. There was silence again for a moment. "You've heard my advice, good King, There is little else to be said."

"Yes, I suppose that is true." The king's dark voice was sullen. "Come, let's go," he said to the others in his entourage.

Paca listened as the royal party left Fada's chambers and shuffled down the tower stairs. They said nothing as they descended. He sat frozen, listening until the sound could no longer be heard and everything was quiet again.

"Pacahara!" Fada's voice was quiet, but it shattered the stillness like a taskmaster's whip.

Paca scrambled to his feet and leapt down the stairs. Was the watcher following? It seemed so, but there was no time or need to find out now. Rounding the corner in the corridor, he saw the light of the doorway beckoning. It seemed like only an instant before he was through the door.

Fada pointed to the chair by the reading table. "Have a seat, son" he said as he turned himself to sit on the bed. "There is much more to be said... What's the matter?"

Paca held out his hand with the small disk in it. He couldn't speak.

Fada stepped up and looked down into his hand. "Where did this come from?"

He motioned toward the doorway and up the stairs. Fada grabbed the disk and bolted past him. Paca had never seen Fada move so quickly. In two steps he had reached the door. In another two he had disappeared up the stairs. Paca tried to follow, but he was shaking and his knees felt weak. Before he got to the door, Fada was back.

"There is no one up there now," he said. "You found this up there?"

"Yes, I heard it fall as I was going up. I found it when I sat down."

"You think that someone was up there?"

"I am sure of it. But I didn't know what to do—I mean the king was coming—"

Fada stared at him. "Did you hear anything else?"

"I thought I did, but I was never sure. I had the feeling that I was being watched several times."

Fada turned the small disk over and over in the light of one of the lanterns. Fada looked up. "Do you know what this is?"

Paca could see that it was iron, inlaid with gold on both surfaces. It was about the thickness of two coins and shaped like a star with a hole through its center.

"It's a signet star, used by the kings of Tessamandria to prove the messages from the king were genuine. The hole through the middle fit only certain keys which the recipients of the messages had. By matching the key to the star, the bearer was assumed to be delivering a royal message." He held the star up to the lamp and Paca noticed for the first time, that the hole was irregularly shaped. "The only time I have ever seen these, they were carried by Mankar's generals. They wore them around their necks, on small chains. In Lutaka's kingdom, they were the messengers. It brings back memories I would like to forget."

There was a faraway look in Fada's eyes for a moment before he shuddered and looked back at Paca. "Whoever it was seems to be gone now. We will have to wait for an answer on this—and not be afraid—as I was saying, sit down, there is more to be said."

More to be said? Paca had so many questions. Most of what he had heard in the corridor was as new to him as it must have been to the king. Fada had never told him much of his history—only what related to him directly. Fada stared at him calmly as if he was expecting Paca to initiate the conversation. Paca decided to wait.

Fada broke the silence. "Tomorrow morning at dawn, you must meet the princess outside the castle gates. The coming and going will be easy because of the festival. The gates will be open, but you should not be seen together inside the castle. The princess should go on foot. A horse would attract too much attention.

"She should dress as normally as she can." He smiled as if he had made some kind of a joke. Paca smiled back and shrugged to show that he had understood the humor of it. "You must travel together to Haniah's soddy. The princess can show you the way; she has been there many times. Wait there until you know it's time to return." Fada stood up, moved over to the south window, and stared out into nothingness.

"How will I—I mean, we—know what are we supposed to do there?"

"I'm not sure. I've told you all I know. You are to wait there. You will know when it's time to return." The way he spoke indicated more was coming.

"Many things happening right now are falling together according to some greater plan. I know only what is given me, and you know only what is given you." Fada turned toward him and leaned casually against the wall by the window. His tall frame seemed even larger than reality as the soft light of the lanterns on the table threw his shadows up on the wall behind him. "It's a time to trust the El in you, and time to act on this trust; to see that our lives are much bigger than just us, our minds, or even our imagination; that history is being formed and that the greater good of all Immerland hangs in the balance."

Paca knew vaguely what the El was, but he had never thought he possessed it. It was the piece of the vorn that formed the connection between the nephus and Mah'Eladra. There was much controversy about the El and few people he knew believed it was real. Fada was one who believed, but it was more like a knowledge than a belief. He had always encouraged Paca to believe, but had never said it quite like he just did.

Fada shifted his weight and peered out into the vast darkness behind the window. "Did you hear my conversation with the king?" he asked suddenly. "All of it?"

"Yes, I did,"

"And what did you make of it? Was there anything peculiar about it?"

It seemed to Paca that there were a thousand unanswered questions, but was there anything peculiar? Anything odd? "Only that the king did not ask many of the obvious questions that I would have had!"

"Would have had? Or *do* have!"

"Well,—*would* have had if I were the king—but that I *do* have as your son."

"And what do you make of the fact that the king—as the king—did not ask them?"

"Perhaps the king is afraid of your knowledge about a situation that he can't grasp?"

"Afraid? Yes!" Fada's animation heightened as he turned from the window and stepped toward him. His hands got involved in the conversation. "But not of me or my knowledge. He's afraid of believing the truth about me, afraid that if he finds out this truth, it will make him *less* rather than *more*!" There was a glint of strength in Fada's eyes that Paca had never seen before. "There are many men who spend their lives trying to fabricate their own truth by hiding from the truth that surrounds them. It's a terror to them and they are trapped by their own fear. One can see it in their eyes, in their faces, in the decisions they make, in the simple act of not grasping for the truth when it's offered to them so plainly." Fada stood two steps in front of Paca, with his hands clenched, eyes full of the forge's fire. "Paca, never be afraid of finding truth!"

Paca met his gaze and they locked eyes. "I'll never be afraid of finding truth!" he said.

Fada turned, walked back to the window, and leaning against the sill, faced into the room with his legs crossed in front of him.

"Now—ask me the questions that the king should have asked!" he demanded.

"Can I start with a question he did ask, that you didn't answer?" Their eyes met. "Why did you come to *Immerland* through the portal after Sessasha's death?"

Fada crossed his arms and a dark expression spread over his face. "When my father was slain by Mankar, I escaped, and I carried with me the singular knowledge of how those swords were forged and how they could be destroyed. That's why Mankar hunted me so ferociously. In my vorn I had made two vows: First, to never make another tool whose design was the injury of another man, and second, to track down the swords my father made and destroy them. When I fell through the portal into The Dawning I escaped his pursuit, but also left the swords behind."

He turned to gaze out the window again, as if looking into the far distant past. "Remember I mentioned to the king about my friend with Lonama's map?" He turned again to Paca. "Well, using the map, we were able to track the swords to the Age of Waiting, that's now. They are somewhere here in Immerland. I knew exactly where they were, but the trip through the portal plays tricks on the memory, or at least it seems to, and when I arrived, the specifics were cloudy. I was twenty-two years of age, and needing a job, I managed to sign on with the queen's stables while I set about tracking them down. It was my hope that my blade smithing would eventually lead to their whereabouts. This has to be done before they fall into the hands of the wrong beings. In the wrong hands, they could once again terrorize Tessalindria."

"What is needed to destroy them?"

"Another sword, forged as a destroyer. Fearful it will be, and not meant for any other purpose. Since I had taken a solemn oath never to create another sword, I was never quite sure what I would do when I found the others."

"Does anyone except you suspect that they're here in Immerland?"

"Not that I know of. Only I—and you—and Verclan."

"Verclan?"

"Yes, he knows. It's partly why he continues to supply me with his finest steel and coal. We have to be ready when the time comes!"

Paca thought he saw a flaw in Fada's plan. "Have you ever wondered whether Verclan's purpose in helping you is pure, I mean, perhaps he is just hoping to find the swords and use them to *his* advantage?"

Fada was staring out the window. "I've wondered that. It would be a fearful thing, but I trust Verclan, more than any other man I know. I don't trust the king." He turned to face Paca. "The king and the princess must never, not ever—never, never, never know what I told you here tonight, do you understand?" There was that look again, only this time it *was* intimidating.

"I understand," said Paca.

"Never ever!" whispered Fada and turned again to the window. He stared silently. He seemed to be waiting. For what? For the next question?

"Why didn't the king ask you about what you discussed with the princess?" queried Paca.

"A good example of not wanting to know the truth. I would have gladly told him, but he fears that his daughter is betraying him. Instead of confronting and being guided by the truth, he would rather let *suspicion* drive his actions. The suspicion belongs to him—he owns it—so he justifies himself in its use. It's a vicious circle. It leads only to trouble."

Paca dreaded the next question. Perhaps he didn't want the truth any more than the king. He had to fight for it now. "Why have you not reprimanded me for breaking my oath to you about the king's sword?"

Fada turned from the window, stepped to the bed and sat down on its edge. His eyes were level with or slightly below Paca's and they locked into his. Paca noticed how gray they really were as he was waiting for the answer. "There was much confusion that day. I really did not expect the king to take me as a prisoner. In a moment of distrust, I tried to get you to commit to a conviction that you did not have the basis to accept."

"Distrust?"

"Yes, distrust of how the vorn of a man must be shaped. It cannot be done with promises. It takes time and experience. I didn't have time, you haven't had the experiences. I tried to shortcut your education by extracting a promise. It was doomed to fail, and fail it did."

Paca broke away from Fada's eyes and looked down at the floor. "You said something about learning from the consequences of what I did."

"Yes." Fada stood up. He returned to the window. "When a weapon is designed for the destruction of another person, it won't be long before the design intent is realized. Someone will die! Who? How? When? Where? For these, we must wait." He leaned against the window frame facing Paca again. "And wait we will. But there is something much bigger happening here. I can sense it. Some purpose in all this that I cannot identify. The El in me tells me it's good, but it's too vague to see. This is often the way it is in the making of history."

"Did you ever see the Eladra that trained your father?" Paca had only heard of the existence of the Eladra as legends, stories from ages past to give credence to the incredible exploits of the Great Fathers. According to the legends, it had been at least seven hundred years since Lutaka died, but Fada claimed to have been born then and believed in the Eladra. Out of respect, any question should acknowledge that belief, no matter how strange it seemed.

"On occasion—although one does not really see them most of the time. It's more of a luminous presence—better seen out of the corner of one's eye than looking directly at them. Occasionally they take the form of a fully present being, no different in appearance than you or I."

Fada waved out the window as he spoke. "Paca, come here."

Paca rose from the chair and made his way to the window.

"Look at the tower on the opposite side of the courtyard—where it meets the wall, on the left. On top of the last merlon of the parapet—do you see anything?"

Paca shook his head. He wasn't sure whether Fada wanted him to see anything specific.

"Don't look directly at it, but look a little to the left, but concentrate on what you see on the merlon."

Paca tried to do what Fada said. There was a faint wavering luminance, dancing on the top of the stone. "I think I see something."

"How about over to the left, in the corner of the drawbridge tower, just to the left of the door. Don't look directly at it."

Paca looked a little to one side of where Fada had indicated. "Yes, yes. I see it!"

"Eladrim warriors," Fada said. "They've been here since I arrived. There are about twenty of them guarding the castle. If you look around, you will see most of them."

Paca was astounded. "Why are they here?"

"I'm not sure, but it's a great comfort that they are. It means that we are well protected. If this signet star represents what I think it may, we would be in grave danger without their presence. They may be watching to keep evil out of the castle or contain it within."

Fada turned from the window and continued his description. "They speak the original language and one only hears them if they are addressing you directly." The faraway look in Fada's eyes returned and his voice softened into almost a whisper. The description came in fragments with long pauses in between. "My father saw them often, sometimes in groups. They would visit his smithy, mostly at night. It was they that taught him the forge poetry, in the evenings. It was then that he did his greatest work. The Mankar swords were all done after the other smiths had left—in the stillness—in the darkness."

Paca stood by the window, not moving.

"As I recall—though it isn't very clear—the Eladra stopped visiting him when he started the swords. The poetry for the swords came from somewhere else. It just welled up, almost from within himself, perhaps from his own nephus. I don't know for sure how, or where it came from."

It was time to speak. "I...I think I know that feeling. That is what happened to me in the smithy—when I started the sword for the king."

"*And* the sword for the princess!" Fada turned, and his words cut deep.

Paca couldn't look at him; he stared at the floor. "Yes, and the sword for the princess," he said, realizing his shame for not admitting to it earlier. He looked up again to meet Fada's eyes. "How did you know?"

"I was the one who sang the poetry for the swords as you were making them the second night," he said matter-of-factly. "I also got a chance to handle the king's sword—he brought it here to show me—and it was a fine blade, but it isn't the blade that was the object of the poetry that night."

"How do you know?"

Fada's intensity rose again. He paced back and forth in front of the window with his left hand on his beard, staring at the floor. At Paca's question he stopped and looked up. "There are things that we know without knowing how we know them. This is part of trusting the El. The person who refuses to acknowledge this type of knowing limits his possibilities. He always wants proof. Consequently, he always doubts. This doubt scares him into something less than he could be. The realization of the existence of the second sword was unexpected, but once it occurred to me that it might exist, it was obvious that it had to."

Fada opened his mouth to continue and stopped suddenly, as if what he was going to say needed to remain unsaid. "It's late and we have talked enough for this time," he said after the pause. "There is more, but it must wait. You need sleep for tomorrow's journey. Do you remember what needs to be done?"

Paca recited back to Fada the plans for the next day's trip with the princess.

"Good. You must tell the princess before the morning. Now go! Go quietly. Let no one see you. Return here to sleep."

Paca hesitated.

"You're thinking that you don't know where to find the princess? Paca, you do know! Don't fear your apparent ignorance—it's false."

Paca knew it was time to go. He hugged Fada and left without speaking. He knew somehow, that he would find Vrengnia, but was unsure exactly how.

Chapter 12

Plans

"Whose folly is greater, the fool who shouts 'Aha' when he has learned nothing, or the blind man who says, 'Now I can see,' but refuses to open his eyes?"

Hispattea,
The Essences of Corritanean Wisdom

Sandihar didn't like what he was thinking. He tried to think about something else, but it didn't work. Why had Vrengnia been to visit the smith? Was she in league with him? Was there something she was supposed to do for him that he had communicated through the singing? He didn't like these questions because he was afraid that he wouldn't like the answers either. Instead of asking the smith directly, he was now left to avoid them himself, which he found difficult. He changed the subject.

"Why do you suppose that the smith so carefully avoided my question about why he came to Immerland?" His advisors shuffled quietly along behind him as he headed back to his chambers. "Well?" he pressed, glancing back over his shoulder to see if there was any reaction from his entourage. He caught Carnados's eye.

"Sire, it was a most peculiar and informative conversation. Apparently, we not only have a taralang, but a portal walker as well—"

Sandihar whirled to face his followers. Carnados stopped and the others ran into him. "And you believe that? The portals are legends. Portal walkers are the same. Son of Lutaka's smith, indeed!" Sandihar peered into Carnados's eyes. "You believe him, don't you? All that nonsense about his father making Mankar's sword, falling through the portal, seeing Sessasha's death, Lonama's map. Come now, my trusted friend, we—"

"Sire, may I finish speaking?"

Sandihar wasn't used to being interrupted. Carnados stood firm. Sandihar read his eyes as they stared at each other. "Yes, you may," he conceded, "but in my chambers." He turned. They walked in silence the rest of the way through the dark halls.

Sandihar sat on the edge of his huge bed with his shoulders drooped and his chin in his hands, his elbows resting on his knees. He stared into the eyes of the three advisors in turn as they sat on stiff-backed chairs facing him. "Well?"

"Sire," said Carnados, "I would speak of legends as plausible history..."

The advisor was setting up a scenario without saying anything, a common tactic for delicate conversations, but Sandihar allowed him to go on, in spite of his disgust for such maneuvers. "Lutaka is an historical figure. We know he was the last of the Great Fathers, and that it was during his reign that Mankar rose to power and ushered in The Grayness. It has never been clear how he managed to wreak such havoc on the fabulous achievements of the Great Fathers. The only explanation ever propounded was his acquisition of the great sword and the swords of his generals—"

Sandihar shifted, stretched, and resumed his baleful chin-in-hands position.

Carnados continued: "His killing of the smith that made the swords is part of the legend. As to whether the smith had a son, there's no written record. Indeed, after Lutaka was deposed, any written history would have been under the influence of Mankar and it's likely, that if such a son did exist and eluded Mankar's grasp, it would be a sufficient embarrassment that it wouldn't be recorded."

"Could be," Sandihar conceded.

"The existence of the portals is woven into every legend we have. Our lack of direct experience with them would never be a valid criterion for rejecting their existence." Carnados paused. "We've done some checking on our smith and have found no genealogical history. The first record of him in Immerland is his service to your mother. He seemed to have been about twenty years of age. There is no record of any smithing apprenticeship, but when he came to the stables, he was quickly recognized as one of the best smiths ever seen in Immerland."

Sandihar rubbed his face. He didn't like what he heard. He had no logical reason to reject it, and he had no historical fact to contradict the advisors' research, but the truth pointed in a direction he didn't want to face. "So now we have a smith with no history and a captain of the guard with no history. Who's next? You, Carnados?"

If Carnados noticed the sarcasm, he didn't show it. "No one has ever disproved the existence of Lonama's map, but almost all portal-walker legends attest to it."

"What, exactly, is Lonama's map?" Sandihar interrupted. He stood up and started pacing back and forth in front of the bed. He wanted more detail.

Mindar spoke: "Details are scanty on this subject. It isn't clear whether there is one map or perhaps several—but it seems to be a detailed map of Tessalindria that includes temporal information—"

"Temporal?"

"Yes. It's a map of Tessalindrian time as well as geographical details. We don't know much about it because those who possess it, or them, have kept the secret well. The map somehow includes the location of the time portals and where they go, both in location and time. The smith's claim, that a "friend" who had such a map helped him to come to Immerland, is certainly plausible, if the map exists."

"Yes—if!" Sandihar stroked his chin. "If! If this is true, then it's likely that the smith is on some kind of mission, wouldn't you say?"

"Exactly, Sire." Carnados rejoined. "The smith's implication, that Immerland-now was a conscious selection, was subtle but real, in my opinion." The others nodded. "This would indicate a mission."

Sandihar dropped back onto the edge of the bed. "Any reasonable scenarios for such a mission?"

"Well, we've all found it peculiar, that given his claim to have witnessed his father's death and his refusal to make a weapon of any kind, that he continues to pursue the development of his blademaking craft."

"That is what he does well. Why wouldn't we expect that he would enjoy it and pursue it?

"We think that there is more to it, that's all," said Cordas. "We don't know why, but we think this is part of his mission."

"Why?"

"We're not sure. It's simply an idea to consider."

Sandihar's frustration subsided in the pursuit of the logical explanation for the smith's presence. "Missions are often quests, aren't they?" The fog lifted and he snapped his fingers. "He's looking for something perhaps—but what?" He paced back and forth. His advisors waited. "Maybe another person, another portal walker—maybe an object, lost in our time—in the map!"

His pacing had carried him from the bed to his dressing table and back several times, before he paused, and leaned on the table itself, looking down. He picked up his new sword and smiled. "He's looking for the Sword of Mankar!" he said in triumph. He laughed aloud at the expressions on his advisors' faces. "He thinks it's here, in Immerland! He may make me a believer yet. I mean, I'm not sure I believe all this, but if the sword of Mankar is here—now, then...come, we have little time to lose!"

"Sire?" It was Carnados.

"What?"

"If the sword of Mankar exists and is here, it would be best to leave it alone. Its terror is legendary, and it's a terror we wouldn't want to unleash on Immerland."

"On Immerland? Hah!" Sandihar laughed. "We would unleash it on that NarEladra Verclan!"

"Sire—"

"What?" There was so much to do. He didn't *want* to stop and listen.

"Sire, you have seen the influence of the smith in all these events. The singing, your birthday and Verclan's activities—may be a confluence of some sort—the culmination of the smith's quest. It wouldn't be prudent to interfere—"

Sandihar interrupted his advisor. "Interfere? Can't you see? I'm part of this confluence as much as the smith! How could I interfere? Perhaps my finding the sword is *exactly* part of the plan!"

Cordas spoke, "Yes, Sire, perhaps. Nevertheless, Verclan seems to be part of this confluence also. Perhaps he already has the sword. It would make him a formidable enemy!"

Cordas was right. There were multiple paths to the future. A wave of fear swept over Sandihar. He needed some way to know with more certainty what path was best.

Another thought occurred to him. His sword! He had seen its power, now it was time to show his advisors. There was a large iron lamp stand on the dressing table. The lamp had been removed for some reason, perhaps a cleaning. Sandihar put both hands to the handle of the sword and swung it suddenly at the lamp stand. There was a flash of blue light as the blade slipped through the thick vertical shaft of the stand as if it were a cucumber. The top of the heavy stand hardly moved under the impact. It tottered momentarily and then crashed onto the desk.

With both hands on the sword, Sandihar turned slowly toward his speechless advisors and smiled. Holding up the sword so that it divided the chamber between him and the others, he scanned its perfection from hilt to tip. "It was a gift from my daughter, forged by the smith's son. It, too, is part of the confluence!"

Carnados opened his mouth to speak, but Sandihar held up his palm.

"We'll confer at dawn. Get some sleep!"

His advisors filed out of the room.

Sandihar still held the sword as he stared out the window toward the mountains. "Verclan, my friend—my enemy—soon we must meet." He uttered it slowly, not even sure where the thought came from. He turned, laid down the sword and strode to the door of his chambers, and looking both ways down the corridor, stepped out unattended into the semidarkness.

"Tears are drops from the bottle of pain within us, poured from the open window of our nephus to be washed away forever."

Old Tessamandrian Saying

Paca sat on the ground, leaning against a stone pillar across the moat from the castle gate. It was half an hour before Asolara's rise, and the sky to the east behind the mountains brightened: yellow at the horizon, then orange mixed with pink and vermilion which faded into an indescribable blend of blues. Overhead a few brilliant stars still decorated the deep violet of the retreating night sky. Warm damp air bore the gentle scent of the newly-cut grass on the fields bordering the road that wound into the low fog in front of him.

The previous night was distant; unreal; except that he sat outside the castle waiting for Vrengnia. He had found her chambers the night before by some miracle, though he was sure Fada would have postulated otherwise. The door had been bolted from the outside. He had unbolted it, and informed Vrengnia of the plans for the morning. He left the door unlatched so she could escape to meet him.

Sleeping on the stairs had been fitful, and he still felt stiff from the cold stone, in spite of the blanket Fada had given him. There had been no further sign of the watcher, but the memories of the experience had kept him restless.

He had made his way down to the courtyard and was passing through the portcullis to the drawbridge when he felt someone watching again. He stopped. This time he knew where it came from. He looked to the left, and met the eyes of the gatekeeper directly. He was a huge man, dressed head to toe in heavy armor, and he stood unmoving at his post by the trigger to the portcullis. It was the same man who had turned him away several times when he wanted to visit Fada.

The giant didn't speak, but his eyes bore into Paca. For a moment they stood, with eyes locked, until Paca dropped his stare and continued out onto the draw-bridge. The keeper made no move, but his eyes followed him until he had crossed the drawbridge where the feeling vanished.

Paca looked back. The gatekeeper still stood at full attention, staring across the gateway at the nothingness on the opposite wall. Paca turned and sat down to watch the sunrise while he waited for Vrengnia.

In the middle of a mental review of Fada's history, he heard the slow, ambling hoofbeats of an approaching horse. At first, he couldn't tell where it came from. There were other people about, merchants mostly, working their way into town, anticipating the festivities of the day. This horse, however, approached him from inside the castle .

He stood up to get a better view. It wasn't a horse, but a lone donkey, wandering across the drawbridge on her way out of the castle. Paca looked at the gatekeeper. He hadn't moved. Paca turned, sat down again and leaned against the pillar, facing the sunrise. Whatever the she was up to, Paca didn't have to worry about an unattended animal; she probably just got loose from the hand of a drunken merchant and decided to leave the castle to feed on the lush grass in the field outside the moat.

The animal was just even with the gate pillar when she stopped. Paca turned to look. She was looking straight back. He turned away. She started moving, but instead of heading down the road, she made straight for Paca and, coming around in front of him, swung her head down and began grazing on the grass beside the moat. He tried to ignore her, but every few mouthfuls, she would pause and look up, as if she were studying him.

Was this the same donkey that he had encountered the night before? He hadn't taken note of any distinct feature that would identify this one from any other donkey. The next time she interrupted her munching, Paca made the point of looking straight into her eyes.

She looked like the same animal, but what would she be doing here? She stopped chewing and swung her ears forward so that her full attention was focused on him, and this time, instead of lowering her head to resume grazing, she ambled up close to Paca and nuzzled his hand gently with her nose. It must be, but why was she here and where was her owner? She returned to refreshing herself with the grass by the moat, leaving Paca to his own thoughts.

"Good morning, my friend." Paca jumped at the sound of Vrengnia's voice. He hadn't heard her coming. "I brought some water and a couple of sweet rolls from the kitchen. It's likely to take a while without horses—Hey! Why is this donkey here? I shouldn't bring my horse—but you brought this donkey?"

"I didn't bring her," Paca protested. "She showed up a few minutes ago. Probably just wanted some fresh grass outside the castle." He didn't want to explain his encounter with this animal the night before. "Are you ready for a hike?" he said.

"Let's go. There'll be plenty of time to talk along the way."

They started off, walking side by side in the cool light of pre-dawn. It was glorious and refreshing; unthreatening, as if the whole world were safe and peaceful.

They hadn't taken ten steps when Paca heard the footfall of the donkey behind them. He turned. The donkey stopped and stared at him. "Come on," he said to Vrengnia, turning away from the beast. The donkey followed.

Vrengnia laughed. "It seems she wants to tag along," she said thumbing backwards with her hand.

Paca brooded. It wasn't so much that the donkey was following, but that he had misled Vrengnia about knowing the donkey previously. He wasn't sure how to explain it now. He turned back to the animal and walking up to face her, told her to go back to the castle. She didn't flinch, and kept watching him, her ears turned forward. He knew that she heard him, but he had no way of knowing whether she understood.

Vrengnia laughed again. "Perhaps she's supposed to come with us." Paca whirled around, embarrassed by the situation. Vrengnia continued, "What could it hurt if she tags along? She may have heard the taralang and this is what she is supposed to do."

Paca threw his hands in the air. "All right, let's go—again! If she wants to follow, let her follow!"

They walked for some time before Paca broke the silence. "Actually, last night, just before you came out of the castle to find me, I did meet this donkey on the road. She was trying to listen to the taralang, but her owner was giving her a hard time about it. I forced the man to let her listen."

"So it *was* the same animal."

"Huh?"

"When I found you on the road, you were standing right beside her. I thought it looked a little odd, but there have been so many odd things happening lately and getting you to your father was so urgent, I paid it no mind. So when I saw her this morning, I was a bit curious."

"How did you know it was her?"

"I know horses—and donkeys, Paca. I never forget an animal. That's just the way it is."

"Not sure what happened to her owner. He was a bit sore when I drubbed him last night and made him let her listen."

"Who knows," Vrengnia said, "but it seems that when the taralang speaks, and tells someone, or some animal, to do some thing, it always works out for them to be able to do it, no matter how strange. I think we should be satisfied that, if she is now free of her owner, and following us, it's proof enough that it's in response to the taralang's message. Otherwise the whole situation doesn't make sense."

Paca forced himself to change his attitude toward the affair and said warmly, "Your wisdom exceeds your years. It is a queen's wisdom, and worthy of full acceptance. The donkey is a welcome member of our traveling party." He reached behind and waved to the animal to follow, not knowing whether she could even understand the gesture. She seemed to take heart, and quickening her pace, came up close behind them.

They had passed through the first stand of trees heading south on the road to Mordan when Asolara broke over the mountains. More travelers appeared on the road, streaming toward the castle for the second day of the king's birthday festival.

Paca felt their familiar, comfortable friendship as he and Vrengnia laughed and talked about everything and nothing, oblivious to whether the donkey heard, understood, or cared about the conversation. They were in for a long walk; there was no hurry to talk of anything significant yet.

After several hours they saw the small town of Mordan on the road ahead, nestled in a dip in the endless carpet of fields and clumps of trees. As they came over a rise in the road above the town, Vrengnia grew quiet.

"Everything alright?" Paca asked, wondering if he had offended her in something he said.

"Everything's fine, but I need to talk to you about the swords—" A hint of anxiety wavered in her voice. "I want to apologize for convincing you to make them."

It embarrassed Paca that he hadn't had the courage to bring up the discussion himself. "Didn't your father like his sword?"

"No, he liked it—but a little too much, I think, or maybe in the wrong way."

"What do you mean?"

"I'm not sure, but the whole business of Fada showing it to your father right away. There was something wrong with that. Fada's attitude has shifted slightly, and not in a good way." She stared at the mountains as she spoke. "I almost didn't give it to him, but I didn't have anything else for his birthday and decided that I should finish what I started."

Paca honored her struggle with a moment of silence, then said, "I spoke with Fada about all this."

"Was he angry?"

"He was disappointed. *I* am disappointed, I mean, in myself. I let him down."

"Me too."

"Interestingly, *he* seemed to think it was actually part of a much bigger—some grand plan that is much larger than any of us can know."

"I've felt that also, but wasn't sure about my feelings—what to make of them."

Paca continued: "He said that someone will die because of the sword; perhaps there will be more than one death—that you and I will have to face the consequences for our actions."

"Maybe it's going to be one of us."

Paca had thought the same thing several times. They walked in silence for a while, absorbed in their own thoughts, until Vrengnia opened the conversation again. "Are you afraid of dying?" she asked.

Paca had to think for a moment. "Afraid of dying? Yes. Afraid of death? No."

The silence that followed begged the question.

"What I mean is, the process of dying can be very painful. I fear the pain of dying. But death itself...well, there's not that much to fear, I guess."

"I think Fada is afraid of death." She looked up at him. They walked beside each other with their arms almost touching.

"Your father?"

"Yes. It's the only explanation for his behavior. I've been thinking that this whole obsession with his fiftieth birthday party and with Verclan—I think he's afraid of death. This fear has a strange power over him. He doesn't believe that there is anything after death, so his life is all there is. He wants to hold onto it with all his might. That's easy when you're young, but there comes a time when this fear begins to eat at you."

Paca nodded. He'd always believed in the Infinite: the afterlife for those who understood and walked in the way of the psadeq of Mah'Eladra. Fada had taught this to him since the first day he could remember. It was difficult to grasp the thinking of someone who thought otherwise. He looked down at Vrengnia. "What about you?"

She stared at the mountains. They were close enough that Paca could see the details of the individual rocky peaks.

"I'm not sure. I think I'm more afraid of Fada's death than my own," she said.

"Why?"

"If Fada dies, then I become queen—I'm not ready for that."

"You don't want to become queen?"

"I did—when I was young. Since I'm the only heir to the throne, Fada tried to raise me as a son. For a while it was fun. I got training as a warrior—swords, bows, and all that. Fada was determined to make me like him, but I don't think I *am* like him and don't want to be *made* like him." She turned to look at him. "Does that make sense?"

Paca nodded. "So when did you realize you *didn't* want to be like him?"

Vrengnia looked out to the mountains again. He heard her sniff and looked over to see tears running down her cheeks. When he took her hand, she squeezed his, wiping her eyes with the sleeve of her tunic and sniffing again.

"It's okay, Vrengnia."

"No! It's not," she said, "I need to tell you why; what happened." She looked up through her tears. Paca nodded to reassure her and she squeezed his hand. "It was about four years ago. I went riding on Mahala early one morning, out along the road to Minsora. I wanted to see the ocean before the winter set in. I was alone—I thought." She sobbed between phrases.

He squeezed her hand again.

"I came across four boys, about my age—they were around a bend in the road, hidden by a small grove of trees. They didn't hear me coming and I surprised them." She sniffed again. "I was as surprised as they were. They were standing over a fifth boy, who was badly beaten. He was very still and may have been dead. I thought they were trying to help him." She looked up and grimaced through her tears.

Paca shook his head at the irony of her developing tale.

"I dismounted and asked if I could help. Before I knew it, they had surrounded me and began shouting." A new wave of tears flooded her eyes. "I reached for my sword and one of them hit me in the face and knocked me down...I think he broke my nose...I could hardly see for the pain. I drew the dagger from my boot and when one of the them bent over to grab me, I stabbed him in the shoulder...I still remember the feeling of the knife hitting the bone...it makes me sick to think of it.... In all my training, I never had to actually hurt anyone." She looked directly into his eyes through her tears. "I don't ever want to have that feeling again."

He nodded. "What happened then?"

"He yelled and lurched back...I remember his blood pouring down my arm...and then they started kicking me...it all became a blur of pain and fear. I must have passed out.

"The next thing I remember, I was lying on a blanket in a field. The Asolara was perhaps an hour from setting, and Mahala was grazing on the grass in front of me...through his legs I could see the mountains to the south. I tried to move and couldn't...and I was *so* cold... It was then that I thought for the first time that perhaps I had died and I panicked. I wanted to yell, but I couldn't open my mouth...I remember the fear. I was utterly alone.

"I lay there—it seemed like forever—unable to move, unable to speak. It got dark. Suddenly, I felt a hand. It was very cold...colder than I was. 'Be still, Princess' was all he said. Vishtorath!"

"Vishtorath?" Paca asked.

She was surprised. "The gatekeeper at the castle...the giant at the portcullis." She wiped her eyes with her sleeve again.

Paca thought back to that morning and his strange encounter with Vrengnia's giant, and the times he had been turned away trying to visit Fada.

"I don't know what happened, or how, but Vishtorath found me. I found out later that all four of the boys had been killed. They were found tied to a tree limb by their ankles. No killer was ever found—No one was ever accused. The boy on the road lived, but didn't remember anything. I was so badly beaten, that I wouldn't have survived, had Vishtorath not intervened. He did something...it must have been some kind of miracle, I think, and that night, when we arrived at the castle, I was completely healed."

"You never told anyone what happened?"

"You're the first."

"Even your father?"

"I couldn't tell Fada. He wouldn't have understood. He would have imprisoned me in the castle. I was ashamed of my weakness. I decided that night that I didn't want to be queen. The more I think of it—becoming queen, I mean—the more I see of it, the less I like it."

"Couldn't you be a queen like your grandmother? Isn't that her crest on your tunic?"

"And who will teach me to be like my grandmother? Fada? I am beginning to see that he has no idea about how my grandmother was. His idea of making me a queen is to make me like him. I can't do that. I don't *want* to do that!"

They continued in silence, still holding hands. Vrengnia's tears subsided, and she walked calmly beside him. He sensed her warmth. Her story and her openness about it to him had drawn her close.

"That night I decided that there had to be more to life than what we see around us, more to life than what Fada was teaching me. I didn't know where to go to find answers. No one I knew seemed to really know or believe anything for themselves. Carnados and Cordas know a lot; they know philosophy—and about vornal things, but I can't tell if they *believe* any of it. Vishtorath knows more than he'll say, almost as if he's not allowed to tell me what he knows." She paused and took a deep breath, then exhaled. "Your father has given me new hope," she whispered. "If I could be like *him*, I think I could be queen."

Paca smiled. "If you could be like him, you would be a *great* queen," he said, and squeezed her hand. Nothing else needed to be said for a long while.

The donkey ambled along, five steps behind them. Paca found himself wondering whether the animal could possibly have understood what had been said, and if so, what she might think about all the strange and hurtful things that people do to one another.

"Suspicion is a harsh mistress."

Old Tessamandrian Proverb

The king's irritation leaked through the door to the great hall before Carnados even opened it. How was this? He wasn't sure how he sensed the mood of the king, but he had learned to pay attention to it.

As they entered the throne room, he realized that this wasn't going to be an ordinary meeting. Two of the king's best dors, Galar and Windarad, stood facing one another in earnest, hushed conversation. The king sat leaning off his throne, face to face with Rapahoogin, the wiry chief scout, clad in black. A dark anger clouded the king's face. In his hand, he held a rolled up parchment. The scout's little black eyes sparkled. Carnados felt a wave of revulsion as the scout glanced at him.

There were no chairs. This was going to be one of the king's standup meetings, consisting more of command giving than advice seeking; short, and to the point.

When the king saw Carnados, he stood up and strode forward to meet him. Asolara had just risen and the king's shadow fell almost to Carnados's feet. The halo of rays backlit Sandihar's silhouette and made his approach a little larger than life. Carnados waited with the others just inside the door.

"Come in, come in, my good advisors," Sandihar boomed. His voice carried no trace of the anger Carnados had seen in his face only moments before. Galar and Windarad turned to face the door and the ever-furtive Rapahoogin hovered just to the right of the throne, as if he would disappear behind it at the first sign of trouble. "There's more news from the fields," Sandihar continued, "good news and bad." He pulled the advisors into the room, closing the door behind them himself and beckoning them all into a circle in the middle of the room. "Rapahoogin, come, tell them what we found at the edge of the barley field on the western flank of the raids."

The scout approached, peering suspiciously at each member of the circle in turn with a sneer just forming on his lips. The king handed him the parchment. Carnados had never liked the chief scout. He was good at what he did, but he had a sneaky, guarded, superior air that made Carnados uneasy, and Rapahoogin's voice reminded Carnados of the edge of a knife dragged sideways on slate.

The scout fixed his gaze on Carnados and snapped the parchment open. "To the Good and Noble King Sandihar of Immerland," began the scout, his mocking sneer smearing through his voice as he read what opened like a proclamation.

"We, the people of the mountains, and outlanders to the prosperous and glorious Immerland Kingdom, have gathered a tiny portion of your harvest so that our families will have bread through the winter. No one was hurt. We did no damage to the land. We took only what we couldn't provide for ourselves." Rapahoogin paused.

The king paced back and forth in the circle stroking his chin, his eyes darting from face to face of those gathered around him. "Go on, go on," he said.

"If the good king and his court find this offensive to his sense of justice, be it known that we will gladly meet with him in person to discuss such injustice, at a time and place selected by the good smith of Shiloh." Rapahoogin paused again.

"Read the signatures!" snapped the king.

"Verclan, Omisar, Chron—"

"Verclan!" thundered the king. "By the darkness of the Portals of Tessalindria! This murderer's gall is only exceeded by his insolence! Something has to be done to stop this madness." The king turned and headed back across the circle. "The question is what. I want to hear from each of you. I want an honest answer, so don't patronize me! Galar?"

The dor shifted his weight and straightened before bowing slightly to the king. "Good King, we've tried to apprehend this brigand on numerous occasions, but their horses are bred and trained for use in the mountains. Our men are unfamiliar with the land and unaccustomed to hunting there. There is little avail in pursuing him yet again."

The king eyed him. "I don't want to hear what we shouldn't do. I want to know what we *should* do, Galar."

The dor was quick to the point. "We should accept his offer then, except for the selection of the time and place by the smith, and set an ambush for him and his men. It seems that he is willing to get together after all."

"Dor Windarad?"

"I would favor the thinking of Dor Galar," Windarad said, "but another option would be to challenge him and his men to a more open battle."

"Open battle? Open battle, did you say? And why would he do that? What incentive could we give him to confront us in open battle, eh, good Dor? He holds all the cards. I need a solution! Rapahoogin?"

The little scout was nervous, and he spoke up quickly. "Sire, we should hold the meeting as the enemy has suggested. When the meeting is over, my best scouts will be able to trail the brigands. We will be able to find where they are so the dors can capture them later."

"You've never been able to effectively trail them before," said the king. "What would be different this time?"

"They would all be together. Our chances are much better that we could follow at least one."

The king turned away. "Carnados?"

Carnados wasn't quite ready. Usually, he spoke for all three of the advisors. He wasn't sure whether this was expected this morning. He decided to speak for them all. "Sire, we believe that the best course of action is to accept the offer to meet with Verclan, to try to settle differences between Immerland and the mountain peoples, and between you and Verclan."

Sandihar scowled but he allowed him to continue.

"We should seek peace for Immerland without bloodshed first."

"And what about the Sword of Mankar?"

Galar and Rapahoogin gasped. Carnados wished the king hadn't brought this up. "The sword is legend, as far as we know," he said calmly. "The existence of the sword in Immerland is conjecture on top of that legend. We shouldn't concern ourselves with it in this context, Sire."

"The Sword of Mankar is in Immerland?" interjected Galar in disbelief. Rapahoogin's eyes were dancing.

"What do you know of the sword, good Dor Galar?" asked the king.

"What I know is legend, but the legend is terrible. If the Sword of Mankar is in Immerland, it is a much bigger threat to all of us than a thousand Verclans, Sire."

"What if this whole play by Verclan is somehow connected to the revealing of the Sword of Mankar?" queried the king.

"Why would it be?" Dor Windarad interjected .

"Well," the king began, "Verclan and the smith are in league with one another at some level. Exactly how, we don't know, and we suspect that the smith is on a quest to find the Sword of Mankar—"

Carnados interrupted Sandihar's logical progression: "That's pure conjecture, Sire. We have no proof."

The king stared at Carnados and continued. "In fact, he may already have revealed the sword to Verclan, which may be why he has suddenly become so bold. This also is conjecture...but it seems to me that we must play into Verclan's hands somewhat, until we can find out what's going on."

Carnados sensed that the king would start issuing orders.

"Galar, go to the smith in the prison tower and see what he has to say about a time and a place for such a meeting with Verclan. He has been set free, so if he is no longer there, find him and set up the meeting. After that, find Omberon. I have something to discuss with him privately."

"Windarad, take four of your best and find the young smith. Put him under house arrest in his smithy so he can continue his work, but don't let him go anywhere. And don't let my daughter visit him there."

"Rapahoogin, I locked my daughter in her room last night. Go unlock the door, but don't let her see you. Follow her wherever she goes today and see what she does. Whatever it is, don't interfere."

"Carnados, Cordas and Mindar: Make sure the festival is uninterrupted today. We'll all meet here tomorrow morning at the same time. You're dismissed."

That Carnados had been given a job unrelated to the king's obsession with Verclan, relieved him. He smiled secretly to Cordas and Mindar, and led the way out of the throne room behind Dor Windarad, to make sure the the people of Immerland were distracted by the festival.

"True grace and genuine beauty are matters of character."

Hispattea,
The Essences of Corritanean Wisdom

Patira lay on the moss under the laurels by the stream on the southern side of Haniah's field. From atop the slight rise that separated the stream from the slope into the field, he could see the breadth of it and watch, unseen, all comings and goings. Asolara was high and out in the field it was hot. In the shadows where he lay, the cool, smell of the soil and the moss filled his nostrils and the semidarkness under the canopy made it quite comfortable.

The quiet woods demanded caution. Four of the king's scouts had been caught the night before. The surprise harvest had brought an onslaught of the clever little men, dressed in black, and probably quite good at what they did in Immerland. Fortunately, they didn't understand the woods, and often fell prey to the wood-land tricks that the mountain guards set for them. Two of them had been caught in snares, one in a man-pit, and the other had been spotted and treed by a guard triad. They cut down the tree to capture the poor fellow.

Each of them had been stripped, dressed in a bright red loincloth, and sent back to the king unharmed. Patira smiled as he recalled the look on the face of the one he had seen when they sent him off. He knew the scout would be back someday; probably none the wiser.

Still, caution was the wisdom of the day. It was the wisdom of everyone who lived on the border of Immerland; a way of life. Even in the quiet seclusion of his carefully selected vantage point, Patira's mind was half tuned to every detail of the forest around him.

Patira knew that Fada had sent him for a purpose and though it wasn't clear exactly what it was, even to Fada, Patira lay quietly waiting. He would know when the time came, and he would know exactly what to do. "There are times to trust one's instincts and the El and wait, in spite of the urgency of the situation," Fada had often said; Patira knew that this was one of those times.

He watched for three hours. Haniah had come out of her hut several times. She had gathered some food from the field, washed some clothes, and hung them to dry on the drying sticks. She had gone back into her hut, come back out again to get water from the stream and so on. It was probably a daily routine. He knew her well, but had never even wondered what she did when no one else was around.

She appeared again with a bright cloth under her arm and a platter, laden with tableware. She went to the large table in the field just in front of the hut, set the platter down, and busied herself with setting the table. Patira was curious. Someone must be coming for a meal.

Patira knew Haniah's meals. They were simple and hearty, always enough but never anything left over. Though they had the aroma of the woods and the field, he knew somehow that they would be considered delicate to a well trained palate.

Haniah finished setting the table and headed for the stream for more water. The place where she got her water was a bit over to the right from where he was. He couldn't see exactly what she was doing, but was confident that she couldn't see him because of the shape of the ground and the thick foliage between them. He busied himself with watching the empty field with its flowers and sunburned, late-summer grass.

"Master Patira..." Patira jumped to his feet, but in the same instant knew that there was no danger. Haniah stood not five feet to his right, leaning over to peer through the laurels to where he stood. "It's almost time. You should come out and make yourself presentable to our guests."

He started brushing the bits of moss off his tunic. "How did you know I was here?" he asked without looking at her.

"Well, it *is* my land, and I make it my business to know what is happening on it. Now come, we haven't much time."

Patira followed her as she went back to her water baskets by the stream. She lifted the yoke, as if it were empty and laid it on his shoulders. It was much heavier than she made it look. Without a word, she started toward the hut. Patira followed, chafing under the load.

Haniah was his friend. He knew that she would never do anything to embarrass him. His pride melted away as he walked back to the hut behind his hostess.

Haniah was a study in contrasts, with a simple beauty that Patira had always admired, but she wasn't the type of person one would compliment on it. Her hair was the color of the autumn hayfields, with strong hints of sun just before sunset. Its tightly curled mass cascaded over her shoulders and glistened in the brilliant light of the open field. She was as slender as a steel blade, with a strength forged of experience. Her clothing was simple, functional, clean, and perfectly matched to her place in the fields, to the extent that it was wholly unremarkable.

Haniah worked with her hands. They were her tools. They showed a firmness, a ruggedness of their labor, but still carried a feminine quality that bespoke gentleness.

Patira couldn't see her face as they walked up the path from the stream, but he knew it well. The slightly chiseled cheeks, thin nose and fine straight lips. Her blue-gray eyes were more like windows, but into what? He wasn't sure. He sometimes felt that her eyes made his own eyes seem more like windows into *his* vorn. If this were true, she never seemed to take advantage of what she learned when she looked in.

He guessed that she was about his age, but he thought he remembered her being somewhat older when *he* was younger. It was very difficult to tell. All in all, Patira saw in her a quiet beauty that didn't come from her outward appearance, but more from the firmness of character; her love of life and the gentleness of one who knew her place in a large world.

They were almost to her hut when she broke the silence. "I had a strange dream last night, Master Patira," she said as she helped him get the yoke off his shoulders . She always called men "master" and the women she called "mistress."

Haniah didn't talk a lot. Patira guessed that years of living alone might do that to a person, or perhaps that was why she preferred to live alone. Either way, he waited for her to elaborate if she wanted to as he rubbed his shoulders and neck where they had borne the weight of the yoke.

"I will tell you more, but only after the others have come."

Patira found himself looking into those infinite blue-gray eyes.

"I"m not sure who they are, but there are three—one of them...it's all very vague at this point, but there will be five all together."

"Five what?"

"Lunch guests," she responded, sweeping her hand toward the table. "Why are you here, Master Patira?" she turned to busy herself with paring the beets he had watched her harvest from the field earlier that day.

"May I help?" Patira offered.

"Of course. There is another knife on the table by the berry bowl."

Patira picked up the knife and joined his hostess in the preparations. "My father sent me here. He said to come and watch—that I needed to be here, but he wasn't sure why. I arrived perhaps an hour after sunrise."

"So you saw those two Immerland scouts rounding the far edge of the field not an hour and a half ago."

"What?"

"Two of Sandihar's scouts, short, dressed in black. They cut the corner on the far edge of the field and headed up into the mountains, I would say."

"No, I didn't see them."

"You're slipping, Master Patira."

They worked together in silence for a while. Patira wondered how so many people could know so little about what was going on and yet be so confident that something right was happening. It seemed to be a matter of trust: trusting in one's sense of psadeq and trusting in the El and the leading of Mah'Eladra. Fada understood what this meant, and perhaps Haniah, but he was sure that he didn't, at least not in the same way that they did.

When all the beets were peeled and had been placed in a pot of water, Haniah broke the silence. "The others are almost here. Come, we should wash our hands and gather some fresh parsley and ginger before they arrive. We have just enough time."

She rose and turned toward the soddy in a graceful movement, purposeful and resolute. Patira watched for a moment before falling in behind her as she wended her way around the side of her hut to the large herb garden behind it.

Chapter 13

Arrangements

"In that brief moment, where he stood
When she, with lighted eyes did fire
His vorn, as match is set to wood,
Consuming all with bright desire."

Ramonmara,
The Legend of Mishla Mira

Paca, Vrengnia and the donkey had been walking all morning. Encounters with other travelers had become rare, partly because they were so far from the castle, and partly because many people had gone up to the festival. When they had passed through Mordan, they found it almost deserted. Since leaving it to the north of them, they had met no one.

Vrengnia had told him everything she could about Haniah. From all the stories, she seemed a little larger than life and and now Paca would meet her.

The threesome had made their way up the old dirt road to the hitching post at the trailhead to Haniah's fields. The last couple of miles had been in the full sun, so they stopped to sit in the shade of the large chestnut tree hanging over the small gap in the stone wall. "Do you have any idea why she's chosen to live so far from everyone else?" Paca asked.

Vrengnia smiled. "I've wondered that myself. I don't know, but I'm sure she'd tell you if you asked."

"Maybe it has to do with her relationship to Verclan. I mean, my father chose Shiloh when he left the castle. It's kind of on the fringe. I'm quite sure now that he moved there so he could have contact with Verclan without endangering him. Perhaps Haniah is the same."

"Perhaps. I am surprised that you've never met her. Your father seems to know her quite well. Isn't that where he gets all those herbs he has in your kitchen?"

"I believe so, but he never spoke of her at home, at least not in a personal way. He always spoke of her in a remote, 'there-is-this-person' kind of way. I don't recall her ever coming to Shiloh or him mentioning that he came here."

"Well," Vrengnia laughed, "you"ll meet her in person, if she's here."

"Why wouldn't she be here?"

"Sometimes she isn't. Even when she's not here, it's a wonderful place to visit."

Vrengnia stood up and stretched. "Time to go." The entrance to Haniah's land consisted of an uneven break in an old stone wall. It was clear that few people passed this way, for the path was covered with deep grass that showed little wear. Vrengnia stepped through the gap in the stones, with Paca close behind, and the donkey ambling behind him.

As he first set foot on the path, a vague uneasy thought caused him to look up suddenly. In the deep shade to the left of the trail, an unnatural brightness caught the corner of his vision. When he turned to look at it directly, it vanished. Without a second thought, he plunged toward the spot where he had seen it, not knowing what he might find. In four quick steps he reached the spot and looked around quickly. Nothing stirred. The cool tranquility of the forest shade surrounded him and left no hint of what he had seen.

"What are you doing?" The princess was standing on the path with her hands on her hips, with the donkey behind her. They both stared at him.

"I...I'm not sure!" he stammered. "I thought I saw something moving in the trees here." He started back to the path. "It must have been some trick of Asolara piercing the shade. Let's go." He stepped onto the path behind the princess.

Paca was sure he had seen something in the woods. Now he detected a slight shift in the air...no, in the lighting...no—what was it? There was some very slight, but tangible difference between the surroundings here and in the land before they stepped onto the Haniah's trail. "Wait here," he said. He sprinted back up the path to the trailhead, a matter of ten running steps. At the entrance to the trail he turned.

The donkey, as unconcerned as ever, had leaned down and was munching on some of the grass by the trail. The princess was facing him with a bewildered look on her face. "What is it?" she called, a hint of alarm rising in her voice.

Paca stood for a moment and listened. He inhaled and held out both his hands, trying to grasp some elusive ambiance of the place. He stepped back onto the trail and took several steps. He stopped again, listening, and then, taking a deep breath, he held out his hands again. He could feel the difference. Perhaps feel wasn't the right word; he sensed it, but he wasn't sure how. There was more clarity; the colors were a little brighter, and the air a little cooler and drier. Details were sharper and more penetrating; more *real,* perhaps.

He eyed the princess as he made his way down the trail toward her. He knew he needed to offer some explanation. "Something is different here—on Haniah's land. Can you feel it?"

"I have been here many times and each time I notice a slight difference in the air when I enter, or in the light or something."

The trio resumed their journey. "It's hard to explain," Paca continued. "It's as if we are being watched...or protected...or no—surrounded by something. Something a little larger or maybe stronger—something more real than before we entered." The princess said nothing. The intensity of the tranquility pervaded everything; quiet beyond quietness; almost un-Tessalindrian, yet there was nothing specific that Paca could identify as different.

He suspected that he may have seen one of the Eladra, but since he had only seen them for the first time the night before, he wasn't sure. He wasn't confident enough to say anything about his suspicion to Vrengnia. If they were here, he reasoned, it was a good sign.

They walked in silence along the edge of the field, through a small stretch of sparse forest, and out into another meadow. The smell of the drying grass, intermingled with occasional breaths of wildflower scents in the still air of the late summer field, was overpowering. "What do you suppose we will find here, I mean at Haniah's place?"

"If your father didn't tell you, then he certainly didn't tell me. Perhaps our four-footed friend knows. She's come for a reason, I'm sure; it's too bad that she can't talk." Vrengnia glanced back over her shoulder and smiled. "I think we'll find peace here."

"What do you mean?"

"Well, I've never seen any kind of conflict on Haniah's land. I hadn't thought about it until you mentioned it back there at the trailhead."

"When?"

"Whatever you said back there—about feeling protected or being surrounded by something. I think it's a unique peace that is only found here. I'm not sure, but I *have* felt it here before. It touches my vorn in ways that no other place does, perhaps in the nehpus, though I would be first to admit that I'm not sure what that means."

Whatever it was, Paca wouldn't have described it as peace, but perhaps she was right. He couldn't argue that he knew peace well enough to refute her, nor did he know for sure what something that touched his nephus would mean. The nephus was the most elusive layer of the vorn. There were many who didn't believe it existed at all.

To those who did believe, it was the extension of the vorn, one step beyond the hjarg—it wasn't tied to their life on Tessalindria. The nephus was a layer of existence that transcended time and death; that piece of a being that made one different from an animal. Perhaps she was right because while both he and Vrengnia pondered this sensation, the donkey seemed unaffected as she munched mouthfuls of green grass bordering the path.

They passed through the last stand of trees and into the large open field that surrounded Haniah's hut. Paca had never seen anything like it. The field was wide and still, and filled with wildflowers, and patches of cultivated plants scattered across it. To the left was the small hut, made out of sod and just big enough for someone to live in. In front of the hut, in the open field was a long table, set for five and begging for someone to sit down and eat.

They stopped to assess the scene laid out before them. Nothing moved except the donkey who nudged between them and plodded toward the little hut. If Haniah were home, she would hear the donkey's approach. The donkey was almost to the door of the hut when Paca decided to break the silence. "Come on."

They started forward again, glancing about to catch the first sign of any movement. The donkey approached the front door of the hut and, with a light shove, opened the door and plodded in. "Now that is peculiar," the princess said over her shoulder. "Perhaps she's been here before."

"Could be," Paca said, "let's find out." They were almost to the door when Haniah and Patira rounded the far corner of the hut, startling all of them.

"Haniah!" gasped the princess.

"Patira!" Paca choked.

Paca stared at Patira. Haniah threw her arms around Vrengnia's neck. "Mistress Vrengnia, I was hoping it would be you," she said, tightening the embrace. She stepped back and turned to Paca. "But you *must* introduce me to your friend."

At the same moment, the donkey emerged from the hut with an ear of corn held between her teeth. "Which one?" asked the princess with a smirk, nodding toward the door of the hut.

Haniah whirled and dashed over to the donkey. "Meshabo, my dear Meshabo..." She threw her arms around the donkey with a tight squeeze and turned back to the princess. The light sparkled in her delighted eyes. "Did she come with you?"

"She followed us. Do you know her?" the princess sasked.

"Know her? Why of course—but now you must introduce your *other* friend."

Paca studied Haniah. The same sense of hyper-realness pervaded her presence that he had first felt when he stepped onto her property. Her eyes had a depth and clarity that defied identification. She came up to him as she spoke.

"This is my friend, Paca, the—"

"—the son of the great smith at Shiloh Forge!" Haniah finished. "It's a great honor to meet you, Master Pacahara. Your presence does justice to your father's name." She stepped closer and gave Paca a gentle hug, standing on her toes to brush her cheek to his and then retreating to arm's length. Paca felt the overwhelming sense of realness again, lingering in his cheek where she had touched him and a wave of emotion rolled over him as she stepped back. It was an immediate sense of closeness and desire that he had never felt before, a flush of embarrassment that he should feel such intimacy with someone whom he had known for less than two minutes. He was speechless.

"Come," Haniah said, "it's time to celebrate. We will eat together before we discuss our reasons for being here."

Haniah's presence had made Paca forget Patira. Paca turned to find him staring back. Paca guessed he was thinking the same thing, so he stepped forward to break the ice, embracing Patira. Patira hugged him back. They both stepped back, holding each other's arms and started laughing. "We meet again, my friend, my foe," said Paca with a smile. "Shall we not make the most of our short times together?" He beckoned to the table.

Haniah was busy removing the fifth place setting while Vrengnia poured water into a large bucket for Meshabo. "I knew there were five," Haniah rejoiced, "but I never guessed that Meshabo would be the fifth."

They sat down at the table, Vrengnia and Paca on one side, with Patira and Haniah on the other. Patira brought the food from the hut. He served the party with a style and grace that would have honored the king's best table. There was lots of food, but not what Paca had expected. There were small quantities in a variety of tastes and textures: wild vegetables, roots, nuts, and berries. They were chopped, cut, and brought together, then uniquely flavored with herbs to produce a subtle experience for the palate of a man who was used to eating stew, dark bread, porridge, and dried fruit. There was plenty of fresh water and a light ginger mead that burned slightly as it went down the throat.

They spent most of the meal talking; telling their life's stories, joking and laughing together as old friends. When at last they finally sat back, each pleasantly filled from the meal, Paca realized that there was almost nothing left on the table, but no one seemed eager for more. He was full, yet alert and felt ready for almost anything.

It was at this point that Haniah turned the talk toward the business at hand. "I had a dream last night," she announced, "and I think it concerns all of you, including Meshabo."

"Our dreams hang from threads of reality and truth that must be sought without fear, and without hesitation."

Mortag of Horrinaine,
Of Beings

Vrengnia thought she saw Patira shift in his chair as Haniah began to recount the dream. It was very strange, as dreams usually are.

Haniah had gone to bed earlier than usual and had slept through the night until just before the birds in the south woods began their morning songs. She remembered sitting up. At the foot of her bed stood a man dressed in an ancient warrior's garb. The stranger told her not to move and reaching behind himself, pulled out a parcel: a large roll of leather with ancient markings on it. As he laid it on the foot of the bed and unrolled it, a line of fine swords appeared, one by one. There were seven in all.

"Seven?" Paca interjected. Vrengnia saw Patira's eyes narrow as Paca said the word.

"Yes, there were seven swords and one of them a little larger than all the others. They glowed against the dark leather. When I moved my hand to touch them, I couldn't reach them. They seemed close enough, but too far at the same time.

"The man spoke again, this time asking me to prepare a dinner for him. I got up to prepare it and as I was setting the table, I realized that I had set places for five. I ran back into the soddy; the ancient man had disappeared, and there were four others in his place in an animated discussion over the swords in the original language. There were two women and two men, but I couldn't see their faces. The odd quartet wore ancient tunics that gave no clue to their origins; their faces remained dark and unidentifiable.

"I bid them come to dinner, and they all filed out of the hut, leaving the swords on the bed. They ate in silence. After the dinner was over, the two men stood up and began a discussion, and as it grew heated the two drew their own swords and began fighting. The two women stood up, one of them turned into a man; they joined into the fight.

"Suddenly the first two fighting men vanished, one at a time, but very close in time to each other. The man and the woman who remained stopped fighting and embraced, then, holding hands, walked back to the hut.

"I tried to follow them, but by the time I got into the hut, they had vanished and the original warrior stood by the bed. He told me to lie down again, which I did. He burst forth in song in the original language, but this time I understood exactly what he was saying. It rhymed; its meter was perfect. He said something like this:

"Swords for the ancient master
Hidden in time for no one but the master.
When he comes, by his birthright
Shall he hold them, bend them to his will.
Nary another man should touch them.
Lest in death and wanton destruction
He beat a path into the darkness
A darkness that lasts forever and ever."

"He touched my forehead with three fingers. They were cold as ice but they seemed to burn the words into my mind. He turned and looked straight at me and told me to set the table today—for five, then he strode out of the door, leaving it open.

"In my dream I fell asleep again, but only for a short time. When I woke the door was open. I went to shut it and I noticed his boot prints in the soft soil just to the left of the path."

"His boot prints?" Patira said, sitting up suddenly then jumping out of his seat and running to the door of the hut with Paca right behind him. Vrengnia followed as quickly as she could. Looking back she saw Haniah seated quietly at the table, watching.

The prints were clear. They were a hand's width longer than her own foot and made by an abnormally heavy person.

"Now this is odd! They lead this way and then vanish," Patira exclaimed. Vrengnia tracked the prints. The ground got softer to the east of the beaten path from Haniah's door, but the prints became shallower and smaller so that after about ten steps there was no trace of the heavy stranger's passage.

She saw Patira's eyes meet Paca's. They stared at one another for an instant before Paca swiveled and ran back to the table. "Are you sure this was a dream?"

"I thought it was—but there were parts that were so real—it is all very clear and very vague at the same time," Haniah said, "but here we are, five of us and the footprints of the Warrior are still there. I don't know what to make of it any more than you."

"How big was this warrior?" Patira asked.

"He was no taller than Paca—a bit more robust, but not exceedingly so."

"Did you see how large and deep those footprints are?" Patira's eyes sparkled with alarm. "The person who made them had to weigh twice what Paca does!"

"Yes," Haniah said, "That is probably true, but did you also notice that they get shallower in the softer soil and then disappear altogether?"

"Yes, I've never seen anything like it."

Patira paused and Paca took the opportunity to shift the discussion. "Why are we here then, and what might it have to do with Haniah's dream?"

The reality of the strange footprints had put a crack in the quiet simplicity of Haniah's hospitality, and Vrengnia was eager to mend it. "There are two men and two women, besides Haniah—if you count Meshabo. And we certainly have enjoyed Haniah's fine meal." Everyone nodded and smiled at Haniah. She flushed slightly and smiled back. Vrengnia continued: "I, for one, am in no mood for a fight; I left my sword back at the castle—I'm not even sure if Paca owns a sword—"

Paca picked up when she hesitated: "—but there's trouble brewing, in which all of us, except possibly Haniah, are involved." He looked at Patira who, glancing back, raised his eyebrows in expectation of being addressed. Paca seemed to be choosing his words carefully. Vrengnia guessed that he didn't want what he was about to say to sound inflammatory.

"The unexpected harvest in the southern barley fields has raised the king's ire. Even now he is seeking a resolution to the insult he has incurred."

Patira listened.

Paca continued, "My personal preference, were I the king's advisor, would be for the king to resolve the matter by seeking an audience with his offender. To settle the matter without bloodshed would be the primary objective."

Vrengnia fought back a smile at Paca's formality. Patira answered in kind. "Were I the sole confidant of the mountain people's leader, I would suggest the same," he said.

"Then I propose," Paca responded, "that in spite of not being so positioned—any of us—that we craft such a scenario and make it our business to persuade the leaders to meet for that purpose." As he spoke he stood up and raised his flagon for a toast. "To peace—to justice—to psadeq."

Patira rose to match Paca's stance. The nobility and grace in that simple action caught Vrengnia off guard. Everything slowed almost to a stop as a wave of...what was it...something she didn't understand swept over her. Patira echoed Paca's toast, clinking his flagon gently against the other's, but the movement, the sounds were distant; surreal. She watched him take a draught and sit down.

"Now that's over, what are we really going to do?" Paca said with a smile. They all laughed. It shook away the last vestige of the silent, tumbling reverie that had overcome her.

Paca stood up again. "May I suggest that I let the son of the mountain leader, and the daughter of the Immerland king craft such a plan. You know your fathers best. You have their best interests at heart, and you wield, might I say, more influence than you think. Haniah and I will clean up." He began loading his arms with bowls, plates, flatware, and crumpled napkins, watching to see if the idea would take.

Patira leaned forward and rested his elbows onto the edge of the table opposite her. "It sounds workable. What do you say, Princess?"

"I applaud Paca's wisdom," she said, turning to face him. "To your duties, good Smith—there is man's work to be done here."

Patira's eyes tugged on Vrengnia's vorn. Bringing her forearms up onto the table, she leaned forward to meet them. She thought she heard Haniah laugh, followed by the distant clinking of flatware being gathered from the table. She knew that what they decided would affect the course of history for Immerland and the mountain people, but part of her also wanted to just spend time with Patira. The strange attraction and the conflicting motives made her feel weak, immature and shy, yet empowered, bold and important at the same time. She waited for Patira to begin.

"Mah'Eladra define the nature of psadeq and, at the same time, are confined by psadeq's nature."

Karendo Marha,
Journey to the Infinite

Vrengnia and Paca left Haniah's property discussing the arrangements that she'd made with Patira for their fathers to meet. They chatted through various events of the day, the meal, Haniah's strange acquaintance with Meshabo, and that they had forgotten to ask her how they knew each other. It was light and easy and seemed fitting for the return to the castle in Asolara's warm, mid-afternoon glow.

"What did you think of her?" Vrengnia asked.

"Who?"

Vrengnia laughed. "What do you mean 'who'? Haniah, of course."

"Oh—she's quite different—much different than I expected."

Vrengnia wasn't sure whether Paca was being evasive or if the peculiar male tendency that made him unable to identify his feelings was beginning to surface. "You did spend a fair amount of time with her cleaning up in the soddy."

"I know."

Vrengnia bit her tongue. The best way to get him to talk was to not talk herself. It always worked with Fada, and although Paca was quite different, he was very much the same in this.

"It was a bit strange...I mean, I found myself just wanting to watch her."

The phrases came in stilted, insecure bursts. Vrengnia nodded and said nothing.

"Everything she did...every time she moved, it was graceful and easy. She never seemed...well, she never was in a hurry. It's almost as if her land is an extension of her...no, maybe that she fits it so perfectly...." His voice trailed off and stopped.

They walked on, saying nothing. She had seen his first reaction to Haniah, and was convinced that he had been quite taken. Haniah's energy was compelling and contagious, and she dove into the vorn of anyone she met, free of fear, suspicion and selfishness to the extent that anyone with those weaknesses could easily misread her intentions. Paca was also an open person, with an honest vorn and simple motives.

"How old do you think she is?" he asked.

"I don't know. I'd guess that she is a little older than we are, but that doesn't make sense. According to the old doctor who first told me about her, she has been here a while."

"What do you mean?"

"He implied that he had always bought his herbs from her."

"Hmmm..." Paca fell silent again.

They walked together for twenty minutes without talking. Vrengnia had plenty to think about herself. She wondered about the warrior and Haniah's dream. What were the swords all about? Why had Paca reacted to the fact that there were seven swords? Did the four other warriors represent real people and if so, who might they be? The woman who became a man and joined in the fight and the two who remained holding hands after the battle; what could it all mean?

She found herself particularly troubled with the two fighting warriors and their sudden disappearance. Perhaps it was linked to the smith's statement that at least one, and maybe more, would die because of the swords that Paca had made. She knew she wasn't sure about death and what happened following it. The infinite was hard to comprehend and she wasn't ready to accept oblivion as the finality of all things. The awareness of her ignorance about death crept up on her, and then reared up in front of her. She must have reacted to her own thoughts.

"Are you all right?"

She shook her head and shivered as if she could shake off the feeling. "I think so."

"You looked as if you were about to...as if you had seen a ghost."

"I was thinking about Haniah's dream. It seems to be another confirmation that someone will die. There were four of us there today and four warriors. Two of them die, I think."

She looked up at Paca. He was staring at the horizon to the north. He simply nodded.

"What do you think happens when you die?" she asked.

"That depends."

"It depends? On what?"

"Fada believes that the life of a being is the essence of what he really is and is contained in the layers of the vorn. Our bodies, though part of the vorn are sort of like containers into which the vorn is placed, where it's nourished and protected, like an eggshell that contains the egg and is part of the egg. How we develop our vorn—how we think about our life while we are here—the things we do, determines what happens when we die."

"So?"

"Well, we were created for something much greater than this, just as the chicken develops in the egg and was created for something much greater than remaining in the egg. Our bodies anchor us to the progression of time we call our life span. When the vorn is developed, or when our bodies fail us or are taken away, the deeper layers of the vorn move either into the infinite or oblivion. Our bodies are changed somehow and then reunited with the rest of the vorn wherever it is."

"But what *is* the infinite and what *is* oblivion?"

"Fada thinks that they are different types of time experience. I don't understand his description very well, but he seems to think that oblivion is a state of being completely bound in time and space, sort of like a time prison. One cannot go anywhere or do anything. Whatever we are when we enter it, we are trapped alone with ourselves forever, in both the past and the future, from our current point of view."

"The infinite is the opposite. The infinite, he describes as a state of boundlessness in both time and space. That's the state where we'll understand Mah'Eladra, and we'll be there with all the others from the past and future who are there."

"Do *you* believe that?" Vrengnia asked.

"I *believe* it, but I'm not sure I understand it. I'm not even sure whether I need to or not."

"So who decides whether you end up in oblivion or the infinite? Mah'Eladra?"

"No, you do."

"Me?"

"Well, yes, for you anyway. Every day you face decisions about who you are going to be. You choose, actively or by inactivity, what kind of person you are going to be at the moment your body is taken from your life. The cumulative choice that you make through your life, is your path, if you will. I mean—if you choose to go in a different direction from someone else, don't you end up in different places?"

"Yeah."

"Every step, then, is a decision point at which you either stay on your chosen path or step off it, is it not? "

"And?"

"If you step off, say by accident, or even on purpose, the next decision is simply whether to step back on or step farther away. The farther you get away, the harder it is to get back, right? At some point, when your body is about to be taken, your vorn is in a state that you have created or allowed to be created for you; you have brought yourself somewhere, and—there you are."

"But I don't understand," Vrengnia said. "I guess I thought Mah'Eladra had something to do with it?"

"Many think Mah'Eladra decide what happens to them. I think that's because many beings don't want to take responsibility for the path they've taken. It's always much easier to blame their final situation on something other than their own poor decisions."

"So do Mah'Eladra have *anything* to do with it?"

"I think what Mah'Eladra want is for us to be where *they* are, but they don't want people to be there who don't *want* to be there. The path to the infinite is simply following the path of psadeq with Mah'Eladra. This demonstrates that we want to be with them. When we step off the path, we damage that relationship with Mah'Eladra and with other beings. Mah'Eladra are constrained by psadeq as much as we are, and if we choose to break psadeq, by our own decisions, Mah'Eladra can't intervene. By the very nature of that path, we have chosen oblivion."

Vrengnia began to realize that what she was hearing encompassed a whole different way of thinking about her life. Taking responsibility for every decision in an active and thoughtful way was something she'd never faced and she wasn't sure she wanted to. She realized that it was related to her fear of becoming queen. "I need some time to think about this," she said as she looked up at Paca.

He nodded and smiled back, "So do I."

They were passing through a stand of trees in a shallow valley in the middle of the huge grain fields north of Mordan. Vrengnia was thankful for the respite from the brilliance of Asolara.

She was still pondering how everything that Paca had said fit together. The smith came to mind. He was the source of all this. Paca seemed to be but a conduit for ideas that he hadn't fully made his own yet. This in itself shouldn't be a reason to doubt. Perhaps if she had heard it from the smith himself, she would understand it better, as if in the translation and the incompleteness of his understanding, Paca was unable to transmit the real essence of what he was saying. In the midst of this ponderance, a sudden sense of danger interrupted her thoughts.

Paca stopped and grabbed her arm. They stood silently in the path and waited. Paca had his finger up in front of his lip. Vrengnia's heart pounded as they waited. It was so still under the trees that she wondered how she could possibly have known there was something to be afraid of. Paca's grip on her arm was beginning to hurt, and as she reached across to loosen his fingers, a huge form sprang from the foliage just in front of them.

Paca let go of her arm, stepped in front of her, and in the next instant sprang into the brush where the animal had emerged. Mahala stood before her on the road, looking directly at her. Somewhere in the back of her mind, she heard Paca thrashing through the underbrush as she stood staring at her horse. He was fully saddled and as fresh as if he had just been readied at the stables. He tossed his head and snorted. She knew he wanted her to mount him.

Paca crashed back onto the road.

"What's going on?" she asked.

"I don't know," he gasped as he leaned over to catch his breath. "Someone was holding your horse in the wood. I thought I saw him, but there is no one there now."

"Not anywhere?"

"No. This grove isn't that big. There is no one here. It's very strange!"

"I think I am supposed to get on and ride. I also think that you shouldn't come with me, though I wish you could."

"Then that is what you should do," he said after a moment's hesitation. "I think that it's only about an hour to the castle on foot. I'll follow. There must be some reason that you need to be back."

She swung onto Mahala's back and looked down. "Maybe I'll see you at the castle."

Paca nodded. She swung Mahala around and cantered up the small rise out of the valley. As Mahala emerged into the Asolara's light at the top, he broke into a full gallop. Vrengnia turned to look back. Paca was standing in the middle of the road, staring into the woods where Mahala had emerged. She looked forward, wondering how this piece fit in the huge, evolving puzzle of her life.

"The evil they spread is like an adder's venom in the society of beings that share Tessalindria."

The Tessarandin,
Book 12, (Referring to the NarEladra)

The last dying rays of Asolara slanted across the stone windowsill as Paca looked down from the tower window at the evening revelries. People flowed in and out through the huge open gate. Some were heading home after a long day; others were returning for the evening bonfires that had been lit, casting showers of sparks into the sky from the courtyard. It was an ordered chaos, bright with the sounds of shouting, singing and the hubbub of a crowd with no agenda, bathing in the warmth of the fires and the late afternoon sky.

After Vrengnia left on Mahala, Paca had remained in the small grove for some time hoping to find a clue as to how Mahala got there, and who had been in the undergrowth holding him. He had only seen a brief movement and heard a couple of quick footsteps, but when he had entered the undergrowth, the noise he made would have masked the sound of anyone else who was there. He waited in the road, hoping that he might hear or see something that would give him a clue as to what happened. Having detected nothing, he headed back to the castle.

As it came into view, he had decided that he should make his entrance as inconspicuous as possible. He found a pack of young men about his own age who were returning to the festival along the road from Mordan. Anticipating a riotous time in the castle that evening, they were already overflowing with eagerness and wit, and making it known to everyone within earshot.

There were six in all, and Paca made an easy seventh. As they had approached the gate, Paca suggested that they enter the main gate arm in arm, so they marched through the archway in a line, seven across singing a bawdy song about the boredom of life in a small town. It wasn't Paca's style, but it was good cover.

Several additional soldiers stood under the portcullis, eyeing each passerby. Paca kept his head down and sang loudly. As they swept through the gate without breaking stride, Paca felt the watcher again. He looked up briefly to see Vishtorath staring straight at him. He looked down quickly. It frightened him that he was singled out by this man, and comforted that he didn't seem to be the object of the search by the increased vigilance at the gate.

Once inside the courtyard, he had made his way to the tower. No one guarded the stairway or Fada's chambers, so his access to Fada was undetected, as far as he knew.

Now he was with Fada again, hoping there would be enough time to sift through the events of the day. He didn't know where to start, so after giving

Fada a hug, he opened with the most innocuous thought he had. "I met Haniah today—she was different than I expected."

Fada had seated himself on the bed. An amused smile flitted across the corners of his mouth and his eyebrows rose. "Really? What did you expect and how was it different?"

"Not sure. I figured that any woman who chose to live alone in a sod house in such a remote place would be a little strange. I mean, perhaps she was hiding something or there was something wrong—but it wasn't like that."

Fada said nothing.

"She seemed very normal, confident, at peace with herself, and—it was—maybe as if she actually belonged there—in the field, I mean—and she was beautiful!" Paca flushed as he said it. "It wasn't the artificial beauty that so many women try to make for themselves, but it was simple; straightforward. It wasn't on the outside, is what I am trying to say—she's very attractive, but what made her so was her character, her vorn, if you will."

Fada laughed. "Haniah is remarkable—but what you say is true. Real beauty is a matter of the vorn. If it's ugly, then a woman cannot be truly beautiful. Painting the outside, when one is devoid of character and strength inside, produces no lasting beauty."

Paca nodded. "We got to spend some time together while Vrengnia and Patira talked. I'm not sure I would choose to live that way, but she made it seem very appropriate—for her, I mean. Her land seems to be an extension of who she is. I could feel it when I set foot onto it. A different kind of reality—a brightness—a clarity that I'd never sensed before." He looked straight into Fada's eyes. "It was almost as if she lives in a different world there."

"Did you see anything unusual, anything *specifically* different?"

"A number of things happened that seemed odd. When we started down the path to her house from the road, I am sure I saw an Eladrim being in the woods, not five steps from where I was—like the ones you showed me last night. When I looked directly at it, I couldn't really see it."

Fada's eyes grew bright with excitement. He stood up, strode across the room to the door, and listened intently. Then, turning back, he lifted the heavy oak door and stood it up on end. "Help me," he said, "we must put this back in place for the time being." Paca helped him move the base of the door back into place, and they pushed it into the doorframe so it blocked the corridor from prying ears.

Fada grabbed Paca by the arm and pulled him across the room where they sat down on the bed. The fire still flickered in Fada's eyes.

"What is it?" Paca asked.

"What I am about to tell you, you must tell to no one else. It's part of your education and is for you only. Do you understand?"

Paca couldn't remember seeing Fada's face so serious and full of intent. "I do," he said.

"Haniah's land is a special place. It's the first place I set foot in Immerland when I came here. The entrance to one of the portals opens out onto her land. It's the portal I came through to get here." He stood up and started pacing back and forth between the window and the bed.

Paca was confused. "How old is Haniah?" he asked .

"I'm not sure, but she didn't own the land at that time. I believe it belonged to an old cobbler who lived in Mordan—it had been in his family for years. Haniah purchased that property about twenty years ago. I'm not sure why she selected it, but it was a good choice, for both Haniah and the land."

"What do you mean?"

Fada stopped pacing and looked straight into his eyes. "The portals are carefully guarded by the Eladra. Their presence gives the area surrounding the entrance to the portal the slightly altered intensity that you sensed. What you saw in the woods was probably one of these guards."

"I know I saw something. I think I may have seen another one later—in a grove of trees just an hour's walk south of the castle." He related the events surrounding Mahala's appearance on the road to Fada in detail.

Fada frowned and remained silent.

"What else do you know about the eladra?" Paca continued. "I mean, most people think they are only mythical—part of the ancient legends."

"No. They are very real, perhaps more real than we are."

"Then why do they appear so vague, so fleeting?"

Fada came over and sat down close beside him. "It's not well understood how it all works together. The Eladra are a race of beings, not unlike us. They are servants of Mah'Eladra and have certain abilities that we don't. They can appear and disappear, at will. No one knows how they do it, but *I* believe that they can walk through time as you would walk through this castle. For us, time moves in one direction—its inevitability carries us along, as I have told you before. I believe the Eladra move through time in all directions, forward, backward, up, down, left to right. Infinity for them can be navigated. As you might visit a single place many times, they can visit many places at, what seems to us, the same time. They live in what one might call the eternal present; in the infinite, with Mah'Eladra.

"If they go in the same time direction as we are going, they become visible for the time they are doing that. When this happens, they appear just like us, as I said before. They are heavier, stronger, denser—more—more *real*. They can remain that way if they choose, or are so commissioned. When they do, they are undetectable as Eladra, and appear as you or I.

"If they cross our time stream, we often get a fleeting glimpse. When moving slightly faster or slightly slower or just in front or behind our time, they appear shadowy and vague. Their voices like whispers—a hissing—timeless and remote.

"They speak the original language," Fada continued. "In the eternal present, nothing changes, so the language is unchanged. I was going to say, 'always the same,' but words like *always, never, then, now, before* and *after* don't really apply to the Eladra."

Paca had no idea that Fada knew so much about these matters, but it seemed to fit. Knowledge produces power in authority, and Fada did have that. "Can the Eladra carry things from our world through time, like objects, or people?"

"I'm not sure." Fada stroked his beard and thought for a moment. "We don't know a lot, but I think that is what the portals are all about."

"What do you mean?"

"Well, we know there are seven portals. There are rumors that there are eight, but no one has ever found the eighth. As far as we can tell they were made by Mah'Eladra so that we can move, or be moved, about in time in a limited way—and things, people, animals *can* be carried through the portals. The Eladra guard them, so that they can't be abused. When I came through the portal into The Awakening, I was being pursued by one of Mankar's generals. He didn't make it through, if he even tried. It seems that the portal travel is restricted to those whose vorns fit an acceptable pattern of psadeq and peace as determined by the Eladra, but that is conjecture on my part. Whether the Eladra use the portals I don't know, they seem able to time walk without them."

Several incidents on the day's journey suddenly became clear. "If what you say is true, I think I saw yet another one of them in Haniah's hut."

"Another Eladra?"

"A warrior. At dinner, Haniah had told us a very strange dream she had last night." Paca said.

Paca related Haniah's dream to Fada in as much detail as he could remember, as Fada sat and pondered his story. Paca saw his eyes flash at the mention of the swords.

"I became suspicious about the dream and whether it was really just a dream, when she showed us the footprints the warrior left outside the hut. Haniah and I went inside to clean up while Patira and the princess colluded on how to best bring their fathers together. Once inside, Haniah whispered to me, 'Come quickly, there's something you must see!' She reached under her bed and pulled out a large roll, like the one she had described in her dream—"

"The swords?" Fada leapt to his feet.

"Yes. She unrolled the package on the bed. There were seven swords all together, one a little larger, the others as perfectly the same as is imaginable."

"Only seven?" Fada asked. He paced back and forth, his bearded chin buried in his huge right hand.

"Only seven." Paca confirmed. "The craftsmanship was astonishing. It was hard to see, but they glowed against the dark leather wrapping." Fada was deep in thought, but Paca knew he was listening. "I reached out my hand to touch one of the swords—on impulse—they were so beautiful. Suddenly a gloved hand appeared and grabbed me by the wrist. The grip was painfully powerful and as cold as ice. I cried out and pulled back and the hand let go. As I stood back, I faced a man—a huge man—fully dressed in an ancient warrior's leather. He stared at me for a moment then he turned to Haniah and said something I didn't understand.

When I looked at her, she told me that I couldn't touch the swords; it would be too dangerous."

"An Eladrim warrior," Fada said. He stood at the window now, staring out into the dusk. "Then what?"

"I turned to Haniah. She knew what I was thinking: 'Some of it wasn't a dream,' she said. I asked why she didn't tell the others. She responded that she had been told to only show them to the smith who would visit her that day. 'He would know what to do,' she said. Then she rolled up the swords and put them back under her bed. She told me I was to tell no one except you. *That* was...difficult."

Fada looked at him. "It's essential that you don't tell anyone, especially the princess. They are undoubtedly Mankar's sword and six of his brothers," he continued. "Why they were brought here, at this time is mystifying. We must be alert and wait. That they are on Haniah's land makes them safe for the time being—"

Fada changed the subject. "You know that old signature star you found on the steps last night?"

"Yes."

"It disappeared from the washstand last night some time."

"This washstand?" Paca said, pointing beside the bed.

"Yes."

Paca opened his mouth to speak, but Fada held up his hand. "It seems that we may have a timebound eladra walking among us. Your watcher may have been such. And it may not be friendly."

"A NarEladra?"

"Perhaps."

"Wouldn't the Eladrim guards on the walls know, I mean, wouldn't they be able to see one of their own?"

"I'm not sure, but I think that when they timebind, they become as one of us for that time and may not be recognized, even by their own kind."

"Is it dangerous? For us? Or Vrengnia?"

"Yes and no. Yes, in that the NarEladra always pose a serious threat. They're dangerous and full of evil intent. Their presence never bodes well. However, if your watcher is a *clandestine* NarEladra, he knows that his cover is precarious with the force of Eladrim guards about the castle. He will be very careful. I am surprised at his carelessness in dropping his signature star, if that is the case. Something big is brewing. Each day I see more evidence of forces and activities that move us closer to some significant event. We have to be more vigilant. Keep your eyes and ears open, Paca. There's much at stake."

Paca sat silently with his thoughts as Fada continued to stare out the window. Less than a month ago, he could never have imagined the situation that was unfolding before him. Everything was happening so fast and escalating into something completely unknown that would undoubtedly change his life forever, and he had no way of knowing whether that would be for the better or the worse.

He would have to wait and trust. Fada always said that waiting and trusting with sober awareness was the key to a positive outcome for any situation.

Fada interrupted his thoughts: "Do you know the details that the princess and Patira worked out for the meeting between their fathers?"

"Vrengnia and Patira are to convince their fathers to meet at Haniah's field two days hence at noon. It will be the autumnal equinox. No more than seven people are to accompany each of them onto Haniah's land and they won't be allowed to bring any weapons. The table will be set for the king, Vrengnia, Patira, Verclan, and Haniah, who will serve as hostess and mediator. They thought about having you as the mediator, but feared that the king would be too suspicious."

Fada stared out the window. "That's also Vrengnia's birthday; her eighteenth. Did she tell you whether she has chosen a name yet?"

"No, she hasn't mentioned it. I didn't even realize that was her birthday." Paca suspected that Fada saw something significant in this discovery from the way he stood. He was thinking deeply.

"You need to go home tonight," Fada said. "Sleep in your own bed; you need the rest after a long day. Meet me at dawn on the morning of the meeting, at the Yendel Fork, north of Shiloh. Be well rested; it will also be a long day."

Paca hugged Fada. He felt his strength surrounding him and warding off the fear that was creeping around the edges of his vorn. They said nothing as they pulled the door from its frame and laid it carefully on the floor where it had fallen before.

"Paca," Fada said, "do not fear, and don't let anyone know where you're going."

"I won't," Paca replied and slipped down the darkened stairs toward the court-yard.

Chapter 14

Journey

"Today bounds your life. Do not miss its fullness by worrying about tomorrow, or fretting over yesterday."

Sessasha,
It Is Said

Verclan sat staring into the dying fire in the stone fireplace before him. In all the years of smithing, he had never lost the delight of sitting and watching its steady, consuming nature and feeling the heat on his face and eyes. It was a form of meditation for him; a place to wash out the events of the hours and days behind him and set the course of his life onto a well thought out path of appropriate action, instead of reaction.

Tonight he needed his time with the fire more than usual. Patira had gotten back from his trip to Haniah's just before dusk, and had related the events of the day briefly. The family had eaten dinner together, as they always did when he and Patira were home and they had worked to clean up the kitchen for the end of another day. The girls had been put to bed and now he sat with his wife and son, facing what might be the biggest challenge of his life.

"Do you think the king will accept the terms of the agreement?" Mordara asked, without looking up from the spoon she was carving in her lap.

She sat to the left of Verclan and he could feel her presence with almost the same intensity as he could feel the fire. Her question wasn't an intrusion, but more of an echo of his thoughts, set into words and reflected back to him. He wasn't sure he knew the answer, so he waited.

Patira sat cross-legged on the floor to his right, playing idly in the fire with a long thin stick. It was a habit of his, part of something he had never lost from his childhood. Verclan thought back to his own childhood in Immerland. He had few happy memories. It was mostly work, as he remembered, and lots of busy-ness and hurry trying to help Fada make enough money to feed the family. Fada never had the time to enjoy the fire, and he never had time to talk to his only son. They would come home, eat dinner, and go to bed, day after day, week after week, year after year until he died. His mother had died a year later from grief. He was seventeen.

Patira interrupted his reflection. "I think the princess will convince her father," he said as he stared at the smoldering tip of his stick. "She has a remarkable character and a strong desire to see this happen."

Verclan looked over at Patira, now a strong young man. "Do you like the princess?" he asked.

Patira poked one of the logs in the fire with his stick. "I do," he said. "Our first meeting was a bit awkward. But I think she—well, when we met at Haniah's that afternoon before our dinner there, we were able to talk alone. She'll be a fine queen some day, but right now she is living in the shadow of her father. It's almost as if she hasn't been allowed to find out who she is yet."

"I've yet to meet her." Verclan said. "Perhaps if we can come to some reasonable terms with the king, you'll be able to know her better."

Patira looked up at him. "I am hoping that's true. I think we have a special connection. At first, I thought it was simply that of being the son and daughter of two important men who should have been able to be friends themselves, but now I think it's more than that."

"I'm sure it is," Verclan replied. He turned to his wife. She was busy with the carving, but he was sure she was listening intently. She looked back at him and her eyes sparkled in the fire. "What are you thinking?" he asked.

"I was thinking that I would like to go with you to the meeting with Sandihar."

The thought took him by surprise. She was looking straight into his eyes as she spoke in complete earnestness. "I don't think that's best. I can only take seven—"

"I know. I want to be one of the seven." Her eyes shone with an intensity that Verclan knew well. It only appeared when she was afraid or when she was determined to have her way. Neither happened often. Mordara had an unusual strength of character and didn't seek her own way without reasonable cause, nor was she easily frightened. Verclan couldn't tell which it was tonight. He turned back to the fire and stroked his chin.

Patira spoke first. "This could be a dangerous trip, Mada. The king has already increased the number of scouts along the border and we don't know what treachery is planned. We are hoping for a peaceful meeting, but we have no guarantees."

Verclan turned to look back at his wife. The carving knife and the spoon lay still in her apron on her lap and her hands were on her knees. She was as beautiful as ever and the firelight accentuated her fine features. Her black hair was tucked back around her ears and then hung forward over her shoulders. She, too, was staring into the fire.

She spoke with an undaunted resolution. "It's no more dangerous for me than for you. In fact, it's likely to be more dangerous for each of you than for me, since you, my husband, are the target of the king and you, my son, are his only male heir. We'll be in the mountain woods until we enter Haniah's land, and once we're there, we'll be as safe as we are here. By agreement, there'll be no weapons at the meeting. That'll make it safer yet."

Verclan listened into the pause that followed, hoping to hear something that hadn't been said. He knew that she was right, but he was trying to understand his own reluctance. Was it simply because she was a woman, or maybe that he hadn't thought of it himself? He had assumed that he would take Patira, his close advisors, and fill out the party with warriors. But why?

If it was to be a peaceful meeting and there were no weapons, what would be wrong with having his wife with him? She was by far his best friend and his closest ally. Dependable, strong and insightful, she was particularly useful in diplomacy. "What about the girls?" he asked.

"They could stay with Cordara and Minstar for the day and even the night if necessary."

Verclan nodded. Cordara was one of the village elders.

"Besides, I would like to meet the princess as much as you do. This may be my only chance. Haniah may need my help. You may need my support."

Verclan smiled into the fire. "Hopefully not. But we should sleep on this tonight and make a decision tomorrow." He looked over to his wife and she nodded and smiled back.

It was as if she knew the answer when she spoke. "It's been a long day. I'm going to bed; if you need to stay up a little longer, that would be fine." She stood up and laid her hand on his shoulder.

"I'll be in in a few minutes."

She bent over and kissed his ear, then left without another word to disturb his thoughts.

Patira threw his stick into the fire, stretched, yawned, and stood up. "Me too. I'll see you in the morning."

The deep silence of night settled around him as Verclan sat alone, staring into the fire. His feelings eluded him. It wasn't fear exactly, and it wasn't joy, although there was a significant sense of accomplishment in having provoked the king into finally meeting with him. It was more of a sobriety in the realization that the event for which he had worked so long was coming to fruition, yet it was still complicated by many unknowns.

He hadn't seen the king in nearly twenty years. He'd never met the princess. Passions and vendettas don't die easily, and he wasn't sure what the king's real motives might be, nor what his capabilities and resources were. Why had Sandihar changed his mind so quickly, and had he *really* changed? He had seen men who fought for something for years, suddenly give up and head home, and the king *had* just celebrated his fiftieth birthday. Perhaps that had triggered a recognition of the folly of his hatred.

Patira had told him all about Haniah's dream, leaving a trail of questions. What were the swords about? Could they be some of the Mankar swords that the smith was looking for? The vanishing footprints of the dream warrior had particularly disturbed Patira. Verclan suspected that it was an Eladrim warrior.

Eladra activity had increased lately. Two of his men had been to the festival and had seen Eladrim guards on the castle walls. The arrest of the smith, the singing of the taralang, the sword poetry, Patira's fortuitous meetings with the daughter of his enemy—the thoughts swam in circles in his head. He knew that they were related, but there were pieces missing. No amount of thinking offered a satisfactory conclusion.

The most troubling of all were the hilt guard for Patira's sword and the sataliin. His friend the smith was at the center of all of it. What did he know and how did he know it? Verclan thought it peculiar that throughout all of this, the smith had been inaccessibly locked in the king's fortress. He alone held the answers, if indeed there were any answers at all.

Verclan sat forward and rested his chin in his hands, his elbows on his knees, the cherry red coals of the fire drawing him into its slow demise. Life had never been easy, but it was always easier when he trusted deliberately in the promise of psadeq: that if one always looked for the best in others and fearlessly pursued psadeq with them and with Mah'Eladra, the result, in the grand view of life, was always good. Implicit in this trust was the knowledge that sacrifices often had to be made, and that the outcome was always worth the sacrifice.

So far, little had been sacrificed in the recent spate of activity, and much was at stake. He knew this imbalance was at the core of his apprehension. Although Mordara knew these principles as well as he did, and trusted in the promise of psadeq, he didn't want her to be part of, or witness to, the sacrifice that might be demanded before the peace of psadeq was gained. On the other hand, her peculiar intensity about it may be part of the grand plan, and who was he to deny her involvement? Was part of the sacrifice his willingness to let her be part of it?

In the end, he knew he would have to trust. Right now, he needed sleep. As he set the iron grill in front of the fire for the night, he pondered the nature of sleep. It had a way of purifying thoughts; distilling and refining them into tangible, cogent pieces.

He'd always thought it peculiar that he had been created to *need* sleep. With all the things that seemed so urgent in one's short life, wouldn't it be better if he didn't have to waste so much of it sleeping? He had concluded that its purposeful, rhythmic intervention in the lives of every created being was simply a mechanism that forced the separation of days into manageable slices of time. It gave each being a respite from the unending assault of life's challenges.

When he lived each day within its natural confines, accepting what it offered without regret and giving back as much as he could within its limits, without worrying about tomorrow's challenges, or disabled by yesterday's failures, he remained content.

Today was done. The fire was secure, as was his mind, and he went to bed without fear, unconcerned about what he needed to face tomorrow. When he slipped into bed beside Mordara, she rolled over and laid her hand gently on his chest. He lay quiet for a moment, listening to her steady, rhythmic breath of sleep...

"The desire for control is the stepchild of fear. "

Pratoraman
The Middle Way

Sandihar leaned on the window frame, staring out at the sunrise. He hadn't enjoyed his birthday festival as much as he had hoped. It wasn't that anything had gone wrong. His subjects had enjoyed it with visible intensity, which was good—but the whole affair with the smith and Verclan had cast its pall over his enjoyment of it.

He watched as the servants in the courtyard cleaned up the inevitable trash left by the crowds, and roused those who had slept there overnight, sending them on their way. Two old men busied themselves shoveling ashes from the bonfires into an oxcart, while several women swept the courtyard with large brooms.

There was a warm spot in his heart for the willingness and thoroughness of his servants. There were so many good people in Immerland. *"But,"* he mused, *"I am glad that I'm the king."*

A knock on the door shook him from his reverie by the window. "Come in," he boomed, to make sure it was heard on the other side of the thick door.

The door swung open and his advisors and Dors Galar and Windarad strode in, followed by Rapahoogin. They must have met in the hall and come together.

"My good Dors, scout and advisors. What is the good word for the day?" He tried to speak as warmly as possible, but his words rang apprehensive, hollow, and tentative. The looks on their faces warned him that it wasn't going to be good news as they took their places in the circle from the day before.

Dor Windarad spoke first. "Sire, we went to the smithy in Shiloh, but there was almost no one there because of the festival. We asked about and found the smith's home, but there was no one there either, and no one we asked had seen the young smith. After spending most of the morning there, we returned and I posted a guard at the castle gate to watch people coming and going. Unfortunately, we couldn't find anyone who knew the smith, that is, knew what he looked like, so we never saw him, if he was here at all. We went back to Shiloh after dark, but he hadn't returned to his house."

Sandihar frowned. Little as he liked it, there was nothing to be done. "Rapa-hoogin?"

The scout stepped forward and bowed. A devilish smirk played on his face. Sandihar didn't like this crooked little man, but he was glad he was working for him instead of against him. He couldn't tell what the smile meant so he raised one eyebrow and waited.

"I went to the princess's chambers at dawn yesterday. The door was locked from the outside just as you said it would be. I waited until noon, watching and listening, and there was no sound." Rapahoogin glanced around at the other men, seeking their approval for his thoroughness. "I finally decided to find out if she was there, so I knocked, planning that if she were to respond, I wouldn't let on who I was, of course. No answer. I unbolted the door and let myself in. Everything was in order, but wouldn't you know it: No princess!" That twisted, ironic smile appeared again.

Sandihar's anger rose. "Fool, she left before dawn and drew the bolt from the outside herself!"

"How would she do that—I mean how would she get out, Sire?"

"Someone must have helped her—the smith, perhaps—but how would he know she would be locked in, and why?" Leveling his anger at the little scout was useless. "Dor Galar, did you speak with the smith about arrangements for the meeting with Verclan?"

"I did, Sire, but he was vague. He wouldn't give me a direct answer. In fact, he said that emissaries from you and Verclan were making arrangements as we were speaking."

"And what time was that? I mean, when were you having this conversation with him?"

"A little after noon, Sire. I found it hard to believe, given that—"

"Hard to believe? Of course, it's hard to believe; I sent no emissary. You were all here yesterday. I gave no one else leave. I wanted to hear from the smith about when and where such a meeting could take place." The men standing before him had done their jobs and they had all been thwarted. It all pointed back to the smith somehow. "Who else would I have sent, anyway?" he thundered.

"It was I, Fada." Sandihar whirled around to see his daughter standing in the open door of the hall. How long she had been there he didn't know. Apparently, no one else had seen her either. "I went to make arrangements for the meeting."

"And how did you know to make arrangements for me? Who sent you?" His attempt at intimidation was deliberate. In the past, she would have backed down, but things had been changing recently and he had seen a personal strength emerging in her that he both admired and resented. She stood undaunted by his thunder. His anger raged inside, but he knew somehow that to unleash it now would be pointless.

Vrengnia strode past him into the circle of men in the room and stood tall and straight in the middle. She turned to face him. "I wasn't sent by anyone, and when I left here I didn't know that this was what I was going to do. I took Paca, the smith's son, with me to meet Haniah the herbalist." She turned to Dor Windarad. "Paca had never met her or been to her house and needed someone to show him where to find her. When we got there, Patira was there." Her eyes swept the assembly of men and came to rest on Rapahoogin. He shifted his weight and looked at Sandihar. "That's Verclan's son," she continued. "I have no idea how he came to be there, but Haniah's table was set for five when we arrived. Haniah seemed to know that we were all coming and had lunch prepared."

"Five?" interrupted Sandihar "Who was the fifth?"

Vrengnia told them all about Meshabo and Haniah's dream of four visitors. "Somehow Haniah didn't realize that the fourth visitor was the she donkey." She smiled. Sandihar frowned. The advisors glanced at one another and shifted uneasily in their places.

"When dinner was over, Paca and Haniah left Patira and me to talk, while they cleaned up. By that time it was clear that the purpose of the meeting was to arrange for our fathers to meet. So we did, and—"

Sandihar interrupted her. "Verclan's message to me was to allow the *smith* to determine the time and the place for such a meeting." He didn't like being upstaged by his daughter, and he felt the same helplessness that he had in the presence of the smith. What was happening? "How is it that you took it upon yourself to do such a thing without my knowing?"

"It all fell into place, and I knew that it was the right path, but I don't know how I knew it. I used to think that this was impossible, and it would make me afraid to trust that type of knowledge. But I've stopped fearing. When one stops fearing, she finds that there is real knowledge beyond physical proof, but this doesn't make it any less knowing."

"You are speaking nonsense! Carnados, what do you make of this foolishness?"

Carnados had been staring at the floor, saying nothing. Sandihar needed his support.

Carnados looked steadily into Sandihar's eyes and then at his daughter, "I think that we should summon the smith. While we're waiting for him to come, we should discuss your daughter's plan. If her knowing is true, the smith will confirm it when he arrives. Either way we need to hear from the smith, by Verclan's request."

What Carnados was saying made sense, but Sandihar felt the evasive caution in Carnados's voice. He recalled what the smith had said about "wanting an accomplice" when seeking advice, and felt chastened and annoyed at the same time. "Guards!" he thundered. Two guards appeared at the door. "Bring me the smith from the tower."

He turned to Vrengnia and strode up to face her. He swept his hand around, as if presenting the group of men in the ring to her for the first time. "Now, tell this group of men your plan."

Vrengnia looked straight into his eyes as she spoke. "You and Verclan should meet together at Haniah's table for a discussion centered on a resolution of long-standing conflicts between you. At the table with you will be Verclan's son, Patira, and the king's daughter, me. Haniah will serve as the mediator. You may each bring no more than six additional persons of your choice onto Haniah's property, and there will be no weapons."

"No weapons?" Sandihar said in disbelief.

"None whatsoever," His daughter responded. "They will be left outside of Haniah's property."

"What if I don't agree to these terms?"

"Then you won't meet with Verclan."

"Is Verclan being told the same things by Patira, and if he is, how do you know he will agree to them?"

"He will," Vrengnia said. "I know it."

He was in the process of deciding to ask how she knew, when the smith, followed by the two guards, appeared at the door. He walked in as if he owned the room and had called the meeting himself. "You called for me, Sire?"

"Good Smith, we were all wondering if you have decided a time and a place for the meeting between Verclan and me?"

The smith looked surprised. "Good King, hasn't your daughter told you by now?"

"Yes she has—" Sandihar felt his victory slipping away. "But what do *you* say? Verclan explicitly wanted *you* to select the time and place."

"I did. Your daughter and my son—"

"You sent my daughter?" Sandihar interrupted.

"No, I sent my son. Your daughter was the only one I knew who knew the way to Haniah's hut. I asked that she lead him there."

"You told the good Dor Galar that you didn't know the time or the place."

"I didn't."

"But you then told him that emissaries of mine were making the arrangements—"

"Good King, let me clear up some confusion. When I sent my son to Haniah's I had no clear idea what it was for. I just knew he had to go there on that day. When Galar visited me, I realized why he had gone, but I don't know how I knew. His journey, in hindsight, was to lead your daughter there. She was your emissary. No one else in the kingdom could have gained Patira's trust. Moreover, probably no one else in the mountain clans could have gained Vrengnia's trust. No one else in your kingdom would have your best interest at heart more than your own daughter. She is a fine young woman and loves you profoundly. Could there have been a better choice?"

Sandihar frowned. Why was it that this always got turned back on him? "Perhaps you are right," he said. "But since it was Verclan's request that *you* choose the time, place, and terms of the meeting, please tell me plainly what they should be."

"You shall meet Verclan at Haniah's table at noon tomorrow. You may take seven other persons; one of them is your daughter, who will sit with you at Haniah's table. Haniah will mediate the discussions between you and Verclan. There will be no weapons of any kind allowed on Haniah's land—"

"No!" Sandihar shouted.

"No what?"

"That is what my daughter said!"

"I agree with your daughter." The smith said. "She has negotiated wisely. I wouldn't have selected better."

Sandihar sulked. He was making a fool of himself and sought desperately to blame it on someone else.

"I see," continued the smith, "because we're in agreement, you suspect that I actually told your daughter what to arrange. I assure you, I didn't."

"Enough!" Sandihar snapped. "Verclan will have his meeting with me as arranged—tomorrow at noon at Haniah's table." He looked at the smith. "You may leave, good Smith. I have many arrangements to make."

The smith bowed and turned to the door. The two guards followed him out. Sandihar silently hoped he would never see him again.

Vrengnia broke the silence. "Fada, are you angry with me for making these arrangements?"

Sandihar sighed. "No, Vrengnia, I'm not angry with you. You've done well. The arrangements are fair and the plan is good."

"Then what are you angry about?" She stared straight into his eyes.

He looked at the floor. "I'm angry...I guess...I'm angry because it was done without my knowledge." He looked up and met the princess's gaze with his own.

"Fada, you must understand—when I left with Paca yesterday morning, I had no idea what the purpose of the trip was going to be. I thought that I was simply guiding Paca to Haniah's place as a favor to the smith. Paca didn't know either." Her voice was steady and full of confidence. "I would have told you except that you tried to lock me in my room again. That insulted my trust in you and I left without letting you know. I'm sorry."

His daughter was becoming everything he hoped that she someday would be. Why was this so hard to accept?

During the whole interchange between the smith, himself, and Vrengnia, the other men in the hall had stood patiently, silent witnesses to the drama before them. He turned to them again. "Come, there are preparations to be made. Vrengnia, we will meet about an hour after sunrise tomorrow morning at the castle gate. If you will now excuse us, I need to speak with my advisors in private."

Sandihar thought that this dismissal might reveal a chink in the Vrengnia's newfound strength. Instead, she smiled at him, threw her arms around him, and hugged him. "I'll be there, Fada. It will be a great day together. By the way, I've chosen a name."

"A name?"

"My elder-name. Tomorrow is my birthday, my eighteenth."

"Yes, yes...your eighteenth!" How could he have forgotten? There had been so much going on, but that was no excuse. "What name have you chosen?"

"I will tell you at the celebration."

"Celebration?"

"Sure. After the meeting tomorrow. You celebrated your fiftieth, shouldn't I celebrate my eighteenth?"

Sandihar's defensiveness melted into her smile as she stood before him. "Of course. I'll look forward to that."

She stepped forward and hugged him again, then turned and left immediately, without so much as a look back over her shoulder.

The king turned to the six men remaining in the room. "As I said, we have much to do." He had his own plan forming in his mind. There were many details to be worked out. "Get me Omberon."

Dor Galar shifted and looked up at him. "We weren't able to find him, Sire."

"What?!"

"Yesterday you asked me to find him. He doesn't seem to be in the castle. I have asked around, and no one has seen him since the night before last."

"Did you ask Vishtorath at the gate?"

"I did. As far has he knows, he didn't leave through the portcullis."

"Are you saying he found another way out?"

"No, Sire, just that Vishtorath said he didn't leave across the drawbridge, and we weren't able to find him in the castle. I'm at a loss to explain it."

Sandihar stopped for a moment, trying to assimilate yet another strange event. He struggled to find how this piece fit into the changing landscape of a journey he didn't want to be taking. He looked down and shuddered. "All right," he said, "we need to make appropriate preparations for tomorrow's meeting." He called to the attendants, "Chairs!" It was going to be a long session.

"It is one thing to make a mistake, or to have an evil thought cross one's mind. It is quite another to make a life out of inventing evil."

Pratoraman,
The Middle Way

Paca walked rapidly to keep up with Fada. It had always been that way, for though twenty-five years his elder, Fada was still strong, and there was no time to waste today. They had met at the Yendel Fork in the gray light of the predawn fog. Fada hugged him.

"We have little time," Fada said as he gestured vaguely west into the fog. Paca knew the road well and knew there was nothing except fields where Fada had indicated. "We need to get to Haniah's before the king. There are arrangements I need to make with her before he arrives," he explained.

They plunged into the fog across the fields. Paca wasn't sure how Fada knew where he was going, but he was following vague trails through the fields. Occasionally they would pass a farmhouse and Fada would stop as if remembering something distant. "I haven't been to Haniah's in about two years," he whispered during one such pause, "and the fog doesn't help." Paca opened his mouth to speak, but Fada held his index finger up in front of his lips and whispered, "Not now."

He walked in silence behind Fada, as if the fields had ears. He had many questions, but the need of the hour seemed to be silence. It gave him time to think.

The fog lifted just before Paca and Fada reached the road from the castle to Mordan, near the bridge across Rindara. They paused in a small gully that ran beside the road and Fada held his finger to his lips as he stole up the side of the roadbed. He looked both ways along the empty road, then waved to Paca to follow him. "No sign of the king," he said in the first normal voice since they had started the journey. "We must be well ahead of him. Keep your eye out for scouts, but I think we can talk freely now."

"Why couldn't we talk in the fields? It seems there would be less chance of anyone hearing us there."

"I wasn't afraid of being heard, but we were traveling under the protection of Allimah Ki. It's simply a matter of respect for the people who live there and work the land." Paca knew about Allimah Ki, but had never used its privilege. The ancient Tessalindrian tradition granted anyone on foot free passage across any piece of land. Passage was allowed as long as the passer didn't injure the land or its owners in any way. Though it had been made a law in Immerland by the Great Queen, many landowners didn't respect it, so there was a risk in invoking it.

"I *do* have lots of questions," Paca opened.

"Speak."

"I want to know more about Mankar."

"Something specific?" Fada stared straight ahead as he spoke. They were alone on the road as far as Paca could see. Just above the eastern horizon, Asolara penetrated the clouds, and the last patches of fog that lay in the small depressions in the carpet of fields surrounding them, yielded to its warmth.

"Was it really as bad as the legends say. I mean—"

"It was worse than *any* of the legends." Fada interrupted as he continued to stare at the horizon.

"Worse?!" It was hard for Paca to imagine. The legends told of unimaginable barbarism by Mankar and his generals; brutal acts that went far beyond the thirst for power and control. "How could it be worse?"

They walked for some distance before Fada spoke. "The legends only tell of the heroics of brave men who stood up to Mankar. One might *expect* an evil man to respond to such threats with sadism and horrific injustice." As he spoke, his sentences overflowed with emotion, rolling back and forth between deep pain and anger. "But the legends seldom speak of the torture and indiscriminate bloodletting levied at anyone and everyone in Mankar's path. The evil he carried in his heart was like a sport. Do you recall the legend of Thiadar?"

"Wasn't he the one who led a band of followers against Mankar with pitchforks? He was blinded, deafened and caged in the town square, as I recall, and kept alive in the cage until he froze that winter."

"Yes, but do you know *why* he rebelled?"

"No."

"Mankar and his generals paid a visit to the small town of Mindaquora on the border of Tessamandria. When he arrived the elders of the town were in a meeting in the central meeting hall. He blockaded the building and set it afire. He and his minions took turns beheading the elders as they tried to escape the flames through the front door of the hall.

"Later, they gathered all the heads and boiled them in a large pot in the center of the town. That night, they forced everyone in the town to drink from the unholy brew. Anyone who refused was killed.

"Thiadar was one who drank. Later, repulsed and infuriated by his cowardice, he led his rebellion. He almost succeeded." As his voice trailed off, Paca looked up and saw tears running down Fada's cheeks. "There was so much more...ugly...evil... unbearable."

Paca didn't know what to say, so he said nothing to let Fada continue.

"His crowning insult to justice was the institution of Kli-marana Waru."

"I have heard of it, but I never understood what it was."

"Kli-marana Waru was devised by Mankar to taunt those who would stand against him. It was a fight to the death with swords, one man against another. Each was allowed to choose a second, to back him up. Mankar instituted it as the only legal method of challenging his authority. Many people challenged him, in the remote hope that they could end his reign of terror. They all died—the sword my father had made gave him too much of an advantage. It was a brutal and sadistic thing."

Fada's eyes looked beyond the horizon. "When Mankar disappeared, Kli-marana Waru was outlawed. Its memory was too vile to allow its practice by any nation on Tessalindria. The Moorimans practiced it for a while, but even they abandoned it."

"What *did* happen to Mankar?"

"We don't know exactly. There's much conjecture, but little evidence. Several of his generals had been killed by daring men who paid with their lives. At some point, his sword was stolen by the Twins of Huravag, along with the swords of his generals, and Mankar and the generals who remained disappeared. Many think that the Eladra were involved in his overthrow. If the swords you saw the other day are what I suspect, it's of great interest that there are only seven. It means that six others are still lost."

"Why didn't the Eladra get involved sooner?"

"That's a tough question, Paca. There are many things about the Eladra that we don't know. There's a lot about Mah'Eladra's plan that we don't know. Many think that the NarEladra were supporting Mankar, and if *that* is true, then it all makes a lot more sense. Their penchant for evil against the mankind would explain much of what happened. It's possible that the rise and reign of Mankar was the extension of a much bigger conflict between Mah'Eladra and the NarEladra."

They fell silent. Fada remained deep in thought and Paca was trying to assimilate the conflict between the bits of what he knew and the dark events surrounding Mankar's history. So much didn't fit; so many pieces had no place in the puzzle.

Asolara burned away all remnants of the fog, and banished the clouds from the sky overhead. Despite Fada's brisk pace and the fresh exhilaration of the bright new morning, the conversation left Paca with an overriding sense of darkness. He shuddered and forced his thoughts elsewhere.

Vrengnia and her father were probably on the road somewhere behind them. Patira and Verclan were making their way down some mountain trail toward Haniah's. Paca busied his mind imagining what they were thinking as they all traveled toward Haniah's table.

"Loneliness is not measured by the absence of other beings, but by the absence of friends."

Hispattea,
The Essences of Corritanean Wisdom

Vrengnia woke early. It was still dark, but the air in her chambers told her that the morning was heavy with fog. The stirrings of the castle rose up from the courtyard. Whenever Fada left the castle, it was a big affair, so it started while it was still dark.

Horses stamped and snorted as they were led out onto the cobblestones with the grooms trying to calm them down in the darkness. Cart and wagon wheels clattered on the stone as various voices alternately gave orders and cursed. She peered down into the dark mist, but could see nothing, except the faint bobbing of lanterns that moved about the courtyard.

In her vorn, Vrengnia knew she'd wanted this for a long time. Fada was a good man, but this cruel obsession with vengeance on Verclan was twisting much of his goodness. Perhaps today it could be mended, even if it was only in the slightest way.

It was peculiar, though, she thought, that amidst all the uncertainty of what might happen, she felt no fear whatsoever. She was beginning to understand the way the smith looked at his world and as she tried to imitate it, she found herself becoming more and more confident, relaxed and at peace. Today she felt unusually strong.

It was also her birthday. Today she would be twenty and she liked the sound of it. Twenty: long ago she had chosen it as her favorite number. There was no particular reason; she just liked it and that was all that mattered.

Many other things had begun to change from her association with the smith, Paca and Patira. She'd been thinking lately about shedding the image of the Pied Princess. She had no recollection of her mother, and many of the images she had of queens were based on legends and were those of weakness and overindulgence in the feminine mystique of excessive and impractical clothing and makeup. She'd resisted any such "queenly" thinking.

The exception to this was her grandmother, about whom she knew relatively few details. Recently, she had developed a new image for what a queen could be, and her confidence in her ability to create this image was at the point where she was ready to try. *Perhaps today should be the day*, she thought as she stared into the wardrobe.

Her attendants lit the lanterns in her chambers and busied themselves with other chores about the room. She dismissed them so she could work out the details alone.

She would wear her best for Fada. He had ordered many clothes for her, hoping that she would wear something more in line with his vision of a princess. He had tried everything, so she had every color, arrangement, and style except the feminine extreme, which she loathed without prejudice, so he had never even bothered to offer it to her.

Her wardrobe was filled with many outfits which she had never worn. She began pulling them out and examining them. She didn't have time to deal with all of it that morning, so she worked through the wardrobe until she had found a suitable outfit: light gray pantaloons, made from a sturdy light cloth that looked like satin, but wasn't. She also found a black blouse with long loose sleeves and a wide-open collar. It matched perfectly with her tunic. The gray and the black accented the yellow sunburst and the blue slashes, and made them stand out.

She decided not to wear her hat. She held it for a moment and smiled. It seemed out of place now, and she wondered briefly at the years of silliness when the hat was her statement of who she was. Who she was would change today. She tossed it aside and turned to the large oval glass beside the wardrobe. If she wore no hat, what would she do with her hair? She pushed it to one side, then the other, then straight back. "This is the hard part," she said. She'd always worn it tucked up under her hat. It wasn't long enough to braid. She brushed it all straight back and held it behind her head. That seemed to fit, so she rummaged through the top drawer of her dresser until she found a single bright blue leather thong.

She brushed her hair back and tied it with the thong so that it hung loosely behind her neck. "That's it," she said and smiled.

She grabbed a long blue riding cloak to stem the chill of the morning mist. It was full length and would fall over Mahala in such a way as to capture his heat and keep her warm.

As she headed for the door, she saw her sword lying on the entrance table by the door. She paused and picked it up. *No*, she thought. *Today is to be a day of peace.* There would be no need for any sword.

By the time she reached the courtyard, the darkness had given way to the slow gray light of morning and the mist had risen slightly so that she could see almost to the other side. Many people, horses, and carts filled the courtyard. Fada sat on his horse in the middle of it all, calling out orders that sent men and women scurrying in all directions at his bidding. She headed straight for him, working her way through the busy-ness to reach him.

She caught his eye as she approached and he stared at her for an instant. "Vrengnia! The hat—"

"It's gone, Fada," she said as she smiled. "Forever. What else needs to be done?" It was then that she noticed Fada's attire.

He was dressed for battle. Under his cloak, he wore chain mail and his new sword hung at his side in a new scabbard. She couldn't see it very well because of the cloak. He wore his fighting boots, plated with bits of steel to protect against errant swordplay. The riding pack on the back of the horse looked as if it held his war helmet.

"Fada, I was thinking that this meeting today was to be one of peace. Surely you won't need your sword and armor!"

Fada frowned. "I can take no chances. We'll leave our weapons at the trailhead onto Haniah's land, as agreed."

"We?" The princess looked around and realized for the first time how many soldiers were in the courtyard. "Fada, you may only take seven others," she said.

"Onto Haniah's land, you said. The others will wait outside." A faint gloating smile curled around the corners of his mouth.

An indignant anger rose inside her. She turned away, intending to find Mahala. Could Fada really be so small-minded? He was up to something of his own design. A sad disappointment that he wouldn't let this happen the way it was meant to happen, crept over her vorn. He always had to keep his control and have his way in everything. What was it? Something was wrong, but she couldn't put a name to the wrongness of it. Until she could name it, she didn't feel adequate to confront Fada.

The old groom with whom she had spoken in the stables, held Mahala's reins. He looked at her directly as she approached and she felt him saying something. "What is it?" she asked. "Speak freely.

"It's fear," he said as he turned to settle the restless gelding. "Your father is afraid, with good reason. But it's not Verclan he fears."

She was puzzled. "What do you mean?"

"Your father is afraid, but not of Verclan. The fear he feels, he can't name; so he won't admit it to himself."

"I...I think I felt the same thing just now, as I left him" she responded.

"Yes, you did. I saw it in your eyes as you approached. Good and fair Princess, don't give way to fear, even if you can't name it."

"I know that, but how?"

"Fear is a strange enemy. We allow her in, and she feeds on herself, becoming larger, and more looming than she could possibly be. She weakens your sense of purpose, cuts off the El in you, and begins the slow task of eradicating your nephus. Sessasha once said, 'She robs you of yourself, then turns what's left into everything you hate.' You mustn't let fear get a foothold in your life."

It made too much sense to be wrong, but she felt confused by the knowing. The old man gently brushed Mahala's coat as he talked. "You must trust in what you know is right; trust in the El and act on it. To do otherwise is to give in to fear."

She stared at him. "I'll have to think about that—are you coming with us today?"

"No, good Princess, I will need to stay at the castle." He looked at her steadily for a moment. She thought he wanted to say more.

"Up you go," he said cheerfully. "It's a bit of a ride, I would say. We packed some food in the saddle bags in case you get hungry before you get there. Farewell, my good friend."

"Farewell, and thank you. You've been kind and helpful. I'll see you this evening when we return." The princess sat in the saddle looking down at the old man. There was something special about him. She suddenly realized what it was. *He* had no fear.

She shook the reins and urged Mahala forward. The old man didn't move, but raised one hand as the gelding carried her forward and out of his sight in the shuffling mass of the crowded courtyard.

From atop Mahala in the growing light, she could see more of the activity clearly. There was at least a dozen carts, filled with many things: tents, blankets, food baskets, tools and other miscellaneous provisions for an overnight journey. If there weren't seventy soldiers, there must have been fifty: all on foot, all dressed for war. She counted twelve dors. She recognized seven or eight of them, including Galar and Windarad, but couldn't recall all their names. Several of them she'd never seen before.

The advisors sat on horseback, near the king, and as she approached, wending her way through the crowd, she could see that they weren't happy. A clump of scouts huddled near the gate, dressed in black, talking to each other.

It was a grand scene in some respects, but out of proportion for her expectations of a short day-trip to Haniah's farm. This was going to be a parade. It embarrassed her.

As she approached Fada again, he stood up in his stirrups and raised a horn to his lips. The sound burst forth, clear and startling in the mist and rattled off the walls of the castle. The crowd hushed as he shouted:

"Today, we travel to Mordan and south, to meet Verclan and the mountain people, to seek resolution. May Mah'Eladra be with us. May we return in victory!"

The crowd cheered, and those between the king and the gate fell back to leave a path for his entourage. Dors Galar, Windarad, Luracon and Mondarta led the procession, followed by Fada and her, beside one another on their horses. The advisors fell in behind, with the rest of the dors following them. Foot soldiers filed forward rapidly to either side, forming a wall to the left and to the right of the party. The princess looked back. The carts followed behind the dors. The scouts had vanished. It was a strange procession, and she wasn't sure whether she was being escorted or held prisoner by the rows of men surrounding her. She was the only woman.

As they marched under the portcullis, she looked over to see Vishtorath. He wasn't there. A chilling loneliness swept over her. She couldn't remember a time that he hadn't been there. Where were Paca and his father? She hadn't seen Paca since yesterday, and there was no indication that they had been invited to join in the king's entourage.

"Is everything all right?" Fada asked as they started across the drawbridge.

She looked at him. This was Fada, the King of Immerland, perhaps the person she knew best in the whole land, but his words were distant; lifeless. "I was hoping that Paca or his father would be with us, but I don't see them anywhere," she said, injecting a hint of disappointment into her last words.

Fada looked straight ahead. "I invited the smith last night. He declined to join our party, though I have a sense that he'll be there today. We've not seen so much as a hint of his son. He seems to have vanished."

Vrengnia didn't want to look at Fada anymore. On the surface, everything seemed right, as it always had in his presence, but increasingly, a reality that went much deeper than the surface filled her vorn. In that reality, something was very wrong. She didn't have enough experience to know how to define it. "Fear," was what the old groom had said. *Is it fear?* she thought.

"You really like this Paca, don't you?" Fada droned.

This Paca! The words stung her heart. *Is that the way you think of my friend? "This Paca"?* She marshalled her self-control. "He's my friend, Fada," she said at last. "I would've liked to have him with us. His father is quite remarkable, as you know. I would think that *you* would have wanted *him* here also."

"I did want him here!" Fada said. She thought she saw him looking at her out of the corner of her eye. "He refused to come with us!"

"He would've come if he sensed a genuine desire on your part, but something's wrong. Something's twisted. I don't know what, but I can tell. I can only hope that no one gets hurt."

Neither spoke. They entered the woods south of the castle in silence except for the steady tramp of the soldiers' boots, the horses' measured gait, and the creaking of the wagons trundling along behind them.

Chapter 15

Convergence

"True leadership is earned before it is assumed."

Hispattea,
The Essences of Corritanean Wisdom

Patira listened to Fada as he faced the clutch of hunters and mountain warriors gathered in the clearing. Mada stood behind Fada. She had dressed for riding, with a long brown-gray mountain cape nearly down to her ankles and her hair pulled back behind her head so that it covered her ears, allowing only the small silver earrings to show, accentuating the stark simplicity of her visage. Even in the dusky light of the fog-bound morning air, she stood out in the party like a beacon of grace and beauty.

"We don't know what will happen today," Fada said. "I, my son, and six others will meet the King of Immerland today at noon. It's my hope that we may make some progress toward peace, toward some mutual agreement that will benefit us all. We must all hope this and we must set it in our hearts to do the best we can to achieve it.

"But we must also be wise. We have reports that the king is bringing at least fifty armed soldiers and that his scouts will be watching the area around Haniah's land. By agreement, there will be no weapons on her land. Outside these boundaries, there are no rules.

"We will travel as a group until we reach Morahura. There we will head north to the stream bounding Haniah's land. After the eight of us enter her field, the rest of you must retreat and remain hidden in the woods to the south. You are free then to make decisions concerning your own safety. Be careful. Be alert."

Patira could tell the men were restless. It was hard to know if it was eagerness to be off on the adventure, or uneasiness about the danger that lay before them. Each of them represented the best and most faithful of Fada's warriors and trackers. Each was a skilled woodsman and easily a match for any three of the king's soldiers, particularly in the woods. It was hard to imagine that they were afraid.

To Patira, those going to Haniah's land had the most to fear. They would be more exposed if there was any treachery by the king or his men. They would have to have the greater trust in the plan he had worked out with Vrengnia.

Fada seemed at ease as they climbed onto their horses and headed down the trail toward Morahura. He rode behind Fada and Mada followed him. Three advisors rode behind them and they were flanked by about twenty warriors and guards on foot, moving through the woods without a sound, five paces off the trail.

The woods were quiet. The thick carpet of fog rolling down from the mountains gave a sense of seclusion and safety. Any invader would be worse off in the fog than these men. They moved swiftly, talking and laughing in low voices and enjoying their camaraderie.

"Do you think it's a good plan, Fada?" Patira asked.

Fada looked back at him and smiled. "I couldn't have thought of a better one. I don't know for sure, but I believe the Eladra are watching over Haniah's land. If this is true, then we are safer there than anywhere else. I have much hope that today we'll witness the dawn of change where the mountain people must no longer feel as outlanders to Immerland's wealth and glory."

"Why do you suppose the king is bringing soldiers?" Paca asked.

"I don't know. That troubles me more than anything. I have to trust that he's just fearful. His fear of me has always been somewhat irrational."

They rode together for a while, each engaged in private thoughts. Patira knew Fada had brought his sword and he had brought his own. He was hoping he would never have to use it. It still had the strange hilt guard that the smith had made. "Did you bring that thing the smith made for you? The...the..."

"The sataliin?"

"Yes, that's it. The sataliin. Did you bring it?"

Fada was grave. "I did. I thought that if the smith made it, it must have a purpose. My greatest fear is that today will be the time I need it. But it doesn't make sense."

"What doesn't make sense?"

"Today should be a time for reconciliation and everything points that way: the way you and the princess worked out the details, your friendship with her, that we are meeting at Haniah's place, that the king agreed to meet on the terms specified. All of it's positive, what I have hoped for over many years. And then the smith sends me this sataliin. And your hilt guard, the curious way it attached itself to your sword—"

Patira watched Fada as he spoke. There was a faraway tone in his voice, as if he were seeing a future on the horizon that Patira himself couldn't see: a sort of inevitability to which their horses carried them. There was no apprehension, only the nagging curiosity about the pieces the smith had given them. They were pieces that didn't seem to fit, but somehow he knew they did.

"Fada," said Patira, "do you suppose the smith knows the details of what will happen at Haniah's today?"

"No, he doesn't."

"How are you so sure? I mean, some of the things he has done are so specific—he must know something we don't."

Fada turned and looked into Patira's eyes. "The smith listens to the Eladra and the El within him, and he does what they ask him to do. *They* know what will happen. It's likely that the smith has done many things by their instruction, but even *he* doesn't know exactly why."

"The smith has seen the Eladra?" Patira had never heard of anyone who had actually met an Eladrim being. He knew little of them. They were a vague legend to him: stories, told as history, but lacking an anchor in reality, as they were to most people of his acquaintance.

"I don't know the details. He arrived in Immerland when he was about twenty. No one knew him and we never knew where he came from. He taught us things that we'd never seen on the forge—things from somewhere else, but he never talked about it.

"He told me once that he had learned bladesmithing from the Eladra. I laughed. He didn't. I don't think I offended him exactly—he never took offense at other people's ignorance—but it was clear from his reaction—that look in his eyes, that he was sincere in what he had said." Fada paused and was silent for a time.

Patira let his mind slip into his imagination on what the Eladra would be like. The legends were legion. Many of them had been read to him as a child. They were written and told in such a way as to never deny their truth, but never to affirm it either. It was as if it was understood that each person was honored with the right to believe or doubt; that one's belief or disbelief would be confirmed and that any position on the issue was accepted without contention. He found it curious that he didn't know exactly what Fada, who had read the stories to him, believed. Even this last statement about the smith carried no judgment whatsoever about the validity of the smith's claim.

Fada's voice broke into his thoughts. "I saw one of the Eladra once. The smith often worked late on the forge, doing his own work after the stable work was complete. I had left one evening and he was still working. There was some piece of bladework he was doing. I don't remember what it was. I had eaten my dinner with the grooms and stable hands when I remembered something I had left at the smithy. As I approached, I heard the smith singing in the Kor-Alura. It was beautiful, but I couldn't understand a word of it.

"I didn't want to interrupt so I crept up to see what he was doing. As I looked in through one of the windows, I could see the smith at the forge. He held a long blade in his hand, examining it carefully. On the other side of the forge was another man, well, a being, tall like the smith, but almost an apparition. He, or she, I wasn't sure, was also examining the blade and speaking to the smith in the same original language.

"The smith would listen and then go back to the forge and anvil, and do something else to the blade while he sang. The other looked on. They were like teacher and student. I watched for about fifteen minutes, but needing whatever it was I had come for, I finally went to the door and knocked. As I entered at the bidding of the smith, the teacher had vanished completely. I never asked the smith about it. The smith never offered."

Fada stopped again. The fog had lifted and the warriors had become silent as they trotted along beside the horses. There was no sound except for the gentle rhythm of the horses' feet on the trail, the dripping of dew off the trees and an occasional bird. In the far distance, they could hear the faint roar of the Morahura.

Patira had always loved Morahura. The giant cascade plunged close to a hundred and fifty paces straight off the edge of a vast rock outcropping on the side of the mountain. At the top it was a sheet of glassy water that fell off the edge of the world. At the bottom, it was a thunderous chaos of foam and spray as it carved its way into the rock. Thousands of years of such pounding had chiseled a bowl at the base of the mountain. No one knew how deep it was. No one wanted to try to find out, but it was easy to sit for hours and marvel at its power and majesty.

Out of the bowl at the bottom of the falls, the water dashed north, bringing its life-giving flow to the plains of Immerland as the river Rindara, where it nourished the land in its path. To the people of Immerland it was much needed water. To the mountain people, it was a symbol of power and life.

The falls could be seen top to bottom from the fields of Immerland, but few of the Immerlanders made the effort to go there. Morahura belonged to the mountain people. It was their pride and their identity.

Today the small band heading to Haniah's hut for the meeting with the king would stop and rest at Morahura. Patira was eager to be there. Fada had led them on the high trail to the falls, avoiding the lower road. The high trail would be much safer for the mountain men. It was narrow and winding, switching back and forth along the side of the mountain as it approached the falls. With every step, the roar grew louder until one could hear nothing else.

As they approached the opening from the trail onto the huge rock plateau at the base of Morahura, Fada stopped his horse and listened. With a swift motion of his hand across his chest the warriors vanished into the woods. Patira knew how it happened, but he was always amazed at how they were gone. All who were left on the trail were he, Fada, Mada and the three advisors, all on horseback. Then, as though nothing at all had happened, they started on their way again, allowing the horses to amble along.

Coming out onto the stone plateau always took Patira's breath away. It was a single piece of rock, a hundred paces across in both directions, and wet with the fine mist of the falls. A column of white water, ten paces wide, fell from above straight down into the bowl carved in the black rock. It boiled like a cauldron before spilling over through a shallow gorge in the northern edge of the plateau.

The riders dismounted and led their horses to the edge of the cauldron to drink. Hand signals were the means of communication; one's voice would be useless.

They stared at the falls, everyone had a drink, and they smiled at each other, slapped each other on the back, and laughed unheard in the din of the falls. Patira saw Fada raise his hand and twist it slightly. In unison, they all turned in behind him as he led the way across the plateau to the gorge.

They were approaching from the west. On that side of the gorge a staircase, cut from living rock, led down the face of the plateau to where the river started on its way north to Immerland. At the base of the stairs, sheltered somewhat from the direct fury of the cataract behind them, they stopped again and waited. They could talk here, but barely.

"What was it back there, Fada?" Patira shouted.

Fada held a finger to his lips then pointed to the trail coming out of the woods along the river. Three hunters were struggling along the path, carrying something among them that looked as though it didn't want to be carried. It wasn't a difficult guess as to what it was.

"Scouts" shouted Fada, smiling at Patira. He pointed again, this time to the right at the base of the cliff. Four other warriors were dragging another figure, clothed in black, by the arms. By the time all the warriors had returned, there were four scouts in all, and none of them was happy about his plight. Patira knew them all by sight. They had been captured before, but let go by Fada's order.

As the scouts stood before them surrounded by woodland warriors, Patira hid his smile, but it *was* a laughable sight. Fada eyed each scout, and with a simple hand sign, had them bound hand and foot by the warriors, who took great delight in the task.

Fada remained stern. He delivered two more signs to the entourage and they all started down the trail away from the falls, each scout walking between two warriors along the broad trail. The horsemen walked this time.

Patira loved Fada, but times like these made him admire him profoundly. There was such loyalty from his men, such command in a simple hand movement; so much authority based in his knowledge of the woods, of horses and men. Patira wondered if he could ever be like that.

As they traveled, each man remained fully focused on the woods around him, scanning and rescanning the details for the slightest disturbance. Half way from the falls to the border of Immerland, the trail cut through a small meadow that was waist deep in brilliant wildflowers.

In the center of the forty pace diameter clearing stood the Ebondar. The Ebondar was a huge stone, perhaps two paces in diameter at its irregular base and seven paces tall. Its presence dominated the meadow, giving it a solemn reverence.

Fada halted the group and circled it around him to one side of the stone. The scouts were shoved into the middle with him, and he stood facing them. He stared at them for a moment, as if he were trying to chart the best course of action.

"Do any of you know what this is?" he asked pointing to the huge stone. The scouts looked down at their feet. "Answer me," he commanded. "Do you?"

The small men shook their heads. Patira loved to hear the story of the Ebondar. He hoped Fada would tell it again.

"Then look at me and I will tell you, so you may never forget. Look at me!" The scouts looked up.

"Fifteen years ago, less than a hundred paces from this place, the mountain clans fought their first unified battle against King Sandihar's army. It wasn't pretty. Fourteen mountain men were killed by Sandihar's arrows. Eighteen more were wounded. My three advisors, whom you see behind you, were there.

"After we drove Sandihar's soldiers from the woods, back into Immerland, we buried the dead, bandaged the wounded, and grieved on this spot. You are standing on the graves of men who were killed confining the greed of your king." The scouts looked down at their feet, but said nothing.

"Look at me! It took us a day to finish the task and at the end of the day, those who were left dragged this stone to the middle of the clearing. Our plan was to erect it the next morning. We slept in the woods so that we wouldn't dishonor the noble deaths of our brothers. When we woke in the morning, the stone was standing, as it still is today and each of the new graves were overgrown with wildflowers, the ancestors of those you see here today. No one in our party knew how the stone was raised.

Out of honor for those beneath us, speculation about what happened is forbidden as is the picking of flowers growing here. Each mountain man who sees the stone ponders what he will, and cherishes the memory, but no one speaks of it save the facts of the story.

"The Ebondar stands as a testimony to the strength of the mountain people. Until it falls, we will resist any evil that tries to take our land."

Fada paused. No one spoke or moved. The Ebondar cast its immense shadow in all directions as the party stood; the woodsmen with their heads high and the scouts staring at the ground. Patira believed the Eladra must have raised the stone, but he had never asked or heard anyone else say it.

Fada changed the tone abruptly. "Each of you has been captured before, am I right?" The scouts nodded. "Some of you, several times, no?" Two of the scouts nodded again and shifted their weight. "Ordinarily, I would send you home in loincloths with some witty note for your king, but today is no ordinary day." He paused for effect and began pacing back and forth rubbing his chin. "No, today I meet the good king Sandihar face to face at Haniah's table for a discussion about peace between Immerland and the mountain clans." Fada turned to his advisors.

Omisar smiled, "No, good Verclan, you make no mistake." Chronista and Phartang laughed as Fada turned back to the scouts. He walked down the line looking at each one.

"But the good king sends his spies before him. Why?" At first, he seemed to be throwing out a simple rhetorical question as he paced down the row of frightened scouts. His face turned dark. "I want to know why!" The scouts looked at the ground. Patira watched as Fada turned away and, as fast as one could comprehend what was happening, he whirled, drew his sword and lunged, the tip of the sword stopping just as it grazed the throat of the first scout in the line. The little man was too scared to move. "Why?" shouted Fada. No one in the ring around the scouts was smiling any longer. Patira had never seen Fada so angry. He knew the scouts could be clever, but they weren't very brave. Verclan held the sword steady, looking straight into the scout's eyes.

"He...he is afraid, Sir."

"Afraid? Afraid of what?"

"Of you, Sir—and your men."

"How many armed soldiers accompany the king?"

"Fifty, Sir."

"Were they given orders to do anything else except wait for the king? Were they told to surround Haniah's land?

"I don't think so. I mean, I didn't hear it if they were."

Verclan lowered the sword. Relief flowed over Patira like the first rays of Asolara after a cold night.

"This is what I am going to do. I will say it once." Fada grabbed the youngest of the four scouts, and with a quick and sudden movement of his hands stripped off the little man's shirt. "You. Go intercept the king and tell him I have these other three. Any move by the soldiers other than waiting for the king, will result in their deaths before nightfall." Fada nodded, and one of the warriors stepped forward and unbound the little man.

The young scout, terrified as he was, didn't hesitate to take his leave. The warriors parted as he scampered out of the circle and disappeared quickly down the path by the river, heading toward Immerland. "Bind them." Fada's order was terse and gentle at the same time.

Two warriors tied the three scouts together with leather thongs so the possibility of escaping was eliminated, but they could still walk. With a quick movement of Fada's hand, the party started off again leaving the Ebondar behind them. This time, they separated. Several warriors followed the horsemen with the scouts, but the rest moved off in bands of three or four and disappeared into the woods.

"There are eyes that see and understand, and there are eyes that only see."

The Tessarandin, Book Six

Paca and Fada approached the trailhead into Haniah's fields when Fada broke the long silence that had prevailed since the conversation about Mankar. "Paca, we weren't invited to be here today by either Verclan or King Sandihar, so I must go ahead and speak with Haniah on several things before either of them arrives. You must wait at the trailhead until I return. Keep yourself hidden so that the king and his men won't be able to see you. Is this clear?"

"Very clear, Fada."

"What will happen today is unknown to me at this time, but I know that today's meeting will determine the course of history for Immerland and the mountain clans. We must be watchful and patient. We can't be hasty. We'll both be tested." He looked at Paca and continued, "There'll be a time to take action, and it'll be very clear. You must be prepared to act."

"How...how will I know?"

"You'll know. If there's any doubt, then don't act!" Fada's emphatic assertion of his ability to know reassured him only slightly.

When they reached the trailhead, Fada paused as he surveyed the wooded area to the left of the trail. "Don't go onto Haniah's land. Hide up in that chestnut tree. It's a curious thing about Immerland people that they never think to look up into the trees. No one will see you there, and you'll be able to see the king's approach. When you see them come over that rise in the hill, whistle."

He laid his hand on Paca's shoulder. Their eyes met. "Do not fear. Do not fear anything." He turned and headed down the path. Paca watched him until he disappeared around the stone wall on his way into the second field.

Paca breathed deeply. There were so many riddles, that he decided the only way to handle it was to take each event as it happened and supress his fear. There were plenty of reasons for fear, but Fada's words implied that there were others he wasn't even aware of.

He made his way over to the large chestnut tree that stood just to the left of the trailhead. It stood like a sentinel. It was the first tree at the edge of the woods and the expanse of Immerland fields that led up to it. As he climbed up the first branches, he pondered what Fada had said about the Immerland people. It was true. He would never have thought to look up into the tree. The thought frightened him, but it comforted him to know that, up in this tree, he would be safe.

He climbed to a spot where he could see the road as it came over the rise Fada had indicated. From there, he could also see the area immediately in front of the trailhead. A large limb afforded him a comfortable seat where he could rest against the trunk, and he sat on it, waiting.

The world he could see was still, as if everything was waiting in anticipation of the meeting at Haniah's table. An occasional insect flitted by on some busy errand, but no breath of wind stirred the leaves of the tree. No trace of the morning fog remained, and the cloudless sky extended in all directions. From his perch in the tree, Paca could see both Immerland and the mountains.

To the left was Haniah's land, quiet, serene and brilliant with Asolara's beams and the early changes of autumn color that had started settling over the mountains. To the right was Immerland, its golden fields and rolling meadows sloping gently upward with its castle far in the distance on the hill. Aside for small clusters of trees interrupting the view here and there, it was all field.

Paca watched and waited.

The first thing that interrupted the stillness was a hurried conversation coming from below and behind him. He couldn't make out the words but he caught sight of three of the king's scouts on the edge of the trees. They were in an animated conversation and seemed to be having some sort of disagreement. He wished he could get closer, but any movement could have caught their attention.

After several minutes, the group broke up. One scout headed up the trail to the east that skirted Haniah's land. The second went the opposite direction, coming almost directly under Paca's perch before moving along the stone wall that divided the Immerland field from Haniah's meadow. The third plunged into Haniah's woods and disappeared.

About two minutes had passed when there was a sudden, frightened yelp, followed by a frantic thrashing about in the woods below him. A tall warrior, dressed like the one Paca had seen in Haniah's hut, was dragging the scout through the woods by his upper arm. When they got to the edge of the woods, the warrior hurled the scout out into the field, where he tumbled like a sack of grain. The scout was up in a flash. Not wanting to see what would happen next, he started running down the road that led into the heart of Immerland.

As the warrior turned to move back into the woods he looked up, straight into Paca's eyes. Paca froze. The warrior nodded. When Paca blinked, the warrior vanished with a slight hiss.

Paca settled back against the tree to watch for the king. The presence of the scouts disturbed him, but he wasn't sure why. Perhaps the king was planning something devious under the cover of a peaceful meeting with Verclan. On the other hand, a little precaution on the part of the king could be expected, given his longstanding antipathy for the mountain leader.

Paca didn't have to wait long. Judging from Asolara's elevation, he guessed it was about an hour before noon when the first movement appeared on the road as it crested where Fada had indicated. He sat forward and with two fingers in his mouth, gave a long, shrill whistle.

He sat back to watch the little black knot of men and horses trudging down the road toward where he sat hidden. They were about fifteen hundred paces away and he couldn't make out who was in the party. The princess would be there and Paca wondered what she would be thinking. How different it must be from two days ago when they ambled together down the same road in the warm sunshine, at about the same time of the day. He thought about Meshabo, too. What had told her to come along with them and why? What had become of her? It was all very strange, but comforting compared to the approaching entourage of the king.

The group was no more than three hundred paces away when Fada appeared at the end of the stone wall. Paca caught a glimpse of him as he ducked back into the woods and vanished. All was silent again, except for the distant hoofbeats of the approaching horses. Suddenly Fada was at the base of the tree. With a single swift leap he gained the first limbs and pulled himself up beside Paca. Paca felt his hand on his shoulder and turned. Fada had his finger to his lips.

There were four dors in front on horses, followed by the king and Vrengnia, side by side. More dors followed and behind them the king's advisors along with a collection of carts pulled by donkeys. On either side was a row of battle-ready soldiers protecting the flanks of the procession.

When they were about fifty paces from the trailhead, the two leading soldiers from each flank suddenly broke rank and started running toward them. One of the dors in the front began shouting at them and two others spurred their horses into a gallop. Fada's breath whispered into his ear. "Eladra! This should be interesting."

The two soldiers stopped at the trailhead and turned to face the approaching dors. As they turned, Paca caught a clear glimpse of the one on the left. It was Vishtorath, the gatekeeper. They drew their swords and crossed them across the trail, a symbol of denial of passage to anyone approaching. A piece fell into place in Paca's puzzle. Vishtorath was an Eladrim warrior, guarding the gate for all those years; watching out for the princess. Now he was guarding the gate to Haniah's land. He wondered if perhaps he had been the watcher in the tower.

The two dors reined in tight just before the two Eladrim guardians. "What is the meaning of this, Vishtorath?"

"This is the trail to Haniah's domain. No armed man or woman shall pass. Only the king and seven others will be allowed." The words were in the original language, but Paca understood them perfectly. He was sure that the dors did also, maybe even the horses. Their faces fell and the horses started scrambling backward. The dors wheeled them around and cantered back to the king, who had halted the procession. A hurried conversation followed.

Paca had a moment to assess the group on the road. In addition to those he had seen before, there were several scouts. One of them was the one he had seen routed by the Eladrim guard an hour before. A second one had no shirt, his skin comically white where he always wore black. Paca watched the princess. She was listening to the conversation between the dors and the king. They were about thirty paces away and he could see her face clearly. He was surprised that she wasn't wearing her hat and that her clothing was simple and uncluttered. *She looks more like a princess ought*, he thought.

The king broke away from the group and approached the two guards. Vrengnia followed him, but the others remained behind. The guards still had their swords crossed and remained motionless as the king approached. At about five paces the king and princess dismounted. The guard on the right nodded to the princess.

The king stood facing Vishtorath with an odd expression on his face. "You would disobey me, Vishtorath?" he asked.

"Only when there are higher orders, Sandihar of Immerland."

The king paused. "I am the king!" he thundered.

"Only of *Immerland*." Vishtorath countered.

The king stepped back, glancing briefly at Vrengnia. "You are my gatekeeper!"

a gatekeeper. You ordered me here, O King."

"But not to bar my way!"

"I'm not barring your way, Sandihar, I am keeping the gate. I am here to see you and your elect safely onto Haniah's land according to the agreement."

The king looked down and frowned; confused. "We've come for a meeting with Verclan of the mountain tribes. We ask passage into Haniah's domain."

"You may enter here," said Vishtorath. "You must lay down all weapons before entering. They will be safe here until you return. The princess may enter also, under the same conditions, and then six others."

The king paused for a moment and looked from Vishtorath to the other guard. "It will be as you say," he remarked as he turned and walked back to the waiting dors. There was another quiet conversation, and he emerged, followed by the two dors, three advisors and an older looking scout. All of them had dismounted, leaving their horses with soldiers. They approached the path on foot.

When they arrived in front of the guards again, the king bowed, and laid his sword on the ground in front of the guard on the right and stood up. The guards uncrossed their swords and the king stepped between them. Suddenly, the guard on the left leapt forward and in one quick motion, almost too fast to see, reached his hand into the king's tunic and pulled something out. A long thin dagger flashed in Asolara's rays as it came up under the king's throat.

The terror in the king's eyes was masked by his surprise. The guard stared into his eyes, unmoving for several seconds, before he turned the blade over in his hand and with a single, swift motion, sent the dagger spinning through the air. It hit the trunk of the tree where Paca and Fada were hidden and buried itself to the hilt in the wood. He turned back to the king and shoved him onto the path.

The princess stepped forward. She hesitated as she looked directly at Vishtorath. The giant stared back, as if speaking to her without words. In the next instant she looked up into the tree and met Paca's eyes and then, as quickly as she had looked up, she looked back. It was so brief that no one else saw what happened. The king was still nursing his wounded pride and the dors behind the princess were busy removing their weapons. A smile lingered on her face as Vishtorath and his companion nodded. She stepped between them untouched.

Paca exhaled as Fada laid his hand on his shoulder. Paca took comfort in the strength of Fada's hand and the knowledge that Vrengnia knew he was there.

The dors laid down their swords as well as the small knives they often carried in their boots, and stepped between the watchful eyes of the guards. The advisors and the old scout passed though without even a glance from the guards. The king was silent. No one spoke to him. No one needed to. Paca watched him as he turned and headed down the trail with the others following. Vrengnia was behind him and she seemed unusually tall compared to her father for that brief time before they disappeared out of sight around the stone wall.

Paca looked back to the others whom the king had brought along. They were milling about. One of the other dors had assumed command and had ordered them to do something. They seemed to be just making themselves comfortable for a long wait.

Fada leaned over and whispered again. "We must wait a little while longer, then we'll go."

Go where? Paca wondered. Were they just going to clamber down out of the tree? If not, how would they sneak down? They were so close to the guards. ..so they waited. The guards never moved. The soldiers, dors, scouts, and cart handlers, milled about, chatting and laughing, and lying about in the warmth of Asolara. It was as if they had come all this way for something, but now they weren't allowed to do it, so they were trying to do nothing. Paca was uneasy. He wanted to know what was going on in the field in front of Haniah's hut. For now, he just had to wait.

They didn't have to wait long. Fada touched his shoulder and whispered, "Follow me." They began climbing down the tree. It was only two or three branches before they dropped to the ground five paces from the guards. They didn't even flinch. Paca saw one of the scouts pointing excitedly and two dors stood up, drawing their swords. Fada headed straight for the guards, and Paca followed as the dors ran to meet them, yelling. As Fada stepped between the guards, they bowed to him and gestured to him to pass through. Paca followed. Vishtorath looked him in the eye, but didn't move to stop him.

He had only taken a couple steps past the guards when he heard the brilliant clash of two swords just behind him. He turned to look. One of the dors was running back to the shelter of the group sprawled on the grass. The other stood holding one hand in the other, his face contorted with pain and his sword lying on the grass in front of him. The Eladrim guards stood motionless, their swords crossed across the front of the path.

Paca turned back to follow Fada who was now ten steps ahead. It looked like he had never even looked back. There were so many questions spinning in Paca's head: How did Fada know when to leave the tree? Why had the Eladrim guards bowed to Fada? Why had they let *him* pass? It took a few running steps to catch up. They walked together down the path without speaking.

"Submission to the larger forces that define our path, is born in strength, and breeds a strength that is greater still."

Pratoraman,
The Middle Way

Vrengnia struggled with her terror about Fada's motives. The dagger that he had hidden in his tunic was the most disturbing. Perhaps "why" was the wrong question, because it was clear enough that Fada hated Verclan and intended to harm him if he had the opportunity.

The discovery that Vishtorath and the other lead soldier in his caravan were actually not under his command had shaken Fada. In spite of all this, he had still tried to get past them with the dagger. How did they know he had it? She had never seen anything as quick or as powerful as the way it had been taken from him and thrown into the tree.

In their hurried conversation with Fada, the dors had said these guardians were Eladra, but it was in that one moment, as she looked into Vishtorath's eyes before she stepped between him and the other guard, that she really understood who he was—who he had been—all these years. This Eladrim being, the gatekeeper, with his ever-watchful eye, had been guarding the castle gate. He had been guarding her. Now he stood guarding the gateway to Haniah's land, as solemnly as he had guarded the castle. What was he looking for? What was he really guarding? Perhaps the answer lay in Haniah's field.

She wasn't sure why she looked up. It was just one of those things that occurs so unexpectedly that it was over before she knew it was happening. Paca and his father were in plain sight, sitting in the tree and watching the entire strange affair. It was comforting to know they were there—she wanted them to be there—but why were they in the tree? How had they remained unseen by everyone else, especially the Eladrim guards?

All these events led her to a single undeniable conclusion: something much bigger than the conflict between Fada and Verclan was at work here. In the midst of it all, what amazed her most was the impervious mind of Fada: blind to everything except his vendetta.

She walked behind him. He hadn't spoken since they had passed the guards. Whatever he was thinking, it wasn't promising that she would find out. He led the tiny procession down the path, walking upright and dignified as a king ought, but she couldn't help be a little amused at how, having been stripped of everything he had brought along for protection and control, he was now just another man, walking a quiet path with seven others: almost naked, exposed, humiliated perhaps, and forced to face his sworn enemy and himself for the first time in twenty years.

The trees, the grass and the warm soil exuded a thick, rich smell that rolled up from beneath them as the noonday rays of Asolara bathed the landscape. Its warmth permeated her shoulders and hair, its certainty comforting her with an enduring faithfulness in times when everything else seemed so uncertain.

It wasn't until they were entering into the last stand of trees that Fada spoke. "Why do you suppose the smith selected this Haniah as the mediator?" he asked over his shoulder.

Vrengnia winced. "Have you never met her?"

"I've never had the occasion to do so," he said.

"Well, I'm not sure exactly why the smith selected Haniah. I might guess that it's because she owns the land and is somewhat neutral."

"But why *this* land? It seems a bit remote."

"Remote? Father, it's on the border of your kingdom—less than a day's march from the castle. You can't seriously consider it remote." It suddenly occurred to her how provincial Fada really was. He had never been very adventurous. Perhaps anything outside of his immediate control would be considered "remote." Here, he wasn't the ruler, and the seven others that accompanied him offered little protection. He was out of his element. He needed reassurance, so she tried to offer it. "It's beautiful here, Fada, and Haniah's land seems to be well protected."

"What do you mean?" he snarled.

"Well, if there are guards like the ones we met, protecting this property—and from what Rapahoogin said, it seems that there are—then we really have nothing to fear."

"I guess." His voice was sullen.

"I think you will like Haniah."

Fada turned. "Why?" He stared into her eyes.

A certain rage rose in her throat. She wanted to say "Fada, grow up!" but hesitated. A counter-rage rose also, a queen-like instinct—coming from where? She looked into Fada's angry eyes. "There are times, Fada, when even the king must accept his place in the greater order of things. This is one of those times."

Fada stared at her but said nothing.

There was more to be said. "Haniah is a woman worthy of your respect. She listens well and doesn't use words lightly. She is generous and thoughtful—and she is knowledgeable in many things. She has done you no harm and, by being the mediator today, she is doing the kindest thing she can do for her king: helping you to face your enemy in a place that is safe, without the need to fear. You mustn't bring your fear to the table."

Fada looked down at the path. Vrengnia held her ground. What she said had struck deep and she watched his struggle without moving. He needed to face it himself. He looked up and there was a small tear in one eye. "You're right. Let's get on with it." He turned and started out of the trees into the brilliant light of Haniah's field. Vrengnia exhaled. A newfound strength welled up within her. She wondered at it, but decided to accept its almost imperceptible tide. She fell in step behind Fada as the others, quiet and reserved, followed without hesitation.

Chapter 16

Haniahs's table

"Come, eat. When the food is gone we will concern ourselves with life again."

Mirradach,
The Tiger in the Tree

The approach to Haniah's table lay through one remaining row of trees at the edge of her field. Verclan wanted to be there, but he was finding it difficult to imagine facing the king in person after so many years. Twenty years it was. Twenty years of exile for something he had never felt was his fault.

If banishment from Immerland weren't enough, he had also felt the continual antipathy of Sandihar through the endless stream of scouts who had invaded the mountains over the years, and through the armed confrontations with Immerland soldiers. It was true that some of these had been in response to food raids he had orchestrated on Immerland fields, but he knew that there was more behind the attacks than that. Now, he was going to face Sandihar at a dinner table. Each would be without means of harming the other, and if his suspicions were true, they would be protected further by the Eladra.

The two guards by the stream where they had entered Haniah's property must have been Eladrim warriors. They had spoken to him in the original language when he approached them. During the half-hour they had to wait until these guards let them pass, he had observed them carefully. They stood still as statues, with their swords crossed in front of them as if they were guarding the gate of the infinite itself, and they were dressed in ancient warriors armor.

Verclan had little personal knowledge of the Eladra. As most people of his time, he only knew the legends, and since they were just legends, he couldn't know what truth lay behind them. From what he did know, why would they be here *now*? In the legends, they showed up at significant times and places, usually when there was a great confluence of forces that punctuated a change in the course of Tessalindrian history. Perhaps it was just that such events were talked about and passed on, but still, in all his lifetime, except for the one occasion with the smith, he had never been aware of encountering an Eladrim being.

There was no turning back now. The small party behind him had passed through the last line of trees and had started up the gradual rise across the field. He could see Haniah's hut and now the table in front of it. He and his family had often come here to visit Haniah and to get advice and medicinal remedies of various sorts for the mountain people. Sometimes they stayed and had a meal with Haniah. Her hospitality was contagious and hard to refuse. He knew today would be the same and yet it would have to be different.

"No one else is here," remarked Mordara. The words startled him. She was walking beside him, but he had been lost in his own thoughts.

"It curious, isn't it?" Verclan's trained eye would have noticed any motion. In front of the hut, an old donkey grazed on the tufts of green grass interspersed between the sunburned late summer grass.

"There—on the other side of the field," said Patira, "just coming out of the trees."

Verclan's eyes followed Patira's finger. He could tell that they had also noticed him and his men. "I think that Sandihar is leading. That's the way he walks," he said.

"Are you ready for this?" Mordara squeezed his hand.

"I'm not sure there is any way to be ready, but I think I am."

She smiled. "You've faced tougher men."

It wouldn't be long before they would meet. What should he say? What should he do? They had been friends at one time, close friends, at least as close as a king and his best farrier could be, but Verclan felt the tug of a deeper kinship than even that would explain.

There was so much to like about the king, and yet he had been forced all these years to regard him with a certain dislike. What was it? He also had many reasons to hate this man: his exile, the accusations of his killing Viarda, the distrust and attacks through the years, the hard life in the mountains, the near starvation every winter...

Yet he had received blessings that the king had never known: standing at the foot of Moruhura or watching the stars from the top of Mount Eliia in the Crown of Tessalindria...sitting around a fire with the mountain princes and hearing their songs and stories...tasting wild boar roasted on an open fire, served with the mangar roots, salt brush and mountain mead...and hearing the cacophonous migration of the orwilla in the spring.

Verclan probed feelings that he had hidden for years as he watched his...his...there was no word, no thought, no right impression that correctly categorized his relationship with the king. Soon they would meet, as men. Perhaps it wasn't necessary to name the relationship accurately. There was a task to be done, a discussion to be had, and a negotiation to be hammered out, perhaps like a horseshoe or a new wheel for a cart; a simple emotionless task finished by facts and reason. But perhaps it was a tortuous and slippery trail, full of emotion, missteps and pain. How could he tell? Mordara squeezed his hand again.

Both parties were twenty paces from the table when Haniah burst from her hut. Verclan was instantly distracted from the king by the explosion of energy. She ran to the table, grabbed something from it, and ran headlong toward Verclan. Without a word, she threw her arms around his neck and hugged him. Her weight nearly threw him off balance. She stepped back and slipped a wildflower garland around his neck and then just as quickly, turned and bolted toward the king, repeating the same ritual.

Verclan wasn't sure if this was some quirky strategy to break down the barriers, but it didn't matter. Haniah's energy, as she raced back to the table, drew the two parties toward one another like magnets. She stood at the table, beckoning both groups together.

Haniah grabbed his hand and the king's hand and put them together, holding both of their large hands cupped between her own. "To the good Immerland King," she looked the king in the eye, "and the fair Mountain Prince." Her eyes penetrated deep into his vorn. "Welcome to my table. May you sit in peace. May you eat in peace. May you leave in peace."

Verclan locked eyes with the king. "Greetings, good King Sandihar of Immerland."

The king stared back. "Greetings, fair Prince Verclan of the mountains," he droned.

Haniah stepped between them and started seating the guests. Verclan counted the seats. She had set the table for nineteen: nine on each side and one at the end. "Master Verclan, shall sit in the middle on this side," she said, pointing to a specific chair, "and King Sandihar, there." The king was directly opposite him. "The fair Mordara, beside the king, on his left, Master Chronista on the other side—Master Carnados, right here." She had her hands on the back of the chair to Verclan's right, "and Master Cordas, here." She stepped behind him, lightly touching the chair to his left. So it continued, until each person was seated beside two others who were sworn enemies. Haniah knew every name, even those whom Verclan was certain she had never met.

Verclan's single warrior and the king's dors were at the far end with a single, empty seat on each side at the end. When everyone was properly seated, she took her seat at the head of the table with Princess Vrengnia on her right and Patira on her left.

No one spoke, but Haniah made no effort to break the pall that settled over the table. Verclan looked at the king. Sandihar stared back. His eyes revealed how uncomfortable he was. It made Verclan want to laugh. He decided it would be inappropriate, but that decision was useless. It came up slowly, from somewhere down inside, like a volcano, as the absurdity of the situation overwhelmed him from the inside out. The smile emerged first, wriggling up the corners of his mouth until everything collapsed and the laughter burst forth like water from a breached dam.

The king turned red as others began to snicker, cough and choke on their own laughter. They were all looking at their plates. The scene went from absurd to idiotic in seconds as everyone at the table gave up and joined in with him. Finally, the king himself, unable to contain it any longer, smiled, then laughed heartily.

Haniah stood up. "Drinks," she called above the din. Two young men and two young women came out of the hut with pitchers. "The finest wine for the mountain men—aged mountain cider for the Immerlanders—for the bold of heart, there is maclin." The conversation broke down into small chattering clusters as the flagons were filled, and they began to realize that those sitting to either side of them were just like them: insecure, prideful, resentful, but none with any reason behind the feelings save the feud between the kingdoms.

Somewhere in the midst of all this, Verclan saw the smith and his son arrive, without fanfare or introductions, almost as if none were needed. They strode across the field and without hesitation seated themselves at the end of the table in the two empty seats. Verclan was relieved that they were there. He could only guess what the king was thinking.

Verclan had once heard a wise man say that a party would last only as long as the food. If this were true, they were in for a long one. He wondered where Haniah had obtained the quantities and quality of food that poured out of the hut. There was every imaginable preparation of vegetables and herbed salads, subtle combinations of fruits and seeds, bowls of grain, flavored with ginger and thyme, and delicate meats, for those who chose them...prepared where? Haniah had a simple wood stove and very few of the utensils that would be necessary for such a preparation. Mountain men tasted the finest cuisine of the kingdom, while their neighbors tried the heartiest of mountain stew and bread.

Verclan, between mouthfuls of food and words with Carnados and Cordas, observed the servers. They were tall, thin and quiet. They did their job with peculiar efficiency without calling attention to themselves. Where had Haniah found them? How did she get them to come *here*?

He noticed that Patira and the princess were engaged in an animated discussion with Haniah most of the time. They looked comfortable with each other. His advisors were relaxed, and he took note that his warrior made it a point to try everything on the table and made continual efforts to convince the king's dors to do the same.

The only one who looked uncomfortable was the king's scout. He guessed that if a man's business was snooping around, looking for ways to get others in trouble, it must be miserable when those around him are enjoying themselves. The little man was seated between Patira and Omisar, dwarfed by their presence, and he fiddled with his food, glancing furtively around the table.

The king was affable, but preoccupied. Verclan felt it here and there in the words he chose and an occasional odd emphasis in his phrases, but it wasn't strong enough to be called resentful.

As dinner slowed, the servers cleared the table for dessert. When the servers arrived with dessert, it was altogether different than he expected. Pies! He had never seen pies served for dessert, and apparently, neither had the king or his party. They all glanced at each other and raised their eyebrows. Verclan looked at Haniah, and she smiled a knowing smile. The servers then cut the pies into pieces. To everyone's surprise, the pies had some sort of fruit in them! How strange. He had seen meat, egg and vegetable pies, but no one in their right mind would make a pie with fruit. The servers put the pie onto plates and distributed them around the table, a plate in front of each person.

Haniah was amused. He looked at her. "What is it?"

Haniah laughed. "You all must try it. It may seem quite different, but I can assure you, it's rather good." She put her fork into it. As she lifted a bite to her mouth, her face lit into a smile of mock ecstasy as she tasted the dessert in front of eighteen pairs of curious eyes. "Ummmmmm," she intoned, closing her eyes to enjoy the first taste.

Everyone sat and stared. Verclan laughed again. With deliberate, exaggerated motion, he mimicked Haniah's tasting exhibition. The warm, spiced and sweetened fruit was a totally new and otherworldly taste that was hard to describe, but pleasurable. He leaned back. "Ummmmmm." He looked up. Everyone was staring. "Ho!" he laughed, "this is incredible," and he plunged his fork into the pie. "Everyone, you must try it!"

His warrior was next, followed by the king's dors, then the king himself. Everyone crowed with delight and marveled at the new idea of a *fruit* pie. The conversation resumed as they all finished their unusual dessert.

Haniah rose. "And now good folks, we've come to the purpose of the meeting here." The servers whisked away the tableware and vanished into the hut while Haniah outlined the plan for the discussion between him and Sandihar.

"Fear cannot penetrate the armor of perfect love."

The Tessarandin, Book 6

A sparkle lit Verclan's eyes and resentment flared in Fada's as Haniah outlined the plan. The two leaders were to remain where they were and each was to select a single advisor to remain beside him. "The smith and I shall remain here to moderate the discussion. Everyone else must leave the table. You may go anywhere you'd like, but you mustn't leave my property. I will blow a horn when we are ready to have you back."

Several men stood up, stretched, stared at one another, and tried to think of something to do. An uneasy silence settled over the group. They slowly gravitated into groups of two or three and wandered off.

Vrengnia looked across and down the table at Fada. His eyes were empty and cold as he looked off into nothingness. She got up and came around the table, approached him from behind and gave him a hug around the neck. She thought he might need it. He tensed and shrugged her away. It didn't leave her with a good feeling about what was about to happen. Fear rose up in her belly, curling its way up into her chest.

On the other side of the table, Patira and Paca had paired up and headed south toward the stream. As she started around the table to head after them, she noticed Mordara sitting beside her husband, watching her. Mordara rose slowly and moved to intercept her. She glanced toward Paca and Patira, now twenty paces away and engaged in an intense conversation, then looked back to Mordara.

The beautiful Mordara, riding instructor to her mother and wife of the man Fada had accused of murdering her mother, made her way around the end of the table. She moved with grace and purpose, never breaking eye contact until she stood directly in front of Vrengnia, where she dropped her eyes. With a brief bow, she spoke: "Fair Princess. May we speak?" It was said in a way that allowed no room for refusal and no time for hesitation.

"We may. Shall we walk?"

"Perhaps the herb garden would interest you?" Mordara's gentle statement folded into a question.

"Indeed." As Vrengnia turned toward the hut and the garden behind it, she glanced over her shoulder. Fada had chosen Dor Galar who was sitting beside him, but his eyes followed *her*. He gave her a questioning, angry look that implied that she was betraying him. She shrugged and turned away.

She was also angry. It coiled up inside her like a snake and churned all through her. She wasn't sure what it was, or why it had to be this way, or why her father couldn't see the opportunity before him.

"Are you okay?" Mordara's firm, confident voice broke the grip he had upon her.

"Yes—well, no, but thank you for asking."

Mordara raised her eyebrows.

"No, I'm really fine. It just my father—he—my father just doesn't get it." Her own voice surprised her with its vehemence.

"Get what?"

"It! The opportunity he has to get something straightened out. He...he treats all this as...as a threat. I mean, what is he afraid of, really?"

Mordara remained silent. Vrengnia decided she had said enough. She had to trust that the smith knew what was going on. Of all the people in Tessalindria, Haniah and the smith would be her first choices to resolve this conflict, and both of them were there. She had to trust; had to wait. She turned to look back. Haniah was standing. Her father leaned over the table, gesticulating at Verclan. It didn't look good.

"I have wanted to meet you for a long time," said Mordara.

Vrengnia was thankful for the distraction. "I have wanted to meet you also, though I have only known about you for a short while."

"When Patira came home and told me that he had met you, my heart leapt for joy." Mordara's dark eyes sparkled. "I don't believe we were meant to be strangers. Now perhaps we don't have to be."

Vrengnia stared away to the mountains. "I hope so." Her mind puzzled about why this near stranger seemed to be so easy to talk to. Mordara had gained her trust with the first words that she spoke. Perhaps it was because she was a woman in the company of so many men, but that couldn't possibly explain it all. Something about her manner and her unassuming openness drew Vrengnia in.

As they came around the corner of the hut to edge of the extensive herb garden, Mordara asked, "Are you afraid, Vrengnia?"

There it was again. It seemed that all the people who knew who they were in this world were concerned about fear in other people. The smith had reminded here not to fear several times. She thought she understood it in the context of their conversations, but it was completely unexpected from Mordara. "May I ask you a question about that?"

Mordara had knelt down to smell the orange-yellow blossoms of one of the herbaceous shrubs beside the path as they entered the garden. She looked up. "About what?"

"About fear. I mean...it seems that many people recently have been concerned about whether I was...or am, afraid. I don't *want* to be afraid. I'm not sure if I am or not, but the way it's asked, it always seems to entail more than just being afraid. As if...as if there is some dimension of fear which I don't understand, that...oh, I don't know..."

Mordara was silent. She looked back at the blossoms and lowering her face into the bush, inhaled deeply, then standing, she faced Vrengnia. "Fear is a formidable enemy. Perhaps it is the greatest enemy of all, because when we fear, then the enemy is inside us. Everything else is outside, but fear eats us up on the inside and weakens us." Mordara's eyes sparkled as she spoke. "Fear destroys psadeq, with others and with Mah'Eladra."

"Why did you ask me if I was afraid just *now*?"

"There is much to be afraid of here," she said as she turned and stepped farther into the garden. "The king—your father—has much fear. It is in his eyes. It will interfere with his judgment and wisdom. If you are fearful, you face the same danger."

Vrengnia knew she was right but her rightness brought up another question: "Are *you* afraid?"

"I've chosen not to be."

"Just like that? You simply *choose*?"

"In essence, yes. One always makes a choice, but it's not simple. One has to learn how to choose and then it takes much strength."

"How did you learn?"

"From my husband; from Haniah; from the mountain people."

"And how did your husband learn?"

"The smith—when they were together in the—in your grandmother's stables."

It all came back to the smith. Vrengnia sensed that he was the focal point of all that was happening. "How would I learn?"

Mordara had knelt down beside a small clump of purple flowers growing close to the ground. "You are already learning. I can tell. Have you spoken much with the smith?"

"A couple times—"

"And Haniah?"

"Many times."

"*They* have been teaching you."

"But I don't remember them saying anything specific about fear—other than to not give in to it."

"Courage is not learned by teaching *about* fear. If you think back to conversations you have had with them, you will see common elements that, when grasped, teach us how to deal with fear."

Mordara stood up. She held a handful of the small purple flowers. "Smell this."

Vrengnia bent over and smelled the blossoms. It was a pungent, aromatic fragrance that made her nose tingle all the way back to where it met her throat. "What is it?"

"Faganwort. Its aroma heightens anyone's perceptions. The mountain warriors and trackers use it when they are on patrol to help stay focused on their surroundings."

As Vrengnia sniffed the small bouquet again, she felt the subtle effect of the smell. It engendered an awareness of detail that was stunning. She looked up at Mordara. New details of her facial features were suddenly visible: the glint of the Asolara on her hair and the fine, faint lines of her face. Vrengnia looked down. The garden sprang to life before her, and new scents and colors flooded over her as she stood still with wonder.

"Take these with you. They will help you not be afraid."

"How?"

"Awareness helps us control fear." Mordara turned away and started down another row of herbs.

Vrengnia remained where she was, clutching the small bouquet in her right hand. She thought she understood what Mordara had told her as she tried to think back over the conversations she'd had with the smith and Haniah. They flooded together, indistinct and vague. She had never thought of them as teaching. Teaching was something that was done by "teachers."

It occurred to her quite suddenly that maybe real teaching was subtler, that all her life she had been being taught indirectly by the people that surrounded her.

Perhaps the teachers in her life, having lacked focus, plan and purpose, had left her as unpurposeful and unfocused at *they* were.

Having now encountered several others who *did* have genuine depth and direction, the teaching, though still indirect, produced noticeable changes in her life. The thought was profound and new, and so different from the way she had always thought, that it was hard to place it and realize it.

She sighed heavily. Mordara turned to look at her and opened her mouth to speak. She was interrupted by the clear, resonant sound of a ram's horn, floating around the side of the hut from the direction of the meeting table. Mordara looked directly into her eyes. It was too soon. They couldn't have come to a resolution so quickly. The words sprang to Mordara's lips, "Something's wrong!"

Mordara slipped her arm around Vrengnia's waist. "We ought to get back, Princess." Vrengnia detected a slight tremor in her voice, but wasn't sure if it might be her own sudden distress. Mordara pulled her gently and they started back to the table.

As they came around the corner of Haniah's hut, Haniah, the smith, Dor Galar and the king were all standing. Verclan remained seated at the table with Chronista, his fingertips pressed together and his mind deep in thought.

"Oh, the surprise, the wonder, when one we consider to be but a beast, speaks to us with wisdom beyond our own."

Mortag of Horrinaine,
Of Beings

Patira ran in front of Paca and was almost to the table, as were several of the other men. They approached the table from Fada's end so Paca couldn't see his expression, but Haniah's face was stern and tight. Verclan was still seated. The king's eyes stormed with darkness and a deep anger loomed there. Paca didn't know the king well, but one doesn't always need to know a man to recognize the distortion of hate in his face.

They were all waiting, but for what? They could have been statues. The king's advisors were the last to arrive around the table, sweating and breathing hard and looking as if they were cramping in their stomachs.

Haniah stood up a little straighter and motioned for silence. It seemed to Paca that the whole world held its breath in anticipation for what she was about to say. "Good men and women," she began. Paca didn't know this woman very well, but the tone and intensity carried a formality that was out of character for all he knew. "The King of Immerland has challenged the mountain prince to a contest of Kli-marana Waru." The king's advisors gasped and shook their heads. "The mountain prince has accepted the challenge."

Paca looked at Fada who looked back at him. A grim darkness that Paca had never seen shadowed his face. How did this happen? He turned to Vrengnia. She looked terrified, but seemed to have no inkling of the significance of the statement.

Haniah continued. "The Immerland King has chosen his daughter, Vrengnia, as his second. The Mountain Prince has chosen his son, Patira."

The various pockets of men began to stir and look at one another. Whether they were just stunned or ignorant of what was happening, Paca couldn't tell, but no one spoke aloud.

"Stupid, foolish king!" The voice was nasal and rolling, possessing a kind of staccato tremor as it rolled over the crowd. It was the original language, but everyone around the table understood it. Paca could tell by the looks on their faces.

The king's face flashed crimson as he slammed his fist to the table. "Who said that?"

"It is I," the voice continued as the old gray donkey nosed her way into the circle of bewildered onlookers. Paca gasped. Vrengnia threw her hands to her mouth, throttling the name. "Meshabo!" she whispered. Paca looked at Fada again, and thought he saw the hint of a smile. He looked back to the king. The redness of his face had been replaced by an ashen white and his jaw hung loosely.

"What you are doing...is one of the stupider things...that I have *ever*...seen a being do," continued the donkey.

Everyone stared.

The king was being insulted. It was his responsibility to defend himself, no matter how surreal the situation. "I won't be told by a dumb animal that I am stupid!" he thundered, some color returning to face. By this time, Meshabo was standing nearly beside Verclan facing the king across the table.

"I am obviously not dumb," said Meshabo. There were snickers in the circle somewhere, but it was hard to tell where. "If you meant a 'stupid' animal...then I should ask you...a question: Who is stupider...the man who lays down a challenge...that leads to his own death...or the animal who tells him...that what he is doing is stupid?" Meshabo had to pause and breathe frequently. The nasal voice fluctuated up and down as she spoke. Between the original language and the strange intonations of Meshabo's voice, it should have been hard to understand, but it wasn't. Meshabo waited patiently for the king to respond, flicking a fly off her back with her tail, and twitching her ears slightly. She was looking straight at the king.

"How would you know the details of this situation—to pass judgment on my actions?" the king snarled.

Meshabo remained impassive and aggressive. It was hard to tell what she was thinking. All the usual body language that accompanied human discussions was foreign; there were few facial expressions. "I passed judgment on you...the day you pushed your wife...causing her death."

The king eyes flitted around the circle. Paca guessed he was assessing the damage done by that statement. No one moved. Each person was watching Meshabo. The donkey continued: "I was there...a young foal...you blamed Verclan...you have continued to do so..."

"Stop!" snarled the king.

Meshabo was undaunted. "Your self-deceit has...fed on itself for years...now it destroys you...it's arrogant...as well as stupid...Kli-marana Waru?" She spat on the ground, stamped on it with her left front hoof and turned away from the king. As she made her way out of the circle, she was just a donkey again.

It was one of those moments when history hangs in the balance, history that would be defined by the next decision, the next words proceeding from one man's mouth.

"The challenge remains!" declared the king.

A murmur rippled through the circle, Verclan shook his head and looked at the king in disbelief. Haniah sat down suddenly. It was then that the smith spoke: "The challengers will retire with their seconds to prepare for the contest. We will meet here again in one hour."

Paca noticed Mordara, standing behind her husband, with both hands resting on his shoulders. As Verclan rose, he turned to face her and she followed his eyes as their level rose above hers, until she was looking up into them. He bent forward and kissed her and she threw her arms around him putting her chin over one of his shoulders. She was looking at the sky as a single tear rolled down from the corner of her eye. Paca looked down. He knew that even in the midst of all the other people this was a private moment.

A deep anger rose inside him toward the king, whose selfish pride was the cornerstone of Mordara's sorrow and the source of such conflict and divided relationships. It rent the fabric of psadeq in so many directions all at once.

Vrengnia stood not five feet from Paca. Her eyes were full of tears and questions. It was obvious she had no idea what was about to happen. He stepped toward her and hugged her around the shoulders, leaning over to whisper in her ear. "You must not fear. Listen to the El in you." He wasn't sure why he said it. The sound of it wasn't even right. It was hollow and weak, pathetically inadequate to the situation.

She turned to look at him, wiping the tears back, with her fingers. "Thank you," she said. She broke away from him and headed off to join the entourage of her father's men heading back to where they had entered Haniah's land.

Verclan's men were filing off in the opposite direction. Paca watched, hoping to catch Patira's eye, even for a moment. They were about twenty paces away when Patira looked back. Their eyes met before he turned away. Paca kept watching, but Patira didn't look back again.

"History's threads are spun by those who value the greater needs of civilization over their own."

Mindar Colloden,
The Great Fathers

The small procession was silent as they traversed the ground back to the stream where they had left their weapons with the guards. Patira wondered what was happening. Each seemed preoccupied with his own thoughts, fears, guilt, and perhaps anger. He wondered what Mada was thinking. Surely, she hadn't prepared for what was developing around her.

When they arrived at the stream, the guards were standing under a large tree. None of the rest of the party was around, having scattered into the woods when Fada and those accompanying him had left for Haniah's field earlier. Fada whistled and two warriors leapt out of the woods. "Set the scouts free. Strip them and send them back to the castle." His words were short and without feeling. All his emotional energy was concentrated elsewhere.

"What is Kli-marana Waru? And what does it mean—that I am your second?"

Mada was helping Fada as he adjusted his war belt about his waist. "Kli-marana Waru was Mankar's cunning method of enticing his enemies to challenge his leadership. He invented it during The Grayness. His enemies were so terrified of his army and his power, that he established it as a way to engage them in one-on-one combat with him."

Patira's skin crawled across his arms and up onto his shoulders.

"It's very simple, really," Fada continued. "A man challenges another. Whoever wins the contest is heir to all the other's dominion and authority."

"What happens to the loser?"

Verclan looked him straight in the eyes and stopped adjusting his belt. "It's a fight to death." He looked away and continued his adjustments. Patira looked over Fada's shoulder at Mada. She looked back at him, her eyes full of life and determination.

"And the seconds?"

Verclan laughed. No one dared challenge Mankar alone. He established seconds to make it seem a more fair fight." His eyes glittered cruelly as he spoke. Patira had never seen this side of Fada.

"How does it work, then—these seconds?"

"You stand to the side. If I get in trouble and call for seconds, you come and join the fight."

"I fight to the death also?!"

"Yes." Fada was grim and matter of fact. "But only if you're needed."

"And I could end up fighting against *Vrengnia*?"

"If it goes that far...you could."

Patira's anger flared. "Why did you agree to this? Couldn't you have just left? The king has no authority over you."

Fada looked up into his eyes. There was a new softness. "Patira," he said, "for nearly twenty years I've been exiled from my homeland by an irrational man who has no intention of seeking peace, at any price. You saw what happened with the donkey, did you not?"

Patira nodded and looked down as Fada continued. "It's time to put an end to this tyranny. It's become clear that, even given the opportunity to change, the king won't rest until he has killed me, and he will continue to drag others into his misery until it's settled. If I kill him, then I inherit Immerland as the new king."

"You're a much better fighter than the king. He must know that. Why would he challenge you to a one-on-one contest? And choosing the princess as his second...it doesn't make sense."

Fada continued his adjustments and took his time with his answer. "The princess is well trained, but I have the same questions," he said at length. "Either the king is so consumed with fear and jealousy that he is lacking sound judgment, or there is some treachery involved. I think this is the key." His hand moved quickly and the sataliin suddenly appeared between them.

"What...how?"

"I don't know, but now isn't the time to fear."

"What if the king kills you *and* me?"

"Then the king will inherit the mountain kingdoms and they will become part of Immerland." Fada read his fear and spoke before he had time. "Isn't this what we wanted anyway, to be accepted into Immerland, to be able to trade freely, to travel freely, to share in the crops?"

Patira, though not wanting to fear, felt it inside him.

"Put on your weapons, Patira. Inevitability stalks us. We must be ready."

"But won't there be further vengeance by the king on the mountain clans and princes?"

"I don't intend to lose. But if I do—and you do—then I think that the king will be satisfied. He hates *me*, not the mountain clans, nor the princes. If he wins, a peaceful accord will follow quickly."

The picture was clearing now. Fada was willing to sacrifice himself if necessary, realizing that the king's antipathy was leveled only at him, but he wasn't willing to do it without a fight. The king's invitation for the one-on-one contest afforded Fada the arena to finish the antagonism, one way or the other.

"How is it that I have never heard of Kli-marana Waru before?"

"It was forbidden as a practice when Mankar was finally defeated. It was seen as shameless arrogance."

"So how can the king invoke it now?"

"He's the *king*. The fact that he invokes this barbaric practice is testimony to his arrogance. It was believed that Mankar's sword gave him much of his power. When his sword was stolen, he was so arrogant, that he believed he could still conquer without it. Some believe that he was finally defeated in his own contest, though no one is sure." Fada's voice trailed off. He lifted the sataliin again and examined it closely. Patira saw his eyes narrow.

"What is it, Father?"

"Get dressed. You have to be ready. There is more to this than we can see. Come, we have very little time."

Patira adjusted his belt and checked his armor as Fada explained the consequences of this contest to the mountain princes. Mada stood behind him, unmoving, looking up at the sky through the trees. The princes were angry, but understanding of the situation. They wanted to help, to be part of the fight, part of the resolution, but Fada made it clear that they were forbidden. They would have to stand and watch. They wept and hugged Verclan and Patira. Patira knew their love and respect. He wished he had their strength of character. He wasn't sure he did. Everything was uncertain, except Fada: determined, bold and unwavering, he held them all together. With great spirit and resolve, he led the small procession across the stream back toward—what?

The Eladrim guards watched keenly, but made no move to interfere.

"He who strikes by the sword, seeks his own death by the sword strike of another."

Hispattea,
The Essences of Corritanean Wisdom

A large circle, fifteen paces in diameter had been drawn in the soft soil of the field. Paca had helped Fada draw it. They had talked briefly while they worked with two hoes that Haniah had brought to create the break in the sod that formed the perimeter. Fada had explained the rules. They were simple, and it only took a few sentences. Paca perceived that he didn't want to talk very much. He was preoccupied with something other than the upcoming contest. Paca sensed that he accepted the turn of events with little fear, but there was something else.

Haniah had disappeared into her hut while they were outlining the contest field. Paca assumed she was continuing to clean up after the dinner. When they were almost finished, she came running out and ran up to Fada. After a hurried and guarded conversation, she disappeared into the hut again.

Fada strode up to him. "No matter what happens, don't interfere."

"Why sh ould I?"

Fada laid his left hand on his shoulder and spoke gently. "A trial like this isn't just a test for the contestants; it is a test for every observer as well. The penalty of interference by a non-contestant is death. There's no second chance. Now, take your place on the circle."

"I understand." Paca guessed that Fada knew something else, but it wasn't time to ask about it.

The two parties were nearly to the circle by this time. Paca made his way to the side where Asolara was at his back so he would be able to see everything more clearly. Fada stood in the middle, impassive and waiting. Two Eladrim guards, quiet and austere followed each of the small bands.

It was then that Paca first noticed the dark clouds moving in from the east. They hung low and towered in huge billows, rolling over one another as they made their way toward them. In the distance, they seemed to be moving slowly, but Paca knew they were coming fast. It would be a matter of only half an hour before they would be overhead. He looked back toward the makeshift arena before him.

The thin circle of turned soil posed a clear barrier that no one crossed as they filed quietly around its perimeter. The Eladra took stations equally spaced to the north, south, east and west around the circle. Vistorath fell in beside Paca. They stood with feet spread apart to the width of their shoulders and the tips of their swords resting on the ground between them.

Haniah had returned. She stood on the opposite side of the circle beside Mordara. Aside from Vrengnia, they were the only other women, but that wasn't the thing that caught Paca's attention. Haniah's eyes sparkled with a bright eagerness. In anyone else, he would have assumed it to be bloodlust in anticipation of the carnage that would soon happen in the circle, but with Haniah, there was something different. Perhaps she knew the outcome. Perhaps either way, there would be a settling of accounts. Paca found himself staring at her, not wanting to look away.

Fada moved, waving to the king and to Verclan, ushering them into the circle. He gestured to Vrengnia and Patira, inviting them in also. Paca glanced at Vrengnia and waited until she looked back at him. Her expression was blank. He wasn't sure whether it was terror or bewilderment. She didn't acknowledge his eyes as she looked back into the circle.

A light helmet covered the top of her head and ears from glancing blows, but a direct hit would probably be lethal. She had put on a light chain mail shirt, covering both arms and her torso almost down to her thighs, which were protected by leggings with small steel disks on the sides and front, with plated foot guards. Fine mail gauntlets covered the outside of her hands and wrists, leaving her palms free to grasp her sword, which she held in her right hand.

The sword! Paca could see every detail and it burned in his memory. The matte finish glowed in the low afternoon rays of Asolara as she stood rigidly watching her father. How did she have her sword? Paca was sure that she wouldn't have brought it herself. He guessed that her father, in his schemes against Verclan, must have brought it without her knowledge.

Her father was dressed similarly, but his armor was heavier, designed to take a more substantial impact, and he carried a small shield on his left arm. He seemed large, standing in front of her. His sword, held tightly in his right hand, gleamed.

Verclan and Patira were clad more lightly. Their armor was dark plates of steel strategically sewn onto snug leather clothing, designed for flexibility and silence. They were the color of the soil from head to foot. Their swords were shorter but had both edges sharpened. As they hung in their hands, their tips came only midway between their ankles and their knees. Each wore a leather helmet, with steel straps over the top and ears, with a fine weave of leather and steel rings hanging down behind their necks. Their feet were unprotected except for the dark leather moccasins laced up over their ankles. Their grim faces focused on the challenge ahead of them.

Without a word, Paca's father stepped back from the center of the circle until he was standing outside with the rest of the onlookers. Verclan and the king advanced until they were about three paces apart and stopped, eyeing each other. The king looked tense; Verclan was relaxed, but aware; each was ready to move—to respond to the slightest hint of an attack from the other. The clouds were moving fast now and the brilliance of the scene before him, fully illuminated by Asolara from the west and the gray boiling clouds in the east, created a surreal image he would never forget.

They circled slowly—carefully. Paca looked again at Haniah; her light hair shone and the same peculiar sparkle still read in her eyes. They were fixed on Verclan. Vrengnia was as still as a stone. She was rigid and vertical, like the statue of a queen, captured forever by a gracious sculptor. Patira stood like a cat ready to spring; his sword was ready. Everyone was silent and still, waiting...waiting.

The king lunged. His sword swept the air. Verclan dropped like a stone and the sword sang over his head. Paca was startled by the sound. A gasp followed the otherworldly whistle-singing of the blade. Vishtorath raised his sword suddenly and then stopped. Verclan had rolled to his left and was back on his feet. Paca saw the king sneer. The secret was out. The sound of the sword had had its effect, and Verclan's eyes narrowed as he stepped back.

As the king lunged again, Verclan slid to the left. The king slashed the air with the sword, three times, back and forth; it wasn't a strike at his enemy, but merely for the effect of the sound. Verclan stepped back again. He seemed to know that the danger was greater than he had anticipated.

The king thrust forward again, but where he should have struck Verclan's body, there was only air. Verclan's sword swept in, and the king barely had time to raise his shield to meet the blow. They separated and circled. The king's sword sang again. Verclan raised his weapon to challenge it and the two swords collided. There was a bright flash and a gasp from the observers as Verclan's sword was severed, a third of its length remaining with the hilt. He wasted no time and dropped the useless piece as he stood facing the king.

Paca stood horrified. The weapon he had crafted, that he had shaped and hardened, moved at the whim of a determined killer. His hands went to his face. The horror of the moment sank into his heart like a slung stone. He looked again as the king pressed his advantage with a smile full of malice.

"Ha!" the king shouted. Paca felt the impact of the evil intent like an arrow through his liver. He wanted to cover his face again but could not. Verclan backed up empty handed. *Call for seconds. Call for your seconds,* Paca's mind yelled, but the words never came. Patira waited. Paca wondered what he must be thinking, feeling.

The king lunged and swung. Verclan ducked and rolled toward the king and came up just in front of him. His hand flashed and a fist full of dirt flew in the king's face. The sword sang, but Verclan wasn't where the king thought he should be. The king couldn't see. He cursed and struck blindly. Verclan ducked and rolled away. As he stood up again to face the king, he held a strange piece in his right hand. Where had it come from? Paca's mind was racing. He had never seen anything like it. It was short and broad, like a fan. The king had wiped the dirt from his eyes, and the two stood facing one another again.

Both were breathing heavily, the king worse than Verclan, and there was a fury in his eyes. He stepped forward and swung his sword with both hands. What happened next was so unexpected that Paca was never sure exactly what happened. Instead of ducking, Verclan seemed to step into the path of the sword; there was a clash, a bright flash, and Verclan's left fist smashed into the nose plate on the king's helmet. The sword flew from the king's hand and did a strange dance in the air. The King staggered backwards. "Seconds!" he roared as Verclan stepped toward the king, the sword swinging from the device in his hand. With a quick thrust and a strange twist of his wrist, Verclan sent the tip of the sword slicing through the chain mail of the king's right shoulder with a flash and a puff of yellow smoke.

It was then that Paca saw the princess. The king's sword had fallen to the ground and the king was on his back. Verclan reached for the sword as the princess arrived. She swung mightily and Verclan rolled. The sword's song was fiercer than that of the king's. The blade hit the ground where Verclan had been. It flashed yellow and smoke burst forth from the explosion. Verclan leapt to his feet, the strange tool still in his right hand, waiting for the princess's attack. She was undaunted. Stepping over her father, she swung her sword down. Verclan raised his weapon, and the princess's sword met it on the way down. There was a flash and a yelp of pain as the blade swept through, severing the steel like celery and slicing off half of Verclan's hand. Verclan dropped and rolled back. Somewhere in the middle of the roll there was a muffled yell. "Seconds!"

Patira plunged into the battle. He came in from the side, moving fast. The princess turned and Paca could see her eyes. They flashed and danced, strangely drunk with the passion of battle. Patira brought his sword down with all his might. The princess stepped nimbly to the side and swung her sword in horizontally to meet Patira's chop. Her sword caught the tip of his. With an ear splitting squeal, her blade ran the length of his, splitting it in half on its journey toward Patira's belly. There was another bright flash as her sword stopped against Patira's hilt guard.

Paca held his breath. Everything had stopped except the clouds that boiled high above them, defying Asolara, their dark shadow crawling across the mountains. The king lay on the ground on his back unmoving. Verclan was sprawled face down and bleeding from his right wrist. Patira stood beside the princess, both of them frozen for that instant as the reality of what was happening struck them. It seemed like an hour. It was probably less than a second.

The princess looked into Patira's eyes and he into hers. A tear ran down her cheek. "No!" she said with a firm tenderness. "No, no, no!" she sobbed. She yanked the sword out of the cleft in Patira's blade and turned toward her father on the ground. He was two steps away. She took one step, and in a sudden mighty effort plunged the blade into the ground. There was another flash, a shower of sparks and smoke, and she leapt to her father's side. When the smoke cleared, only the handle and the hilt the sword remained above the ground.

Patira stepped back. He looked bewildered and unsure what he should do. He dropped his useless sword and ran to his father. "Fada—Fada!" he shouted, rolling the fallen prince onto his back. It must have been in about the same instant that the king and Verclan both opened their eyes. Vrengnia and Patira both shouted. "Help, somebody help." Paca stepped forward involuntarily. A huge fist crashed into his stomach, knocking the wind out of him. He remembered little else, other than being dragged out of the circle by Vishtorath and left to recover on his own outside the circle, flat on his back, as the clouds occluded the sky above him.

Chapter 17

Challenge

"The sword of malice makes a deep wound."

Old Tessamandrian Saying

Fada opened his eyes. Vrengnia saw the pain. "Help, somebody help!" Her words were distant and hollow. She thought she heard someone else saying the same thing. Fada opened his mouth to speak, but there was no sound. Vrengnia leaned forward to hear him better.

He could barely manage a hoarse whisper. "It's cold...so cold," he gasped. The sword had sliced the mail and cut a swath perhaps an inch deep across the front of his left shoulder, but the pain was overwhelming him. "It's cold," he gasped again and shuddered.

A large hand took her hand. She looked up. It was the smith. She looked into his eyes through her tears. "*You must be brave. Do not fear,*" he said; his lips never moved. He reached down. Everything was in slow motion. He removed Fada's helmet carefully. Fada gasped again. When he saw the smith, he tried to lift his head, but it fell back, exhausted. "You!" he whispered, "So...cold."

Vrengnia heard but didn't understand, "Why is he cold?" she sobbed. "What is wrong?" She looked hopefully at the smith.

"*He has tasted the blade forged for his own death,*" the smith said with his eyes. "There is nothing else that can be done," he said aloud. "Stay with him. He needs you now." The smith rose. The sword—*why had Fada brought his sword? Why had he brought her sword?* She had left it behind on purpose. The irony of the scene before her wrapped its arms tightly around her chest, making it hard to breathe.

Vrengnia grabbed the smith's right hand. "Get Haniah, she can help—"

He looked into her eyes again and stroked her head with his left hand. "No, Haniah cannot help. You must be brave. You must let him know you love him." He pulled his hand free. As the smith stood, she collapsed onto Fada's chest. "Fada...Fada..." Everything else was just a blur as a grave darkness settled in around them.

"The darkness of death brings many things to light."

Oratanga,
Passages

The cold crept up Verclan"s arm. He had never felt anything like it before. It wasn't just the cold; it was a strange brightness that was creating the shadows all around him. He could hear Patira. "Help, somebody help!" but no one came. Somehow, he knew no one would. They couldn't. There was no help. It must have been that sword. It sliced right through the sataliin; right through his hand, but now it was all cold and an intense light shone so brightly it nearly blinded him. "Don't shake me, Patira," he tried to whisper, but he wasn't sure the words made it out.

Another shadow. The smith? My friend? My enemy, perhaps? Who are you anyway? Why did you do this to me?

"Tell Mada I love her. Your sisters...tell them to be strong." Did Patira hear me? Did I even say it? "Please let me know that all this has been worth it." Where are you carrying me? What is happening?

Verclan was alone with his thoughts, when suddenly the cold receded slightly. The brightness abated, and he felt someone holding his left hand. It was a firm grip. He tried to move his head—had to move his head. Who was it? He screamed inside and with everything he had, swung his head to the left to look. He saw the king. "No!" Panic surged through him.

"I am...sorry...I am sorry...my friend." The voice of the king came out of the brightness. He struggled to open his eyes. He could barely see in the brilliance. The king was looking at him. "I am sorry...so sorry."

Verclan knew that it was genuine. He moved his mouth to speak. Nothing happened. He must speak now. Everything he had, everything. "I am sorry...too."

There was a sudden clatter of hoofbeats. A shadow darkened what he could see of Asolara for a brief moment, and his sight faded into the all-encompassing light. He heard Patira calling and weeping. He felt Patira's hand, but it was far away.

"The specter of an evil past continually haunts the future."
Mindar Colloden,
The Great Fathers

Carnados would have considered himself a skeptic if anyone had ever cared to ask. No one had, so he had never had to explain where he stood on all the questions that suddenly confronted him. The king sought his advice, but seldom listened and never, *ever* asked his personal opinion. It was only about facts, and it always was centered on the king's immediate situation.

The line between the facts, as he knew them, and these new realities was suddenly blurred. He had seen things today that he had only heard of in ancient legends, hardly a reliable source of truth. Starting with the guards at the trailhead, the donkey who had confronted the king, the terrible power of the king's and princess's swords—the "facts" stood on shaky ground.

Both the king and Verclan were close to death. The four soldiers, who had appeared to be guardians of the contest ring, had carried them to the edge of the ring. The princess was weeping over her father, and Verclan's son held his father's hand, gently stroking his hair. Haniah stood behind both of them, her face buried in her left hand. She too, was weeping. She held Verclan's wife's hand, whose face was turned toward the sky as tears streamed down her cheeks.

Dark clouds swept overhead, heading west on a collision course with Asolara, but there was still no breath of wind on the ground. Carnados looked up when the first thunder cascaded down from the mountains across the fields of Immerland. Was all this significant?

The smith was in charge. He had attended to both the injured warriors and seemed to command the guardians. He was standing in the ring, having picked up the king's sword. As he stooped to pull the princess's sword out of the ground, there was a commotion outside the circle, and the donkey that had confronted the king burst through the outer ring, galloping toward the smith. She stopped. There was a hurried exchange in the original language that Carnados didn't understand. The smith's face turned dark as the donkey galloped out of the ring on the opposite side from where she had entered.

The smith bent down and grabbed the handle of the princess's sword. He pulled it from the ground with his left hand, and the blade sizzled and smoked as it yielded into his hand. He stood up and took several strides in the direction of Haniah's hut and stopped, still in the circle. The onlookers, sensing that something else was about to happen, parted, leaving the path open between the smith and the hut.

The smith looked up and raised both swords to the dark sky, his back to Asolara that still flooded the contest field.

> *Hirath ala rama din kala*
> *Pira holl om kirath dalu*
> *Pissha, dala, omrath mala or*
> *Mahan Kli-marana Waru!*

It rolled off his tongue and a clap of thunder from somewhere behind Haniah's hut punctuated the last words. The smith lowered the swords, crossing them in front of him as he spread his feet apart. Carnados had no clue what he had said except for the final phrase. There was a stir in the hut in response to them; then everything was silent for perhaps ten seconds as the smith and the onlookers surrounding him stood motionless. The brief stillness was interrupted by the first gust of wind from the clouds overhead as it rippled over the field, approaching from the east as the clouds had.

As it passed over Haniah's hut, the front wall of the hut vanished. Carnados wasn't sure that was the proper description of what happened. It appeared to melt; perhaps it exploded into dust or smoke, but suddenly it wasn't there.

The cloud of dust, carried by the wind, swept across the circle. Seven men strode forth from the hut, each dressed as an ancient warrior, and each brandishing a sword. One man was larger than the others, and he walked in front of the advancing line. The four guardians stepped into the ring behind the smith as the others approached.

The six warriors from the hut stopped suddenly as the leader continued to advance. His countenance was fearsome and his face was grim. He stopped two paces from the smith and smiled. Carnados wasn't sure it was a smile; one might rightly call it a sneer—a fierce, mocking sneer. "Ahhhh...the son of Valradica, the smith! We meet at last. Surely it wasn't you who challenged me just now in Kli-marana Waru?" His eyes flickered. The warriors behind him laughed.

"It was I," declared the smith.

"Look here...what is your name, by the way?"

"My name doesn't matter. You will learn it at the proper time."

A suspicious look flitted across the warrior's face and then was gone. "No," he laughed, "I suppose it really doesn't matter, *does* it?" He chuckled and the others laughed again. "But look here, little man, do you see this sword? Do you recognize it?"

The smith didn't move. "I do. My father made it."

The leader looked back over his shoulder with a cruel smile and laughed. "His *father* made it." The six warriors laughed again. He turned back to the smith. "How nice," he said as he examined the sword's edge up close.

Carnados looked around. The onlookers around the circle had drawn back. They remained silent as the smith stood steadfast in the face of the leering warrior. The four guardians stood behind the smith, impassive and ready.

The big warrior continued his taunting. "Do you realize how long I have been looking for this? I mean, it was the best sword I ever had. Whoever stole it, well—never mind. But listen little man, you must know that you cannot stand against it. Yet you challenge me in Waru?"

"I do," said the smith.

The warrior's face darkened. "And these little swords you hold, did you make them?"

"No, my son made them."

"Your son?" The warrior leaned back in mock laughter. "How cute." The other warriors laughed. He looked back at the smith and smiled. "You will need them both if you intend—"

"NarEladra Mankar," interrupted the smith. "Do you accept my challenge?"

Mankar? Carnados stepped back involuntarily. How could this be? A ripple of whispers ran through the onlookers around the circle.

Mankar studied the smith, still sneering. "And what are the stakes?"

"If I am victorious, I will have your sword, and the swords of your generals. If you conquer me, you will have the throne—and Immerland."

Out of the corner of his eye, Carnados saw a sudden movement as Vrengnia stood up. "Immerland isn't yours to wager," she said.

The smith continued, his eyes fastened on Mankar, "Vrengnia, Queen of Immerland, is my second."

Mankar turned and looked at Vrengnia. "The Queen of Immerland, you say?—I would rather have her." He laughed and took a step in the direction of Vrengnia.

The smith's blade flashed in front of him as a warning to stop. "You will have nothing unless you kill me first. Do you accept my challenge?"

Mankar turned to his men and made an obscene, mocking gesture. They laughed and he turned back to the smith. "Look, little man, if you consider your life to be of so little value..."

"I consider my life to be of great value," interrupted the smith. "Do you accept my challenge?"

"With pleasure. I'll even let you keep both your swords." Mankar made a mocking bow to the smith. "When do we start?"

"We start when your generals lay down their swords, you select a second, and step into this circle." The smith never took his eyes off the warrior. Carnados looked at the princess. She stood about five paces behind the smith, straight and tall. The anger had left her eyes, and a deep calm seemed to have settled across her entire being. She looked like a queen.

"Omberon!" Mankar barked over his shoulder. Looking back at the smith but still speaking to his general, he said, "You will be my second. We must hand this impudent little man over to oblivion."

Omberon stepped up behind him; that crooked smile curled across his lips. A ripple of voices cascaded over the edge of the crowd.

Carnados squinted to see better. He felt a choking anger rising in him. His emotions raged, *Traitor!*...but self-discipline arrested his tongue.

The smith stepped back into the center of the circle. "Have the swords thrown into the circle. Vishtorath!" he called over his shoulder. "Give the queen a sword."

Vishtorath walked over to Vrengnia and bowed, handing her his sword. Vrengnia bowed back and accepted the sword with grace and appreciation spoken without words.

"Transcendent strength is found in perseverance in the unfinished task."

Karendo Marha,
Journey to the Infinite

Vrengnia took the sword without a word. Words seemed useless to her right now. Fada lay dying and deep within her, she knew that whatever was happening in front of her was connected to his death; that somehow, the smith's challenge was still key to whatever remained of Fada's life. She lifted the sword. Despite its size, it was light and well balanced. It held her hand.

While Mankar conferred quietly with Omberon, the smith backed up beside her, turned to her, and looked her in the eye. "You know, don't you?"

She nodded. Omberon's betrayal weighed heavy, casting a pall of anger on top of a weight that she was already unsure she could bear.

"Do not fear, princess, and do not hate. There is a time and a place for both, but this is neither that time nor that place. You won't have to fight, but you must be brave for my sake."

She looked into his eyes and nodded again. A strange strength flowed out of their depths and flooded her. The smith looked back toward his adversaries and she followed his eyes.

Mankar and Omberon were in the circle now. The other generals had thrown their swords into the circle as the smith had requested, and they stood in a line along its perimeter with their backs to the hut. Everyone else had withdrawn from them. Vrengnia studied these strange warriors. Wherever there was power, evil men could be found trying to take it and use it. She had seen evil men, but she had never seen it so concentrated.

She wasn't truly "seeing" it, but she could sense it; a sixth sense she had never been aware of was now awake, and the presence of these warriors made it as real as her sense of touch and smell. It was so new there were no words to describe the sensation: acrid, bitter, lonely, empty, black—all came to mind, but none of them fit exactly. They were standing in the full light of Asolara, but even that brightness was dimmed as it reflected off their faces and armor. They looked more like the clouds behind them than Asolara.

She waited, watching Mankar and the smith. They circled slowly, just as Fada and Verclan had circled. Mankar struck first. His sword shrieked as it cleft the air toward the smith. The smith feinted slightly and the sword swept over his head and shoulder without contact. The sword in the smith's right hand flashed, with a lightning quick flick of his wrist, catching a corner of Mankar's gantlet and severing it from his arm.

The smith stood still. Mankar snarled. He wasn't hurt, except perhaps his pride. The smith waited.

Mankar lunged again, a straight thrust. The smith moved so that the thrust passed his right side, deftly glancing it away with the sword in his right hand. There was a shower of sparks as the blades screeched by one another. The sword in his left hand flashed and a piece of Mankar's shoulder epaulette fell to the ground smoking. Bare skin showed itself.

Someone laughed; it was distant and hollow, and the princess couldn't tell who it was. She didn't dare look. Mankar's eyes narrowed as he and the smith continued to circle. "Well, little man...you've been taught well..." He lunged again, slicing downward with his sword. It sang on the way down and there was an explosion as the sword in the smith's right hand came up and met the full force of the descending blow. The smith's sword shattered in his hand and pieces flew in several directions. Fada's new sword was no more and the smith dropped the smoldering, useless stump to the ground. Mankar laughed. His generals cheered.

She never saw how the smith got the strange tool, which he now held in his right hand. It must have been hidden in his tunic somewhere, but it gleamed brightly, reflecting the rays of Asolara like a rainbow. It was similar to the one Verclan had used against Fada, but there was a small flat surface on it that had been polished like a mirror, and the smith was deftly reflecting Asolara's rays directly into Mankar's eyes, taunting him.

Mankar couldn't see what the smith was holding. He cursed and threw obscenities at the smith. Vrengnia had never heard such profanity. It was in the original language, but she understood it perfectly. She remained passive—waiting.

The smith had stopped circling. As Mankar moved, he moved with him, playing his advantage with Asolara's location relative to the battle. The wind was at his back and he scuffed with his feet to send puffs of dust scurrying toward his enemy. One of Mankar's generals called, "Unfair!"

The smith remained unconcerned and calm. "Paca MahMoralda," he uttered. It was soft, but it rang like a bell as it left his mouth.

Mankar stiffened and swore again. He switched sword hands and struck at the reflector the smith held in his right hand. It happened fast, but the smith was faster. His hand rose to meet the descending blow and caught Mankar's sword deftly between the tines of the tool. The force of the blow would have crumpled another man's arm.

"No!" It was a desperate, helpless cry, issued from Mankar's mouth as the sword in the smith's left hand flashed between them. There was another explosion and Mankar was left with only four inches of his sword. "Seconds!" he yelled, leaping back. The smith stepped forward and his sword sang again, slashing across Mankar's right shoulder.

Omberon launched himself toward the fight. "Seconds," called the smith. Vrengnia leapt forward to the smith's aid. His sword flashed again as he lunged into Mankar. Straight into the heart it went. There was a sort of un-explosion, as if all the light reflecting off Mankar was suddenly absorbed. Utter blackness appeared where the sword had entered Mankar's chest. The darkness crawled out and swallowed Mankar and then closed in on itself, disappearing as it flickered out along the length of the sword. The blade of the sword was now pitch black. No reflection whatsoever could be seen on it. At almost the same instant, a ribbon of lightning darted across the sky overhead and spiked downward into the woods to the south of the field, exploding in a blinding flash of light behind the smith. The thunder struck instantly, and the onlookers gasped.

Vrengnia knew she couldn't get there in time. Omberon was approaching fast from behind the smith. He swung his blade horizontally, aiming at the smith's upper body. The smith dropped and the blade swept over his shoulders. As the momentum and surprise of the missed impact threw Omberon off balance, the smith rolled, coming up beside the general before he could recover. His sword found its mark in the NarEladra's torso under his right arm, directly through the heart. The same anti-explosion absorbed Omberon into the blackness of the sword's blade, as another bolt of lightning zigzagged down into a tree on the north side of the field, shattering the wind with its impact.

The smith turned toward the other generals, who had started running toward the hut. "Stop them!" he ordered pointing his sword after them. The four guardians were already running in pursuit. The five remaining generals vanished in flight, fading into dark smoky shapes before disappearing with a hiss. The guardians followed, with a withering luminescence. "They won't get far," said the smith, as he knelt down to the ground and picked up a small gold and black object that had fallen from Omberon when he vanished.

Vrengnia looked back toward him; he stood still, holding her sword in his left hand, looking straight at her as the clouds swallowed Asolara behind him.

"The path to peace is not peace itself."

Paca was badly bruised where Vishtorath had hit him, but he was standing and he could breathe. The battle was over and Verclan and the king, holding hands as friends, lay dying beside each other on one side of the circle, with Vrengnia and Patira comforting them in their final moments. Haniah stood behind Patira with her arm around Mordara and her hand resting on his shoulder.

Fada stood still in the center of the circle. He hadn't moved since he had ordered the Eladrim guardians to follow Mankar's generals into who-knew-where. He seemed to be waiting. Vrengnia's sword hung loosely in his left hand.

No one else moved. No one else knew what to say. Paca didn't know what to say. Life as he had known it seemed to have taken a left turn and the path of history now lay in an uncertain direction. He was guessing that everyone else felt the same thing when his father interrupted him.

"Paca, Carnados, Chronista! Gather the generals' swords. Find all the pieces of Mankar's sword and Sandihar's, and bring them to me. Then come, let us be with our friends." He started walking toward where Verclan and the king lay. Like iron filings to a magnet, the circle of men began to draw together toward the two fallen leaders.

Paca gathered the general's swords while Carnados and Chronista searched for pieces of the other two. They were heavier than he expected. He had to take off his tunic and roll them up in it to carry them all. It was still dark from the cloudcover. As he looked up, it seemed as if the sky was boiling and the wind tumbled across the field in rolls, creating shadowy ripples in the grass of Haniah's field.

When he joined the circle around the two men, it was obvious that they were close to death. Paca had seen dead people before, but he had never seen a man *die*. He had often wondered about that fine line between life and death; the infinitesimal change that happens when the vorn leaves behind the inanimate body. Everything of real value would be gone and all that the man may have valued—his strength, his appearance, his wealth, his intellect, or position—would suddenly be reduced to nothing, and the empty body of the man, devoid of this thing called life, would become an object of dread. What exactly was it that left? And where did it go? Things had to go somewhere, it seemed, but perhaps not. The Eladra had vanished, but they seemed to be going somewhere—another time, another place?

He watched closely. Vrengnia pleaded softly with her father not to leave. Patira was quiet. Tears were streaming down his face as he held his father's head gently, rocking slowly back and forth. The two lives evaporated at almost the same time. Paca saw it happen but wasn't sure what it was that he saw. Patira simply said "No!" and Vrengnia gasped and sobbed. Mordara fell to her knees and buried her face into the fabric of Verclan's tunic. Haniah moved quickly to the ground beside Patira and placed herself so that Patira could hug her. He held her tightly and she whispered something in his ear.

A flicker on the horizon caught Paca's attention and he looked up to see a bright crack tearing the clouds apart from the northern horizon. It looked like lightning, but it moved slowly, winding its way overhead. Paca pointed and gasped and everyone had time to look up. They watched, mouths hanging open as several other streaks joined with it. It passed overhead and hesitated over the mountain to the south for an instant before plunging downward into the forest with a force that shook the ground under his feet. Several seconds later, the thunder smashed across the field with an impact that left Paca's ears ringing. The gusting wind stopped abruptly and the small gathering stood speechless in the still air. No one even breathed until Mordara fell to her knees beside her dead husband and gasped in a hushed cry, "The Ebondar—Oh my husband, the Ebondar is no more."

No one else knew what to do except his father, who knelt down beside Vrengnia and lifted her chin so that she looked into his eyes. He said nothing. He didn't have to. They stood up and she threw her arms around him, sobbing.

Verclan's warrior knelt down beside the fallen leader, removed his own cloak, and spread it over him to hide the now empty body. Carnados did the same for the king. No one else moved for several minutes as each man waited respectfully for someone else to take the lead. The smith spoke first. He broke away from Vrengnia and said, "Come, everyone. There is so much to be done."

Vishtorath and one of the other Eladrim guardians reappeared, materializing with a bright hiss as they strode up to the group. They saluted Fada and took up stations beside the bodies of Verclan and the king.

Fada led the somber procession back to the table. He was carrying Vrengnia, and Haniah walked between Patira and Mordara, supporting them with her singular strength. Paca felt left behind, and found himself angry for not having been more in touch with Vrengnia's trial. Perhaps it wasn't anger, but jealousy that rose from his belly as he walked behind the others, carrying the swords rolled up in his tunic.

Fada set Vrengnia in her father's place at the table, and Haniah led Patira to the place where Verclan had sat. Mordara seated herself beside her son as Haniah returned to her seat at the head of the table. "Everyone sit down," she said. It was clear that she meant that they should return to their previous seating arrangement. "We gathered here today for the purpose of seeking peace between the Immerland kingdom and the mountain clans." Paca watched Haniah's face. The clouds had lifted slightly and Asolara shone obliquely across the table, its yellow warmth flooding over her. She was beautiful, he thought, so poised and purposeful, gentle and firm.

She continued speaking: "The path to peace is not peace itself. Sometimes that path is troubled and elusive, fraught with malice and mischief beyond our planning, and beyond our expectations. Today much pain and loss mar the path to peace, but we have come to the end of the path and seek peace itself. I ask the new queen of Immerland—" She smiled at Vrengnia, "and the son of the mountain prince to finish what their fathers came here to do."

Dor Windarad started the applause as Haniah sat down, but the whole table burst forth and stood up, smiling alternately between Patira and Vrengnia. Vrengnia stood up and motioned for silence. "If the mountain prince would be so good as to give ear, I propose that we end the enmity between Immerland and the mountain clans—" She looked down, struggling to restrain tears that wanted to flow. "—that we find a way to unify our peoples, so that we all may live in peace—" She looked up, wiping a tear back with her hand and sniffing before continuing, "—trade in peace, intermarry in peace and share our resources with each other. It's time that we find strength rather than strife in our differences and in the end, realize how much more the same we are than different." Vrengnia sat down to renewed applause.

Patira stood. "In my respect for the new queen of Immerland, I heartily accept this proposal, and propose myself that we start immediately, and not leave this place until we have a plan for our doing as the queen suggests." He sat down. This time there was no one to interrupt the applause. Paca thought it would last forever.

When it finally died down, the smith stood. "Let us leave the queen, the prince and their advisors to confer with one another. Everyone else, come with me."

Paca rose with the others and followed his father. Haniah took Mordara by the hand and headed off toward where the bodies of the king and Verclan lay, guarded by the Eladrim warriors. When they had gone a short distance, his father dispersed the various men on errands in preparation for the cremation fires that would be required that night. Asolara would soon set: wood had to be gathered, and much of it.

Paca was finally alone with Fada who had reserved the task of preparing the bodies for the funeral pyre for himself and Paca. There wasn't a lot to do, but it was important.

Mankar and his generals had nearly destroyed Haniah's hut, but they entered it and found several empty bowls. As they set off to the stream to get water, Paca looked up. The clouds were rising and turning salmon and green as they thinned out against the azure sky above them.

Paca breathed deeply. There were so many things he wanted to ask. "Did you know that the king was going to die?"

"No, we can never know when one will die."

"Did you know that Mankar would come after his swords?"

"No—not for sure. But there were so many things coming together that I guessed something beyond the meeting between the king and Verclan would take place. You told me the swords were here."

"Yes."

"All I knew about these swords is that it's my job to destroy them. I wasn't given an explanation of how. I think this is true of many things in our lives. We have a purpose. How we fulfill that purpose is often up to us."

"But the swords—Mankar's sword destroyed the king's sword, but then Vrengnia's destroyed Mankar's. How is that?"

"I don't know the details. They have become clearer in hindsight, which is usually the case. It seems that this meeting and its outcome were determined to some extent. When I was prevented from making the swords that would be needed, you did. I made the sataliin for Verclan and the hilt guard for Patira. Each had its perfect purpose. Meshabo publicly confronted the king. It was part of the greater plan, but we may never understand what may have happened if she hadn't done so. I didn't know all these years that Mankar and his generals were NarEladra. It makes sense now, but I doubt if anyone ever knew it. I am sure my father did not."

"He was disgusting."

"He is no more," continued Fada. "The sword you forged was apparently destined for his destruction. I knew there was something special about it, but had no inkling..."

"What happened to Mankar? I mean that blackness...?"

"It was the onset of Oblivion."

"Oblivion?"

"I believe so."

"What about Verclan and the king?" Fada's eyebrows raised. "I mean, when they died. What happened? Where did their vorns go?"

Fada was filling the bowls from the stream. "You know there is much debate about what happens when one dies."

"I know. I guess I meant, where do *you* think their vorns went?"

"I'm not in the position to know the state of psadeq between each of them and Mah'Eladra." Fada paused. "Any attempt to do so would be only conjecture."

They carried the bowls of water back to the area where the bodies of the king and Verclan lay on the ground beside each other. This would be the first trip of many that evening. Fada was silent until they had set down their burdens and were headed back to the stream with more empty bowls.

"Have you ever looked up at the night sky," Fada continued, "and looked at the stars and thought how incredibly many there are?"

"Yes," Paca said.

"Have you ever wondered what is between all the places where there are no stars?"

"No—not that I can remember."

"Suppose one of those countless stars suddenly stopped shining, would you be able to tell it wasn't there by studying the stars that are there?"

"Unhh...No...I don't get it."

Fada looked at him intently. In the gathering dusk, his gray eyes were dark, but they gleamed with energy. "Paca, the decisions we make in our lives, the path we choose that leaves us where we are when we escape our bodies, determines forever whether we shine like a star in the eternal fabric of time or are dark like the space between the stars. This is how Mah'Eladra see us and have always seen us."

"What do you mean?"

"Mah'Eladra see all time as the eternal present. They see the sea of lives as we see the stars that are either shining brightly or they are dark in oblivion. If a life is shining, it has always been shining, if it's dark, it has always, and will always, be so."

"Then how do we have a choice? How could we change one way or the other?"

"We choose by the way we live. Each of us has the responsibility, the privilege, and the freedom to do so. But as our decision unfolds, if one lives in the psadeq of Mah'Eladra, though we move through time in only one direction, to Mah'Eladra, that state of psadeq just *is*, *has been* and always *will be*, in all directions of time at once. You appear as a star, eternally shining before Mah'Eladra. If you turn away and don't live in that psadeq, then that state *is*, *has been* and always *will be*."

Fada paused and looked at him as though he could see his confusion. "Suppose you are walking through a field and find a large stone. The stone *is*. From every direction it *is*. If you lived only in the present, and had no sense of the past or the future, all you could say about it is that it *is*. You wouldn't speak of when it became, because that would be in the past. You are unconcerned as to whether it will disappear because that is the future." He stopped, his inquiring eyes probing into Paca's. "If you came to the same field and didn't find a stone, then no sense that there ever was a stone would be comprehensible."

"I think I see," Paca said.

"Our vorns live in this infinite present. However, our bodies anchor our vorns to a single thread of time, and they are separated temporarily from the rest of the vorn when they have served this purpose. We are limited—confined—so that we are forced to make timewise decisions that define our nature, our character and our destiny. No such decisions are made in the infinite present."

"I seem to remember you saying one time that we keep our bodies."

"I believe they are restored to us in the infinite present, when we enter the Deep Sky, but they are different."

"Different?"

"Yes, different. But I'm not *at all* clear about the details. I think that's left for us to find out then." Fada smiled and breathed deeply.

"I'm going to have to hear more," Paca sighed. He had the vague feeling that this would actually make sense if he had a chance to reflect on it some more. "I'll sleep on it tonight and let it settle. Can we speak again tomorrow?"

"Yes, there'll be plenty of time tomorrow. I think we're settling into a long period of peace between Immerland and the mountain clans. By the way, did you see this?" Fada opened his hand and in his palm lay the gold plated signature star that had been stolen from his night table. "Omberon dropped this as he died. Keep this as a remembrance of all the things that happened here tonight."

Fada dropped another piece of the puzzle into Paca's hand.

"The fires of the dead burn brightest in the hearts of those left behind."

Old Tessamandrian Saying

Patira stood in front of the two pyres built for the cremation of Fada and the king. In his left hand, he held a burning torch and in his right, was Vrengnia's left hand. The assembly of beings on Haniah's land had grown as all those accompanying the king, and Fada's scouts and warriors had been asked to join in the farewell to the fallen leaders.

The smith and Paca had overseen the preparation of the bodies and the building of the two pyres, while he and Vrengnia had talked at the table. They had reached a tentative agreement to cease all hostilities and to open trade between Immerland and the mountain clans. It was a small step, but a first and a good one. Anyone violating the peace would be punished severely by his own people. Time would be given for easing of tensions and progress would be watched. He planned to meet with Vrengnia again in one month to talk further. He needed the time to establish his leadership in the mountains and she needed it to establish her sovereignty.

The smith's voice silenced the muttering and shuffling of the circle that surrounded the pyres. "The time has come. We will honor our fallen leaders. Let no one speak. Let the fire consume what is left behind and deliver it into eternity." His voice rang with strength.

Patira knew the custom. He waited. Vrengnia waited beside him. Aside from his torch and the one in her right hand, there were no lights except Tal and Meekar rising over the mountains behind him. He would wait in silence until he knew it was time to light the fire. Together, he and the new queen would set fire to the wood that would engulf their fathers' bodies. No one would move until they moved, and no one would speak until one of them spoke. It was up to them how long they would pay this tribute to the dead before them.

Patira waited a long time as the still night engulfed the circle, then he turned slowly and looked at Vrengnia. She looked back and squeezed his hand. He felt her strength. She was so different than the first time they had met. She stood straight and tall beside him, with the stature of a queen, her straight hair pulled back behind her, formed a halo around her head, illuminated by the torch she carried. He wanted to lean over and hug her, but this wasn't the time for that.

He nodded and she turned away, dropping his hand and moving toward her father's pyre. Patira turned and walked to Mada. He hugged her with his free arm. Her hug was full of passion and warmth, the pathos of a woman who has lost her husband and though feeling the loss, knowing that life is much bigger than her husband. She let him go and he stepped back, turning to the carefully laid pile of wood.

The flames leapt upward as the fine boughs at the base of the pyre caught the fire of the torch. Vrengnia had set her fire in several places already, and he did the same. By the time he had walked around its base with his torch, the heat of the fire was driving him back. He tossed the torch onto the top of the pyre. Vrengnia met him where they had started. They held hands, as they backed up until they were standing in the circle, his mother on his left and the smith to Vrengnia's right.

Both fires roared and crackled and with each explosion from within, showers of sparks scattered and leapt skyward. The circle of onlookers stood transfixed, mesmerized by the fire and the somber intensity of the moment. Patira looked over at Paca, standing beside his father. He was staring up at the sky, his mouth open in wonder. Patira followed his gaze upward into the expanse above them.

It took a second for his eyes to adjust to see what Paca was seeing. "The stars," Patira shouted, "the stars of the deep sky come to visit us." Even as he said it, he knew it was a strange way to break the reverent silence of the circle. Moreover, the words he chose puzzled him. He had only heard about the deep sky from the legends, but knew little about it. An invisible realm beyond the stars, the deep sky defied the capabilities of the imagination of those who lived in the confinement of Tessalindria.

All around the field, tiny lights that looked like stars drifted toward the ground. As they fell they grew larger and descended faster, like snow, but out of the cloudless crystal of the night sky. He looked around. From all directions the stars fell, faster and brighter with each passing moment. They landed on the edges of the field. As they touched the ground, each flashed brightly. When the brilliance of the flash faded, a luminous being could be seen making its way toward the fires.

They were clothed in white tunics that sparkled like a thousand diamonds in Asolara's light, and their skin shimmered with a faint yellow cast. They sang as they walked, faintly at first, but with increasing vigor and clarity as they approached. The circle around the fire shifted nervously. Patira saw that in a matter of minutes, the gathering ring of beings from the deep sky would dwarf them. "To the King!" he shouted, "To the Mountain Prince!" the circle of men cheered and the singing rose in pitch and fervor.

"The song, the song of the ages
Bringing light to the beings of this world
Bring vision for days to come
That death has culminated in victory
The bonds, the chains, the enmity
Fallen, fallen and falling away
New strength is found
A new purpose in Psadeq
A beginning, a fresh beginning..."

It was the original language, thin and high in quality, an intense resonant whisper that filled the air and seemed to come from everywhere at once.
"Sing O Tessalindria,

Sing with one voice out of the darkness of this night..."

Suddenly, the thin, nasal singing was underpinned by sonorous bass tones that didn't sound like voices at all, but almost as if Tessalindria itself was resonating in harmony with the voices of the approaching circle of light.

"... For the swords are found
Found to be destroyed in the fire
Found that they might trouble Tessalindria no more
And Mankar is revealed and trapped in Oblivion
His minions captured and thrust
into that singular timelessness.
That their evil might no longer
Terrify this world and
Occlude the vision of deep sky ..."

More stars fell and their brilliance outshone the light of the funeral pyres themselves.

Chapter 18

Fire

"...that I might catch even a brief glimpse of the deep sky, behind the curtain of stars; beyond Tal and Meekar, in the infinity of Mah'Eladra."

Mirradach,
The Tiger in the Tree

Tears rolled down Vrengnia's cheeks. The beauty of the voices and the brilliance of the strange beings closing in around the fires caused the tears to flow from deep within. She was unsure whether it was fear of the unknown surrounding her, or joy evoked by the song, but her whole body quivered.

The smith's arm swept around her and squeezed her as the first row of enlightened beings converged on the circle. Tall and thin, they moved with an effortless grace, as if weightless. They passed through the circle without any sound. "What's happening?" she whispered.

The smith looked at her and raised his index finger to his lips. He leaned over. "Just watch," he said in her ear.

Several Immerlanders and mountain people fell to their knees as the bright travelers passed them. One of them stepped between her and Patira like a tongue of fire that licked her left arm and leg, then passed without injury. Deep sobs welled up within her and a new flood of tears poured forth.

"A new queen is found
A queen who will prevail in justice
One who will know Psadeq among her people,
Who will bring peace to her land.
We lift up the queen.
We hold her hand,
That unity, harmony, and peace might prevail ...."

Once inside the circle, they headed straight toward the fire where Verclan's body was being consumed in the flames. They stepped into it and disappeared without hesitation. It seemed to get brighter with the entrance of each one until the white heat blinded her. Vrengnia looked around. The circle retreated slowly under the pressure of the increasing brilliance. Haniah and Mordara had covered their eyes and others squinted, trying to see what was happening.

Vrengnia looked up at the smith. He stood transfixed with his eyes closed, breathing deeply with a faint smile on his lips. She watched him. His strength seemed indomitable, and the sharp contrast of the white light on his face and the deep blackness behind him heightened her awareness of his presence beside her.

A sudden gasp from the circle made her look back toward the fire. The beings still streamed into it, singing, but she could no longer recognize the words. A white column of pure light rose slowly from the middle of Verclan's fire. She looked at Fada's fire. Where there should have been orange flames, all she could see was charred wood, collapsed in a heap of coals that were completely eclipsed by the brilliance of the other fire, so that it seemed to not be burning at all.

The white column rose faster now and when it reached about thirty paces, it shot skyward like an arrow from a bow. As it did, the white beings still left on the ground seemed to be sucked into the fire. The column splashed against the night sky, almost as if it were burning a hole into it. The hole widened, and the edges rolling back until half the sky was missing.

Vrengnia could see to infinity and perhaps beyond. There was no sensation of depth. Creatures defying her imagination swarmed around structures whose expanse and design couldn't be comprehended. The web of pathways leading everywhere at once but seeming to go nowhere in particular obscured all sense of proportion. She felt helpless to grasp even a fragment of its complexity and scope, as the column of the fire poured into it.

The column of light that shot forth into the vastness, exploded into a dazzling fountain of sparks that wound their way down the tangled pathways, shouting with joy. The words echoed and rolled down to Tessalindria in waves, a euphony that defied description. Somewhere in the center of it all, if one could describe it as a center, the brilliance of the light absorbed everything, as if everything were flowing there and from there at the same time. This core writhed with frenetic motion and activity, but Vrengnia found herself unable to look directly into it for its brightness and overwhelming intricacy.

She watched as the rising column of fire pulled itself into this vastness. As the last of it vanished into the infinite brilliance, the night sky rolled back, until, quite suddenly, with a singular last flicker, everything was gone, leaving the speechless circle of awestruck beings staring at the familiar, dark canopy of the silent, Tessalindrian sky.

"For all that's good; against all that's bad; stand I must and stand I will, that my name shall be lifted above the nameless hords that, on the path to the infinite, sat down to rest, and in resting, died."

Erengnira,
The Tiger in the Tree

Patira watched the smith as he stared into the coals of the fire. A small group had gathered there to garner the last vestiges of its warmth against the breeze settling down from the mountains to the south. The others had left for their encampments after the cremation fires had died. He poked a stick into its heart and a shower of orange sparks leapt upward on their journey to the sky.

"I heard that you had chosen your adult name," the smith said to Vrengnia without taking his eyes from the fire. "Perhaps now would be a good time to share it, before Meekar and Tal pass overhead."

"Is today your name day?" Haniah seemed surprised. "I wish I had known."

"Me too." Patira felt a twinge of guilt, although he knew that not knowing was clearly not his fault. It must have come from his desire to know more about Vrengnia than he did.

Paca and Phartang, sitting to his right, nodded, and Carnados, to the left of the smith, on the other side of the fire, sighed and shook his head in frustration, murmuring something to himself. Mordara smiled faintly and continued staring into the fire.

The smith broke the embarrassed silence. "Since we all missed it—and with all the events of the day, it is completely understandable—let's let it go no longer. Come Vrengnia, what is your chosen name? It will now become your queen name as well—" Patira knew this was important. The smith was trying to say it with a gentle encouragement.

Vrengnia stared into the coals for several moments, before rising slowly in acknowledgment of the request. She smiled and opened her hands with a shrug. "I will be Queen Erengnira of Immerland."

Patira jumped to his feet. "'For all that's good; against all that's bad...'" he cried as he started the applause, "Queen Erengnira of Immerland!" The others stood and joined in the applause. He looked around. By the looks on their faces, he could tell that, apart from the smith and Haniah, no one else knew what the name meant.

Haniah stepped forward and hugged her warmly, then stepping back and looking into her eyes with her hands on Erengnira's shoulders, said, "It is a fine name and fitting for our queen. Perhaps, you should tell us all why you chose this name," she said, as she motioned for everyone to sit down. "It is a fine name, and a worthy name, but we want to know more."

When everyone was seated, Erengnira began: "It is from the ancient play, 'The Tiger in the Tree.'" Carnados snapped his finger and his lips curled into an understanding smile. "Mirradach, the hero of the story, has been enlisted by the Eladra for the task of rescuing three foolish young men from a perilous situation of their own making. They had been unwittingly beguiled by the NarEladra to carry out a sinister murder of a foreign prince. Mirradach is sent after them to prevent them from carrying out the task and to bring them back to their senses before they are destroyed by the evil that they are perpetrating. At one point in Mirradach's journey, Erengnira, the daughter of a woodcutter, rescues Mirradach from certain death at the hands of several NarEladra who trap him in a pit in the woods.

"Erengnira's bravery and wisdom inspire Mirradach and guide him through the final hours and trials he faces until he is able to finish his assignment. At the end of his quest, Erengnira dies in a heroic final confrontation with the NarEladra and saves Mirradach again, along with the other young men. The three young men are all saved to live out their lives, altering the destiny of both countries forever. I thought it was a fitting name for a queen—and it almost rhymes with Vrengnia!"

Paca stood up and started clapping again. The smith smiled as he and the rest of the group stood for the applause. Patira thought back to the first time he had ever heard of 'The Tiger in the Tree.' It was around a fire, just like this—"

"Good Smith—" Carnados's words cut into his thoughts. The smith looked up. "Have you ever read 'Tiger in the Tree'?"

"It was read to me once, but I remember it as if it were yesterday. It was part of my education under Sessasha."

"Sessasha read it to you!?"

"No, after I had become acquainted with Sessasha's friends—I was just about the age of our new queen—one of the women in the group could read, and Sessasha had appointed her to read whatever we could get our hands on, out loud, whenever there was time. Her name was Erinshava. In the evenings, she would read legends, stories, plays and poetry—and from the Tessarandin. Everyone who was available would sit and listen. When she was done reading, Sessasha would teach on the reading until late into the night—that was a long time ago." He stared into the fire and poked it with his stick.

"What kinds of things did he teach?" Mordara asked.

"Many things—about many things. He seemed to know everything—everything about life anyway. He never taught about science, or mathematics, or—his emphasis was on beings, what they were about, and what they were like. He taught us about the Eladra and Mah'Eladra. It was from him that I first heard about the deep sky. He said that he—"

"Is that what we saw tonight?" asked Mordara. Her eyes shown in the light of the dying fire.

"I believe so. I have wanted to see it all my life. Tonight was the fulfillment of a hundred dreams, yet it was so brief. But just to get that glimpse..." Everyone was quiet as the smith drifted back to his memories of Sessasha. "His descriptions of the deep sky were always difficult, because there were no words that could describe it. That's what he always said, anyway. Having seen it now, from a distance, I am inclined to agree. Sessasha said he had been there. It was always difficult to believe when he talked about it because no one in the company had ever seen it, but he made it seem so real."

"I guess I don't understand," interjected Carnados. "What was it you saw?"

"When the stars fell and shot up into the sky from Verclan's fire. The sky opened—" Paca stopped in mid-sentence.

Carnados wore a worried frown. "I'm not sure what you are talking about. When we were all standing around the fire?"

"Yes. When that column of fire shot up—didn't you see it?"

"I guess I didn't. I mean, I saw the fire—and the tall beings...were they Eladra?"

"They were," said the smith.

"I didn't see anything like that either," interjected Phartang.

A silence fell over the small group. Paca shifted in the awkward stillness and said, "Perhaps only certain ones of us could see it. It was clear as crystal to me."

"What did you see?" asked Phartang.

The smith jumped in. He explained what the others had seen to a stunned Carnados and Phartang, the only two of the group who had seen nothing. "Sessasha often said that Mah'Eladra reveal things to some without showing them to others. It is somewhat like the original language—some beings understand certain parts and not others. We don't know how—or why—Mah'Eladra choose to do this, but they also teach us not to fear, or be envious when it happens. There is a purpose in all of it, that is sure, but we may never know what that purpose is. Sometimes we know in hindsight. I think we are beginning to see the details of the last few weeks more clearly, even now."

A long pause followed. The fire drew everyone's eyes in like a magnet as each pondered the recent events that had drawn them there. "Sessasha taught us to be thankful," said the smith, his voice gently guiding their thoughts. "Not *about* thankfulness, but to *be* thankful...for the smallest things...and not to dwell on things we don't or can't have, but on what we do have.

"When we are grateful, we are able to recognize gratitude in others. It compels us. It is the root of compassion. It is the foundation of contentment and peace, the 'birthplace of genuine love and psadeq' as he often said. He taught us that when we are thankful for what we have, we are able to realize its value; and when we know its true value, we become less likely to hoard it, but to share it freely, especially with other thankful people."

More silence followed. Patira knew that he would never have explained it that way but thought he understood the simplicity of it. There was so much to be thankful for, even amidst the hardships, and it had always been his experience that, when he was grateful, he was more alive, more alert and more aware of who he was. His mother had taught him this through years of patient counseling. He looked up from the fire at her as she opened her mouth to break the silence.

"I am thankful for my husband," she said without lifting her eyes. It was the first she had spoken of him since his death. "I am thankful that his death was honored by Mah'Eladra." Patira felt the choking in his throat as he watched his mother's tears stream down her cheeks, her eyes glued to the heart of the fire. "My husband was a grateful man...he spoke often of how thankful he was for so many things. He loved the mountains...he loved Immerland."

Haniah put her arm around his mother, but other than this, no one moved. Patira knew she had to grieve and it seemed that everyone around the fire knew it also. They waited as she continued in the slow, tender expression of her pain.

"He said that this might happen—but he felt he needed to make every effort to settle this matter with the king, for the sake of the mountain people—for the sake of Immerland—for us, but it is so much bigger than just us." She buried her face in her hands and sobbed. Patira moved to put his hand on her back and the smith caught his eye and waved him off, with his index finger on his lips. Somehow, he knew the smith was right and he stopped, sitting quietly while his mother wept openly for the death of Fada. He knew it would be his turn sometime; for right now, the moment belonged to his mother.

She wept a long time. The others in the circle stared into the flames, searching their own hearts and feelings without moving. When she finally stopped, and took her hands from her face, she sat up, turned to Patira, and hugged him. "I am all right for now," she whispered. "I love you."

Patira hugged her back.

The smith put his arm around her. "It was a noble death. One that will long be remembered by Immerland and the mountain clans. It is a great price to pay, but the value for which he fought is without measure."

Mordara sniffed. The tears were done for now. "I know—I knew that when we came here—it was just hard to watch." She stood up and stepped toward Erengnira, motioning for her to stand and holding out her arms for an embrace. As the young queen unfolded her arms to embrace his mother, the dams in her eyes broke, and she fell on his mother's shoulder and wept. His mother held her firmly. "It's okay, my young queen. It was the providence of Mah'Eladra that brought you here—that brought us here. Our lives are now safer—and richer. You will see this in time. For now, your tears will purge your fear and anger."

They stood for a long time as Erengnira wept, sobbing deeply. Patira knew that his mother's arms were a healing refuge. He knew that when she was done, Erengnira would make her peace with the horror of this day. So they waited.

When they finally sat down the smith broke the silence again. "It's very late. We have many days of resolution ahead of us. Tal and Meekar have flown overhead and we're all due for some sleep. Tomorrow is nearly upon us. It'll be a new day. Go now and sleep. We shall gather again when we are refreshed."

Everyone stood at once. Each hugged the others, and Patira put his arm around his mother as they headed off into the darkness toward the black line of trees to the south of the field. He looked back once to see Erengnira walking slowly back the other way, flanked by Haniah and Carnados. He knew he would see her again, and that was enough for now.

"The smith stares into his fire, and there he sees his past, his present and his future."

Timmanaeus

The smith was finally alone, sitting in front of the fire. How many hours, days, years had he stared into the fire? Fire was his life, and he never tired of watching it. In its heart, he could see the thousands of blades he had made and unmade. It was the soul of his art, the origin of his trade, the ever changing and infinite source of power that guided much of his life. Fire had consumed the bodies of the king and his friend Verclan. It had allowed his father to fashion the unholy instruments of destruction for which he had searched all his life, and it had claimed the life of his father in the inferno of his own smithy.

The smith leaned close to the fire, and with his stick, raked a piece of metal from deep in the bed of coals. It glowed bright orange as he propped it up on a rock and watched it cool. When he could see no more color in it he turned back to the fire and raked another piece from it. This one was as black as the night sky, like a shadow with nothing to cast it. He spat on it. The spittle should have danced and hissed on the hot metal, but it did not. Reaching down, he tapped the piece with his the back of his fingernail. It wasn't even warm.

He leaned back and looked up at the night sky. There were many questions he wanted to ask, but most of all, he wanted to know what he had to do to destroy Mankar's sword. He stroked his beard and stared back into the fire. He had recovered seven of them. Six were still hidden somewhere in the fabric of space and time. If he had Lonama's map, he would be able to locate them, but he had no idea whether the map existed in Immerland or the mountains or where it might be. His thoughts drifted back to his first encounter with the map.

He remembered it well. It was made of some light fabric, woven so finely that it was more like leather. It was perhaps a pace wide and two thirds high, and the detailed calligraphy defied description in its intricacy and depth. He wasn't sure whether there was only one map or several, though he believed that there had to be more than one copy.

Somewhere in the middle of a thought about the Lonama's map, he was interrupted by the faint hiss of an Eladra engaging his timespace. The characteristic sound was unmistakable, and he turned to see Vishtorath and his old friend Vishtava approaching from behind.

As his eyes met theirs, Vishtorath spoke. "May we join you at your fire, Mah-Moralda?"

The smith stood. It wasn't often that he was called by his adult name. "You are welcome guests. Have you brought a gift?"

"We have many gifts for our friend, if you will have them," said Vishtava, smiling as he embraced the smith. It was a powerful hug. Long ago he had gotten used to contact with the Eladra. For some reason, in spite of their ability to imitate Tessalindrian beings, they were always cold to the touch.

He pulled free and hugged Vishtorath the same way. "Sit down, please," he said motioning to the large log benches beside the fire. The three sat down and the smith waited until the Eladra were ready to speak. It didn't take long.

"Mah'Eladra send their favor for finding the swords and revealing Mankar and his generals," said Vishtava. "It has been a long task, but well noticed. You must now destroy the swords, utterly."

"I'm aware of this, though I must admit, I may not know the poetry for their destruction."

"There are six others, as you know," said Vishtava. "We believe we can find them now."

"How will you find them?"

"We have located Lonama's map—here in Immerland."

"In *Immerland*? Where?"

"There is an old groom in the stables at the castle. He has been there for years. He served under the grandmother of the new queen. We believe that the Great Queen gave him her piece of the map when she died."

"A *piece* of the map?"

The Eladra ignored his query and continued their story. "He kept it secret—as he should. Tonight, he saw the deep sky when it opened, just as you did, and he pulled the map from its box. When he opened it, we were summoned to investigate. He has been told to help you use the map to find the other swords."

"This is a gift beyond asking," said the smith.

Vishtava continued. "You must take all the swords to the Crown of Tessalindria. Queen Erengnira will provide you a suitable escort. In the Verrilain Dale, at the trailhead to the Jualar springs, you will find the Eladrim smith Vishortan—"

"The smith who taught Timmanaeus?"

"The same," said Vishtava. "You, your son and Vishortan must take the swords deep into the heart of the desolation of the Great Margah in the bowl of the Crown. There, on the slopes of Mount Eliia, you shall build a forge. Fire it with wood from the desolation, and feed it with the mountain wind from from the caves of Eliia. Burn the swords in this fire until nothing remains. They contain great evil, and only in the Crown can this evil be dealt with. You will be given the poetry you need when it is necessary."

MahMoralda sat and stared into the fire, envisioning the task laid out before him.

"There is more," said Vishtorath. MahMoralda looked up in astonishment. "The new queen, Erengnira, will ask you to serve in her court."

"Me?"

"She will request you to be her advisor," said Vishtava, "to train her other advisors and to be her personal counselor. You mustn't refuse."

"It would be an honor."

"Your task will be to unify Immerland and the mountain people. There is still much fear and resentment. Like the destruction of the Ebondar, the enmity between Immerland and the mountains will be destroyed. At times, it may be violent and discouraging. Erengnira and Patira don't yet have the maturity to resolve these difficulties."

Vishtorath continued when Vishtava paused: "Patira and Erengnira will wed one-and-a-half years from now, but you mustn't reveal this to them. There will be many difficulties. They will find their course, but Mah'Eladra want you to know so that you wouldn't despair."

"Your son will take over your shop. His cymbic relationship with Erengnira will continue to grow and it will be strong. She will appoint him as master smith for Immerland, to train the other smiths. He will wed Haniah in time and—"

"But Haniah is—"

"We know, but this is the way. She will bring him much happiness and will keep him strong to the task in front of him. The land on which we are standing belongs to the Eladra, and we will guard the portal, but Haniah's assignment here is complete. Paca will help her rebuild her hut, but it won't be permanent."

There was a long pause. The smith, in spite of his long association with the Eladra, wasn't used to such open revelation. It occurred to him that all this activity might have been preparing him for a deeper trust with Mah'Eladra, a more direct conduit into the affairs of this tiny world. It pleased him at some deep level and overwhelmed him at the same time. He had nothing to say.

He looked from one Eladra to the other. They were watching him. As he looked into Vishtava's eyes, the giant smiled. "There is a fifth gift."

Vishtorath opened his huge hand and lying in the middle of if was a small blue stone. It was shaped like an almond and glowed faintly.

"Stand up, MahMoralda." Vishtorath spoke with words that couldn't be disobeyed. Vishtava reached across the smith's chest as he stood up, and pulled his tunic back from his left shoulder, tearing it down the middle. Vishtorath took the small stone between his fingers and pressed it into his flesh. It burned slightly and the smith winced under the pressure as the stone sank into his skin. When the giant withdrew his hand, the stone was embedded in his shoulder.

"The stone of Marhana," he gasped.

"You thought it to be legend only?"

"Yes, that's right." He reached up and touched the stone. It sparkled as his finger made contact. Both Eladra stood up straight in an attentive stance.

"We are your guardians. You shall not fear. Mah'Eladra present this gift to you. When you touch it, we will come to your service. You must wear a covering at all times, that no one may know you have this sign. Is this clear?"

He nodded, looking from one to the other. "Vistorath: will you no longer guard the castle gate?"

"I will, unless you need me more."

"I will need you to guard our young queen. She needs your strength. She needs your watchfulness." He looked at both of the guards. Each had served him well and protected him. Vishtava had saved his life. He knew they were only doing what they were assigned to do, but he had grown to love them. "You both have my undying affection. I thank Mah'Eladra for these gifts." They both nodded.

"We must leave now," said Vishtava. "Be wise, be careful." With a faint hiss, they both disengaged and left MahMoralda alone in his own spacetime by his dying fire.

He smiled to himself. There was much to be thankful for. There was much to be hopeful about. He stared into the fire, and there, deep in its heart, he saw his past, his present, and his future.

The End
(of this part of the story)

<u>**Thank you for reading this book.**</u>

Book reviews are very helpful to authors in their craft and their careers.

- If you are my personal friend on Facebook, it is better to write a review on Goodreads

- Please take the time to write a review on Amazon.com if you can.

<u>**A Bit about the Books**</u>

The "Portals of Tessalindria" Collection is a growing number of books that I like to characterize as "historical fiction from another planet".

They are about Tessalindria, a small planet on the other side of the universe, created by the one creator god, Mah'Eladra, but in the farthest reaches of the science fiction world, no human from earth will ever find Tessalindria or be able to go there. Tessalindria is a lot like earth. The mankind, whom Mah'Eladra created, are basically the same as us, but they have a different history, of course, different culture, different ways of thinking and there are a few other differences. On Tessalindria there are space/time portals that transport people throughout history with Mah'Eladra's message. God is still God, but since He never does the same thing twice, there are other differences between Tessalindria and Earth that are revealed throughout the novels.

The books take place at all different times in the history of Tessalindria so some of them border on medieval fantasy, others more on urban fantasy and some that are futuristic, but all of them develop a view of Tessalindria from their own perspective in time.

Some would classify them as fantasy, but they would not be considered high fantasy, involving magic, swords, dragons, elves, dwarfs etc. There is spiritual power, but no magic per se. Others would like to call them science fiction, but hardcore sci-fi buffs would be disappointed at the very ordinary world that Tessalindria is.

For many years I struggled to find the niche genre for these books. The closest analogy is *The Chronicles of Narnia* and the space trilogy by C. S. Lewis. While this may seem presumptuous, they are much the same: the postulation that there are other places and times where God is working differently than on Earth and how it might be different if God still has to be the same.

The books purposefully challenge many basic and lazy assumptions that we often make about God because of our somewhat Christian culture. These books are for thinkers and ruminators, who are willing to "*Think beyond the horizon and color outside the lines*".

While the books *were* written in a certain order, I prefer to call this a "collection", not a "series". A series implies order. A collection can be read in any order. While the stories overlap, they are separate, but each giving color and understanding to all the others as they are read. The *Chronicles of Narnia* is like this, as well as Lewis's space trilogy, *Out of the Silent Planet, Perelandra* and *That Hideous Strength*.

All of the books are written in the new sub-genre called *nobelbright*. Basically, this assumes that while there is evil, most people are mostly good, but they make mistakes and bad decisions that challenge them and others around them to rise up and become better. In the books, as in real life, there's violence and hatred, anger, bitterness, mistrust, envy, greed and the like, but we can rise above it if we work at it.

When I first started writing, I wanted to create a cross-over collection that would inspire non-religious people to seek God. I have discovered that this is too broad to find my tribe, and have come to see that these books are for believers who are willing to be challenged and encouraged in faith, admitting that they are basically religious in nature.

At the end of the day, with the help of others, I have settled on my genre as *religious soft science fiction*.

I hope that you will find these stories and the world of Tessalindria inspiring and challenging to your thinking, to make your faith more robust and provocative.

Please visit my website (www.immerland.com) and sign up for my newsletter for continued ongoing information about the release of other books in the collection.

<u>Other Books</u>

Please visit www.immerland.com for more indepth and up-to-date information about the release of these books.

A Sword for the Immerlad King – The story of a blacksmith who defies a king's command to make a sword for his fiftieth birthday and the twisted paths to truth that culminate in a significant shift in the history of the natikingdom. of Immerland

Lonama's Map – The story of two teen friends who discover new challenges in life, as they are accidentally transported back in time to discover that the legends of their times are true and how their friendship is continually challenged as they discover truth from the fiction of history.

Tveeling – The story about the twins of Huravag who are separted for a time as their lives weave into an intriguing tale that leads to the overthrow of the evil king Mankar.

Bitterleaf – This is an urban fantasy about a biochemist who has developed a drug that can offset the effects of aging. But there is trouble when the drug is released to the public early, and Wilner and his family must seek refuge with the Sessashian cult to hide from the reaches of his corporation, that seeks his help in the chaos of the drug's failure.

Earthbound – The story of Mael, destined to be the savior figure for Tessalindria, as he grows to discover who he is, after being transported to a place to learn personally from the master of life, before returning to Tessalindria.

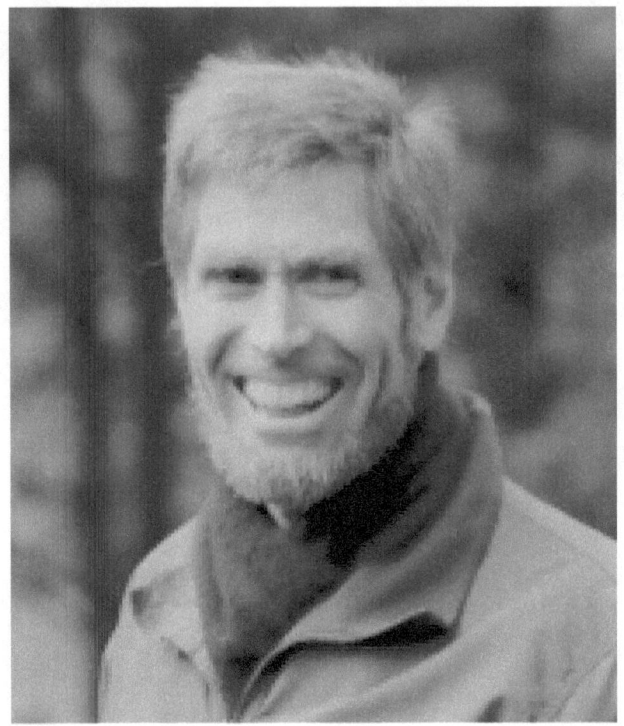

F. W. Faller

About the Author

F. W. Faller was born on Cape Cod in 1955. As a busy child, there was never time for reading until after college. When he discovered the power of fiction to change the world, he began his quest for a writing that would encompass his worldview with good fiction.

The original efforts were sidelined by reading *Lord of the Rings*. Being completely derailed from any original thought by these books for a number of years, other aspects of life took over: work in the church, marriage, children, a demanding job...

In the summer of 1998 he settled down and wrote the opening scenes of his first novel, *A Sword for the Immerland king*.

Since that time he has written five novels in the Portals of Tessalindria Collection as well as a number of satellite shorts and the backstory for the collection. In addition, he has written many non-fiction articles related to spiritual life issues that he publishes on his website for the curious to peruse.

Currently, he is retired and living in Portland, Maine with his wife of thirty-four years and focusing on his family, the strength of the church, and writing his legacy of thought into the best fiction he can muster for future generations to enjoy.

If you would like to contact F. W. Faller you can reach him in the following ways:

- Home web page –Immerland.com

- Author email address – f.w.faller@gmail.com

- Facebook – Friends of Immerland group

If you would like to hear regularly about what is happening in Tessalindria and get other special opportunities, please sign up for my monthly newsletter.

I never share my email list or individual emails with anyone else and you can always unsubscribe with the link at the bottom of each newsletter.

SIGNUP FOR NEWSLETTER

If you cannot access this link, go to www.immerland.com and you will find a button to sign up for the newsletter.

www.ingramcontent.com/pod-product-compliance
Lightning Source LLC
Chambersburg PA
CBHW020946260626
47169CB00006B/1848